C.C.

OF FAITH & FLAME

THE PROPHECY OF SORIN TRILOGY

Of Faith & Flame

Publisher's Note: This is a work of fiction. Unless otherwise indicated, all the names, characters, businesses, places, events and incidents in this book are either the product of the author's imagination or used in a fictitious manner. Any resemblance to actual persons, living or dead, or actual events is purely coincidental.

Cover design by: Fantastical Ink

Developmental Edits: Megan Records Editorial

Line Edits: Whitney at Empowered Writing

Proofreading: The Word Faery

Interior Art: Stardust Book Services

Published by Author C.C. Tyler

www.authorcctyler.com

1st ed. March 2024

E-Book ISBN: 979-8-9895549-0-4

Paperback ISBN: 979-8-9895549-1-1

AUTHOR'S NOTE

Please note this book contains content that might be upsetting to some readers, including violence, murders, mature language, death of loved ones, anxiety, and sexual content. It is not intended for anyone under the age of eighteen.

DRYSTAN
LAND OF VAMPYR
THE VOID
THE SAPPHIRE SEA
MORROW
SORIN
THE NEW WORLD
NŪA
CITY OF WITCHES
DRENGR VILLAGE
THE VADON MOUNTAINS
WEREWOLF TERRITORY
CIRRILLO

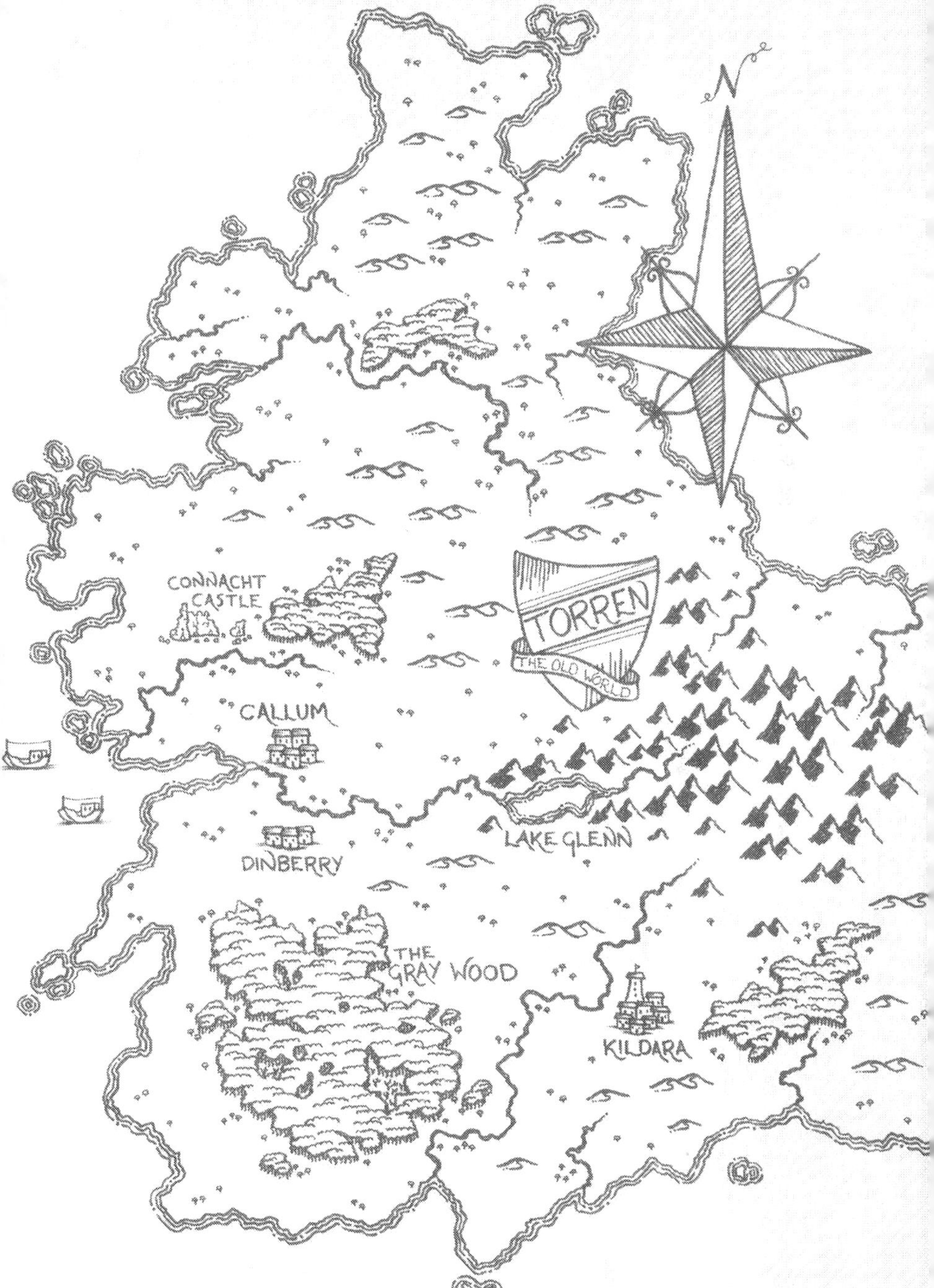
N
CONNACHT CASTLE
TORREN
THE OLD WORLD
CALLUM
LAKE GLENN
DINBERRY
THE GRAY WOOD
KILDARA

CONTENTS

For those still learning to believe.

CHAPTER ONE

EVELYN

THE FIRST SHRED OF light peeked through Evelyn Carson's dingy window. Dirt and mold spores splattered the glass, making it impossible to see clearly through it. But the orangey blur of the morning sun broke over rolling waves of incredible green.

Not even an aged window could dampen the view of the grassy hills of Callum. Bright and lush, they went on and on for miles, surrounding the small coastal town, bleeding into the rest of the continent of Torren, or the Old World as some called it.

Evelyn didn't have time to appreciate the beauty. The hour only meant one thing—it was time she left.

Evelyn gripped the strap of her leather satchel, one she'd risen early to pack. Not that it mattered. She had few belongings: her money pouch, an extra sweater, a thinly knit blanket. At least traveling light made packing easy. Most of what she owned she currently wore. She'd tucked her collared blouse into her high-waisted trousers, and her navy cloak draped behind her like a moving, breathing shadow.

She tiptoed to the door in her worn leather boots, treading cautiously over the rickety hardwood. She tucked her stubborn obsidian hair behind her ear, which she placed flush against the door.

On the other side, nothing moved about. Not a single patron stirred in the Runaway Radish Inn. No one afoot in the kitchens or pub downstairs either, surely empty this early of barmaids and Miss Patricia.

At the thought of her boss, a pang of sadness shot through Evelyn. Maxie danced between her ankles and then paced the humble room, restless. As her witch's familiar, the cat was attuned to her emotions. Unlike other familiars, though, she didn't share a likeness with her witch. Maxie had fiery red fur instead of Evelyn's black hair, and all-knowing yellow eyes, not gray. The cat blinked at her, and Evelyn faced the fact she'd miss this place.

Despite the itchy hay mattress and the nippy draft from the window of her room, the inn had been one of the nicer places she'd stayed the last two years. It beat the stables in Cirillo where it'd taken weeks to rid her clothes of the manure smell. The food surpassed the watery porridge she'd eaten during her journey on the ship, Oilliphéist. She'd been able to earn some coin here too, the full pouch adding weight to her satchel.

Evelyn gripped it tighter and took a calming breath. She was tired. Tired of running. Tired of new places. Tired of starting anew with only fragments of herself. Except she'd already been in Callum far too long. Three months. A full season. She'd enjoyed the summer warmth of the coastal town but couldn't afford anyone from her past catching up, which meant she needed to keep moving. Running protected everyone in her homeland, and Evelyn had every intention of sticking to that plan.

Even if she ran for the rest of her life.

Evelyn eased open the door so the aged hinges didn't squeak. Poking her head out, she assessed the hall. Something clattered against glass, and Evelyn stopped. To the left, the wind howling outside blew a tattered flag against the window. Relief washed over her. Thank the Goddess, no one was about. Goodbyes were difficult. Stuffy. Something Evelyn liked to avoid.

Maxie pushed under Evelyn's cloak, nudged between her legs, and darted through the sliver of opening, her red fluffy tail flicking behind her. She turned to Evelyn and perched on the edge of the stairs. Her yellow eyes glowed like orbs in the candlelit hall and gave an expectant look as if to say, are you coming?

Evelyn sighed. She made one last assessment before she entered the hall and closed the door behind her. She glided over the wooden boards, landing her boots with a methodical softness, and sent a small prayer to the Goddess that she'd risen early enough.

She'd learned a few things while on the run. Stay quiet and say little. She'd mastered the latter, becoming experienced in giving half-answers, but currently struggled with the former thanks to her rambunctious cat who, of all mornings, wanted to leap from table to table in the pub, knocking over candles and clay mugs.

"Maxie!" Evelyn hissed as she descended the stairs on the balls of her feet.

The cat ignored her and continued along her path to the back door. Evelyn hurried and scooped her up before she began scratching at the weathered wood. No doubt her familiar hoped to have a taste of the fresh milk left on the doorstep as she did every morning.

Evelyn's chest tightened and her eyes stung as she thought of her morning routine at the Runaway Radish. Collect the milk, bake barmbrack loaves, wash bowls of berries. She'd miss its simplicity. Her routine had become a daily dance, and she'd started to look forward to it.

Evelyn soothed Maxie with gentle strokes down her mane. Her eager familiar had become accustomed to the routine as well, expecting her morning milk, a sure sign they needed to leave. They could make it out of Callum before the townsfolk filled the streets if they skipped breakfast. But where to next?

Evelyn stopped at the cusp of the kitchen where a copper plaque depicted a map. The contours of the continents, sea, and mountains had been hammered into it. She rubbed her thumb over home, Sorin, the continent to the west, but set her sights east. The Sapphire Sea stretched across the center, separating her home from the current continent she traveled. Torren lay on the eastern side of the map;

Callum nestled into the coast. Would she travel farther north into the woodlands or farther east into the grasslands?

A crackle and flicker of light caught her attention. Behind her, spots on the blackened logs in the kitchen's hearth glowed orange. The bricked back glistened in a sheen of black soot while snowy ash piled on the bottom. The last remaining flame pulsed in its final moments. Then it died. The lack of fire and light left the kitchen bitter cold.

The tightness in Evelyn's chest returned, leaving her hollow and numb. Evelyn knew she needed to leave soon if she wanted to get out of Callum without anyone spotting her exit, but the dying fire was a painful reminder of the magic she'd lost

The Sun Goddess has given you a gift, Evelyn.

Over the morning chatter of birds filtering in from outside, Evelyn's late mother's sweet, calm voice resounded in her mind. She still possessed the innate abilities of a witch. The ability to cast spells. Recite enchantments. Brew potions. She'd lost her bronntanas, a power unique to her. Other witches possessed bronntanas, too, but Evelyn had flame, a power granted by the Sun Goddess that defined her duty and destiny.

And she'd lost it.

The dying fire haunted her. Dread pierced her chest like an arrow dipped in sorrow. Evelyn had been here before, rooted in the hope that she could conjure back her flame. Goddess, she'd tortured herself with so many failed attempts to bring back what she'd lost. And yet, she still stared into the hearth, wondering if she could summon her flame. She wanted to bring it back. Create warmth and light again in the small cozy kitchen.

Her gaze darted between the cooling hearth and the Runaway Radish's back door as her stomach sank with indecision. Doubt and hope wrestled one another until Evelyn dared a step toward the hearth.

She raised her right hand, opened and closed it over and over, and willed her flame to come forth. It did not. She felt her flame, like the flickering of the dying hearth. But it was unreachable, buried so deep Evelyn couldn't conjure it.

You're nothing without your flame.

Evelyn shut out the memory but believed the words to be true. The shrill voice only fed her doubt like an obstinate weed while her hope wilted away. Maxie purred in her hold, providing some comfort. It did little. Evelyn sank into the hollowing absence of her flame, the reason she ran, the reason she had left in the first place, the reason she needed to move on to the next place.

She rushed from the kitchen and let Maxie down. The cat, for once, understood the initiative and headed for their exit. Unlike the night before, the pub was empty, silent, and cold, the platform where the band played abandoned. The mismatched rickety chairs were empty and solemn.

"Good morning, my dear!"

Evelyn jumped at the sound of Miss Patricia's cheery voice.

The owner of the inn didn't miss her reaction. Middle-aged eyes assessed Evelyn's attire, lingered on her cloak, and spotted Maxie by the door.

"You're leaving," she said, her face falling. Not a question but a fact.

Guilt sliced through Evelyn. She hadn't wanted to disappoint the older woman who'd been so kind to her these last three months. She'd given Evelyn a job and a roof over her head and never asked questions.

"What gave me away?" Evelyn said with a meek laugh.

"I run an inn. I see people come and go every day."

Again, Evelyn's guilt rose to the surface. She'd hoped to leave and avoid this confrontation. *Fucking flames*, her morning was not going as planned.

"I'm sorry." It felt like she'd been saying this over and over for two years, even to herself. *Goddess*, another thing she was tired of. Here she was letting someone down, yet again. Like her parents, like her people. It almost felt like it was the only thing she was good at.

"Aye, think nothing of it. I knew the moment I met you, Saige Ferriwether, you'd be here for only a short time."

Evelyn's fake name echoed as loud as any band that played at the Runaway Radish, and Evelyn tugged at the collar of her blouse.

"At least let me send you off with some fixings," Miss Patricia said.

Evelyn nodded, afraid of disappointing her boss any further.

Miss Patricia placed her basket of fresh eggs down on the kitchen counter, feathers bouncing off the top. Her ruddy cheeks were darker from exertion and her wheatfield curls frizzed with sweat. She wiped her hands on her floured apron. In no time, she put together a parcel of barmbrack slices, a few hard-boiled eggs, an apple, and even two cured lamb sausages.

"I added a sprinkle of salt to the parcel in case you come across any faerie during your travels. The grains will distract them."

Evelyn fought a smile, biting her lip. "Thank you."

"Aye, now what did I tell ya?" Miss Patricia raised a brow.

Evelyn tensed, gripping her satchel and parcel of food close. Maxie popped in between her legs and meowed at Miss Patricia.

The inn owner tsked and pointed a finger at Evelyn. "Always say hi to a lone magpie, keep a cat, keep the faerie out back, and don't dare disturb a faerie fort."

Ah, Evelyn's skin tingled, and her ears perked. She'd heard the innkeeper's jolly saying about faerie before and how the enduring presence of the ancient faerie gave the wind its howl and the air its chill. Not that Evelyn believed a word of it. In her homeland, those tales were told as bedtime stories. Here in Torren, they had a millennium-old history, and if accounts were true, the humans had driven the faerie underground and they'd yet to resurface. Miss Patricia, along with the rest of the town, whispered about them as if they were still around, but Evelyn hadn't seen evidence of that.

Slowly, Evelyn nodded. "Of course. Thank you again. For everything."

Sadness flashed in the older lady's eyes, but she managed a warm smile. "You'll be missed, dear," she said and pulled Evelyn into a hug.

Evelyn's innate magic zapped, feeling the goodness of the woman's soul vibrating through the air. A witch's magic was tethered to their soul, weaved into its making. It sensed likeness and the essence of others, whether they had magic or no magic. It gauged one's true nature.

As she hugged Miss Patricia back, she bristled. Not from the older woman's warm kindness but because she hated goodbyes. They reminded her of those she'd left behind. Those she'd never had the chance to say goodbye to. Likely never see again. Like Miss Patricia and the other kind townsfolk of Callum.

As they parted, a breeze charged with a haunting chill escaped from the outside and through the open door. Evelyn's magic sensed the darkness, the threat lingering outside the inn, looming in the morning.

A scream rang out.

Gut-wrenching terror. Raw pain. And pure panic.

Evelyn rushed outside the Runaway Radish, searching the town square. At the center, Brenna McCarthy, an older woman who ran a farm with her husband, knelt under the clock tower, her stare fixed upward. Her features contorted with anguish, and she let out another horrific cry, as if the worst pain ailed her.

Evelyn's legs moved, her boots clattering against the cobblestones. An instinct she'd left dormant awakened, propelling her forward. Maxie and Miss Patricia followed close behind her as townsfolk began to flood the streets. Half still wore their nighttime clothes while others looked half-dressed in Callum's signature knitted wool.

Brenna sobbed, unaware of the crowd growing around her. Her braided hair streaked with gray wisped in the wind while a stream of tears cascaded down her lined face. Shocked murmurs rang out around Evelyn, and she followed the distraught woman's gaze.

A whaling-hook protruded from a young woman's chest, securing her to a rope that dangled from the bell tower. The sharp tip was stained, stark and grim against her white nightgown. Her arms hung lifeless at her side, her head bowed, and her matted hair obscured her face, making it difficult to determine who she was or what had happened.

"McKenna, my poor sweet McKenna!" Brenna wailed.

Goddess, it was McKenna McCarthy, Brenna's daughter. She couldn't have been more than twenty, five years younger than Evelyn, and by the looks of her stiff body, she'd been dead for some time.

Evelyn had seen death many times before, but those of Callum were jarred, riddled with shock and horror. Mothers shielded their children. Some wept. Others retched and prayed to their spirits. Murmurs trembled through the crowd.

Who would've done such a thing?

McKenna McCarthy was the beauty of the town, with dark ringlet hair and jeweled eyes, and every young man had yearned for her heart, the one no longer beating.

Evelyn looked at the entire town congregated around the bell tower. She couldn't fight the pull to say something, *do* something. Her magic thrummed with anticipation. Unlike the humans around her, witches followed a strict birth order practice that determined their role in their coven and greater society. Gender didn't matter, and as a third-born, Evelyn was a protector—or at least, she'd *been* a protector, her urge to help just as innate as her magic.

Miss Patricia comforted Brenna McCarthy as best she could, and Evelyn focused her attention back on the body. There was hardly any blood, not a drop on the nightgown. The young woman's bare feet peeked out from under the white nightgown, and Evelyn froze. She shook her head and blinked a few times to regain her focus. Evelyn grew colder than the air, disbelief coursing through her.

It can't be.

"Move aside!" a thunderous voice boomed.

Charles Doyle, Callum's commissioner, barreled through the crowd, wearing a leather tanned trench coat with a large silver brooch sewn above the right side of his chest, above his heart.

He looked between Brenna and McKenna's dead body.

"Cut her down!" he yelled.

Some townsfolk hurried up the bell tower. The young woman's body twirled as they worked to cut her down. She dropped like a puppet, once, twice, a third time, before she reached the ground.

At this distance, Evelyn saw the unmistakable pale blue hue of McKenna's skin. *Fucking flames*, she'd been killed by a vampyr. Evelyn took a step forward, wanting to explain what she saw, but stopped.

She couldn't.

Heat prickled on Evelyn's skin. She clenched her jaw and balled her fists. It was evident McKenna had been killed by a vampyr, the very enemy Evelyn had trained all her life to fight against, but the people of Callum didn't know she was Evelyn Carson.

Third-born.

Protector.

Daughter of the Goddess.

Destined to marry the Son of the God, Kade Drengr, a third-born werewolf, and prophesied to defeat the darkness.

She hadn't faced a vampyr since the day her parents died, and she hadn't used her true name and title for two years, unworthy of it after losing her flame and failing her parents. She wasn't the protector she once was.

Maybe she was wrong. Maybe the lack of light during the morning hour or the distance between her and the body only gave the appearance of a vampyr attack. Callum sat on the human continent, far out of reach of the vampyr. Traveling from Drystan, their homeland, across the Sapphire Sea would be impossible between the harmful sunlight and their hunger for blood.

It's not possible.

They laid McKenna out on the cobblestones. Her head angled south, looking away from the crowd. Evelyn kept sight of her feet and hands—robin's-egg blue skin and a blatant lack of blood on her body, as if she'd been drained.

It didn't matter how hard she tried to deny it. Vampyr bites held a poison that turned a victim blue. Evelyn's magic felt the familiar darkness that surrounded vampyrs, too. No matter how much time had passed, she could never forget the sharp coldness, that feeling of wretched darkness.

The growing questions of the crowd snapped her out of her thoughts. Some were terrified, hoping for answers. Others were angry, demanding retribution. She battled between wanting to help and wondering if she even should. Was it worth the risk?

You're nothing without your flame.

The words had her falling farther back into the crowd, farther into herself, and away from McKenna's body. She'd left her life as a protector behind for good reason. She'd failed ones she'd loved. Her parents. Her sisters. Her betrothed. And without her flame, she wasn't good enough.

Three things killed a vampyr: a stake to the heart, beheading, and burning them with fire. Evelyn's flame, the part of her magic she could no longer wield, was the perfect weapon against them. Evelyn flinched, the teachings of her childhood tutor replaying in her mind. Her flame was a gift from the Goddess, a beacon of hope for witches and werewolves, and ultimately the only way to defeat the vampyr.

Without it, what was she?

Rain began, and the steady drizzle drove the townsfolk away. Droplets traveled down Evelyn's neck as uncertainty crept through her. It didn't matter how much time had passed, the impulse to protect never stopped raging within her, but Evelyn reminded herself she'd also left to protect her people.

Her flame wasn't only a weapon but a beacon of hope. If anyone were to learn she'd lost it . . . Evelyn shuddered, imagining how devastated witches and werewolves would be, how disappointed her sisters would've been. Even worse, if the vampyr king ever learned she no longer had her flame, Sorin would be on the cusp of a dangerous possibility.

War.

The vampyr king and his army hadn't entered Sorin in a calculated attack since she and Kade were born. Other than demons and scáths crossing the Void, war had ceased for twenty-five years. There'd been one union preceding Evelyn and Kade, formed almost a century before. Though unsuccessful in defeating the darkness, they'd created the strongholds at the Void and the Wall around Nūa. Some wondered if the efforts had paid off, keeping the king and his armies out. A few feared the vampyr king grew stronger and waited until the right moment to strike. Most believed he feared the prophecy, and the promise of a marriage between Evelyn and Kade protected them.

For that reason alone, Evelyn could not allow any vampyr to learn of her lost flame and risk a war the witches and werewolves could not win.

Maxie meowed and rubbed Evelyn's lower legs with her cheek, as if asking, *what are you going to do?*

Evelyn considered.

The blue-tint of McKenna's skin taunted her, egging her on to do something. Say *something*. Yet, two years ago, she had tried to do something, save her parents from vampyrs, and had failed in the process. Her power of flame had been extinguished, had left her, and they'd died. Her failure had cost her parents their lives, and she'd never forgiven herself. Despite wanting to help, the weight of her failures was far too heavy, burdening Evelyn's tired being and spent spirit. If she wasn't good enough to protect her own people, what good would she be to Callum?

"Best we leave," Evelyn whispered, scooping Maxie up and heading for the hills surrounding the town.

Chapter Two

Kade

Kade Drengr hated boats.

He'd much prefer the bite of a *nathair* demon or even a week's worth of patrolling the Void in his werewolf form than the sway of the sea. Full of darkness and demons, the Void stood as the desolate divide between Drystan, the land of vampyr, and the continent of Sorin. Kade would face that sliver of chaos willingly, but *stars above*, not a boat.

His sense of unwavering duty had driven him onto the ship, and now, as he made his way down the dock of Callum, the ebb of waves still locked into his knees, Kade sent a small prayer to the Moon God that the four-week voyage had been worth it. Waves crashed against the dock and his stomach heaved at the sound. Worse, the stink of fish and salt hung in the wind, and his werewolf sense of smell couldn't escape it.

The townsfolk stared as Kade made his way farther from the ships. His traveling leathers and billowing cloak contrasted to the wool everyone wore, down to their hats. Kade's large stature and towering height didn't help. Few came up to his breastbone, craning their necks to get a better look.

He had at least wrapped his sword to hide the hilt and pocketed the brooch that usually secured his cloak. Nothing gave away his name, and thanks to Evelyn's middle sister, Blair, he wore an enchanted necklace to hide his werewolf magic. Kade could still feel his inner wolf, a strong magic that enhanced his senses and allowed him to shift into a beast, but others were none the wiser.

Over the last few months, he'd adapted his disguise. The black color distinguished him as a huntsman, a human traveler and mercenary who slayed demons and beasts for hire. He prayed his disguise would be enough when he and Evelyn finally came face to face.

Bleu, Kade's war horse and only companion, walked beside him at a steady pace as if he too wanted to put as much distance between him and the Sapphire Sea as he could. Together they towered over the humans working on the docks, Bleu's hooves clattering against the wood planks. The people of Callum continued to stare with curiosity but not suspicion.

The rolling clouds from the sea cast a gray, ominous hue over the hilly land and colorful town, so different from the lands of his people, full of pines, mountains, and lush with life.

Kade sighed, smoothing his hand over his thick beard. He missed home. He'd been traveling for almost a year and craved fresh pine in the air and the cooing of songbirds, the ability to shift into his wolf form and feel the plush forest floor under his paws, guided by the moonlight bleeding through the canopy above.

Instead, he was on this seemingly endless search for Evelyn Carson, Daughter of the Goddess, and his betrothed. She'd left just before they were to unify their souls as husband and wife, setting in motion a prophecy that had been given four centuries ago.

The truest of unions between the third-borns of the Sun and Moon will defeat the darkness.

Kade believed in the prophecy. Breathed it. He swore by his duty, recalling what his Mother had taught him. She'd been the third-born in her family, too, the only daughter but a protector, nonetheless. When Kade's life had been threatened during a vampyr attack ten years ago, she'd distracted the beasts, sacrificing herself and giving him the chance to live so he might fulfill the prophecy. Evelyn, on the other hand, had abandoned her duty as Daughter of the Goddess, run not only from their union but their people, and jeopardized the chance to defeat the vampyr.

With each step up the docks, he shook away thoughts of the sea and resentment toward Evelyn. He'd come all this way, searched all this time to find her, convince her to return so they could fulfill their duty once and for all. Festering in his frustration did him no favors.

Kade ducked, and Bleu bristled as a fish flew over them. Another flew from one boat to the other. Crewmen unloaded ships and pushed barrels down ramps. Captains argued with other captains as respective crewmen eyed the opposing group. Merchants traveled down the dock with their carts. Crates of fruit and grain lined the walkway. Currents of people came and went.

He pushed onward, guiding Bleu as he did until, finally, they left the docks and entered what appeared to be a harbor market. He circled through it, passing vendors using tents, tables, and wagons to sell goods of various types: produce, linen, baked items. Compared to the bustling dock, few townsfolk shopped at the vendors.

Sea wind barreled past, and the hairs on the back of Kade's neck rose. His inner wolf, an animalistic magic that gave him strength, the ability to shift, a tracking specialty, and heightened senses, detected something amiss in the air, a tension bristling beyond the smiles of the townspeople. The clouds from the sea continued to roll in, each darker than the last, as evening approached. Even the waters seemed a darker shade of blue and the air grew brisk. Kade sensed *something*, but he didn't assess any further as he weaved through the market, shoulders back and eyes ahead.

He was here to find Evelyn.

Kade had followed a trail of moonstones over the last six months, and he'd learned that a dark-haired woman used ten of the precious gems to pay for passage to Torren on a ship called the *Oillipheist.* Kade grimaced. Not only had she run from her duty, but Evelyn had used the moonstones from her wedding dress as payment, trading and bartering them while on the run, as if the dress meant nothing. Her actions demonstrated how little she cared for their union and the prophecy.

Bleu nibbled the leathers on Kade's shoulders, as if to say, *Don't worry about it,* but all Kade could do was worry. What if she wasn't here? What if, yet again, he was weeks behind her?

Sighing, Kade pulled Bleu along.

Compared to Sorin, Callum felt older, stuck in a time of simplicity. Squat and tall hodgepodge buildings of blues, yellows, and pinks lined the coastline, so unlike the gray stone and wood-lodge homes of Kade's homeland. Small and quaint, the sheer size of Callum would've fit snug into a single base of the Vadon Mountains.

He went down street after street, the small town closing in on him. He peered at the young women as they passed, reaching out his magic to sense if they were witches, but few with magic walked through the market. None of them had the signature dark hair of the Carson coven, but what if she was disguising herself? What if she had cloaked her magic just as he had? Besides, despite the description Blair had given him, he didn't know exactly what Evelyn looked like. He'd never actually met the woman he was supposed to marry.

It was no use.

Clenching his jaw, Kade pinched the bridge of his nose and took a calming breath. It had been the decision of the Elders, leaders of the witches, and Alphas, leaders of the werewolves, who thought it best he and Evelyn never meet until their wedding day. In Sorin, witches and werewolves traded, did business, and allied together against the vampyrs but lived separately. Werewolves inhabited the west, focusing their efforts to protect Sorin at the Void and in the Vadon Mountains. Witches maintained the east, protecting the plains, coastline, and city of Nūa at the Wall. Due to the separate efforts, Evelyn and Kade never came across each other, but now more than ever, Kade struggled with the decision of the Elders and Alphas.

If they had met, perhaps Evelyn would never have left.

A group of young men walked past. Sweat and brine clung to their skin and clothes, invading Kade's senses and roiling his stomach.

Sailors.

As they headed down the cobblestone street, an idea struck. He'd learned two ways to get people to talk while searching for Evelyn. Money and alcohol. Since his funds were running low after a year, he needed to find the busiest tavern in town. Kade followed the group of sailors.

After three blocks, Kade almost smiled.

Ahead, a three-story building sat in the heart of town, its windows glowing orange from the light inside. Laughter and song spilled out into the streets, and those going in wore grins of glee, while those leaving stumbled with even bigger grins.

The name Runaway Radish had been carved into the beam above the doorway, and a wooden carved sign painted rosy pink depicted its namesake. The sign squeaked on its hinges as the evening wind blew from the coast. Kade tied Bleu to a post amongst other horses and threw a copper coin to a stableman. Bleu grunted, displeased but happy to eat the hay laid out in bins.

Kade left him and walked into the inn's rambunctious crowd. His boots stuck to the sticky floors, and he smelled sweet mead in the air. A few cast wary glances his way, his stature eating up the space beneath the low-hanging ceiling, but most were enraptured by the jolly jig the band played.

He reached the bar, and a familiar scent hit him. Vanilla and burning cedar sat stagnant in the area behind the bar. Old but there, nonetheless. Kade had first detected it in Evelyn's apartment in Nūa, then in remnants left in the cities and towns she'd bounced between. *Her* scent. Kade's wolf howled, his beastly magic awakened, but Kade reigned in his wolf, taming it, calming it.

Did she work here? Perhaps luck was on his side and they'd cross paths. But how would he know for sure? They'd never met, and like him, she'd most likely cloaked her magic. Kade needed answers, but he had to be strategic. Calculated and patient.

An older woman with ruddy cheeks and curls the color of a wheatfield handed trays of drinks to barmaids and turned to him. "Well, I've never seen your handsome face before, lad," she said. "You look like you could use a whiskey."

Kade nodded. "Please."

The older woman obliged and pushed over a generous pour. Kade sipped and listened to the chatter. By the time he'd downed half his whiskey, he'd heard small town gossip, business talk, and flirtatious whispers, nothing of Evelyn and no sight of her, for that matter, but he'd observed one important detail.

The captain of the *Oilliphéist* was at the Runaway Radish, and thanks to the defeated souls who exited the gambling room, Kade knew where to find him.

He nodded at the double doors. "Is the gambling room open to anyone?"

The older woman nodded, planting her hands on her hips. "Aye, it is. No funny business in my inn. You play fair or you don't play at all, I don't care how handsome you are."

"Yes, ma'am," Kade said, unable to hold back a small smile. It was the first in some time, and his muscles felt stiff.

"It's Miss Patricia." She swatted her towel at him. "I'm far too young to be a *ma'am*."

Kade laughed. "Of course, Miss Patricia." He gave her a kind nod and headed for the double doors.

He found silence on the other side. A table of seven sat huddled over cards and black dice, a game Kade had never seen before. One man cursed while another, smoking a pipe, grabbed gold coin from the center table.

"Better luck next time, Sam," said the smoker.

As they gathered their earnings from that round, their attention fell on Kade.

"Fifty coppers to buy in," the one with the pipe said, one arm slung over the back of his chair. A wide-brimmed hat with a feather hung from the chair, and his skin stretched like leather across his frame, dark and tight from years in the sun.

Was this the captain of the *Oillipheíst* he'd heard others mention?

Kade joined the table, taking the last empty seat. "How about fifty coppers and instead of cards you answer some questions, Captain?"

The man's eyes darted downward in a movement so slight only Kade's werewolf sight caught it. The rest of the table stiffened. Kade sensed their wariness as if it perfumed the air. He threw fifty coppers onto the mountain of coin in the center of the table, redirecting the crew's attention. All eyes twinkled with the promise of more money.

"I'm looking for a passenger who boarded your ship four months ago," Kade said, crossing his arms.

The captain snorted, taking a puff from his pipe. "I suppose at that price I can entertain ya. Who you lookin' for?"

"She wouldn't have used her real name. Early twenties. Dark hair. Traveled with a large cat." Kade cringed. Why would Evelyn choose a feline companion to travel with?

The crewman named Sam huffed a laugh. "Aye, I don't think any of us would forget such a fine beauty. Could we, lads? Eyes of steel with an ass—"

"Careful," Kade said with lethal calm. He locked his eyes on the crewman, his wolf growling below the surface. "That is my future wife you speak of."

The captain slapped Sam upside the head. "Are you daft, boy?"

Sam winced and rubbed the back of his head, sinking into his chair.

The captain sighed and said, "Aye, the young woman you speak of was on my ship. Boarded it with red hair and a black cat, but her hair changed to black as night for the rest of the trip, while her cat was a fiery red thing."

Another crewman nodded in agreement. "A witch in disguise, if you ask me."

The story fit, and Kade didn't hear a hint of a lie in the captain's tone. He itched to pinch the bridge of his nose, a habit when he worried, but remained calm in his seat. He'd already considered that Evelyn might be using a disguise, but he felt like a fool hearing it out loud. He himself masked his wolf. Why wouldn't she do the same in more ways than one? Kade remained still as stone in his seat, worry and frustration weighing him down. He might as well be trying to catch the wind at this point.

"Did you not think to ask about this said disguise?" Kade asked, letting some of his frustration leak through his tone.

Another crewman, seated to the right of the captain, narrowed his eyes. "Not our business, and I'm not entirely sure it's any of yours, future wife or not."

Moons, the prophecy and his duty *was* his business, and as Daughter of the Goddess, Evelyn was tied to it. Kade mastered his temper and threw an extra three coins, this time silver, onto the table, diffusing the growing tension. "What else can you tell me?"

The crew and captain shared a silent conversation with looks and nods. Kade's patience wore thin, until the captain sighed.

"Not much, I am afraid. She stuck to herself. Spent some time on deck during the day but stayed in her room most of the journey. Seemed on edge the first few days but boarded the ship with rigid determination. Definitely running from something." He paused, took a puff of his pipe, and eyed Kade. "Or someone."

Kade ignored the jab, again not wanting to face the fact he may be the reason she left. If so, convincing her to come back would be more difficult, but Kade had learned from his mother's sacrifice that what he and Evelyn wanted did not matter compared to their duty.

He *had* to try and convince her of that.

"Have you seen her in town?" Kade asked.

The captain nodded. "Aye, of course, Saige's a barmaid here."

Kade's wolf howled. She *was* here, in this very establishment.

A crew member clicked his tongue. "True, Captain, but I haven't seen her at all tonight."

"Aye," another crew member chimed in. "Perhaps she left after the McCarthy girl's murder."

"Shame, that is," the captain whispered.

"A murder?" Kade asked.

Had that been the tension he'd felt earlier at the docks?

"Aye, a young woman drained of blood. They sayin' it was a vampyr. Can you believe that? A vampyr in Torren, let alone Callum of all places." The captain shook his head.

Kade's brows furrowed, and he scratched his beard as the crewmen began discussing the oddity of the murder and how the body had been hung from the clock tower for the whole town to see. Horrific, but Kade doubted a vampyr was in Callum. He'd never heard of a vampyr crossing the Sapphire Sea, let alone boarding a ship. Their darkness had started and spread from Drystan alone, an affliction of the New World in Sorin.

The captain grunted, bringing Kade back to the present. "If she's not here, she's probably headed north or east. Not much work farther south and not possible to travel west, not for a few months anyway."

Kade stilled. "Why not west?"

He hadn't expected Evelyn to travel back home. Why would she when an entire ocean separated her from those looking for her, those who *needed* her? Yet, the captain made it sound like she couldn't.

"It's storm season. Not a single ship will be leaving this harbor for ten weeks. Us sailors stay. Find work on the farms ramping up to harvest or other jobs in town." Seeing the confusion on Kade's face, the captain smiled warily. "Wait, don't tell me you had no idea it was storm season?"

Kade gritted his teeth. He hated boats and had never cared, but he'd heard of the sanction that prohibited travel between continents during the late summer months before autumn. Stars above, his maddening search for Evelyn had made him forgetful.

Kade wrestled with worry and frustration. He'd already been gone a year, longer than he'd intended. Months after Evelyn had run away, Blair had traveled to the Drengr village, imploring Kade to search for her. The Carson coven had exhausted all options, and the last person Evelyn would expect to come looking for her was him, the betrothed she'd never been allowed to meet and who was required at the Void.

Kade's eldest brother Eldrick, the interim Alpha as their father's health continued to decline, hadn't agreed with the decision but offered to cover Kade's absence. He and his team would be stationed at the Void under his orders, their efforts keeping them from home for an extended period of time. Four seasons had come and gone, and Kade doubted his brother had been able to keep the ruse for that long. The Elders and Alphas had to know by now he'd disobeyed orders, and he couldn't imagine the headache his brother, team, or Blair—for that matter—endured.

Internally, Kade cursed. With storm season, he was stuck. He couldn't fulfill his duty here, not an ocean away from the efforts against vampyrs. But what good were his efforts without Evelyn? How could they fulfill the prophecy apart? Time wasn't on his side, a nagging reality twisting his gut.

Yet, a realization hit him like a gust of the sea's wind, and hope filled Kade again. If Evelyn was still in Callum, she would be unable to leave the continent of Torren. At least she'd be stuck here, too. Storm season gave Kade plenty of time to find her and finally convince her to come home.

Satisfied with what he'd learned about Evelyn, Kade stood, his cloak unfurling behind him. "Thank you for your time, gentlemen." He threw a small pouch, and a loud *thunk* echoed in the gambling room as more coin landed on the wooden table. "For your silence. We never spoke; I never asked questions."

The crew and captain nodded and continued arguing amongst each other whether the vampyr was rumor or truth. Kade hadn't faced a vampyr, demon, or any shred of darkness in twelve months. He'd been away from his duty, away from his team, away from the efforts at the Void, and his protective instinct ached to be unleashed, but he was here to find Evelyn.

Kade left the gambling room and entered the chorus of folk music, laughter, and whisperings of the murder. He eyed each of the barmaids delivering food and drink to tables. Was Evelyn using a disguise that aged her ten years? Did she sport russet hair? He could ask Miss Patricia, but now that he knew she worked here, he risked Evelyn learning he was looking for her.

Kade grabbed the reins of his tracking ability. Only he could see his magic at work if he attempted it. He planted a single hand on the bar top, steadying himself. His chest puffed and nostrils flared as he rallied his breath. His magic assessed the space, but time and emotions beat against him.

Purple happiness. Red desire. A pulsing yellow of fear. Too much time passing, too many emotions filtering through. It would be impossible to ground himself enough in the space to paint a picture clear enough to help him find Evelyn.

Kade pinched the bridge of his nose and headed for the exit. He stepped out into the descending evening light. Still tied to the post, Bleu eyed him, bored, as if mocking his failed efforts.

A clock tower rang, booming across the town square. Candles and bouquets of flowers lined the base of it. Was that the clock tower the *Oillipheist* crew had mentioned? Kade sighed, running his hand down Bleu's back despite his horse's judgment.

Kade wavered between his purpose here and his engrained duty.

He'd come to find Evelyn, and he was *so* close, but he could not risk the threat of a vampyr in Callum, even if he didn't believe it. He debated finding Evelyn first, but what if she was already gone? What if convincing her to come back took too long and the vampyr killed again?

Deep in his bones, Kade knew learning more about this murder and the possible presence of the vampyr was the right thing to do.

"Who guards the town?" Kade asked the stableman.

"That'd be the commissioner, Charles Doyle," he said.

"Where could I find him?"

The stableman explained which direction and what streets to take. Kade thanked him and hoped the commissioner would be willing to discuss the murder. Maybe he'd even have the body for Kade to inspect.

Once assured the vampyr whisperings were nothing but rumors, he'd refocus on finding Evelyn.

Chapter Three

Evelyn

Evelyn's journey smelled of salt and grass. She planted her dragon bone staff into the tufts of earth, patches of buttercups sprinkled in her path.

Her staff hummed with magic, the ancient remnants of power from the dragon bone, and instead of giving her stability, it gave her direction. It reached across the land and led to the next destination, using the best route. The dragon bone also withstood the heat of her flame—the perfect weapon with which to wield her power.

Not that it mattered now with her flame gone.

Evelyn gripped the bone material tighter, burying the reminder of her lost power and what that loss had cost her.

She headed northeast, tugged to her final destination of Kildara, a two-day journey on foot, if she kept a good pace. The small town known for its fast and agile horse breed wasn't too far or too close to Callum. New people. Same secrets. Less questions. Not too long a journey and far enough that the chance of coming across someone from Callum would be slim.

The briny wind whipped and whirled over the hills, creating waves of green glinting in the sun. The rain was long gone now, Callum a mile behind her. The sun shone in a cloudless sky while Maxie led up ahead, her red and orange coat like a ball of fire scurrying across the green grass.

The wind barreled into Evelyn again. Her hair came loose from her low bun and twirled across her face. She sighed, turned back to Callum, and braced against the wind.

An hour ago, she'd gazed up at McKenna McCarthy's dead body. Chills crawled across her skin. The stiffness of the dead always made Evelyn uneasy. She shut her eyes, trying to forget the sight of McKenna's blue-hued skin. It had to be a trick of the light. Vampyrs did not cross the Sapphire Sea. Vampyrs resided in Sorin, the New World, not the Old World.

No one knew for certain how vampyrs came into existence. Demons had roamed since the times of Gods and Goddesses across both Torren and Sorin, creatures of darkness, and though vampyrs shared a likeness with them, they'd only emerged five centuries ago, at the same time the land in Sorin split, the Void cracking into existence. Some theorized vampyrs were humans who tried to gain power and bargained with the faeries. Others wondered if it had been witches corrupted by dark magic. A few blamed the faeries altogether, saying it was the ancient ones corrupted by their own trickery.

But there was always a constant in their origin story.

Witches' bones.

Evelyn shivered, the wretchedness of the vampyrs crawling up her skin. No matter the hills she walked or the minutes that passed, she could not shake the horrific but blatant truth.

There was a chance a vampyr was in Callum.

Evelyn thought of Miss Patricia. The other barmaids who worked at the Runaway Radish. Mr. Finn and his fish shop. The baker who sold blueberry muffins from a wagon. The farmers who sold to weavers.

Goddess, the quaint, humble town of Callum had grown on Evelyn, and she could not imagine a vampyr wreaking its bloodthirsty wrath on them all. Guilt gripped her by the throat. Leaving Callum had seemed like a wise choice, but now it reminded her too much of running two years ago.

Letting down those she loved. Fracturing a hope her people thrived on. Abandoning her duty.

Believe, Evelyn, her father had told her, his last words before the vampyr used its claws to shred open his throat.

The sickening memory had Evelyn halting in her tracks. Back then, leaving had seemed right. She could not help her people, not without her flame. Sorin had werewolves defending the Void and witches defending the plains and Wall. Yet, Callum did not have those defenses. Dread bloomed in Evelyn's belly. She doubted they knew how to stop a victim from turning into a vampyr.

Burning the victim's body.

Maxie rejoined her at the base of the hill, threading through Evelyn's legs and brushing her cheek against her high-waisted trousers. Her familiar's bright yellow eyes would not meet Evelyn's and instead stared down at Callum. Evelyn assessed those coming and going from the south entrance, boats sailing in from the horizon before storm season started, and white-as-snow gulls circling the perimeter. Evelyn sighed. She scratched Maxie behind the ears and supposed her familiar already sensed her decision.

Resolve twisted in her gut. She'd been running for so long she'd forgotten what it really meant to protect others. From her birth order to duty to the prophecy, being a protector mattered above all else. Unable to help against the vampyr, she could at least warn Callum of the threat they faced.

She'd find Commissioner Doyle, admit her suspicions about a vampyr, and advise them to burn the body.

And then finally leave Callum as she'd always planned.

"Let's make this quick." Evelyn sighed and turned back down the path. Using her innate magic, she shrank her staff to the size of a hairpin and slid it through her bun, out of sight and unknown as a magical weapon to others.

Maxie meowed in agreement, and together they traveled back to the coastal town.

Chapter Four

Evelyn

When Evelyn and Maxie reached the outskirts of town, it bustled with the same midday activity Evelyn had grown used to, but townsfolk appeared solemn, weary with their thoughts. McKenna's death lingered in the air like a haunting ballad.

Maxie dashed out of sight, and Evelyn guessed her familiar had gone searching for a snack near the ships. Thanks to their linked souls and magic, Maxie would find her later as she always did.

Evelyn weaved through the harbor market, cutting across to reach the far side of the town to visit Commissioner Doyle's office. A large horse lumbered across her path, and Evelyn grimaced and went around it. She detested horses, hating how tall they stood off the ground, hated how they reminded her of the last time she'd ridden one.

A horrible, wretched day.

She passed a young woman sitting with a little girl, weaving on a loom, and paused to watch them work. Chestnut-colored yarn depicted a willow tree, and after a few rows, the young woman turned over the next two rows to the little girl, nodding words of encouragement and directing her when she hesitated.

Evelyn's chest swelled at the sight, remembering the times she'd sat next to Blair, her middle sister, and Mirella, her eldest. Witches possessed innate magic, a part of a witch as natural as breathing. Unique abilities outside of innate magic, like Evelyn's flame, were considered bronntanas. Not all witches possessed one, but Evelyn's sisters, like her, had their own. Blair wielded wind like their father while Mirella possessed healing. Unlike innate magic, bronntanas were like a muscle. They needed to be worked, trained, challenged, used, but also rested.

Like the skill of weaving a loom, row by row, tapestry after tapestry, or blanket after blanket. The little girl's hands moved slower than the young woman's, hesitant and thoughtful, but she stayed focused and smiled after finishing a single row. The young woman beside her beamed, smile and eyes just as bright as the gold bangles on her arm.

In between her two sisters, Evelyn had practiced bringing forth her flame at her fingertips or lighting and dimming candles. The young woman smiled at the little girl with encouragement as Blair had smiled at Evelyn, and she corrected the girl's movements like Mirella had corrected her younger sister. Evelyn had felt that adoration before. From her parents, her sisters, her coven. Even from her people as she'd walked the streets of Nūa.

"That'll be you one day," Evelyn's mother had said as they'd strolled through Fearrington Park where the Third-born Union statue stood. Just like the little girl, full of excitement and eagerness, Evelyn had gazed at the copper figures, stained mint from age and elements.

"Tell me the story, Mama!" she'd asked.

Her mother had smiled and obliged.

"The Sun Goddess planted the seed to create our world, giving us life and light. The Moon God watched over us, giving us strength and courage. After the Great Burnings, witches came to this land. For years, we prospered. But then darkness took root in the north: the vampyrs. Though we are not alone, not then and not now. Our friends and allies, the werewolves, lived in the great forests of the Vadon Mountains, and their Moon Seers saw what our Sun Seers saw: 'The truest of unions between the third-borns of the Sun and Moon will defeat the darkness.'"

It had felt like a fairytale. With the power of the flame and the strength of the wolf, Evelyn would save the world. Yet, unlike the little girl learning to weave with the cold coloring her cheeks and a tutor beside her full of affection, at the age of six, Evelyn had been turned over to a tutor who had been cold, cruel, and relentless like the southern wind that gusted through the harbor market.

Evelyn wrapped her cloak closer around her body, dismissing the harsh words of the past that fed the doubt rooted within her like an obstinate weed. She may not have been good enough to be Daughter of the Goddess, but she *could* warn Commissioner Doyle and Callum thanks to her knowledge of the vampyr.

Evelyn walked three more blocks, passing the back of the Runaway Radish, hearing the cries and cheers filtering from the gambling room. Escaping the back kitchen door, the promise of parsnip soup sweetened the alleyway air.

After three more blocks, Evelyn arrived at the commissioner's office, a singular squat brick building. The size of it still baffled her. An entire wall, twenty feet tall, surrounded Nūa to protect and defend witches, but Evelyn knew that Callum had little crime or violence.

The most Callum saw were drunk quarrels at the Runaway Radish, petty thieves in the market, and the occasional pirate ship squatting at the dock. Tales of demon sightings in the hills and farmlands were whispered over pints of ale. Like faeries, Evelyn hadn't seen a single one, but according to Miss Patricia, huntsmen handled that particular problem.

One hadn't traveled through Callum in months and they'd only been passing through to help with a demon in Dinberry. Evelyn sighed, certain Callum had a single line of defense with their commissioner and this quaint building. Evelyn entered the doorless entrance, finding the front office empty. Floorboards creaked under her arrival. A petite fireplace provided heat from the side of the room, and a small empty desk stood to the left. A cell, smelling of stale beer and sweat, took up the right wall. At the center, an entry led to a hallway lined with doors.

"Commissioner?"

No one answered. Except silence and the presence of death.

Evelyn didn't need to see to know. Her magic sensed that McKenna's body had been brought here.

"Commissioner?" Evelyn called again.

Evelyn checked outside but found the street empty. This close to the town's edge, it was quieter with less foot traffic.

Evelyn sighed. If she waited any longer, she'd lose daylight before reaching the next town to rest in. She couldn't risk using magic to light her travels either, as no one knew she was a witch and she wanted to keep it that way. Whispers and rumors traveled fast, even with an ocean between her and Nūa.

Her innate magic urged her forward, curious to investigate the darkness seeping from the back, but it wasn't just Evelyn's magic that was curious. Evelyn had seen victims of vampyrs for years, as long as she could remember. She'd witnessed them attack, seen them feed. The horrific sights had fueled her need to protect her people, her desire to ensure she could prevent others from suffering similar fates.

But she'd never seen today's sight. Not once had a vampyr displayed its kill in such a way. They killed for blood, not for show. They ravaged villages. Ran crazed after prey. Slaughtered anything with a heartbeat. The way McKenna's almost pristine corpse had been displayed suggested it had not been a vampyr, but her blue-hued skin suggested otherwise.

Evelyn crept to the hall and stopped at the first doorway. Inside, a white sheet covered the silhouette of a woman. McKenna's hair spilled out from under it and over the table. Her head, feet, and hands stuck out, blue contrasting with the sheet.

The dead always sucked the energy from a space with their stillness, as if the darkness surrounding them consumed everything.

Back home, Evelyn had been trained as a protector like all other third-borns. Birth order, witch or werewolf, determined one's duty. Firstborns were leaders, while second-borns were scholars. How they fulfilled their duty depended on their skills and magic. Mirella, as the eldest, was a leading healer. Blair as second-born had become a highly esteemed scholar in one of the most decorated libraries in Nūa.

But Evelyn wasn't just any third-born; she was a third-born *daughter*. Children were rare amongst witches and werewolves. Two children were a blessing. Three was a miracle. To have all three be daughters or sons, consecutively for that matter—well, the rarity, the scarcity, the blessing befitted a prophecy. It had only happened once before, a union between a third-born daughter named Carena and a third-born son named Finton. They'd died before they could fulfil the prophecy, and Sorin had gripped onto the hope that a new union would be born.

One hundred and fifty years later, Evelyn had been the third consecutive daughter born of her Carson coven parents. The moment she'd drawn her first breath, she'd earned her title as Daughter of the Goddess. Four months later, Kade Drengr, a third-born *son* of a werewolf pack, was born, earning him the title as Son of the God, promising their eventual union.

As a protector, Evelyn had been trained to be on the Guard, a group of elite witch soldiers who protected Sorin. That part of her life came back in flashes. Missions. Marks. Rescues. The memories left her empty, hollow, because she hadn't done anything like that since running away.

Standing in the commissioner's office, waiting to inspect a victim, felt like being on the Guard again. Evelyn itched with old habits—inspect for bitemarks, study the hue of their skin, ask for any witnesses, determine if it was demon or vampyr. Yet, she wasn't on the Guard, she was on the run. She decided it was best to wait to talk with the commissioner, and perhaps Miss Patricia had seen him around town.

Evelyn turned to leave, her magic sensing something new, like the gentle caress of night. She stepped through the doorless entrance, only to collide with a wall of muscle, knocking her off-balance. Leather-gloved hands caught her forearms, steadying her as she stepped back into the commissioner's office.

"Apologies, miss," a voice with a deep timbre said.

Evelyn looked up, craning her neck as she did so to take in the full length of the tallest man she'd ever seen and one she hadn't crossed paths within Callum before. She herself stood inches taller than her female peers, but this man stood over a foot taller than her, having to duck his head through the entryway as he entered the commissioner's office.

Eyes made of liquid gold, like warmed honey, stared down at her. He raked his hand through tousled, sun-kissed brown waves that curled past his ears, glinting from the light of the fire. Leather traveling trousers and vest, not of Callum craftsmanship, conformed to every inch of his long, muscular legs, and a black cloak billowed around him, the contrast of dark and gold ensnaring her.

Evelyn's magic bloomed, as did a foreign heat in her belly. The wide distance between them bristled with the static of her magic. Thankfully, only she could feel it, but she tried to rein it in. She didn't like the way her body or magic reacted to his voice and amber stare. Not one bit. It knocked her off-balance worse than their earlier collision, and she'd forgotten her plan to find the commissioner and warn him about burning McKenna's body.

"You're not the commissioner," he said.

"How observant of you," Evelyn said, putting on the indifferent mask she'd mastered over the years. *Stay quiet and say little.* Best to remember that.

The man raised a single brow, his bearded jawline tightening as he assessed her.

"If you'll excuse me," she said, stepping forward.

He stepped back, but only enough for her to pass by with a feather-breadth of air between them, their chests almost flush. Evelyn's magic, relentless, fluttered with independent interest around him. It compelled Evelyn to chance one more glance.

She certainly would've remembered those eyes, looking her over as if he saw every truth, lie, disguise, and title she possessed.

"Have you seen him, perhaps?" he said in a rush.

Evelyn stopped. "Who?" she asked, despite reason screaming for her to stay quiet and say little.

She found no traces of magic belonging to him. The beautiful man before her was human. Yet, why did it feel like a spell was at play? Perhaps he was hiding his magic like her? The black leathers, the larger build, the sword. Evelyn recognized his profession.

A huntsman. They passed through Callum from time to time looking for jobs. No magic to speak of.

Evelyn shifted from foot to foot. No, she didn't like this one bit. Nothing, no one, never a man before had caught her attention like this.

"The commissioner," he said, walking farther into the small space. He took in the desk, peered down the hall.

"No, unfortunately." Evelyn paused, looking toward the room with McKenna's body. Goddess, the body needed to be burned before it was buried in the ground, activating the vampyr curse. Evelyn's hesitation caught the man's attention again. "He wasn't here when I came looking."

She needed to get out of this office, out of this room and away from the orbit of this man, whoever he was. He made her forget her wits.

Say little, stay quiet, find Commissioner Doyle, and leave *Callum.*

The wind blew in from outside, as if reaching out its hand and beckoning Evelyn to move on with her plans. Ready to be on her way, she stepped forward and her boot skidded across the floor—

"Wait," the man said.

An unexpected *something* pulled at her magic, and she stopped.

Turned.

And faced his devastatingly beautiful amber stare.

Chapter Five

Kade

Suspended, off-kilter, Kade attempted to rally his thoughts and intentions.

Stars above, Evelyn Carson, Daughter of the Goddess, stood before him, and Kade had almost missed it. The wind pushed through the small room again, and the sweet scent he'd detected earlier assaulted his senses.

Vanilla and burning cedar. Evelyn's scent.

Her gray eyes, a silvery shade of blue, bewitched him and his wolf. He stood there, his heart hammering in his chest as his feet rooted in the room, needing time to take her in, like a wonder he wanted to marvel at.

The sunlight made her obsidian hair resemble spilled ink, wavering between blue and black. Twisted into a low bun, loose strands framed her flushed face, high cheekbones, rosy lips, and austere brow. She wore a high-necked blouse tucked into wool trousers that were high-waisted and tapered around muddy boots. A deep blue cloak, tattered, worn, and rimmed with the same mud of her boots, draped over her tall and lean frame, bringing out the blue in her eyes and hair.

An ethereal beauty, like that of the full moon in a cloudless sky, encompassed her. For a breath, Kade wanted to revel in her beauty—*No*. He locked his knees tight and clutched his anger. This was the woman who'd abandoned her destiny and her people, the woman he'd been hunting for twelve months, scouring every village, town, and city on the continent of Sorin.

A woman had never once compelled him like this, and even before he'd realized who she was, Kade hadn't wanted her out of his sight. *Something* within him couldn't bear it; an itch, an inclination, an instinct drove him to keep her close, whoever she was, and yet—

He'd traveled on a boat to find her. She'd *left*, and Kade wouldn't allow the sadness in those eyes to lure him into forgetting. He seethed, battling the urge to toss her over his shoulder and demand answers, but he couldn't. He couldn't make a scene after finally finding her.

"Saige? Is that you?" a burly man boomed as he entered the office. A metal broach reflected off his chest. Tiredness gripped the man's eyes, and he wore a frown so deep it appeared etched into his skin.

"Commissioner Doyle!" Evelyn said.

"Aye, that's me. What are you doing here? Miss Patricia said ya moved on from Callum." The man removed his leather cloak and hung it by the door, his gaze catching Kade.

Kade froze, an icy chill cementing his muscles in place. He assessed Evelyn. The mud on her worn cloak and boots. A filled satchel and tied parcel slung over her shoulder. Her cheeks were rosy as if she'd been kissed by the wind. She'd been ready to leave, perhaps already put her boots to the road. But if so . . . why had she returned?

Evelyn eyed Kade up and down, then darted her attention back to the commissioner.

She swallowed. "I came to warn you that I believe McKenna was killed by a vampyr. If so, you'll need to burn the body to stop the curse."

"Vampyrs are only in Sorin." Kade spoke before he had time to think.

His betrothed's silvery eyes narrowed. Her lips fell into a thin line as she raised a brow. "Have you seen the victim's body, Huntsman? The evidence might challenge that notion."

Commissioner Doyle clapped a hand on Kade's shoulder. "A huntsman? Now, the timing couldn't be any better, I tell ya!"

Kade ran his hand through his hair and cleared his throat. Thank the Moon God his disguise had worked. His hands itched to touch the enchanted necklace under his tunic for reassurance, but he resisted, falling into the disguise in a breath.

"Can we see the body, Commissioner?" he asked.

"Of course. Follow me."

Kade waited for Evelyn, holding out his arm for her to go ahead of him. Now that he had found her, he wouldn't dare lose sight of her. After a beat, she followed Commissioner Doyle into the back room, ignoring Kade entirely. Her muddy boots squished on the stone floor, and the drenched hem of her cloak dragged across it.

Shaking away the urge to blow his cover and demand answers from her, Kade joined them in the small, candlelit room. His wolf hearing detected an intake of breath from Evelyn, her heart skipping a beat. Did the sight of the dead unnerve her? Intrigued and focused on getting a better look at this supposed vampyr victim, Kade peered over Evelyn's shoulder.

Unease swept through him. The young woman's eyes had been removed. The murder victim—McKenna, he gathered—lay there with a crimson, hollow gaze and her skin tinged a robin's-egg blue.

Stars above, she had been killed by a vampyr.

His duty snapped into place, worry and resolve twisting in his gut. How in the *moons* had a vampyr crossed the Sapphire Sea?

"How long ago was she killed?" Kade asked, rounding to the other side of the table.

Vampyr poison interfered with the natural process of decomposition, and even Kade's werewolf sense of smell couldn't determine McKenna's time of death. The petrified state preserved the body until it was buried deep in the earth, covered by mud, worms, and darkness, allowing the vampyr curse to take root and turn the victim into a scáth.

"From accounts of when she went missing, we think she was killed last night," Commissioner Doyle said.

Kade pulled the sheet farther back, revealing a wound not made by a vampyr—a puncture from a sharp object in the center of McKenna's chest. There was barely any blood at all surrounding the wound.

She'd been drained.

"She was found dangling from the clock tower, a whaling hook in her chest," Evelyn said, sparing him a quick glance. Her brows furrowed as she returned her attention to the dead body. Her other features lay blank. Even breathing, even heartbeat. The Daughter of the Goddess was unreadable, and Kade could only guess she thought the same as him. As Son of the God, Kade had encountered hundreds of vampyr victims, but he'd never seen one displayed like this or with missing eyes.

"She won't turn," Evelyn said, a sliver of relief in her tone.

Kade nodded. "Without her eyes, she can't."

Turning someone into a vampyr, much like spells and enchantments, hinged on preciseness. First, a vampyr victim needed to be entirely drained of blood for enough venom to enter the system and activate the curse. Injuries or mutilations before death could be healed by the vampyr curse, but a victim's body needed to stay intact after death.

Minimal bruising rimmed McKenna's eye sockets, indicating they'd been removed after she'd been killed.

"We don't need to burn her?" Commissioner Doyle asked.

Both Evelyn and Kade shook their heads.

"That's a relief," he said. "But I'm not convinced a vampyr did this."

Evelyn shook her head again, pulling the sheet back over the young woman's chest. "Her skin is blue from the poison of a vampyr."

"Aye, we may know little of vampyrs here in Callum, but there are no bite marks." The commissioner gestured at McKenna's bare neck.

"We have more arteries than that, Commissioner. May I?" Evelyn asked.

The commissioner nodded, and she pulled the sheet up, revealing the young woman's naked legs, hued blue but unscathed. Not even a bruise. As Evelyn assessed, Kade took the moment to reach out his wolf and sense Evelyn's magic. He met a blanket of heat, like the comforting rays of the summer sun, but nothing else. In fact, his wolf didn't even detect magic, just a sense of power. If he didn't know better, he'd guess her to be human.

Then he smelled it. The musty herb wolfsbane. Evelyn's slim fingers hovered over the victim's thigh, a bracelet of leather and vegetation woven together around her wrist. She, too, masked her magic and true self. Kade wasn't surprised. She'd evaded discovery for two years, and this explained her success.

Again, Kade's wolf wrestled within. The sight of the bracelet, the use of wolfsbane—an outlawed plant amongst the werewolves—angered him. He hated her actions. Masking her identity. Constantly on the move. She didn't give a damn about her duty as Daughter of the Goddess. Evelyn never wanted to be found. But then . . . why had she cared about McKenna enough to seek out Commissioner Doyle?

Evelyn pointed to the puncture wound on McKenna's inner thigh. "She was bitten here."

Kade inspected the wound smudged with black dirt, close to the dead girl's covered sex—an intimate area, not typical of a bloodthirsty vampyr who went for the neck or wrist.

Back home, bit marks were routinely inspected after a vampyr attack. How many bite marks scarred a victim's body determined how many vampyrs had attacked. Vampyrs bit once, drinking blood from a single source. More than one bite meant more than one vampyr. But the type of vampyr could also be determined. The deeper the blue, the more venom, and scáths, newly turned vampyrs, didn't have control over how much venom they used. Mature vampyrs left their victims a lighter shade, but Kade had never encountered a "mature" vampyr.

They hadn't crossed the Void in over two decades.

Kade pinched the bridge of his nose. McKenna had been drained by one vampyr—odd enough an ocean away from Drystan—but she was also a lighter shade of blue, not the evidence of scáths, the vampyr he, or Evelyn for that matter, were accustomed to. The details of the vampyr murder became more and more confusing.

Evelyn pulled back the sheet to cover McKenna again. She blinked and gave nothing away, appearing almost bored, but then she swallowed, eyes darting back to where the bite was.

Evelyn Carson wore a mask.

She tried to come across as aloof and indifferent, when in fact she felt far more than she let on.

Miss Patricia said ya moved on from Callum.

Evelyn had left Callum, or at least had tried to. Leaving, running, moving place to place, constantly avoiding her duty. Anger seared through Kade. Again, he fought the urge to demand answers.

Yet, why had she come back? Was his betrothed as concerned about the murder as he was?

Before Kade could ask anything more, Commissioner Doyle cleared his throat. "I'll hire both of ya to find the vampyr and kill it."

Kade balked, remembering he posed as a huntsman. Staying and finding this vampyr had not been his plan. It was not his duty to protect those in Callum. But he'd been fighting the vampyr most of his life, and leaving, putting his own wants before the threat, felt wrong.

He'd wanted to find Evelyn and bring her back. Convince her to unify their souls and fulfill the prophecy, yet that prophecy connected Kade to his duty. Defeat the vampyr, regardless of what he wanted. His mother had sacrificed herself for that duty, and now he'd seen something he'd never thought to see. A vampyr in Callum. A victim with missing eyes. An intimate bite. These weren't like the killings back home. Kade's wolf sensed the difference, and the way Evelyn appeared lost in her own thoughts, he wondered if she sensed the same.

Commissioner Doyle continued. "I have a feeling it won't be the last killing. But we aren't equipped here in Callum for vampyrs. We have our own demons, our own monsters, but this is new for us."

"I . . ." Evelyn shook her head, setting her shoulders back. "I'm sorry, Commissioner Doyle, but I can't help."

As she turned to leave, a flash of defeat and even guilt mixed with the sadness in her silver eyes, the first light of emotion Kade had witnessed.

Kade needed to stay and find this vampyr, despite the complications it caused. He couldn't lose Evelyn, but revealing who he was may drive her away. He needed her to stay and work on this murder with him. That way, he could prove they could be a team and possibly discover why she'd left in the first place.

"Frightened?" Kade called.

He baited her, knowing damn well fear wasn't an emotion he'd scented on her. Accounts of Evelyn had never depicted a frightened young woman but instead a witch who faced demons, darkness, and vampyrs head-on.

She halted, spinning around so her tattered cloak billowed about her. "No."

Kade raised a brow, scratching his beard. "Fooled me. Usually, those who are scared run."

He'd hit a nerve.

Evelyn's eyes widened. She gritted her teeth, then sighed. "What's the pay?" she asked Commissioner Doyle.

Money would be her deciding factor? No. Evelyn bluffed again, deflecting the real reason she'd decided to stay. A *why* swam in her eyes, a determined curiosity. She needed answers just as he did.

Commissioner Doyle made for the door, leading them out of the room with the dead body. "Captain's pay, if that'll suit you. I pay by coin every week."

Evelyn nodded. "I'll start first thing."

"*We* will start first thing," Kade corrected.

Evelyn scoffed. "I don't recall agreeing to work with you, Huntsman."

Her rejection bit, but Kade brushed it off.

"I don't care if you work as a team or solo. Find the vampyr. And kill it," Commissioner Doyle said.

Evelyn left, walking from the building and out of Kade's sight in three long strides. He caught up to her, following her down the street.

"It would be better if we worked together," he said, his tone far too desperate for his liking.

"Not going to happen." She continued walking, not even sparing him a glance.

Stars above. Kade struggled to rein in his anger and frustration. "Our chances—"

She stopped and swiveled to face him. For a witch with flame, her eyes could freeze the world solid. "I work better alone. Trust me. Stay out of my way, and I'll stay out of yours."

Evelyn blended into the growing crowd, becoming lost in the busy market. Kade tried to follow, pushing aside the townsfolk. Quick, light on her feet, she danced like flames out of his sight.

Kade stopped. He didn't like Evelyn gone yet again, but she'd stay to find the vampyr.

They were bound to cross paths soon enough.

Chapter Six

Evelyn

Usually, those who are scared run.

Fucking flames, the huntsman's words had reminded her far too much of running from her duty two years ago, but she hadn't run out of fear. She'd run because she wasn't good enough to defeat the vampyr. She had no flame.

He didn't need to know that, but she in no way could allow him or Commissioner Doyle to believe she was frightened. The word enraged Evelyn and her magic. It had risen to the surface, itching below her skin. She'd remained calm, considering her options.

She'd meant to leave Callum, move on to the next place. Staying was risky, but even though McKenna's body wouldn't turn, a vampyr had killed her and could still be in Callum. No, she didn't have her flame, but this was different than facing the threat of vampyrs or the Void's darkness back home. With the resolve of her urge to protect, Evelyn could handle one vampyr. She still had her innate magic and two decades of training behind her. She'd figure out how to kill it the old-fashioned way, severing its head and burning the body.

Evelyn sighed, anxious thoughts tumbling through her. McKenna's missing eyes and the intimate area of the bite. And she still wanted to keep her identity as a witch hidden. She'd have to be tactful, secretive with her investigation, work alone. And the reason she'd said no to the huntsman . . . She couldn't afford him learning she was a witch.

At the thought of him, her heart quickened.

Goddess, she hadn't noticed the opposite sex since she'd gone on the run. Not to mention, she was betrothed to a werewolf an ocean away.

Evelyn shook away thoughts of the huntsman and sighed again. She stopped at the edge of the docks, the greasy scent of Finn's Fish Fry teasing her with the promise of a salty and vinegary snack. After buying herself a large order and taking a seat on the rock wall overlooking the sea, Evelyn sent out her magic to Maxie, calling her back.

Thankfully, storm season brewed on the horizon. Dark clouds, like puffed mountains, flashed with lightning in the distance. Wind, fierce and cold, blew off the waves. Ships at the docks appeared abandoned, not a soul on them and sails gone. For ten weeks, Evelyn could be assured no whispers of the vampyr would make it across the Sapphire Sea to Sorin.

Enough time to find the vampyr, kill it, and move on from Callum.

By the time Evelyn finished her salty, meaty snack, fingers greased and belly full, Maxie appeared and scurried up the docks. Her familiar rubbed up against her legs, Maxie's purr vibrating through her. She jumped up onto the wall, pacing over Evelyn's lap and meowing nonstop.

"All right, all right," Evelyn said, unwrapping the fish scraps.

Tired, weary, and fresh off a ship with serious sea legs, she'd had her first meal in Callum at Mr. Finn's, and the shop owner never forgot Maxie's parcel of scraps.

Evelyn scratched behind Maxie's ears, laughing as the cat devoured her dinner. Maxie meowed and flicked her tail in contentment.

"Evelyn?"

Her true name froze her blood and quickened her heart rate.

But the woman's voice—

"Tovi?"

A wide-brimmed lavender hat obscured most of her best friend's face, but Evelyn would recognize that snowy blonde hair anywhere. Decked in the finest garments, Tovi stood tall and proud and appeared regal in a full-length petticoat the same pale shade of cream as her skin. She stood a few feet away, her mouth agape and tears welling in her jade eyes.

They both burst into a run, crashing into a hug and holding each other with endearment and heartache.

Two years.

Evelyn hadn't seen her best friend, let alone anyone from home, in two years. She held her willowy friend close, disbelief replaced her heart-pounding fear of being discovered by someone who would drag her back.

Evelyn pulled away but didn't dare let go of her friend. "What are you doing here?" she asked, voice breaking. *Goddess,* she cried with joy.

Tovi put her hands on Evelyn's cheeks, running her thumbs across her tears. Comforting her like she had after Evelyn's parents had died.

"I . . . I'm here on business for the trading company," she said in a rush. "And please tell me you are not crying!" Tovi teased.

"It's the wind," Evelyn said.

Her friend laughed and raised a questioning brow. "Ah, yes, the wind!"

"I see tears of your own, Tovi!" Evelyn said.

They laughed again, and a sense of comfort washed over Evelyn like the gentle warmth of the afternoon sun. Laughter had always been woven into their relationship.

The first time they met, Tovi had leaned over and whispered horrible jokes about the history professor until Evelyn thought she might burst into a fit of laughter after holding it in for so long. Tovi had offered Evelyn distraction from the stares her title as Daughter of the Goddess had gained her in the classroom. Her friend was the only one who'd never paid mind to that.

Tovi was human, the only daughter of a wealthy trader. His wealth and influence had secured Tovi a spot at the university in Nūa, which accepted a handful of humans each year, despite his wishes to marry her off for business alliances. Tovi did not care about Evelyn's title or magic, but she understood duty and family expectations. She'd worked hard at university and earned her place helping run her father's business, instead of being a pawn in it.

"I can't believe you're here," Evelyn whispered.

The last time she'd seen Tovi, it'd been at her parents' funeral. Nūa had been overcome with grief and dreadful rain, and Tovi had held Evelyn as she cried herself to sleep for days. Mirella had been busy stepping up as Coven leader while Blair assisted with the transition, and yet Tovi had stayed.

To this day, she was the only one who knew Evelyn's secret.

As if sensing Evelyn's thoughts, Tovi pulled her into another hug. Despite her willowy frame, she possessed considerable strength. She released Evelyn and kept her hands on her shoulders. "It's good to see you, Evelyn," she said.

Evelyn almost smiled but the sound of her name felt like a whip. She covered her friend's mouth with her hand and shushed her.

Her friend blinked and then looked around. Not a soul walked the area they stood in. She swatted Evelyn's hand away and pulled her to the side. "What?"

"Saige. My name is Saige Ferriwether in Callum," Evelyn said.

Tovi's shoulders drooped, but before she could comment, a hiss sounded below them. Maxie sat between Evelyn's legs, her yellow eyes slits as she stared up at Tovi.

"Still not friendly, I see," Tovi said.

"Maxie isn't friendly with anyone."

"Except you."

"She's my familiar—of course she's friendly with me." Evelyn shook her head.

"Come," Tovi said, taking Evelyn's hand. "I want to hear everything. Where you've been. How you are. All over a glass of wine."

Evelyn laughed, following her friend down the street with Maxie in tow, a feathery lightness easing her shoulders.

If she had left Callum, she wouldn't be here now in the presence of a friend.

The early darkness of night descended in the small parlor inside a townhome situated in the northeast side of town. Riven, Tovi's twin brother, had purchased it weeks ago after planning to stay during storm season and ensure their new trading route ran smoothly come the winter months.

Evelyn and Tovi had finished an entire bottle of wine while discussing the last two years. How she changed her name in every place. Used moonstones from her wedding dress for bartering. The odd jobs she'd taken to gain money or lodging. Disguising her magic with an enchanted bracelet.

Evelyn held it up for Tovi.

"So, witches can't sense you," Tovi said, her eyes widening.

"Or werewolves," Evelyn said, twirling the bracelet around and around. The magic laced within it hummed. "I added wolfsbane."

A few lone grapes and slices of cheese still sat on the plate of snacks Tovi had laid out, and the candle on the table had a skirt of wax on the hilt of the candelabra.

With the black curtains and tinted windows, it was difficult to tell how much time had truly passed. The dreary lighting had to do with printing, ink, and drying times, according to Tovi. A beast of a machine sat wedged in the corner, its copper and iron parts gleaming in the candlelight, and stacks of trading pamphlets, advertising goods sold through her father's trading company, sat waiting to be handed out in the harbor tomorrow.

"I'd have you stay here, but I've taken over Riven's spare room," she said, her tone dismissive at the mention of her brother.

From what Evelyn knew, her brother was like Tovi's father—demanding and harsh. Unlike for witches and werewolves, birth order meant nothing to humans. No leader firstborns, no second-born scholars, no third-born protectors. Instead, gender meant everything, and as the daughter, Tovi was expected to marry, something Evelyn's best friend cringed at the very mention of. Tovi had never wanted to fulfill her father's demands, but Evelyn *couldn't* fulfill her own family expectations and those of the prophecy. It'd been Tovi who'd encouraged her to find a different way.

The two friends had sat on Evelyn's roof, days after Evelyn's parents' bodies had been laid to rest, drinking a bottle of wine. Evelyn could still taste the tannins biting her tongue and the rawness under her eyes from so much crying.

"You could protect them in a different way," her friend had said.

At first, Evelyn had blamed her wicked idea on the wine. But her friend's words had rung in her thoughts for days. Her plan manifested itself, deeply rooted in her desire to protect her people. Like Tovi, who'd found her own way in her father's business, Evelyn had found a different way to fulfill her duty.

Leaving.

"Do you have news of home?" Evelyn had wanted to ask at least ten times during their conversation, but the words had turned to ash on her tongue, leaving her anxious and with a dry mouth.

Tovi sighed. "The efforts at the Void and at the Wall are the same. Demon attacks have worsened, but at least vampyr attacks have lessened."

Evelyn nodded but was too guilty to feel relief. She'd expected as much, seeing as no news had traveled to the shores of Torren since she'd arrived, but she often wondered about the state of her homeland in her absence.

"And what have I been up to?" she asked with a scoff.

Tovi gave her a weak smile and rose from the table. At the desk in the back, her friend sifted through various papers. A moment later, she handed Evelyn a Nūa pamphlet dated from five weeks ago.

"It's the last one I got before boarding a ship here."

Evelyn read through the columns of news. Art festivals. Holiday parades. Shifts in leadership. The latest fashion. And a single paragraph about the "secret mission" that she and Kade "couldn't disclose but felt confident in."

"I see they've been able to keep up the ruse," she muttered, throwing the pamphlet back onto the table.

Witches and werewolves back home believed Evelyn and Kade had solidified their union. Right under everyone's noses in a village north of Nūa, Evelyn had first read about her wedding in a paper a month after running away. At first, she'd been angered they'd used her like some story, some tale to add to the paper for witches to read over their morning coffee, but she understood it for what it was.

Damage control.

She'd run, and neither the Elders nor the Alphas would ever let witches and werewolves—or the vampyr king, for that matter—know they'd lost the Daughter of the Goddess. Her flame was a beacon of hope to their people and a weapon against the vampyrs.

Tovi leaned across the table. "I have to ask, but did you ever . . ."

"Try to get it back?" Evelyn sighed. "I did. After exhausting the library in Nūa before I left, I sought texts elsewhere. Nothing. No witch loses their bronntanas. Sure, it can become weakened and need rest, but it's never . . . *gone*. So I traveled to the mages, visited temples, prayed to the Sun Goddess." Evelyn shook her head. "All I heard was the voice of my father, his last words to me before he died."

"And what were they?" Tovi asked.

"Believe," Evelyn whispered.

"Well, sometimes the strongest magic is belief," Tovi said, laying a hand over Evelyn's.

A bitterness coated Evelyn's tongue, and she wasn't sure she agreed with Tovi. She believed plenty. In the prophecy. In the Sun Goddess. In the efforts against vampyr. Why had she lost her flame? Perhaps, because her bronntanas had been gifted by the Goddess herself, the Goddess had taken it back.

Tovi shifted in her seat, pulling her hand back. "Speaking of Kade, has your 'valiant' and 'courageous' betrothed come sniffing about?"

Her friend mocked Kade's portrayal in the pamphlets, and Evelyn managed a laugh.

"No," she said. "He'd never betray the 'wishes of the Elders.'"

Considering he hadn't attended her parents' funeral, this wouldn't be any different. Evelyn couldn't explain why, but his absence had left a sour taste in her mouth. If they were to be husband and wife, shouldn't he have come to offer support?

Evelyn shook her head. It no longer mattered. She'd run from her duty and their union. She was here as Saige Ferriwether and no longer third-born Daughter of the Goddess.

"Have you heard of the vampyr in Callum?" Evelyn asked.

Tovi straightened, and her mouth fell open. "A vampyr? Evelyn, how in Goddess's name would they make it here?"

Evelyn shrugged, still wondering the same thing. "I don't know, but a young woman was murdered. I saw her body today. All the signs fit."

Tovi sipped her wine, licking her lips and swirling the burgundy liquid. Sultry, bashful. Tovi possessed an air that demanded attention. Men at university had followed her like bees to honey, but she never seemed to notice.

"Well—"

"Tovi, you failed to mention your friend is a striking sight," a gruff voice said.

Evelyn turned to find a rake of a man leaning against the doorframe. Jade eyes—twins to Tovi's—zeroed in on her, trailing her from head to toe. Riven possessed the same allure as his sister. Tall, thin, and limber, with his long, pale blond hair pulled to the side, a few thinly braided strands throughout. Gaunt cheekbones, a curved smirk of a smile, and a walk more like a prowl.

As he reached the table, he outstretched a hand stained by printer ink. Evelyn expected a simple handshake, but he planted a kiss on her knuckles, his jade eyes never leaving hers.

"Tovi also failed to mention her brother is a flirt," Evelyn said with a raised brow.

He laughed and his eyes flashed, *Goddess*, with determination.

"Riven, Evelyn is off-limits, and you very well know that." Tovi stood and invaded Riven's space, pushing him from the table as she gathered their wine glasses and empty bottle.

Riven's gaze still flicked over Evelyn, conveying interest. "Well, from what you told me, Tovi, Evelyn is a runaway bride, which, I believe, contradicts your last statement."

Shocked, Evelyn looked at Tovi.

A look of guilt crossed her face, and then she waved her hand. "Riven knows, but don't worry. He has no friends or any acquaintances to even blab to."

"Well, that's a relief and a trait I don't doubt," Evelyn said.

Riven placed his hand over his heart and pretended to wince. "You wound me, Miss Carson."

Tovi grabbed her coat, and Evelyn gathered it was time to leave. Her magic sensed the tension between the two siblings. Tovi had explained earlier that she'd arrived to keep Riven in line as he operated the business during storm season, but Riven didn't enjoy being monitored.

Evelyn stood, putting on her coat by the door.

Tovi joined her and turned to Riven. "Evelyn was telling me about a vampyr murder in Callum," she said. "Who did you say it was?"

"McKenna McCarthy."

Riven moved toward the table of pamphlets, calling over his shoulder, "I already heard. Nasty business, but a single murder won't interfere with my deployment plans, sister."

"Right," Tovi said. She led Evelyn out of the townhome and into the night without a backward glance at her brother.

"I can see the brotherly-sisterly affection," Evelyn said.

"Yes. Our regard for one another has no bounds."

Evelyn scoffed but noted the sadness in Tovi's jade eyes. "It was good to see you, Tovi."

"Don't you dare say it like it's a goodbye." Tovi's brow furrowed, her eyes flashing. "We *must* have our weekly wine nights again."

Evelyn paused. The promise of a wine night, like they used to have, brought about a comfort she hadn't felt in so long. But could she enjoy a relaxing night with her friend like old times? She planned to solve McKenna's murder and leave as soon as she could. Except Evelyn didn't want to let her friend down.

"Of course," Evelyn said. "I'll let you know when I'm free."

Evelyn parted with her friend and headed into the center of town to start her investigation.

Chapter Seven

Evelyn

Sitting beside the still copper bell at the highest level of the tower, Evelyn had a bird's-eye view of Callum's shingled roofs. Chimneys sprouted like brick trunks. In the direction of the sea, blackness ranged for miles. Above everything, the moon shone, lighting the grassy hills in a silvery green. Below, the music from the nightly band at the Runaway Radish filtered outside, along with laughter and singing.

The bell tower had offered as much evidence as Evelyn expected. No signs of a struggle. No signs McKenna had been killed there. Other than the leftover rope from the whaling hook tied to a post protruding from the tower, there was no sign of the murder.

Which meant McKenna had been killed somewhere else, which begged the questions where and why hang her body from the bell tower? A killer would display a body like this to send a message or to mark their territory, but that wasn't the nature of vampyr.

It didn't fit.

Evelyn sighed. The few clues pointed to a murder rather than a vampyr attack. She needed to learn more about McKenna to learn more about her death. Tired, Evelyn descended the tower in the hopes Miss Patricia had her old room still available.

Despite the late hour, the Runaway Radish was filled to the brim with guests. Beers and cheery tunes appeared to have brought the town out of the dark mood it had been in since McKenna's body had been found. Between seeing Tovi and acquiring a job that let her use her training, Evelyn entered the Runaway Radish with a spring in her step. Even her magic thrummed at her fingers. She felt closer to her roots, protecting those around her as if she were back on the Guard.

She headed straight for the bar.

Miss Patricia, cheeks ruddy, beamed as she saw Evelyn. "My dear!" She rounded the bar and gave Evelyn a hug. "Here I thought you'd left!"

"About that . . ." Evelyn began. She filled Miss Patricia in on her new job with Commissioner Doyle and asked if she could get her old room back, promising rent and a few shifts in the tavern if needed.

Miss Patricia frowned. "I'm sorry, dear, but I gave your suite to another this evening. I have a spare room for guests you can use tonight, but I unfortunately don't have anything long-term left. Stom season's a busy time."

Her stomach sank. She'd taken on a job but now had nowhere to stay. Even though Tovi didn't have a spare room, maybe she'd offer the couch until Evelyn killed the vampyr. Not ideal, but she'd slept on worse over the last two years: stables, forest floors, wagons. Plus, she'd only be here temporarily.

Evelyn sighed and gave Miss Patricia a small smile. "It's all right, not a worry."

"Ya know," Miss Patricia said, "I have a niece with an apartment available."

Evelyn had made fair money as a barmaid, but she doubted she could afford an apartment. Nor did she need something so official or long-term. Although having a space of her own sounded nice. Back at home, she'd had her own place with a lovely view of Nūa's city skyline. A kitchen, a dining room. Bookshelves stacked and stacked with endless stories. She'd had her favorite bakery three blocks over. Maybe her new captain's pay would be enough.

"I'll check it out," she said.

"Perfect," Miss Patricia said. "Now, don't forget a room comes with dinner and a drink." She nudged Evelyn's shoulder. "I'll give you an extra spoonful and slice of bread." She gave a parting wink and rounded back behind the bar.

Evelyn smiled, unable to hide her delight at Miss Patricia's kindness. She saddled up on a wobbly stool at the bar, her smile dropping as her gaze connected with the new bartender.

The huntsman from earlier raised an expectant eyebrow and walked over. Her skin grew hot. Couldn't anything go right today? Her plan to leave had gone to shit. A vampyr had killed a woman in town. She didn't have lodging. Of all things, Evelyn didn't want to deal with the huntsman's pursuit or irritating questions.

"Aye, Cyrus here will get your supper for the evening," Miss Patricia said, patting his broad chest. She barely reached his elbow. "Thomas Banks is here tonight, and I better save Maisey the trouble."

Evelyn nodded as Miss Patricia walked off, then she met the huntsman's stare. He no longer wore his cloak or traveling leathers. Instead, he wore wool trousers and a loose cream tunic untied at the center so that the tanned skin of his chest peeked out.

"Cyrus, is it?" Evelyn asked, keeping her sights eye-level.

He nodded. "Cyrus Skender."

"And how exactly does a huntsman end up being a bartender? The commissioner's pay not enough?"

Cyrus shrugged. "Pay's fine. Miss Patricia offered a room for a few shifts a week." He shrugged. "Seemed like a fair trade while I'm in town."

Evelyn crossed her arms. "So you're the one who took my room," she said, using a sarcastic tone.

Cyrus tilted his head, his eyes the same color as the whiskey bottles on the shelves behind him, amber and gold. "I heard you'd left."

Evelyn narrowed her gaze while her stomach churned. She didn't like being reminded of that. "Changed my mind."

Cyrus nodded again. "The stew is rabbit this evening. Does that work for you?"

"Works fine."

He threw a dishrag over his shoulder and sauntered off. Evelyn blinked, trying to refocus her attention on what she'd discovered in the bell tower and not his eyes or the way his biceps flexed when he lifted his arm.

Goddess, what had gotten into her?

Sure, Evelyn had had her fair share of exploratory fun during her time at university. She also had a type, muscle and man, and Cyrus . . . She shook her head as if she could shake off the heat starting in her toes. Evelyn couldn't afford a distraction of any kind. Besides, she was, after all, betrothed to Kade Drengr, and though she never planned to follow through with that engagement, it didn't sit well with her to start relationships while on the run. It disrespected the werewolf she'd never met, and it wouldn't be fair to anyone.

Or herself.

She exhaled and plastered an indifferent scowl on her face as Cyrus returned with her stew. "Thank you," she said.

"Miss Patricia's dinners always come with a drink, I've been told. What will you be having?"

"Honeysuckle wine, please." Evelyn stirred her stew, turnips and carrots bobbing in the rich broth. She took a sip and detected the gamey taste of rabbit, mouth watering at the promise of a hearty, meaty meal.

"How long have you been in Callum?" Cyrus asked.

The question made Evelyn's defenses go up. *Stay quiet and say little.* It'd kept her safe thus far, and entertaining questions and conversations like this with those she didn't know made her nervous.

Yet, Cyrus wasn't looking at her as he cleaned a pint glass. His demeanor was relaxed, as if he was merely attempting conversation with her while he worked. He filled two pints of mead for a waiting barmaid who flashed him a dazzling smile.

He either didn't notice or didn't care, because his reaction was passive. His gaze landed back on her as he leaned against the bar and crossed his arms, waiting.

Oh, right.

She'd forgotten to answer him. *Fucking flames*, what had gotten into her?

"Three months."

"You know the town well?"

Evelyn shrugged. "Spent most of my time here at the inn but know it well enough. Why?"

He slid a piece of parchment over to her. Black ink gleamed under the pub light, and Evelyn read an address scribbled in impressive penmanship.

"It's the McCarthy farmstead. Could point me in the right direction?"

Evelyn *could* point him in the right direction, but so could Miss Patricia or anyone else at the inn. He was baiting her. Again. And again, it worked.

Curious, she asked, "Are you planning to talk with the family?"

Cyrus nodded. "Makes sense to learn more about McKenna."

She'd been planning the exact same thing after coming up short at the bell tower. "Their farm is north of the town—not too far, really."

Cyrus leaned over, bracing his hands on the bar top. "You know, it would make more sense if we went together."

Evelyn shook her head and took a sip of honeysuckle wine, the faint sweetness coating her tongue. "I already told you; I work better alone."

The lie was more difficult the second time. During Evelyn's time back home, she *had* worked primarily alone, but not because she was better that way. She'd been training as Daughter of the Goddess, betrothed to Son of the God. It didn't make sense to waste time working with others in the Guard when she'd eventually leave. The irony of it was not lost on Evelyn. She had left in the end, just not as everyone had intended.

Cyrus looked unconvinced but changed the subject. "You checked the bell tower today?"

Evelyn nodded. "Didn't find much, but I don't think McKenna was killed there."

Cyrus raised a brow. "I came to the same conclusion myself."

Evelyn shook her head. "It doesn't make any sense. It's as if . . . as if the killer, the *vampyr*, left the body for everyone to see."

"Or to show it off," he said, his tone bitter.

Vampyrs were cruel, ruthless creatures. They destroyed, tore bodies apart. Never had Evelyn seen a body left in the way McKenna's had been.

"Again, it doesn't make any sense."

Cyrus sighed. "No, it doesn't." He remained braced at the bar, golden-brown waves falling over his face. The ends in the back curled slightly, and Evelyn suddenly wanted to run her hands through them. "Why are you doing it?" he asked.

"Doing what?"

"The job."

Evelyn mused over the question. *To protect those in Callum*, but she couldn't tell him that. No. She couldn't allow anything related to the Daughter of the Goddess to come to light. Even something so slight as revealing her knowledge of vampyr had put her at enough risk.

"Pay," she said. "I need the money."

Say little. At least she'd told the truth, too. She'd already sold the last of her moonstones, and the money she'd made as a barmaid wouldn't last long. She took a long gulp of honeysuckle wine, sweet and floral.

Again, Cyrus appeared unconvinced. "The vampyr will kill again. They need to feed every three days. The sooner the vampyr is killed, the sooner the town is safe again."

True. Evelyn had been able to recite the blood-feeding habits of vampyrs at the age of seven to her tutors. Yet, Cyrus brought up a good point. She needed to find the vampyr sooner rather than later, which meant working with Cyrus was the right thing to do.

"All right," she said.

Cyrus lifted off the bar top, a sly smirk spreading over his handsome face. He crossed his arms, and Evelyn wished he hadn't, fearful his flexing muscles might rip the fabric of his tunic into shreds.

"All right what?" he asked.

Fucking flames.

"I'll work with you. If you're going to the McCarthys' farm tomorrow, I want to go with you."

He nodded. "Deal. I can get us there quicker than on foot. Partners, then?"

Evelyn's heart hammered in her chest. She hadn't fought a vampyr in so long, let alone worked with someone. The prospect frightened and excited her, and it had nothing to do with the huntsman and those eyes of his.

She could help Callum. Solve McKenna's murder. Kill the vampyr. Then leave.

"Partners," she said with a nod, determination she hadn't felt in a long time swelling inside her.

Chapter Eight

Evelyn

Evelyn checked Miss Patricia's note. That morning, she'd run into Cyrus over the Runaway Radish's communal breakfast. He'd promised to find Commissioner Doyle to ensure they could meet with the McCarthys, and he'd agreed to meet Evelyn back at the Radish before noon. In the meantime, Evelyn had decided to check out the apartment Miss Patricia's niece owned.

She walked through the misty streets of Callum, and the chilly air tightened her lungs and hardened her knuckles. The cold gave her energy, a dash of speed as she twisted down the cobblestone streets.

Fog so dense the town appeared to be on the cusp of a white abyss blanketed the sea. All around the town, the fog crept over and down the hills like ghosts, and the crisp moisture in the air stuck to Evelyn's cheeks and dampened the loose strands of her dark hair.

She turned onto a row of colorfully painted shops. Blues, yellows, pinks, and purples lined the street, with no one shop painted like the other. One as pink as a dawn sky displayed dresses and thickly woven blouses in a window. Women rushed in and out of the store, their cheeks rosy from morning chill and their hands full of shopping bags and clothing boxes.

Next to the boutique, a carved wooden sign in the shape of a boot hung over a men's shoe store painted the shade of lilacs. Inside, a man smoothed and hammered the leather of a loafer on a workbench. Evelyn continued, detecting cinnamon and vanilla. A robin's-egg blue bakery beckoned customers with tea and small cakes, and seated outside under an umbrella, a couple shared a rolled pastry and laughed together.

The street buzzed with activity. The young and playful energy reminded Evelyn of Nūa's shopping and arts district, where she'd owned an apartment. It had been her first independent venture while attending university. Something of her own. A place to rest. Surprisingly, the similarity did not make Evelyn sad. She hadn't had something stable in a while, and the sense of familiarity allowed her to hope this apartment could be promising.

At the corner of the street, a shop painted a luxe green shined like an emerald even in the misty morning. The storefront window—"Pages and Leaves" written on it in delicate, gold cursive—reflected Evelyn's silhouette as she stood out front. Through the glass, she saw that greenery took up a majority of the interior. It felt as if she stared through the window of a garden and not a shop. A large plant, tropical in nature, overtook half the window, while vines with leaves the shape of stars dangled behind the gold lettering.

Again, Evelyn read Miss Patricia's note. The shop's name matched. Taking a step back, she looked up and noticed the second level, contrasting the green with black brick. Matching black wrought iron bars wrapped around a balcony overlooking the street.

Maxie would love it.

Evelyn sighed. Hopefully with her savings and new weekly salary, she could afford it. She pushed the door open, the bell chiming her arrival and—

Her magic detected another's magic. Every molecule in the air vibrated with it, tickled and caressed Evelyn's magic in greeting. Gentle, vibrant. Petals and leaves fluttered around her like butterflies and soared to the ceiling. Pink and dainty, cherry blossom petals landed on her nose and cheeks, while dark and moody ones, made of dried oak leaves, landed on her arms.

Evelyn turned and found the witches' creed above the door. Right where it should be.

"Our eyes to the Sun, and hearts full of fire, minds open, and hands for good."

Carved into the wooden doorframe, the four-stanza creed etched a symbol of guidance over the exit and entry, like any other home, shop, or property belonging to a witch.

A worktable made of pine sat in the center, cluttered with piles of soil, uprooted plants, and empty pots. Behind it, a counter lined with terracotta planters full of flowers ranging from cherry to marigold ran along the back wall. On the left, three rows of floor-to-ceiling bookshelves, crafted from the same pine, were stacked with books. Vines of ivy slithered and grew down and around the books, twisting and curling with activity as they restocked the shelves from volumes piled high on a cart.

Transfixed by the beautiful magic of the shop, Evelyn almost forgot—there must be a witch nearby. Despite her excited magic, thrilled to have met another, disappointment crashed through Evelyn. She couldn't stay here. Not when she wished to keep her identity as a witch hidden. Doing so under the nose of a fellow witch would be a challenge.

Avoiding witches entirely was impossible. They resided in the New *and* Old World, which was why Evelyn wore her enchanted bracelet to hide her magic. Many had fled Torren during the Great Burnings, but some stayed. After six centuries, witches and humans lived peacefully in Torren, but there were few witches left. Magic needed to be worked and kept strong, but as witches used their magic less and less, there was less and less magic in the following generations.

Evelyn took a step back to depart, but the round, wide-eyed face of a young woman her age popped up from under the cluttered table.

"Can I help you?" she asked.

The witch's magic . . . it was so bright and kind, much like her russet-colored eyes that brought out the faint freckles scattered across the bridge of her nose. Her hair, ringlets of copper and red, had been cut to her chin, bouncing as she made her way toward Evelyn. She wore a thick turtleneck that matched the color of her shop, a dark green with daisies embroidered on the front.

Too shocked, too scared to be discovered by another witch, Evelyn said nothing, frozen with fear. Witches in Sorin and Torren lived and governed separately, but all witches prayed to the Sun Goddess. She was the Goddess of growth, light, and prosperity and had given witches the first kernel of magic in their souls. Because of that one commonality, Evelyn had to be wary of the prophecy tying her to the Sun Goddess.

Some witches were fanatics when it came to prophecies, like Elder Black, who had touched her shoulder in the streets of Nūa as if she were divine herself. Others left gifts upon her doorstep, oblivious to the concept of privacy. Evelyn shuddered. It was why she kept her identity as a witch hidden. No doubt, witches like those would haul her back to Sorin to complete her union and fulfill the prophecy.

Evelyn adapted her mask of indifference as she placed her arms behind her back and clasped her bracelet, feeling the twine threaded with magic. Forget the apartment. She needed to get out of here quickly.

"I'm just here to shop around," she said.

The shop owner blinked, those wide eyes soaking her in. Then she smiled, and guilt washed over Evelyn for treating the witch as a threat.

"Here at Pages and Leaves, we offer two sorts of excitement: plants and books," she said.

Evelyn didn't think the fellow witch's eyes could get much bigger, and the bounce in her curls only grew as she herself bounced with each step around the shop. Excited, bubbly. Her energy further ignited the magic in the air.

She twirled toward the bookshelves, snapping her fingers. The vines froze, their leaves swiveling toward her like little faces, as if they turned to look at her. The witch kept her hand out and open until the vine returned with two books. One was small, maroon, with an embracing couple depicted on the front, the other thicker, bound in leather like some sort of manual.

"Romance or recipes?" she asked.

Evelyn had no words. "Um . . ."

The witch frowned, handing back the books to the awaiting vine. Without even looking, her magic enchanted the vine to place the books back on the shelves. Evelyn wasn't just in the presence of a witch but a powerful one, with an earthly bronntanas tied to plants and vegetation.

Earth bronntanases were rare in Nūa. During the Great Burnings, covens tied to the earth had an easier time blending in, manning farms, and raising livestock. Many of them stayed instead of fleeing to Sorin, thriving in Torren during peace.

A tinge of loss twisted in the pit of Evelyn's stomach, witnessing a witch wield their bronntanas, the power deeper than their innate magic, with ease. Years ago, she had been so similar with her own bronntanas, her flame. Before family suppers, she'd ignite the candles from afar, burst the hearth into a roaring fire, even man the stoves as they cooked brisket. Fire, flame, heat. It had all been a part of her everyday life, being, and personality.

The witch scrunched her brows. A beat passed, and her eyes went wide. Evelyn couldn't decide who to watch: the witch twirling through the shop in lime green rain boots or the vines awaiting further instruction.

She followed, captivated. It'd been some time since she'd been in the presence of another's magic. Her magic danced in her blood, but her flame didn't even flicker. A dormant reminder of why she kept her identity hidden. Evelyn's chest tightened.

Spinning back and almost knocking Evelyn into a fig tree, the witch leaned in far too close. At her small height, her head came level with Evelyn's chest, her neck craning fully back to glance up.

"What's your name?" she asked.

"Saige," Evelyn whispered.

"I'm Aster."

"So . . . why books and plants?"

Aster shrugged. "Plants are the perfect company for books. Of course, they're watching, but they keep their opinions to themselves."

She tapped her chin and turned her attention to the shelves stacked with potted plants. Evelyn gaped as they turned toward the shop owner, leaves and flowers twisting. Her own magic danced in delight. She couldn't deny being happy. Like called to like, the magic in her blood singing at the feel of another. Evelyn clamped her eyes shut and shook her head. She couldn't get too excited or stay too long.

Another vine-like plant touched her arm in passing. Evelyn stopped to admire the round white flowers that glowed brighter as she stepped closer.

"Are you looking for something that's easy maintenance or a little more exotic?" Aster asked.

"I'm not sure what I am looking for." Evelyn clenched and flexed her fists. What she needed was to find something to buy and then to leave, but her magic warred within her. She'd missed being around other witches. The magic. The closeness. The bonds. Witches weren't perfect. They were proud and gossiped. Yet, they were strong and loyal.

Evelyn worked a lump in her throat, ready to tell Aster she wanted a pathos, a plant she'd adored back home, nestling several onto her bookshelves, when she noticed those russet eyes studying her attire. From her boots to her cloak, they roamed over her.

"Wait," Aster said. "You're one of my aunt's barmaids."

"I—"

Aster gasped, jumping up and down. "You must be the one interested in the apartment! She came early this morning to tell me. Why didn't you say that?"

Evelyn shook her head. "You must have mistaken me for someone else."

"Oh, I don't think so." She waved her hands about. "I have a sense for things, like I have a sense you're a witch."

Evelyn balked, but she didn't step back. Instead, she shifted into her indifferent scowl. "Again, you're mistaken—"

Aster snatched her arm, inspecting her bracelet.

Icy panic shot through Evelyn, and she yanked her arm away. "What do you think you're doing?" Her words came out like a bite, fierce and pitched.

Hurt flashed through Aster's russet eyes, and regret replaced Evelyn's panic. She didn't detect any threat or malice, only pure curiosity from the fellow witch.

"I . . . I'm sorry," Evelyn said.

Aster's lips twitched into a small smile. "It's okay. You're scared. I sensed that, too."

Evelyn teetered, eyeing Aster. Nothing felt like a threat. Nothing sat in the air. Nothing coming off the witch.

"How did you sense I was a witch?" she asked.

She pointed to Evelyn's wrist. "Your bracelet is enchanted well, but my bronntanas can feel through whatever you made it out of. But I wouldn't worry. I sense more than others."

"You don't say?" Evelyn said with a raised brow. She looked around the shop. "Your magic is powerful."

Aster shrugged, her cheeks blooming with a blush. "Why deny you're a witch? Is it because you're in Callum?"

Evelyn shrugged. "Something like that."

"Well, you shouldn't worry about being a witch in this town. We're a friendly bunch."

Evelyn scoffed. Witches were welcoming. She didn't doubt that. Yet, one word of a dark-haired, mysterious witch from Nūa with secrets would make it to her sisters. For all she knew, her coven had already written to covens an ocean away to keep an eye out. Even though Tovi said the Elders had fabricated some stories, who knew what had changed over the course of two years?

At present, she had a vampyr to find and a murder to focus on, no time for lying her way out of a conversation with a witch.

"Do you mind keeping the fact that I'm a witch between us?"

Aster's brows pinched with disappointment, and then her eyes went big. "Are you on the run? Are you hiding, by chance?"

Evelyn laughed again, her throat going dry. *Fucking flames*, she enjoyed Aster's energy, but she feared the witch *sensed* too much.

"I should leave," Evelyn said.

"How about a proposition?" Aster paused, wringing her hands. "A trade of sorts?"

"A proposition?"

"Rent the apartment above my shop, and I won't tell anyone you're a witch."

Evelyn took a step back and laughed. "Proposition is an interesting word choice for blackmail."

Aster swallowed, twisting her fingers. "All right, it is. But I desperately need someone to rent out the apartment above to help pay off the shop and you need somewhere to stay with someone whom you can trust not to tell anyone you're a witch."

Aster was a witch, and she seemed kind. Would she be so kind if she knew who Evelyn was? If she learned she was Daughter of the Goddess? Although she never needed to find out.

As the books floated from shelf to shelf, another plant continued to play with Evelyn's hair, and the petal butterflies flew around, the shop's magic, as well as that which ran in her blood, beckoned her to take the risk.

"All right," Evelyn said, crossing her arms. "How much?"

"Two hundred a month."

With her captain's pay from the commissioner and the little she'd saved as a barmaid, she could certainly manage that and have money left over when she readied to leave for the next place. That only left one predicament.

"I'll take it," Evelyn said. "But month to month. I can't promise I'll rent it long."

Her words sent Aster into a frenzy. She jumped up and down and launched at Evelyn, startling her as her hug squished Evelyn's arms to her sides. Unsure how to reciprocate, she stood unmoving until Aster released her.

"Oh, well, isn't this the start of something fun!" Aster said, clapping her hands.

Interesting . . . not the word Evelyn would have used but difficult to disagree with, nonetheless.

Chapter Nine

Kade

While waiting for word from the commissioner about visiting the McCarthys, Kade ran errands. He first visited a blacksmith, requesting his Drengr crest be welded down to a smooth surface on his brooch, sword, and dagger. The request cost him his spare dagger with a moonstone hilt, but desperate measures ensured his huntsman disguise stayed intact. The blacksmith guaranteed it'd be done by midday, and Kade would have his weapons before they started investigating.

Kade released a breath. He weaved his way through the harbor market, finding his next stop near the watchtower. A messaging post was nestled into the stones, and the courier who managed the birds listened to Kade as he explained his request.

"It'll be ten silvers to get a letter over to Nūa, and I'm half tempted to charge ya extra with the risk of storm season," the courier said.

Behind the thin, hook-nosed man, birds of various species sat caged: owls, ravens, pigeons. They fluttered their wings and stared at Kade, their eyes watchful and screeches full of warning. The animals sensed his wolf.

Yet, the single *iolair*, a beast of a bird far too big for a cage, paid no mind. With talons large enough to crush a man's skull, it slept, unbothered by the chaos around it.

Ten silvers for a single letter was steep, but Kade wanted to deliver a message across a great distance. The *iolair*, with its feathered wings and leathery body, could make the trek across the Sapphire Sea, but the rarity of the bird always jacked up the price.

Frustration simmered through Kade. He had never intended to be gone for so long, and his funds were running thin. Paying to learn about Evelyn had cost him. The captain's pay would help, but at present, paying a ten silvers to chance a letter to his brother would be a risk.

He sighed, staring at the folded parchment. He'd written to Eldrick with the news of finding Evelyn and how he planned to stay behind to find and kill the vampyr in Callum.

The letter weighed a hundred pounds.

Wind from the hills delivered more fog out to the sea, and Kade caught the scent of cedar and vanilla. He searched the crowd, catching Evelyn weaving through the vendors. She nodded to the town's folk, her smile lighting up her features and knocking him off balance.

She appeared happy, so different from the day before. Kade wondered if she'd found a place to stay with Miss Patricia's niece, and the letter began to weigh even more, along with something her sister Blair had given him.

Tucked away was Evelyn's muince, a necklace every witch had. At the age of sixteen, they created it with their own magic as a rite of passage. Evelyn's stone pendant reminded Kade of the moon, pearly and ominous, but when the sun hit it just right, an iridescent rainbow glinted as it swayed. Kade had heard Evelyn had formed the stone from her flame itself, creating a piece of her magic in solid form. The pendant hung from a platinum chain, the silvery white metal a common pairing with the Carsons's navy emblem, signifying Evelyn's coven. She'd left it behind, and Blair had told him that, when the time was right, he should give it back to her.

She wandered the streets, apparently unaware of him, her obsidian hair twirling in the wind. For whatever reason, sending the letter felt wrong, and yet Evelyn had fled her duty, run from her people. Why did it matter what he did? His brother deserved to know. *Moons*, her coven deserved to know. He deserved the satisfaction of telling those back home he had finally found her.

Kade oscillated between what was right and what he wanted to do. At this point, he owed Evelyn nothing. She'd left, abandoned their people, but he was already deceiving her about his identity. The letter felt like further, unnecessary deception.

He tucked the letter back into his cloak, reminding himself the price for the bird wasn't yet worth it.

"When's the last day you'll send the *iolair* out?" he asked the courier.

The man searched the horizon. "Aye, *iolairs* are tough and smart beasts. They can fly through anything, but the price changes if there's the scent of storm in the air."

Kade nodded. "Thank you. I'll keep that in mind."

The *iolair* opened one eye, a black fathomless bead, and stared at Kade.

Hopefully, he and Evelyn would soon find the vampyr and burn it. Then, by some stars-blessed miracle, he'd convince her to go home, and *then* he'd write to Eldrick.

Chapter Ten

Evelyn

By midday, Evelyn had moved her few things into her apartment above Aster's shop. She'd left Maxie basking in the sun on the windowsill, jealous she could soak in the clear sky in the comfort of their new home.

Home.

Evelyn hadn't used that word in a long while. It didn't matter. Callum wasn't her home, nor could it ever truly be. She could cancel the lease with Aster whenever she wanted, and once she solved McKenna's murder, she'd have to leave anyway.

The McCarthys had requested Evelyn and Cyrus visit them after their daughter's burial. Evelyn didn't want to delay the investigation any longer, but their child had died. Evelyn understood loss and respected their boundaries.

She and Cyrus would visit them tomorrow instead.

In the center of her new apartment, Evelyn pushed chairs in at a sturdy wooden table. Miss Patricia, who had no children of her own, had boasted about her niece, a shop owner *and* landlord. Evelyn's landlord, to be exact. And Commissioner Doyle had reassured the town he'd hired reinforcements to work on the vampyr case.

The news took no time at all to trickle through the entire town. A couch from the baker had shown up outside Pages and Leaves. Miss Patricia had visited as well, leaving behind her a table and a single chair. One rain shower later, three more chairs appeared with a box full of dishes.

Evelyn pushed in the fourth and final chair, smoothing the green weathered paint under her fingers. The left stood taller than the others, while the right one was too large to fit fully under the table and blinding yellow. Each chair was different, and the table a wobbly scrap from the Runaway Radish, but Evelyn didn't care, and a small smile graced her lips as she took it all in.

A decent-sized bed took up the west wall, facing the entire apartment. Naja, Callum's finest weaver, had gifted her a monstrous wool blanket threaded with various shades of blue, creating an effect of shimmering sapphire. It beckoned Evelyn to have a slow morning, to cozy up into the layers of blankets and sheets and rest.

She'd repay the town's kindness by protecting them from the vampyr.

On the north wall toward the west end, a patchwork sofa of various maroons, greens, and navies added more color to the space. Evelyn hoped she and Tovi could sit and chat over a bottle of wine on the sofa soon, just like old times.

The apartment wasn't as big or as cohesive as Evelyn's apartment back in Nūa and far more colorful than her usual monochromatic color choices, but it possessed charm, and a sense of home flooded through Evelyn, like the space anchored her in rightness.

As if this was right where she was supposed to be.

The front door eased open. Her stone wards, the first items she'd situated in each corner, glowed with a faint green light. Still in their spots, they didn't rattle with alarm. Aster's head peeked through, and the stones' green glow dimmed back to black.

No threat to tarnish the smidge of sanctuary Evelyn had gained.

Aster let herself in. "I come with a gift."

Evelyn found she liked the earth witch's company. Positive, bubbly, and beautifully kind. With her magic and personality, Aster and Pages and Leaves would flourish in Nūa. Evelyn could envision it already, lines down the block in the shopping district, witches bursting to meet Aster Arkwood and snag a new book and plant.

Aster handed her a green and white spotted plant, three vines of heart-shaped leaves cascading over the edge of a squat pot.

"A pathos—my favorite." Evelyn took Aster's gift, lifting and spinning it. "How did you know?"

"I may have noticed you staring at one the first time you visited the shop." She shrugged. "They also symbolize good luck and fortune, and I figured it would fit with your new apartment."

"Thank you, Aster. It's perfect. Now, you're the expert—where should I put it?"

Aster smiled, eyes glowing as she did so, pleased with herself. She pointed to the bay window. "Closest to the sun. Water it once a week and it'll be a happy camper."

Evelyn tiptoed past her kitchen, and Maxie emerged from under the sofa, meowing. She danced between Evelyn's steps, gazing up at the pathos with bright eager eyes.

"Don't you dare eat this, Maxie. It's a gift from a friend." Evelyn peered down at her familiar, brow raised in command.

Maxie hmphed, her eyes slitting to slivers of yellow as if insulted Evelyn would insinuate such a thing.

Below, Callum's shops bustled with activity. The promise of a rain shower approached over the distant hills while the sun beamed over the bay. Thrilled to have her first decoration, Evelyn proudly placed the pathos in the center of the wide windowsill. Maxie jumped up and, despite the mischievous gleam in her eyes, hunkered down into a sleeping position next to the pathos, yawning her way into a second nap. The sight made Evelyn think this was indeed, at least for now, home.

Evelyn sighed. What a cruel notion to hold on to. She would be leaving after she killed the vampyr. She knew that.

"Again, Aster," Evelyn said. "Thank you."

The fellow witch walked around the apartment. Dressed in velvet emerald overalls and a mustard turtleneck, she made Evelyn think of Blair's own colorful fashion sense; she and Aster would get along well. Evelyn missed her sister's bold clothing statements. She'd always wished she had enough courage to stand out like that. Her title as Daughter of the Goddess brought enough attention as it was, so she'd always chosen clothing to help her blend in. Aster's red hair and matching rain boots tucked under her overalls did no such thing. What fashion had Blair worn these last two years? What sort of fashion fads in Nūa had come and gone?

Aster skipped past her, twirling through Evelyn's apartment with wide, russet eyes.

"The place is coming together nicely, and the apartment looks good on you."

"As my new landlord, you have to say that," Evelyn said.

Aster shrugged. "Not landlord. I'm your new friend. Who you happen to pay every month."

They laughed for a moment.

"All right then, friend," Evelyn said and meant it.

Aster teetered, a faint blush overtaking her freckled cheeks. "I have to meet my parents halfway today. They grow the saplings of the plants I sell at Pages and Leaves on their farm. I wondered if you wanted to join me? Figured you could ask townsfolk questions along the way."

It wasn't a bad idea. So far, Evelyn hadn't had the time to ask around Callum yet. Cyrus had started scoping out the land and town with Commissioner Doyle, searching for places the vampyr could be hiding out in. Joining Aster would help while they waited to talk with the McCarthys.

Evelyn gathered her cloak and boots, readying herself for a day of walking. "Actually, I'd love to join you."

"Perfect!" Aster jumped up and down, clapping her hands in delight.

Evelyn smiled as they left her apartment and began journeying outside the town. She enjoyed the company, having a fellow witch by her side after so much time.

Evelyn's enjoyment quickly turned into frustration. She and Aster had traveled the merchant's path, a wide road big enough for horses, wagons, and carts to travel into Callum, brimming with farmers, traders, and merchants alike. But no matter how many she talked to, she gained no insight.

No one had seen the likes of a vampyr. Most believed vampyrs couldn't be in Callum—a problem of the west, they called them. Others didn't even know what one looked like. It was a foreign concept to Evelyn, that these people considered this land and themselves immune to the threat of vampyr. They didn't even fear them. For those in Torren, vampyrs were a legend from the west lands they never had to worry about.

If Evelyn didn't find it and kill it soon, that peace would shatter.

Evelyn walked alongside Aster, spent from asking questions, as they neared an outpost-like tavern. A couple with the same flaming red hair as Aster stood waiting by a horseless wagon, filled to the edges with small plants and supplies.

The couple waved them down, and Evelyn learned where Aster had got her enthusiasm from. As they neared, Aster's parents' warmth and kindness bubbled in the air. Clearly, it was an Arkwood trait.

"Mama and Papa," Aster said, giving them both hugs. "This is Saige Ferriwether. My new temporary tenant."

Both parents hugged Evelyn warmly and without warning. Stiff as a board, she wavered foot to foot and endured their embraces.

"It's good to meet you," she said.

Mr. Arkwood sighed. "How about you both join us for an early dinner before you head back to town? Jim's got his famous roast lamb with a mushroom cream sauce on the menu." He nodded at Evelyn. "And Miss Patricia's my sister. Let me know you're quite a fan of the honeysuckle wine."

Evelyn straightened. "It's divine."

Aster giggled. "It's my father's brew. Half of Torren sells it in their pubs and taverns."

"So you're famous?" Evelyn said.

The entire Arkwood family laughed as Mr. Arkwood shook his head. "Me? Famous? Nah, lass. But my honeysuckle wine might be."

Evelyn smiled, appreciating how humble they were. A wine like that would overtake Nūa and Sorin, and the witch's fame would be celebrated. Evelyn preferred the simplicity here, the lack of showmanship.

Over the course of a delicious dinner, Evelyn learned the Arkwoods were truly the kindest witches. Their coven resided in Ferry, another day's walk from Callum. Unlike witches in Sorin, they didn't talk of prophecies or the Sun Goddess. It was nice to be in the company of magic without being discussed as a prophesied savior.

Birth order didn't apply in Torren either. Aster was the firstborn. In Sorin, she would've been expected to take over her parents' farm, following in their footsteps, a leader in the family line. Yet, her parents were proud she'd set out to be a business owner in Callum.

A similar magic Evelyn had known growing up vibrated between Mr. and Mrs. Arkwood. As they waved goodbye down the road, Evelyn turned to Aster.

"Are your parents fated?"

Aster nodded with a smile. "Indeed, they are. Met in the forest in Ferry. Papa says his magic led him on a walk, and he found Mama foraging for mushrooms." She shrugged. "They knew immediately."

Evelyn's parents had been fated, too. They'd collided when Evelyn's father, who had been a professor at the university, studied the magic of the Wall surrounding Nūa, and her mother, a Guard on the Wall, had been his guide and escort.

Sitting by their living room fire, they'd told Evelyn and her sisters the story often when they were children, and Evelyn remembered the way her parents' eyes—her mother's brown and her father's blue—had stared into the other's with love and adoration, as if it were the first time all over again each time they recounted the tale.

Fated were witches whose souls were mirrors of the other, and since magic was tethered to one soul, it could be *felt*, the bond witnessed by others.

Jim's inn grew busier behind them as travelers settled in for the night. Up ahead, the Arkwoods grew smaller as they journeyed toward the horizon. The sun hung low, threatening to dip into night as Evelyn and Aster ventured back to Callum. Alongside them, Aster's wagon traveled without a horse. Two lemon trees manned the front, their sturdy branches growing and reaching the wheels to push it into motion. Aster's petal butterflies fluttered at the front, as if guiding the lemon trees in the right direction.

The lively magic brightened the road, and the two witches walked in silence for a while as Evelyn's thoughts tumbled one after the other. Her nerves shook as much as the rickety wagon on the bumpy path. No matter where she went or where she turned, reminders of what she'd run away from always found her. Like a phantom weight on her chest, the reminders pushed and pressed a heavy guilt onto her.

"I heard you're working with that handsome bartender," Aster said, red welly boots squishing along the muddy path.

Evelyn scoffed. "I have no idea who you're referring to."

Aster gaped, russet eyes growing as wide as her mouth. "You can't be serious! The dangerously tall, bearded man now working for my aunt? I heard he's also working on the vampyr case."

Evelyn tripped through the mud at the mention of the huntsman. "You mean Cyrus?"

"Cyrus? I'm not sure that name suits him." Aster shrugged. "Well then, what's he like?" Aster wiggled her brows.

Evelyn couldn't hold back her laughter. Was this girl talk? She'd forgotten how it went, and the topic of conversation didn't exactly excite her. She'd rather not talk about him at all.

"I don't know. He's a beast of a man—"

"A beautiful beast," Aster corrected.

Evelyn rolled her eyes.

"Damn dandelions, Saige. All the single women in Callum have taken note of him. Are you trying to tell me you haven't noticed those eyes of his?"

Fucking flames.

Evelyn rolled her eyes as warmth spread across her cheeks. "No."

"What about those arms? The biceps!"

Oh yes, she'd seen those. In action. Now warmth spread in her belly, the kind that elicited wicked thoughts. But she wasn't about to let Aster know that.

"Again, no," Evelyn said with a wave of her hand.

"You're a liar, and you know it!" Aster yelled across the path.

"I *work with him*," Evelyn said, but laughter seeped into her tone.

Aster threw up her hands. "That makes it all the more fun."

"You can't be serious!"

Aster shrugged. "I must be a weaker woman than you, Saige, because I'd be tempted."

"The scary thing is, you're being serious."

"Damn dandelions, I sure am. Do you have another man out there? Is that why?"

Evelyn snorted. She hadn't been interested in a man, let alone in a relationship with one, in two and half years. Most of her relationships had been the *physical* kind, and though that kind suited her on-the-run lifestyle, it didn't sit well with her since she'd run from her betrothed. But surely Kade Drengr had had women in his life, too. They were in their mid-twenties. To think they'd sworn off the opposite sex until marriage was unrealistic.

She'd run to protect her people, not to start a new life. Men, emotions, flings—Evelyn didn't have the emotional bandwidth to navigate any of those things, and she wasn't sure she could without thinking about Kade and that she'd abandoned their union.

Guilt pressed on her chest again, and Evelyn struggled to breathe evenly. Their union had been one of the main reasons she'd run. Not to run from a man she didn't know. Evelyn had been ready to marry him for the sake of the prophecy.

According to the Elders and their belief in the prophecy, for Evelyn and Kade to be their strongest, their magic needed to be connected.

Unlike Aster or Evelyn's parents, they weren't fated. It wasn't possible for witches and werewolves. But with the help of spells crafted by both witch and werewolf scholars, Evelyn and Kade would have tied their souls together during their union in a forced bond, all for the sake of a prophecy.

But according to one particularly cruel Elder, the one who haunted Evelyn's dreams and thoughts, Evelyn's success at defeating the vampyr hinged on her flame. *That* power, *that* gift from the Sun Goddess, destroyed them instantly. Darkness couldn't outmatch the power of the Sun.

Evelyn's breath became shallow. Her chest constricted, ribs squeezing her heart and lungs like a room growing smaller and smaller with each breath.

Like the time her tutor went to desperate measures reciting the importance of her flame. Everything she'd learned, trained for, breathed had been about her flame. The prophecy depended on it.

Not her, but the power given by the Sun Goddess and Moon God.

The vivid reminders of her tutoring heightened her nerves, and Evelyn couldn't stomach bringing Kade down with her when her flame was gone. What if it hindered his werewolf magic? What if, once they were tied together, whatever ailed her ailed him, too? Evelyn had already failed and let down so many others. She couldn't add Kade to the list.

Evelyn sighed. Aster still waited on her answer. "No, there is no other man. Cyrus and I work together. That is that. More importantly, he isn't my type."

The Goddess knew that was a lie, but her unexpected and intense attraction to the man hardly mattered. Even if she wasn't promised to another man, a man she'd ruin if they bonded, her life would never be stable enough for a relationship of any kind. Evelyn's stomach rolled. She also had a murder to investigate and a vampyr to find before she left Callum. There was no need to entertain anything with the huntsman and drag him into her mess. Besides, she kept others at a distance for a reason. Her secrets, her loss of family, or her absence, for that matter, could never reach the shores of Sorin with the risk of war with the vampyrs a possibility.

All of it landed on Evelyn's shoulders, leaving her empty and hollow as she walked alongside Aster.

The earth witch sighed. "How about I tell you my favorite tales of Callum?"

Evelyn nodded with a small smile, and Aster enlightened her with unique tales of faeries and kings and princesses. With each story, Evelyn allowed herself to be more distracted, forgetting her failures, secrets, and attraction to the huntsman.

Chapter Eleven

Evelyn

The next day, Evelyn inhaled the salt of the sea and the earthiness of the grass. Callum was bright. Townsfolk smiled, their eyes twinkling with recognition as Evelyn passed, her jitters making the brisk air colder than it was.

Though Callum was older than home, stagnant in time, the town possessed a level of magic. It was unlike the magic that Evelyn was used to in Nūa, the city of witches, brimming with modernity and innovation, but she found the simplicity charming.

At the corner before the town square, a woman wrapped in a wool shawl handed out parcels of baked goods. The sweet, bready smells reminded Evelyn of the bakery a few blocks from her apartment in Nūa. Instead of the pastries she'd have found at home—lavender blueberry macarons or peach brioche—bread-like scones, biscuits, muffins, and loaves lined the shelves of the wooden cart. Hearty and warm, the fixings were perfect for the weather.

"Good day to ya," the woman beamed. "Anything ya fancy?"

Berry muffins, fruit bursting on their bulging tops with brown sugar, caught Evelyn's eye. An idea struck her.

"I'll take two of the muffins, please."

Evelyn paid, left with a parcel of two large muffins, and went on her way.

Cyrus stood outside the Runaway Radish with a horse.

A *single* horse.

Evelyn stopped, her mind reeling.

"Good morning," he said with a glance, brushing a hand down the massive horse's mane and along its back. "Bleu, this is Saige. Saige, this is Bleu."

Cyrus stood a half foot taller than Evelyn, and yet Bleu dwarfed him. Its bulging leg muscles trembled as it stood. Feathered black hair hid its hooves, and the rest of its coat appeared gray and shimmered a shade of blue when the light hit it.

Evelyn had never seen a horse like it before, and fear crept up her skin.

"Everything all right?" Cyrus asked.

Evelyn nodded and buried her nerves. She teetered from foot to foot, glancing again at the horse. No cart, no wagon. *Goddess*, was she expected to ride the beast? Why had she not asked? Of course a huntsman would have a horse.

"I got you a muffin," she said, handing over the parcel to Cyrus. Her words came out in a rush, cracking with her fear. Evelyn hated riding horses, not because of the animals themselves but because they were so damn goddesses high off the ground.

Evelyn Carson, Daughter of the Goddess, was petrified of heights.

Not vampyrs, not demons.

Heights.

"Thank you," Cyrus said, taking the muffin from her. "Are you sure everything's all right?"

Evelyn turned to his handsome face. Leather trousers gripped his strong thighs. The sun reflected from his eyes like light through honey. Evelyn shook her head. He made her insides fuzzy, and she couldn't afford the distraction, even if it took her mind off the horse.

Instead, she looked to the verdant hills that swelled and surged, a shade of green like no other. White stone jutted out every few spaces, ancient ruins of faerie civilization. Patches of yellow swayed in the wind, the last of the summer buttercups holding out.

"Saige?" Cyrus's brow was raised. "Is something wrong with the horse?"

"I . . ." She couldn't very well admit heights terrified her, and then the idea of surrendering to this beast as it carried her so high off the ground . . . *Goddess help her*. Her first day, and Evelyn was exactly what he'd called her a day ago.

Frightened.

"When you said 'means of transportation' last night . . ." Evelyn fumbled with her words. Flustered, she tried to find a reasonable excuse. "I didn't realize it would be *just* a horse." Evelyn gestured at Bleu.

Cyrus laughed, and if she weren't so embarrassed and heated from his reaction, she'd appreciate the sound. But his tone mocked, jabbing at her, and she fought the urge to call off their entire partnership.

"My sincere apologies that Bleu doesn't meet your standards, princess," Cyrus said.

Evelyn saw red. "What did you call me?"

"Princess." Straight and stoic.

The word shot through Evelyn, and if she'd had her flame, she would have scorched the entire square in anger. She hated the word, having heard it used loosely throughout her life. The Daughter of the Goddess was *not* royalty, but it didn't deter some witches from treating her so, in positive and negative ways.

"Don't call me that." Evelyn bit out the words, fighting the urge to scream.

Cyrus appeared intrigued rather than deterred. It only made Evelyn angrier. Why did his appraisal rile her?

"You're acting as if Bleu isn't good enough—"

Evelyn threw up her hands in frustration. "It is not the horse. I expected maybe a wagon or a carriage."

"You mention a carriage, and yet I'm not supposed to call you a princess?" Cyrus assessed her while he adjusted the saddle of the horse, large enough for two. He followed her gaze and hmphed. "If it's sharing a saddle that worries you, I will keep a respectable distance."

Evelyn's eyes widened at his suggestion. *Fucking flames,* this couldn't get any worse. "It is not you, Huntsman."

He shot her a smile. "Good." He didn't believe her, that was clear. "Or maybe you've never ridden a horse before? Is that it?"

She shut her eyes and shook her head. At this point, he was toying with her, and they were wasting time. She pushed past him, grazing his shoulder. She gripped the saddle, jumped, and swung herself over in one fluid, athletic move.

Evelyn averted her gaze and focused on the town's buildings and hills beyond—*not* the distance between her and the cobblestone ground. Fear coursed through her like acid, but she kept it at bay, masking it with an indifferent scowl. She couldn't show Cyrus her fear. Leaping up onto the horse at least helped, and Evelyn appreciated the surprise on Cyrus's face from her successful mount.

"Care to join, or do you plan to walk alongside us?"

Something glinted in Cyrus's eyes, but Evelyn couldn't place it. Mischief? Triumph? She didn't have long to wonder, as Cyrus gripped the saddle and joined her atop Bleu.

With their combined weight, the horse took a few steps to adjust. He huffed as Cyrus reached past Evelyn's waist, keeping a respectable distance as promised, and tugged on the reins to start their journey.

For an entire hour, neither of them spoke. Evelyn focused on the sights around her, so very different from Sorin. They kept to the northern path, passing whitewashed cottages and humble farms. Sheep grazed like long fallen clouds on the hills, while ancient castle ruins jutted out of the earth as if they grew from the dirt like buttercups. Moss-marred stone painted the land with another shade of green.

Callum possessed a rich magic, and Evelyn loved it.

She relished its ability to be ancient yet fresh, from the vibrant grass to the salty wind. Life buzzed even outside the town, as if the land manifested it deep in its core. Perhaps the tales of the faeries retiring underground held some truth.

The sights only did so much to distract Evelyn from Cyrus pressed against her back. Even though he leaned a little away from her, sticking true to his word, they could not avoid touching while riding double. His strong thighs ran parallel to hers, and Evelyn shuddered, cursing her very wicked thoughts. She prayed to the Goddess more than once that Cyrus had a dagger in his pocket that kept grazing her backside and not something else entirely.

Aside from being mortified, a festering fear made her sick to her stomach. During the last two years, she'd walked hundreds of miles, hitched rides on wagons, and even sailed on ships. She had her staff, and that was all she needed. Not once had she traveled on horseback. The last time she'd ridden one had been the day her parents had died.

Evelyn blinked the memories and emotions away. No matter the time that passed, it all felt raw and fresh, a wound that refused to close. She and her parents had ridden from Sorin with a small guard to meet the Drengr pack, her betrothed's family, and discuss wedding preparations. It all seemed so silly now, how she'd fidgeted on her saddle under the blazing sun, annoyed Kade wouldn't be there, thanks to "the guidance of the Elders," when in the end she'd lost her parents.

Bleu trotted over loose rock, and Evelyn stiffened. The rocks clattered behind them, but she didn't dare look down. If she didn't see the distance to the ground, sometimes it helped.

Cyrus tightened his hold on the reins and, as a result, his arms around her waist. "Saige, you're tense. What is the matter?"

Sincerity laced his tone, and Evelyn's shoulders lightened.

She sighed. She couldn't tell him that being on a horse reminded her of the day her parents died, but if they were to be partners, she could be honest about one thing.

"I . . ." She swallowed. "I hate heights."

Behind her, Cyrus stiffened as if he were surprised by her admission.

"So, like I said, while Bleu is adequate, he's a little farther off the ground than I like."

Cyrus was silent for a moment, long enough for Evelyn to feel foolish until he said, "Why didn't you tell me in the first place?"

Evelyn shrugged. "I didn't want . . ."

You're not good enough.

The words of her tutor vibrated through her skull, but Evelyn tuned them out.

"I didn't want you to think less of me or to think I couldn't help with the investigation because I was afraid of something so silly."

"I would never think less of you because you fear something. In fact, I respect you more."

He meant it. She didn't need to see his expression—his voice said it all, the gentle timbre of it behind her.

"Why?"

He shrugged, the movement drawing his chest closer to her back. "Fears make us real."

Surprise shot through her, making Evelyn sit a little straighter on the horse.

"I hate boats," Cyrus said.

Evelyn turned, looking up at him. "What?"

He seemed to smile. "Boats. Well, truthfully, I'm terrified of the water. Being out at sea." He shook his head. "Therefore, I hate boats. Loathe them. Loathe the very thought of bobbing up and down in an endless body of water."

Impossible to believe someone like Cyrus, who appeared strong and agile, was afraid of something like water, or of anything at all. It made her fear of heights feel normal, relatable.

"Thank you for telling me," she said. "But I must request we share no more secrets."

Cyrus looked down at her, one eyebrow raised. "Why?"

Evelyn shrugged. "If we are to be partners, we must establish boundaries."

Cyrus leaned closer, his chin brushing her shoulder. "I think after this ride, there is not much left for boundaries."

Their eyes locked, and Evelyn didn't turn away. The wind whipped around them, blowing Cyrus's golden hair in the wind. The way he spoke, the way his words tickled down her neck . . . She shook away the idiotic feelings. She was reading too much into it. He was teasing her. After all, they were partners and nothing more could come of it.

Luckily, their destination came into view at the end of the path. The farmer's cottage was made of clay and painted with a thick, white paint. Reed thatch, arranged like overlapping shingles, created the roof. Rocks tied to ropes dangled at the bottom edge, keeping the thatched roof in place. They swayed in the breeze, clattering off one another and making a gentle chime in the wind. Stacks of stones and horizontal beams lined the perimeter in a hodgepodge and randomized fence. In the center, a direct path led to a red-stained door.

Cyrus dismounted first and helped Evelyn down from the horse. She stepped off to the side as he tied Bleu to a horse's post. Cyrus squinted at the house, his eyes slivers of honey while his lips thinned into a flat line as if he were deep in thought.

Leather britches, tan with red undertones, molded to his muscular legs. His dark blue tunic contrasted in color. The sleeves ballooned but gathered tightly at his wrists. His torso filled out the tunic, more muscle straining against fabric. He wore a belt of the same leather, fastened at the center with a buckle. Something of its size and metal type would be a considerable price all its own. He'd secured a sheathed dagger beneath his cloak. It appeared ordinary, mundane against his clothes, until she noticed the hilt had been melted down, the etched crest buffed beyond recognition.

So richly attired, he must be quite the successful huntsman. Those who traveled for hire to kill demons in the human lands could make good money but surely not enough to afford his clothing.

"Done staring?" he asked.

Evelyn jumped. She had been staring. *Again.* Goddess. She swallowed and met his gaze. His eyes glistened with amusement, one brow arched upward inquisitively.

"Let's get on with it," she said, heading toward the cottage.

The gate screeched as they pushed it wider. Aside from the clucking chicken that scurried across the lawn and the distant moos of the unseen cows, the cottage sat quiet and unnerving. Past the house, tools, wagons, and wheelbarrows surrounded a weathered barn. A wreath of lilies hung from the door. The unmistakable color and symbol for mourning reminded Evelyn of why they were there.

Cyrus stood rigid and alert. He knocked, deliberate and quick. Not too long after, Brenna McCarthy swung the door open, and Evelyn's stomach sank. Brenna's eyes were swollen, rubbed raw from crying. Her braided hair had unraveled, and gray strands wafted in the breeze. She wore the same high-necked dress from the morning she'd stood under McKenna's body, the same shawl falling over her shoulders. She appeared to have sunk into madness on a tide of grief and shock. Her rumpled clothes had not been changed in days, her frenzied hair left unbrushed.

"You must be the ones Commissioner Doyle mentioned," she said, her voice a brittle, broken rasp.

"Who is it?" a man's voice boomed in the back.

"Ma!" another shouted.

A young man, about the age of sixteen, entered the doorway. Days of crying showed on his face, too. Evelyn recalled that the McCarthys had a son and daughter. He was McKenna's brother.

"Mrs. McCarthy, do you think we could come in for a moment?" Evelyn asked.

"We don't want to answer any more questions. Leave," the young man said.

"Daniel!" Brenna chided.

"I know this may be difficult, but we want to learn more about your sister," Evelyn said.

"And do what?" Daniel said.

"Make sure it hopefully doesn't happen to anyone else," Cyrus said, his tone soft, not an ounce of impatience or authority.

"Yes, of course, please come in," Brenna said.

She opened the door wider, and Daniel led them into a small kitchen area. An older man, whom Evelyn recognized as Jack McCarthy and McKenna's father, sat at a wooden table.

Brenna motioned for Evelyn and Cyrus to sit. "I'd offer ya some tea, but seeing as the last two days haven't been, well . . . We've not had much time to go into town and get groceries."

Jack regarded them wearily as everyone took seats at the wooden table, except for Daniel, who leaned up against the kitchen counter, arms crossed.

"First, we're sorry for your loss," Cyrus said, again his voice soft, even gentle.

During the beat of silence that followed, Evelyn's magic sensed the sorrow, the absence in the home.

"She was only twenty," Jack whispered more to himself than anyone else.

Brenna nodded, but her eyes were absent, constantly searching around the house, unable to sit still. The McCarthy family receded into themselves, a darkness settling around them. The clay walls appeared to be cast in shadow. The house was in disarray. Empty mugs and bowls scattered about. Furniture upturned. The table cluttered.

The fire crackled to Evelyn's left, the familiar sound fueling her resolve. The flame was dying, the tin bin beside the fireplace almost empty of wood.

Evelyn sighed and started. "Can you tell us anything about McKenna's day-to-day? Did anything change recently?"

"McKenna was a clerk in Callum," Jack said. "Got the job at eighteen. Too smart for her own good sometimes."

Brenna's smile was tight, as if it hurt to even attempt speaking. "She left shortly after the sun came over the north hill and always returned an hour before it fell."

"McKenna was a good girl. Sassy at times, but sweet most of it."

"And recently?" Cyrus asked. "Did she mention seeing anyone? Being followed, perhaps?"

Both parents shook their heads, but Evelyn's magic detected unease.

Daniel's eyes darted between his parents, and he seemed undecided if he should cross his arms or put his hands in his pockets.

Brenna's sudden tears pulled Evelyn's attention back to the table.

"Have you heard the wretched rumors?" Brenna said through streaming tears. "They sayin' McKenna brought this upon herself, too independent for her own good. The rumors have been cruel."

"The Kerrys can rot," Jack muttered.

Evelyn recalled the Kerry family name, a well-to-do merchant who supplied most of Miss Patricia's stock at the Runaway Radish. In small towns like Callum, gossip flitted on the wind like pollen. Once it spread, it couldn't be stopped. A victim of unwanted gossip herself, Evelyn understood the stain it left, the whispers as harsh as a brand on one's character. She'd always been *too* something, according to her tutors, not *enough* to other witches. But like pollen, it was best to brush it off and move onward.

"Right now," Evelyn said, "we are trying to understand patterns, learn anything we can about McKenna. When did you discover she was missing?"

"Wednesday morning," Brenna said.

That was the morning McKenna's body had been found.

"She never came in for morning tea. She always sat with me before she left for work. I went to check on her, and she wasn't there. I thought maybe she went in early for the day. Her bed was made. Satchel gone. Something in the air didn't feel right that morning—a mother knows—so I decided to go into town to check."

The cottage went still as they waited for Brenna to finish.

"Then I found her, dangling in the town square. *Dead*. At first, I didn't believe it. Not my McKenna. I kept tellin' myself, that poor soul looks like my sweet, smart girl. But like I told ya, a mother knows. My very soul knew it was her as I walked down the street. My McKenna."

"Our poor daughter, dangling like some sort of meat meant for the butcher. I dunno how we're supposed to go on. Don't know how we are supposed to even breathe right."

Cyrus and Evelyn remained silent, too nervous to interrupt the grief. They locked eyes for a brief moment before Evelyn flicked her attention to Daniel and back. Cyrus followed her gaze, assessing in silence. After a moment, he turned back to Evelyn and nodded in agreement. It was slight, barely a twitch, but Evelyn felt him agree with her.

"Daniel, what about you?" Her question shattered the silence in the gloomy cottage.

His eyes grew wide, and then he found the floor suddenly interesting.

Evelyn looked to Cyrus for help, not wanting to push the grieving family. The brother knew something, Evelyn sensed it, and they needed clues in order to find the vampyr.

Cyrus cleared his throat. "Were you and your sister close, Daniel?"

Sadness entered Daniel's eyes. "Yes."

"Is there anything you may have noticed? Anything out of the ordinary?"

Daniel pursed his lips, hesitant yet again.

Jack turned to his son, noticing his silence as well. "Daniel, what is it?"

McKenna's brother sighed. "For about two weeks, McKenna'd been slipping out in the middle of the night. Some nights she'd come back after only a few hours, and other nights she'd be gone until right before the sun came up."

Both parents whirled to face their son.

"You never thought to tell us?" his father demanded.

"I didn't . . . I didn't think anything of it. And I'm not sure if either of ya cared to notice, but McKenna was happy. Smiling more than she already did. She's a grown woman, and I didn't think it was my business to rat on her."

Jack's cheeks grew so ruddy he looked like he might burst with anger, but Brenna laid a hand over her husband's. "I suppose he's right. McKenna was a grown woman. She could do whatever she liked."

"But she was my little girl," Jack said, rising from his seat and leaving. Daniel followed him, unable to meet his mother's gaze.

Evelyn's heart twinged. She'd seen the look of loss before, trudged through its sticky ambiance. Had met with families of vampyr victims. Had consoled those who grieved.

And yet, this was different.

Back in Sorin, vampyrs attacked and killed like a horde of demons, ravaging a village or town with only the thought of blood to fuel them. The death and loss were the same, but witches had each other to lean on. McKenna's death was more intimate, more direct, and shrouded in mystery.

They needed answers. Clues. *Anything.*

"We—" Evelyn started.

"Commissioner Doyle told us you both believe it to be a vampyr that killed McKenna. Is that true?" Brenna asked.

"Yes," Cyrus said. "Which is why we need to learn more about where she's been. Who she's been with."

Brenna shrugged. "I don't know. McKenna used to tell me everything. I didn't know she was seeing anyone."

Evelyn's brows furrowed. Had McKenna been seeing the vampyr? It made sense for the secrecy, at least, but Evelyn couldn't understand why she'd willingly meet with a vampyr.

Cyrus continued. "Is there a place that McKenna thought was special or maybe somewhere she would've gone?"

Brenna scoffed, placing a hand over her chest. "We used to call McKenna our sweet little faerie as she ran through our fields as a child. Even when she was older, well, she practiced the old ways, ones she learned from her grandmother, my Ma." She paused, looking out the window and squinting as if she was searching for something. But her little girl wasn't out there running in the fields and never would be again. "There's a castle, a ruin from the ancient faerie reign. She used to visit and leave trinkets. Told me she felt the ghosts and respected the dead."

"Do others visit the castle?" Cyrus asked.

"Nay, wouldn't pass the crumbled wall, let alone go into the actual castle. There's rumors demons roam there. But the otherworldly didn't bother McKenna."

Which meant McKenna may have trusted a vampyr.

The sun dipped below the hilltops, and evening shadows fell over the table. Evelyn's magic pulled her toward the items sitting there, a tug that beckoned and said, *look here*.

The items were stacked neatly compared to the rest of the house. A bouquet of dried buttercups tied with white lace sat atop a water canteen with the initials *M.M.* on it, a cloth-covered notebook underneath it all.

Evelyn's magic tugged at her again. "Are these McKenna's things?"

Brenna nodded.

"May I take a look?"

"Of course."

Evelyn grabbed the book, flipping it open as Cyrus rose from the table.

"Can I get you anything, Mrs. McCarthy? A pot of tea, perhaps?"

"Doubt there's any left. Barely been able to get out of bed the last two days. Water will do fine."

Cyrus obliged. Evelyn admitted she'd misjudged him as a brute. The huntsman was strong, sure, but he was evidently kind. It was real, too. In his eyes. In his tone. Evelyn's magic sensed the authenticity.

Grateful to have learned more about her partner, she turned her attention back to the book. It was a diary or journal of some sort. Some entries were about McKenna's day-to-day, nothing mentioning a vampyr. Others appeared to be notes, but Evelyn froze, roaming the script over and over. She recognized it. *Olde Witch.* How in the Goddess had McKenna known the ancient language of witches?

As Cyrus talked with Brenna, Evelyn searched the cottage for signs the family were witches. There were none. No dried herbs above the door for good grace when one left home. No grimoire displayed over the fireplace. Not even the simple black candles that even descendants used.

Though if they had been witches, it still would have been unlikely that McKenna would know Olde Witch. Evelyn couldn't even read it. True, Olde Witch was from the Old World, but witches who had fled to the New World had left the language behind and those who'd stayed had lost it to keep hidden. The script was ancient, not even used in grimoires anymore. It had been her sister's role to learn the ancient script as a scholar, not Evelyn's.

Evelyn continued flipping through the pages. McKenna's handwriting had been neat, studious. Evelyn found herself at the last page, and then the air in her lungs whooshed out.

Flame.

Evelyn didn't need to know Olde Witch to understand the drawings McKenna had depicted. The last five pages were drawings of flame, black ink swirling, smudged ink to show smoke.

To be sure, Evelyn reached her magic out to Brenna. She was human, not a hint of magic. But maybe McKenna had magic in her blood? It was not impossible. Rare indeed, but sometimes magic reemerged in faded bloodlines. But had her parents known?

Evelyn couldn't ask. If she did, she revealed knowing the language in the journal. Not many humans recognized the script, and it would be suspicious if she did. Her knowledge of vampyr was already suspicious enough.

"Could I take this with me?" Evelyn asked.

Brenna gave her a hurried nod while Cyrus stared at the book but said nothing.

When they left, they took the somber mood with them. The visit only gave Evelyn more questions. More things to discover. She tried to consider it a win. They had *something*.

But it wasn't enough.

As they walked toward Bleu, all she could think about was Jack's heartache, Brenna's tears, Daniel's loss. Guilt riddled Evelyn to her core. She couldn't ignore that their daughter had been killed by a vampyr. What if the creatures had crossed the Sapphire Sea because she'd left? What if they'd grown stronger in her absence? The questions nagged at her.

But Evelyn was here. Helping. She had to. She needed to.

"What is it?" Cyrus asked.

Evelyn didn't meet his questioning gaze. Instead, she focused on the McCarthy cottage as dusk swallowed it whole.

"There's something I'd like to do."

"Tell me," he said.

So she did.

Chapter Twelve

Kade

Evelyn Carson cared.

From the moment she'd set foot in the McCarthys' cottage, she'd been conscious of their grief, and tactful when asking questions. Kade found his preconceived notions of his betrothed being challenged, and he *liked* it.

Liked *her*.

And then she'd wanted to get the McCarthys food and anything the nearest village could offer. She'd grabbed fresh milk, eggs, tea, and even visited the butcher for stew meat. She picked up blankets, carried as much firewood in her arms as she could. Her kindness reached others. Once they heard who the items were for, they came and offered their own contributions.

Kade knew she couldn't afford to be spending the amount she did. She'd never taken money from her accounts back home in Sorin, according to her sisters. Sure, she'd sold the moonstones throughout the towns she'd traveled through, but he imagined the profit she'd made ran low.

Yet, it didn't matter.

Evelyn never hesitated once when getting things for the McCarthys. She'd ignored him when he offered to buy something, only asking him to load up Bleu like a traveling mule, the horse less than thrilled as his saddle became wider and heavier. It was a two-mile walk back from the nearest village. She didn't once stumble or complain as they returned on foot in the evening light.

By the time they parted from the McCarthys, who hugged Evelyn fiercely with gratitude and couldn't stop their thanks, night had officially overtaken the hills of Callum.

"It'll be too dark for Bleu to take us back to Callum's harbor," he said. "We might have to stay in the village tonight. I saw a small inn at the edge of town."

Evelyn nodded. "All right. Maybe we can ask those in the village if they've seen anything tomorrow."

"Good idea."

They turned north instead of south. The wind whooshed, and Bleu's hooves clobbered on the path. The stars above blinked into existence. The moon, a pearly crescent in the sky, illuminated the path in a silvery hue. Evelyn, with her dark hair, obsidian like the midnight hour, and blue eyes that favored gray, looked ethereal. Kade found himself staring, ensnared by her likeness to the night.

Moons, where would they be now if he'd disobeyed the Elders and gone to meet her before their union? If they'd met as Kade and Evelyn, he wouldn't have denied his attraction to her, and that would've been a dangerous distraction. Except. . .

She left.

Kade still harbored anger, but it was waning like the moon above. The more he watched, the more he learned about Evelyn Carson, the more his anger transformed to curiosity, and tonight he'd at least learned Evelyn wasn't doing this for the money, despite what she'd told him at the Runaway Radish.

Her lie made him all the more curious. Why lie? Why was she doing any of this? If she cared so much, why had she left?

Kade didn't ask any of his burning questions, remembering that he was Cyrus and she was Saige. He needed to wait. Solve this murder. And maybe gain her trust along the way.

The village came into view. After dropping Bleu off at the stables, Kade and Evelyn each secured rooms at the inn. Compared to the Runaway Radish, the patrons were quieter in the tavern with no live music.

"Potato soup is on the menu. Can I fetch you some bowls?" a barmaid asked.

Kade nodded. "You?"

Evelyn nodded too. "I'm going to freshen up really quick. Save me a seat?"

"Sure. Honeysuckle wine?"

Evelyn smiled, her eyes brightening. "Absolutely. Thank you."

She hurried off, her boots and cape muddied from their journey. Kade sat at the bar top, ordering himself a pint alongside Evelyn's honeysuckle wine.

"Are you the huntsman?" a woman's voice said next to him.

She was a few years younger than him, perhaps. Her cheeks were rosy, as if she'd run through the cold. She twisted her hands together, and Kade's wolf hearing picked up her nervous heartbeat, pattering away.

"I am." He turned away from the girl and glanced back down the hall but caught no sign of Evelyn.

"My name is Penny. I am—was—a friend of McKenna's."

Kade's interest was piqued. "Can you tell me anything about her?"

She nodded furiously. "Yes, but not here. The town is already gossiping, and I don't want anyone to hear what I have to say."

Kade exhaled, searching for Evelyn again. He should wait, but he wanted to know what Penny had to say and, by the sound of her nervous heart and the shake of her voice, her courage to seek him out would falter soon. Besides, he needed to gain any clues he could to solve the murder, protecting these people from the vampyr.

"All right." He followed her out of the inn and into the side alley.

The wind had tamed, and night had fallen in the smaller village, stars littering the sky with blinking white lights.

Penny checked around them, continuously wringing her hands. "McKenna had a lover," she said in a rushed whisper.

Kade's brow rose. "A lover?"

"Yes," she said.

"Who?"

"I don't know. She never told me his name, and she'd only ever meet him at night."

Kade mused. At night would fit if this "he" was in fact a vampyr.

"I never met him. McKenna was secretive these last few weeks." She shook her head. "She kept telling me they were in love and that he had promised her forever."

Forever.

Kade pinched the bridge of his nose. He'd never known the creatures to form relationships with humans. They killed, slaughtered, drank from them, sometimes took them away to turn them. But falling in love? Promising forever? Kade flushed with frustration, unable to believe what Penny had told him.

Then he remembered something Brenna had said.

There's a castle, a ruin from the ancient faerie reign. She used to visit and leave trinkets.

"Did she tell you where she met him?" Kade asked.

Penny peered around the corner and watched the door for a beat before whispering, "Aye, she did. Connacht Castle."

"Thank you, Penny."

She grabbed his forearm, stopping him in his tracks. "Can I ask ya to keep this to yourself? The McCarthys are good people. They don't need rumors. McKenna's death is enough."

Kade nodded. "Of course."

They parted ways, and Kade headed to the stables to check on Bleu and to ask the stableman about Connacht Castle. Once he learned the directions, he headed back to the inn. He expected to find Evelyn at the bar, but she was nowhere to be found.

The barmaid caught his stare. "Looking for that beauty?"

Yes. He nodded.

"She took her dinner and wine up to her room. Haven't seen her since."

Kade slumped onto a barstool, running his hand over his beard. A sinking feeling filled his stomach as the barmaid slid him dinner. As he ate alone, he reminded himself she'd *left*. Yet, he couldn't shake what he'd witnessed today—Evelyn helping the McCarthys. Solving this murder for money was bullshit. She'd lied to him. Something else drove her, and there was something more to her running two years ago.

He went to bed, determined to find out what it was soon.

Chapter Thirteen

Evelyn

Evelyn draped her mud-soaked cloak over the chair at the writing desk and splashed her face in cold water. She worried for Maxie in their new apartment, but she'd cracked the main window, and her crafty familiar would be fine.

She sighed, adjusting her bun and pushing stray strands of her stubbornly straight hair behind her ears. She threw down her satchel, its weight now inconsequentially lighter than before. Her loss of funds couldn't compare to the guilt tightening her chest.

The truest of unions between the third-borns of the Sun and Moon will defeat the darkness.

Her mother's words echoed in her head, the meaning behind them as empty as the room Evelyn stood in. As third-born daughter, she'd been prophesied to one day defeat the vampyr, and her failure had allowed their darkness to spread as far as Callum, killing and hurting families.

She was a coward, wretched and weak. Running had done nothing. Were her efforts now so different?

Evelyn battled her doubts, allowing them to trail behind her like shadows as she left her room to join Cyrus for dinner. She stopped atop the stairs, an unfamiliar white-hot fury going through her.

A bright blonde beauty whispered with Cyrus. He leaned in close, attentive to whatever she had to say. The young woman's rosy cheeks, the way she peered up at Cyrus, and the way he assessed her . . . As Cyrus looked across the room, she backed up behind the corner, still able to see him but hidden from sight. After some thought, he nodded to the young woman and followed her out back.

Evelyn's gut twisted, but why? They worked together. He'd said kind words about her fears. He'd flirted on the horse. Completely supported her when she'd wanted to help the McCarthys. None of it mattered or impacted how he spent his evenings.

She descended the stairs and headed to the bar, taking her dinner to her room when it appeared, and readying herself for bed in the tunic she wore.

The warm soup, crusty bread, and knee-wobbling wine helped Evelyn to forget Cyrus soon after, and she found herself poring over McKenna's journal. The more she read, the more she wondered if McKenna had been attempting her own grimoire. But there was no magic in the book, not an ounce. Yet, McKenna wrote furiously, passionately. Maybe she believed she had magic? Or maybe the vampyr had made her believe it?

Whoever the vampyr was, McKenna never mentioned it. One word appeared often, and Evelyn racked her brain to remember any Olde Script she may have learned during her training. Was it "white"? She couldn't be sure.

She hunkered deeper into the quilts of the inn's bed and sighed, wishing for Blair's company. As a child, Blair had hidden under blankets and read and read while Evelyn and Mirella had played dress-up. Blair could have read through this journal in no time, offering some clarity and answers. But Blair wasn't here, and the last time Evelyn had seen her sister, it'd been at her wedding dress fitting, two years ago.

For what it's worth, Evelyn, you look stunning.

Her middle sister had been so encouraging, so kind. It ate Evelyn up to know she'd been planning to leave hours after they parted, and she hated to think of how her sister resented her now. They never knew she'd lost her flame, and they'd never know why she left.

Evelyn squeezed her stinging eyes, holding back tears. Exhaling, she shut the journal and placed it on the nightstand. She didn't have time for memories. She'd ask Aster if she had any texts capable of translating the Old Script at Pages and Leaves.

Evelyn buried herself deeper into the quilts as sleep overcame her, burying thoughts of her sisters as she did.

Chapter Fourteen

Evelyn

The next morning, family-style porridge and berries was laid out on the long tables as Evelyn entered the main area of the inn. She hadn't heard or seen Cyrus the rest of the night, and she was still stewing from her own stupidity.

He wasn't at breakfast either.

Evelyn simmered with frustration. She couldn't sit in the village all morning waiting for him, and she wanted to get back to Aster sooner rather than later. A small part of her dreaded meeting the blonde beauty if she appeared.

She gritted her teeth and tried desperately to not give a *fucking flame*, piling her breakfast onto a plate.

Halfway through, the morning light dimmed as a large figure appeared in the main doorway. Cyrus sauntered toward her.

"Morning," he said, chipper and warm.

Evelyn smiled, mastering her emotions to indifference. "Morning."

He joined her across the table. "I was thinking . . ." He spooned porridge into a bowl and topped it with blueberries. "Castle Connacht is on our way back to Callum. We could stop and take a look around."

Evelyn sipped some tea. "Castle Connacht?"

Cyrus nodded. "The faerie ruins Brenna mentioned. I know you have a cat to get back to, so I wanted to make sure more time spent away from Callum was all right with you."

How had he come by the name of the faerie ruins? She was about to ask, but something else made her pause. "Wait, how do you know I have a cat?"

Cyrus paused, looking over his mug. "Miss Patricia mentioned it. Said she missed the free pest control."

Evelyn slowly nodded. "Well, Maxie should be fine a little longer without me."

"Good," Cyrus said with a small smile.

Evelyn stirred her porridge. "So, how was your night?"

Cyrus took a few bites of his breakfast. "Decent, though the bed was a little stiff and small."

Evelyn laughed. "I imagine it would be with two."

Cyrus's brow furrowed. "With two?"

Fucking flames.

His confusion was blatant, and Evelyn realized she'd made a terrible mistake.

She shoveled two heaping portions of porridge into her mouth, waving her hand dismissively. She swallowed. "Never mind."

Cyrus watched her as she rose from her chair, his eyes narrowed and lips in a thin line. Goddess, he wasn't going to drop this, was he?

"I'll meet you at the stables." Evelyn didn't meet his eyes and never gave him a backward glance. She almost ran as she fled the table and Cyrus's assessment.

"Saige, wait!" he called behind her.

She did no such thing, heading out of the inn and into the sunless morning. Gray blanketed the sky, and the promise of rain hung in the air.

She made it to the stables and found Bleu tied out front, saddled and ready for them.

"Do you mind enlightening me as to what that was back there?"

Evelyn turned, inch by inch, wishing away the embarrassing blush on her cheeks. Behind her, Cyrus stood with his arms crossed, waiting and expectant.

She cursed. Why had she said anything? Why had she cared in the first place? She refocused her attention on Bleu's stirrups and reins, checking everything was in order, not daring to meet Cyrus's eyes. "I saw you with the young woman." She masked her tone with indifference and tried to sound aloof while her body scorched as if she'd burst into her own flames.

Cyrus said nothing for a moment and then, "Do you mean Penny?"

Evelyn scoffed. "You remembered her name. I guess that's good." She raised her brow in a taunt.

Cyrus's eyes went wide. "Moons," he hissed so low Evelyn barely caught the word. She didn't have time to think about it, because he laughed and then his next words rocked her. "You're jealous."

"What?" she said, dropping her tone and indifferent demeanor. She tried to recover, fumbling her words. "No. I'm . . . trying to make conversation."

"About a woman you believed I brought back to my room?"

In all her years, Evelyn had never thought she'd die of embarrassment. By vampyr, certainly. By demon, possibly. Preferably by old age. But never embarrassment.

"Again, I was trying to make conversation."

Cyrus's lips twitched into a smile, and Evelyn found herself in deep shit. *Fucking flames*, he was already attractive, but when he smiled, he became devastatingly beautiful. She couldn't stop staring, barely registering his next words.

"If you must know, for conversation purposes of course, Penny was a friend of McKenna's. She sought me out to tell me McKenna had a lover, one she met only at night. Penny also told me they used to meet at Castle Connacht."

Kade dropped his smile, and it all dawned on her.

"Oh."

"It's why I suggested we go there on our way back to Callum."

Oh.

Cyrus strode to Bleu, checking the saddle himself. "So you have nothing to be jealous of."

"I am not jealous!" she said, her voice shrill with exasperation. Evelyn turned, readying herself to mount Bleu.

"Why do you do that?"

She stopped, facing Cyrus again. "Do what?"

"Hide your emotions. Pretend like you feel nothing." He threw out his hand as if the idea exhausted him.

"You don't know me, Huntsman. We met only two—"

"Yes, only two days ago. And you told me you were solving this murder for money, but someone who does this for the money doesn't go spending it all on some family they barely know."

Evelyn's heart skipped. Not only did he recognize her mask, but he saw through it too, and it terrified her. She should run. She should stop working with him and walk away and solve the murder by herself. Getting close to someone, allowing him to get close to her, wasn't worth the risk.

And yet, it'd been so long since she'd been seen. Truly seen.

Cyrus took a step toward her, the air near the stables zapping with his energy. They came toe to toe, his eyes searching her face. "Saige, why are you doing this?"

"I don't understand why it matters."

"If we're going to work together, I want to get to know you."

Evelyn scoffed and shook her head. She couldn't afford to get close to anyone. Not when she planned to leave right after she solved the murder and killed the vampyr.

"You have to choose," she said.

Cyrus narrowed his gaze. "Choose what?"

"Knowing me or working with me. You can't have both."

"Why not?"

"It's complicated."

Cyrus sighed. "All right. Answer this one question, since we both already know you originally lied, and I won't ever ask another."

Evelyn bit her lip and tucked a stray strand of hair behind her ear. She walked on dangerous ground admitting this out loud, revealing her true intentions. Yet, she wanted to say it, to be heard.

"I know what it's like to lose loved ones to vampyrs." The words tumbled out of her. "The heartache and sadness, all because of these wretched creatures. I'm doing it so no one else in Callum has to feel what I or the McCarthys did."

Cyrus stared at her, really stared at her, like he was seeing her for the first time.

She swallowed, waiting for any response at all. Nerves pricked at her skin like the tickling promise of rain still vibrant in the air.

Finally, Cyrus nodded. "Let's go, then," he said. "For those who have lost someone to the vampyr."

His eyes bored into hers, and his absolute tone reached her heart.

Being seen, being heard . . . No one back home in Nūa had noticed the difference after she lost her flame. No one had seen her pain, not a single coven member, not even her own sisters, and no one ever asked why she did what she did—trained on the Guard, went to tutoring. They assumed she did it all because she was the Daughter of the Goddess and never asked what her own reasons were, whether she had her own reasons. But Cyrus had asked and accepted her answers with no judgment. Not an ounce. It was refreshing, wild, and unlike anything she'd experienced.

Evelyn's chest swelled as they rode to Castle Connacht and felt as light as the slow morning breeze.

Chapter Fifteen

Evelyn

The crumbled walls of Castle Connacht flanked the outside perimeter of a single tower. Structurally intact, the tower stretched toward the sky like a stone beacon in the sprawling valley.

Time had left its mark, though.

Moss and ivy traveled over the once sharp architecture, the gray surface withered and rounded. Glassless windows opened to the outside world, and the gateless entrance beckoned them in. A path through the grass speared up ahead, the softened ground evidence the castle still received visitors, despite its fall hundreds of years ago.

Evelyn followed Cyrus, in step behind him on the path. The higher they climbed, the thicker the air became. Not from altitude, but with *other*. Evelyn's magic flicked out and detected the darkness seeping from the castle. It crept up her spine in greeting, curious and cold. Evelyn shivered.

Cyrus stopped on the path. "Is everything all right?"

The wind howled, deep and moody like an omen. It ruffled Evelyn's hair, and she fiddled with her bone staff, making sure it was still secure through her low bun.

"This place . . ." Evelyn shook her head, unsure how to describe it to a human without revealing she possessed magic and could feel others'.

Cyrus frowned. The opening to the castle loomed in shadow, too black to make out what lay ahead. "I feel it, too."

"Darkness?"

Cyrus's expression went grim. "Death."

Evelyn pursed her lips. Whatever she felt surrounding the castle, it made her reconsider Miss Patricia's tales of faeries.

Evelyn and Cyrus passed through the gate and entered a hallway. Mildew and the smell of wet rock permeated the air, as did the silence, more deafening the farther they walked.

At the end of the hall, she could just make out a dim light. Cyrus glanced back, and Evelyn nodded in agreement. She couldn't shake how well they worked together, how in sync she felt with him.

Their footsteps clattered against the stone hallway until they entered what appeared to once have been a grand hall. The ceiling had crumbled above, leaving an open outlet to the cloudy sky. A disarray of rubble covered the dais. Behind it, the last threads of a tapestry hung in defiance, swaying in the breeze that escaped from the open windows.

Evelyn approached the dais, walking around a circle of burnt candles on the steps, melted to stumps, their wax having dripped onto and melded with the stone slabs. Various items were piled in the center as offerings—bottles of unopened wine, wilted grapes, rotten apples.

A single loaf of bread, wrapped in linen, appeared to be recent, not a patch of mold on it yet. Cyrus joined her, then squatted and reached for the bread.

Don't ever disturb a faerie fort.

Miss Patricia's words chimed through Evelyn's mind, and she grabbed Cyrus's wrist in time. Panic quickened her heart.

"Don't disturb the offerings," she whispered.

Cyrus stared at her hand, tight and firm around his muscled forearm. A zap seared through her fingers, and Evelyn snatched her hand away, hoping the dim light hid her blush as she assessed the offerings again.

She pointed to the loaf. "That's fresh. Days old compared to the other offerings."

"Which means someone has been here recently."

"Maybe it was McKenna," she said.

"It would fit the timeline of her death." He paced the hall again. "It's also the perfect place to meet a vampyr. Lacking sunlight and secluded from the village."

Evelyn looked east and west and found passageways leading farther into the tower. "I can take one and you can take the other."

"There's no way we're separating." Something flashed over Cyrus's features, as if he was surprised at what he'd said.

Evelyn thought nothing of it, or tried to, at least. She needed to solve this murder, not over-think her interactions with Cyrus. Not his kindness. The things he said. His touch. None of it mattered. They worked together.

And Evelyn held too many secrets, too much of a past to even risk getting close to him, dragging him into the mess that was her life.

She tapped into her magic and focused on the task at hand. Evelyn made sure to keep her expression and posture neutral so Cyrus wouldn't notice.

The *other* in the castle buzzed, the darkness pulling her to the left doorway. Evelyn sensed the vampyr curse tethered to dark magic. The coldness. The affliction.

A red droplet stained the stone near the doorway. Evelyn crouched down for a closer look; the color was unmistakable.

"Cyrus," she called.

He joined her, his expression turning grave at the sight of the blood.

The trail continued down the corridor, fading into the blackness of the tower.

"We have to follow it," she said.

"We can at least be assured the vampyr isn't here."

"True. It would've smelled our blood already."

Vampyrs fed often, and seeing it was almost night, if a vampyr slumbered here, its hunger would've woken it with them so close.

As they left the once grand hall, their steps echoed in the corridor, and Evelyn tried to keep her footsteps light, fearful her boots would wake whatever did live inside the wretched place.

They passed a series of vacated rooms until a flash of gold caught Evelyn's eye.

"Wait!"

This time, Cyrus grabbed her hand, halting them both in the hall. They stared at their joined hands. Evelyn forgot how to breathe. Her magic flared to life, reaching out to Cyrus with a surge of curiosity. She couldn't think, couldn't meet his eyes as she pulled her hand away, yet again caught off-guard by the searing sensation his touch gave. She snuffed her magic down.

McKenna. The vampyr. Solve the murder. Leave Callum.

She continued to remind herself of those things, ignoring Cyrus's prickling stare on the back of her neck.

A set of golden goblets sat on a maroon blanket, mirroring the wine still in the cups. A wicker basket on the edge lay open, fruit and bread left behind. The scene appeared special, serene, even intimate.

Like the bite mark on McKenna's thigh.

"It's a picnic," Evelyn said with disbelief. Vampyrs were ruthless, hungry creatures. How in the Sun had it accomplished this with McKenna? Evelyn couldn't imagine it. Their razor teeth. Their animal-like movements. The picnic was far too . . . *normal.*

Cyrus dropped to his haunches, assessing the blanket, sniffing the goblets. Wilted flowers rested in the corner while an empty bottle of wine lay on its side.

"It doesn't make any sense. There aren't even signs of a struggle," Evelyn noted.

No wrinkled blanket. The goblets still stood. It appeared as though the lovers had merely abandoned the picnic.

"No," Cyrus said, "but it does fit with everything we know. Daniel McCarthy said McKenna was sneaking out at night. Penny, McKenna's friend, said she had a lover."

In love? With a vampyr? The vampyrs Evelyn had faced were crazed, bloodthirsty creatures who couldn't form sentences. Evelyn shook her head, pacing in the small room. "I don't understand . . . Why hang her body? Why gouge her eyes out?"

Cyrus furrowed his brows as he rose, seeming to consider the same thing. "Maybe to send a message?"

"A message for what? For whom?"

Why did it feel like every time Evelyn discovered something, she had only more questions that needed answers? She struggled to articulate them out loud, afraid she'd reveal her close ties to the vampyrs and shatter the disguise she'd worked hard to build these last two years. Working on this case and with Cyrus was already a risk in itself. Having been on her own for so long, she'd forgotten what it meant to work closely with others.

Guilt spread through Evelyn like ink seeping into paper, quick and permanent. She'd run from her duty to protect her people, but it seemed the vampyr extended their wrath farther than she'd ever imagined. Was she a fool to think she could solve this murder? She'd already failed once. What was to say she wouldn't fail again?

"Where do you go? When your eyes get lost like that? What are you thinking of, Saige?"

Evelyn blinked and refocused. Cyrus watched her. *Intently*. His eyes looked like butterscotch in the dim light, sweet and . . . concerned.

For a fraction of a moment, Evelyn didn't want to lie. The truth sat on her lips, ready to fall and reveal what she could never take back.

"You promised no more questions, Huntsman," she said.

"I'm afraid I may break that promise from time to time," he said with a sad smile. "Tell me, Saige."

Her name on his lips, though it was her fake name, sounded kind and true, like she could tell him anything and he'd listen.

"Where do I go? The past. To whom I used to be." Her words were a mere whisper, but it was as if she'd shouted it into the small, stone-walled room.

"I imagine if I asked who that was, you wouldn't tell me."

Evelyn shook her head and conjured a timid smile. "Not today."

A light of hope flashed in Cyrus's eyes. "Not today, then."

Embarrassment spread through Evelyn at how he made her feel. The small touches. Their stares. His questions. Her honesty. Everything and something brewing between them. Goddess above, she couldn't let this happen. She was Daughter of the Goddess, for one, promised to another based on a prophecy. Despite the fact she'd left that engagement, she'd run away to protect her people, not to start over.

Air. She needed air. And light. Sunlight.

She moved too quickly to the doorway, and her boot caught the wool blanket, tugging it with her. The goblets clattered to the ground, and the wine splashed onto the stone floor. The commotion echoed off the walls and through the eerie castle.

Both Evelyn and Cyrus stilled. Silence rang out for a few deafening moments, hope sparking in Evelyn that she'd not disturbed whatever slumbered here.

Her hope was short-lived.

A thousand creatures screeched, the piercing pitch ringing through the castle. Cyrus's nostrils flared, his eyes flashing dark and determined.

"*Run.*"

His command vibrated through Evelyn's bones, and she didn't hesitate, her years of training clicking into gear. She ran. Her magic surfaced. Flares of it searched for the creatures she'd awakened. The manifestation of claws, tiny yet sharp, scraped through her magic's reach.

Evelyn grimaced, faltering a step. Strong arms caught her, and she paused. They both paused. For only a breath, a moment long enough for Evelyn to look into Cyrus's eyes.

More screeching broke their stare. Down the hallway, a horde of rat-like creatures with blazing red eyes scurried down the walls, the floor, the ceiling. Their misty, black bodies overtook every surface, not a single stone left in sight.

The energy. The *other*. Their misty, black bodies. How had Evelyn not recognized it? Perhaps it had been so long since she had seen it, or maybe it was because she hadn't believed darkness had spread to Torren, this far east of Sorin.

"Demons," Cyrus uttered under his breath, his body stiffening.

Creatures of darkness.

Evelyn grabbed his hand, yanking him along as they ran faster than before.

Demons had once been animals of the natural world, corroded, infested, and forever changed by darkness. Vicious, ghastly, and damn hard to kill.

A yelp escaped Evelyn, her ankle stinging with pain. A single rat clung to her boot, nibbling through the leather with needle-like teeth. Evelyn pulled out of Cyrus's grasp and kicked the rat away. It hissed and bounced off the wall, readying itself to leap again.

It leaped, but Cyrus severed it in two. With his sword out, black blood dripping from the blade, Cyrus had transformed. His shoulders were taut, jaw tight, stare lethal. A beastly energy bristled from him, and Evelyn's magic fought to be used, itched to fight and defend.

She shoved it down. She couldn't use it and reveal she was a witch. Her secret saved lives.

They continued running. Up ahead, the grand hall beckoned them with the promise of freedom, but the opposite corridor filled with more rats, bigger and faster.

"Fuck," Cyrus whispered.

They reached the grand hall and came to a halt, the rats closing in around them from the east, west, and north hall where they entered the castle.

Evelyn let out a stream of her own curses. Rats began to leap at them, Cyrus cutting them down in mid-air. They backed up into the circle of candles, stepping through the offerings as they climbed up the stairs of the dais. Their retreat only made the rats angrier, faster, as they filed into the grand hall. Evelyn kicked the stray ones away while Cyrus severed the others. They were going to be overrun.

"Any ideas on how to get out of this mess?" Cyrus called over his shoulder.

Evelyn needed to do something. They were out of options. *She* was out of options.

Fucking flames, I am the option.

Evelyn didn't have a choice. Damn her secrets. Protecting others took priority. She'd deal with the consequences of revealing herself later, but protecting Cyrus, getting them out of here, and continuing to solve this murder mattered more than her disguise.

"Well, there's something I need to tell you," she said, turning to Cyrus.

"*Now?*" Cyrus swiped across a bigger rat's exposed belly. Its dead body thumped to the ground.

"I think now is actually the perfect time."

"Saige," Cyrus said, unamused.

Evelyn pulled her bone staff free, her obsidian hair unraveling. She twirled the staff through her fingers until she gripped it in her palm, the dragon bone matte against her skin. With a surge of magic, it transformed to its full size, and she slammed the staff into the grand hall's floor, magic shuddering through the stone. It sent a wave of opal energy at the rats, ricocheting them back.

"I'm a witch."

Chapter Sixteen

Evelyn

Evelyn's heart hammered, her insides jumbled with jitters, waiting for Cyrus's reaction.

Time stopped in the grand hall as she waited, the rats unable to break past the waves her staff sent out.

Yet, Cyrus only blinked and . . . didn't seem the slightest bit surprised. Instead, his lips twitched into a smile and his eyes twinkled in triumph.

"Magic sounds like an amazing idea," he said.

Evelyn controlled the magic from the staff, knocking back rats as she and Cyrus advanced toward the exit. Cyrus continued to cut down any rats that scurried past Evelyn's wave of magic, fighting off the bigger ones and annihilating the small ones.

A rat as round and massive as Maxie pounced and clung to Evelyn's forearm, sinking its teeth into her flesh, attempting to compromise the mighty grip on her staff.

Metal slicing through the air rang in Evelyn's ears, and then the rat's hold on her arm loosened. Cyrus caught her before she fell to her knees, blood streaming down her hand.

"Can you heal?" he asked, peering down with unfaltering concern lacing his beautiful eyes.

"Yes," she breathed.

Castle Connacht shook. Debris and dust fell from above, and the bellow of a larger, fiercer demon echoed. The stone wall covered by the tapestry crumbled, and a rat-like creature twice the size of Bleu, with the talons and tail of a reptile, burst into the grand hall.

Evelyn and Cyrus stood back-to-back as the rats around them retreated, and the demon sized them up. Darkness rolled off it, and the smaller rats hissed, waiting for the leader to charge. Evelyn drove her staff down, casting out stronger magic, and Cyrus tightened his grip on his sword.

"Do you think it's pissed we stepped on the offerings?" she asked.

Cyrus raised a single brow, the hint of a smile on his lips. "You're unbelievable."

Together they charged the demon. Evelyn sent out a flare of magic, bringing up debris and hitting the demon. It screeched in pain, distracted long enough for Cyrus to cut its forearm, sending black blood spraying into the grand hall. Back and forth they went, Evelyn assaulting the demon and Cyrus injuring it further.

Yet, the demon caught on to their plan and bucked, swishing its tail at them, hitting them. Evelyn fell with a deafening thump, her staff clattering across the stone and out of reach.

Cyrus had been knocked through her barrier and into the horde of smaller rats. He growled, fiercely and in pain, and gritted his teeth as a rat latched on to his shoulder. He swatted and fought, but there were too many of them as they crawled and overcame him. He rose and fell, killing one only to have two more run him over.

Not again.

Evelyn tamped down her fear and shook away the doubt. She *had* to protect him, had to get them out of this mess.

She swooshed magic behind her, and the rats fell away, giving her distance to reach her staff. She gripped the ancient bone, her magic humming through her veins. It soared. She hammered it into the grand hall and screamed.

And instead of an opal white, red and orange flame ascended from her staff, cascading its power through the grand hall and scorching the rats in its wake.

A feathery warm lightness overtook Evelyn's muscles and hollowed her bones. Her heart soared. Her mind reeled.

Elated. Awakened. Light.

Her flame. She'd conjured her flame. It was wild, twisting and twirling, like a beast left dormant but now free. Evelyn's blood coursed hot, and her eyes almost welled with tears at the familiarity of her power.

She sent it out, controlled and steady, until she reached the rats surrounding Cyrus and scorched every single one. The leading demon bellowed through the hall, descending the dais toward her.

Cyrus joined Evelyn at her side, his leathers tattered but the injuries minor. With his head held high and eyes alert, he gave her a knee-wobbling smile and curt nod. Her flame flared at his proximity as if greeting an old friend.

The demon bared its teeth, a wave of rotten breath assaulting them. Evelyn cast a sphere of fire at its right flank, and Cyrus cut its left. It rose onto its hind legs. Scorch marks sizzled while cuts oozed black. It reared to strike, but Cyrus was faster, leaping from a pile of debris and swiping across its exposed belly.

As it fell, Evelyn slammed her staff one last time, sending a whoosh of flame over the demon. Her power fed on the darkness, ate its way around the demon's body, and devoured it.

The demon withered and died. Evelyn's flame fluttered back into her chest, like a hound returning to its master. All the rats in the grand hall dissipated into dust, vanishing into the wind as if the ruins of the castle swallowed their existence whole. Sunlight poured through the broken windows, and for a few, heaving moments, Evelyn relished their victory.

And then she laughed. Uncontrollably and sillily.

Cyrus stared at her, unsure, until he broke into a smile and laughed with her. Evelyn slumped against the rubble of the castle, beat from the fight, and celebrated her win in stitches.

For the first time in a long time, she was whole again.

Chapter Seventeen

Kade

Kade walked between Evelyn and Bleu, the sun sinking below the horizon of the sea past Callum. Puffs of chimney smoke rose over the town like miniature clouds, and lanterns glowed to life one by one as they climbed down from the hills.

Merchants, farmers, and traders passed as they left the market for the day. Kade nodded in greeting while Evelyn sent them a friendly smile. She'd been silent since they'd left Castle Connacht. Kade chanced a glance or two her way. She'd used her staff with ease, and it fit her. He recognized the dragon bone, the coveted material witches and werewolves adored. Evelyn had color in her cheeks, a sheen to her blue-gray eyes, and more bounce in her step.

It was as if revealing herself as a witch had awakened some side of her he'd not yet seen. Not only had they gained more clues about McKenna's murder, but Evelyn had dropped her disguise. Guilt ate away at him.

Their fight with the demons had driven Evelyn to reveal herself as a witch. Kade hoped it meant she trusted him, but another part of him knew she'd done it because they'd been out of options. The moment the demons had appeared, his wolf had itched to be released, and he should've shifted. He'd feared revealing himself, feared he'd fracture whatever was building between them, and his protector instinct hated that he'd hesitated.

It felt wrong, playing this dangerous game of being Cyrus the huntsman.

"Cyrus, can I ask something of you?"

He hated hearing his fake name on her lips but hid his frustration. "Depends on what it is, Princess."

Evelyn rolled her eyes but didn't object. "I . . ." She paused as a group of merchants passed them on the path. Once out of earshot, she met his gaze. "Callum does not know I am a witch. Well, I take that back. My friend Tovi knows, and I suppose my new landlord does, too, but Miss Patricia, the others, they don't, and I'd like to keep it that way."

Who was Tovi? Why did her new landlord know? Why did hiding her identity as a witch matter so much?

Her brows furrowed with worry, and hesitation laced her tone. She wanted him to keep her secret. She trusted him enough to ask, but he worried about why she wanted to keep her witch nature hidden.

"Saige, Callum would not treat you differently if they knew. There are other witches in these lands."

The Great Burnings had overtaken Torren long ago, but peace now flourished in the Old and New World between those who possessed magic and those who didn't.

Evelyn shook her head. "That's not the point."

Kade sighed. If he pushed her, he could break his cover by coming across overly interested. He'd found her. Gotten close to her. He couldn't risk any of the progress he'd made—it had taken him a full year to find her.

The wind whirled over the hills, and a realization dawned on him. He'd never once found her trail by following clues left behind by a witch. Cirello to Sorin to Morrow, he'd followed the trail of the moonstones, the whispers of a young woman with raven hair, and the rare sightings of a miniature lion in tow, but *never* the sightings of a witch.

No magic, no spells, never flame. It finally clicked.

"Definitely good at hiding, aren't you?" he asked out loud, an unintended assertion.

Evelyn didn't catch his slip or realize his mistake. "It's complicated."

He almost laughed. How ironic. Keeping her magic hidden, going from town to town, not using her flame at least made sense. It was a gift from the Sun Goddess, unique to her as Daughter of the Goddess. But to hide her entire identity as a witch?

Kade remembered the words of Evelyn's scholarly sister, Blair. *She had to have a reason for leaving, and I know Evelyn. She is not selfish; she is not vain. Whatever reason it was or is, she didn't think she could tell me. Her own sister.*

Thus far, Kade had struggled with that notion, but after witnessing her with the McCarthys and now learning she hid so much of herself from everyone . . . There was *something* else—he could sense it. He needed to gain her trust if he ever wanted to learn what that was, and the one way to do that was to agree to her request.

"I will keep your secrets," he said, eyeing her reaction.

Her shoulders relaxed, and she let out a sigh. "Thank you."

As they reached the outskirts of town, Evelyn surveyed the path, and seemingly pleased with the lack of observers, she summoned her magic, her staff assuming its smaller size and landing in her palm. Like she'd done it every day of her life, she slid the now pin-sized staff through her low bun.

Kade slowed his pace as they walked through the first line of buildings, Bleu's hooves clobbering against the stone streets. "So, what's next?" he asked.

Evelyn tapped her satchel. "I think I know someone who can help us read McKenna's journal."

"Why can't we read it now?" he said, pausing on the street.

She tucked a stray strand of hair behind her ear and looked around. "It's written in Olde Script."

Ah. That had been the recognition in her eyes back at the McCarthys' cottage. "You can't read it?"

She shook her head. "Not many witches can. Now if—" She stopped herself and waved her hands, flustered.

Had she been about to mention Blair? Evelyn swallowed and averted her gaze. Stars above, did she miss her sister? Kade grappled with his preconceived notions of her, bile forming in the back of his throat.

He'd thought she was spoiled. Someone with no regard for duty and honor. Or perhaps a woman who didn't want to marry a man she didn't know. Kade understood that. Respected that. He'd been nervous to marry a woman he'd never met, too.

But by the looks of it, she didn't enjoy hiding or being away from her sisters. Maybe the lightness he saw in her was the weight of her secret lifted off her shoulders, even if it was him who'd witnessed her greatness. Why did she live like this? Why had she run? Kade's chest tightened.

What else are you hiding?

"I owe Miss Patricia an evening shift at the bar, but how about we meet tomorrow at the Runaway Radish around lunchtime?" he asked. "Maybe your contact can come along, too, and help us decipher the journal."

"I'll see what I can do." She stepped off to the side, backing toward a brightly painted green building. "This is me."

Kade swore flowers flew in the storefront window, but the gold lettering glinted from the twilight, and he chalked it up to being a trick of the light.

"Have a good evening, Saige," he said.

"You, too." Evelyn ascended a set of wrought iron stairs on the side of the building. Her boots echoed off the metal, her cloak swaying with each step. Her slender frame rocked from side to side, the sway of her strong hips and shimmer of her obsidian hair inky in the low light, ensnaring him.

What he'd give for her to turn back so he could meet those silvery eyes one last time.

Kade waited until she made it inside before returning to the Runaway Radish, and the entire journey there, an unshakable sense of absence followed him.

Chapter Eighteen

Evelyn

Candles lit every corner of Evelyn's apartment, illuminating Maxie's orange coat as her cat sat and stared out the window. Below, the street bustled with a steady flow of night life, younger folks meeting for drinks and couples going to dinner.

It reminded Evelyn of home so much her chest ached. On Fridays, she and Blair would venture out to a wine bar deep in the art district of Nūa that sold the most divine cheese and fig jam. Between the laughs, the cheese, and the tannins of the wine, Fridays with Blair had been the end-of-week event Evelyn had looked forward to, getting her through gruesome and sweltering days working on the Guard.

Sometimes Tovi had joined them too, and her rejection of half the eligible bachelors in Nūa only filled the night with more laughter and their glasses with a second bottle of wine. Those keen, green eyes had broken the strongest of hearts.

Tonight, there was no dimly-lit wine bar bustling with witches or men angling for Tovi's attention and Blair's animated tales, but at least half the company was here. Tovi swirled her wine, the earthy plum liquid streaking across the bowl of the glass. Thin and crystal clear, they'd been a housewarming present for Evelyn's new apartment. She didn't want to think about how much they cost, often forgetting her friend's wealth.

"I have no idea what you're cooking, but it smells divine," Tovi said.

"Breakfast."

"For dinner? It's like old times."

Evelyn's chest ached again as she flipped a piece of bacon. Aster claimed that in Callum it was called a *rasher*. Sliced black and white pudding—traditional oatmeal sausages—sizzled away in another pan. The whole apartment smelled of fat and meat, and Evelyn's stomach grumbled at the promise of a feast. Maybe she *had* cooked breakfast for dinner for old times' sake, seeing she and her best friend were in the same place again.

"The last time we did this was Blair's birthday." The pan hissed as Evelyn cracked two eggs into the rasher grease.

She'd made a mushroom quiche that night, with sausage gravy, while Tovi had supplied bottles of bubbly white wine. Mirella had joined too, bringing cinnamon rolls from their favorite bakery a few blocks from their parents' home. Memories sat so heavy, like stones on her shoulders as she balanced them all.

"You're right. I don't think any of us left your place until the sun started to come up." Tovi's eyes glazed over, as if she too were lost in the memories, lost in a world that no longer existed.

Evelyn faced her friend and found Maxie sending Tovi a withering glare, as if the cat remembered the celebration that had kept her up all night.

It'd been summertime, two weeks before Evelyn rode out with her parents to meet the Drengr pack. The breeze of a summer storm had flitted through her small townhome, continuously blowing out Blair's lopsided birthday candle sticking out of her cinnamon roll before she could muster a wish. The four of them had laughed until their bellies hurt, singing the worst rendition of happy birthday all of Sorin had ever heard.

Evelyn sighed. Blair's birthday, if memory served correctly, had been one of the last times she and her sisters had enjoyed time together. The weeks after were blurred memories leading to the horrific day her parents had died. There'd been no fun then. No breakfast for dinner. Just scrutiny and duty and division between the three sisters.

Laughter, company, meals shared with others. Evelyn shook her head. The lack of those small joys left Evelyn empty, starving for more than breakfast. As she plated their meal, she grasped onto gratitude for having Tovi with her, dismissing all the things she'd missed.

Evelyn slid Tovi's plate across the counter island. "Did you and Blair ever . . ."

Evelyn trailed off, not really sure what she was asking. They'd all been friends. Mirella, the oldest, with a husband and babe, only joined when she could, but Blair, Tovi, and Evelyn had been thick as thieves in Nūa.

Tovi sighed, poking at her fried egg where the yolk ran into the rest of the food. "We hung out a few times after you left, but she stopped meeting me for coffee. Stopped mentioning you altogether. Then the letters came less and less until she ceased to write to me at all, even when I reached out to her multiple times. In the end, I think Blair felt I was keeping something from her."

Which wasn't untrue. Tovi knew Evelyn had lost her flame, something she'd been too frightened to tell her sisters. Tovi wasn't a witch; she didn't judge the way other witches would, partially because it wasn't in her nature, but also because she didn't fully understand. Witches sometimes lost *control* over their bronntanas—the power became too flighty or too docile.

Evelyn had burned a few bookshelves in the Nūa library during her lessons. Blair had created a tornado in their backyard as children. Mirella had healed someone so well, she'd left herself unconscious for two days.

But to lose one's bronntanas completely?

It unnerved Evelyn to no end. Between the prophecy, her title, and the unexplained part of it, Evelyn hadn't told anyone.

Tovi had also been privy to her leaving. Where, when, how—well, even Tovi hadn't known those details until they'd run into each other on the docks of Callum days ago.

Evelyn wasn't sure why she cared. Usually, when it came to her sisters, she tried to forget them, dismiss the memory of them entirely. Guilt nauseated her, and some of their last words stung her eyes. Thinking of it never really aligned with her goal of *running*. Keeping them from her thoughts made it easier, as if there was nothing to look back at while she focused on moving forward.

Until now.

Thankfully, Aster's recommendation had been right. Evelyn's new landlord, who was slowly becoming a friend despite Evelyn's efforts to keep everyone in this town at a respectable distance, declared a Callum breakfast the best in all the land. Evelyn agreed. The sausages, very different from Nūa's, definitely competed with the gravy recipe her family had passed down for three generations.

Evelyn swallowed, taking a large gulp of wine. Why were all these memories rushing back to her now?

"You're doing that thing." Tovi eyed her while cutting into some black pudding.

Evelyn squirmed in her seat. "What thing?"

"That thing you do when you have a secret or something is weighing heavily on your mind." Tovi's eyes never left her as she devoured a forkful of food.

Fucking flames.

Evelyn was a fool to think her friend wouldn't see past her indifferent scowl. She'd yet to tell Tovi her flame had returned, and maybe her friend's presence didn't play into memory lane as much as having her Goddess-given gift back did.

Evelyn raised her hand, thrumming her fingers through the air. As she thrummed them back, she lit each tip of her finger alight.

Tovi spat out her wine, jade eyes going wide. "Goddess, Evelyn! Your flame! It's back!"

Evelyn beamed, the smile spreading across her face. The familiarity of her flame, being whole again—it eased years of tension from her shoulders.

"I don't understand," Tovi said. "How?"

Evelyn gave Tovi a vague rundown of the demon attack. She left out the details about Cyrus, not really in the mood to have that conversation about a handsome, muscular, far too kind for his own good, beast of a man with her dear friend who would sniff out whatever feelings—no, *attraction*—she had for him. Tovi believed the opposite sex to be an unnecessary distraction, or she suspected them of wanting to rob women of their independence.

After they'd finished their dinners and moved to Evelyn's patchwork sofa with their half-full bottle of wine, they continued to discuss Evelyn's flame.

"I can't explain it. It sort of happened. One minute I was using my staff to blast the demons away, and then my flame erupted."

Tovi curled into the cushions. The green patches brought out the jade in her eyes, and the maroon contrasted with her snowy blonde hair. "Sounds like it came back in a time of need. Like an instinct."

Evelyn supposed that theory wasn't far off. She'd needed to save Cyrus, get them out of there before the demons killed them. But she'd also needed her flame while fighting for her parents. Why had it left her then if her flame was fueled by instinct and need? What about this moment had been different?

During the first few months on the run, Evelyn had dedicated her time to getting it back. She'd tried everything. Read every book. Said countless prayers. Used her innate magic. *Nothing* worked. What if having it back was a fluke?

Tovi searched her face. "So, what are you going to do?"

Her friend's words were an echo of Evelyn's own question since her flame had appeared in Castle Connacht. It *seemed* to be back. She'd lit the hearth with it, manned the stove with it, and even lit every last candle in her apartment with one thought. Her flame's warmth was a gentle caress in her blood—was it back for good?

Maybe that lingering question was why she couldn't stop thinking about home and her sisters. She'd left because she'd lost her flame, fearful of not being able to get it back, and now that it was back, did she still need to run? Mesmerized by her own power, she stared into the flames flickering from her fingertips as if the orange whisps held answers.

Or false hope. Doubt nestled deep into Evelyn's core, scratching and screeching like the rat demons she'd faced. What if she lost her flame again? What if its return was a fluke? What if it continued to come and go unexplainably?

She extinguished the flames in a blink, flexing and unflexing her hand, unease tensing her fingers.

"I don't know what I'll do," she said.

"Evelyn, I think your sisters would be happy to have you home again."

Evelyn sank into her chair, nerves sending a chill down her spine. Considering the things Mirella had said before she'd left, and that she'd run away on the eve of her wedding week, she didn't envision the same joyous reunion Tovi imagined.

"It is not just my sisters I would be returning home to." Evelyn took a swig of wine, wishing her slight buzz could drown out her sense of unease.

Her coven. Witches and werewolves of Sorin. Not to mention the snooty, rigid Elders who believed in the prophecy the most.

And Kade Drengr, her betrothed.

With her magic back, Evelyn worried about their union, the magical binding that would tie their souls, and their magic, too. Her dread was cold, freezing her in place.

"What if I lose my flame again?" Evelyn said with a shake of her head.

She didn't even know what had caused it to leave in the first place, so she had no way of stopping it from happening again. Since Evelyn was a witch and Kade a werewolf, their bond would be forced, and what if her faulty flame affected his werewolf magic, or the union didn't even work?

"Evelyn, I know your flame is important, sure, but it doesn't make you any less of a witch without it." Tovi grabbed her hand, holding it tight as Evelyn's anxiety prickled at her fingertips.

Her friend was wrong. She wasn't just any witch. Evelyn was Daughter of the Goddess. Her flame defined her success against the vampyr. No one could question centuries of scholars studying the prophecy. The Sun Goddess had gifted it to *her* just like the other third-born daughter before, except she had lost it.

"What if losing it was a sign, Tovi? I don't know if I can face fucking up my union with the Son of the God in front of our entire homeland." Evelyn sighed. "I can't risk compromising the Son of the God, taking another protector in the event the vampyr king decides to strike. What if I lose my flame again and the vampyrs learn of my weakness? It'll put everyone at risk."

Sorin still faced scáths and demons crossing the Void, threats Evelyn had protected Nūa from during her time on the Guard. Nestled deep within her being, the desire to rid witches and werewolves of those threats pulsed and pounded in her heart. It battled her never-ending unease and questions. Evelyn took a deep breath, centering herself in reality. She'd just gotten her flame back.

"I'm not ready to decide yet." Evelyn met Tovi's gaze.

Her friend smiled back, a relaxed and thoughtful expression that put Evelyn at ease, made her feel seen. Then Tovi topped off Evelyn's wine glass. "Well, I suppose with storm season, you can't go back. Not yet anyway. Which gives you some time to think things through. Process it all."

Her friend was right. Evelyn had time and a murder she needed to solve first. For now, she could help Callum rid its town of a vampyr.

Tovi laid a hand over Evelyn's and gave her a gentle squeeze. "I'm here, though. To talk if you need."

Evelyn scoffed, taking a swig of her wine.

"Or not to talk," Tovi said, rolling her jade eyes.

Evelyn clanked her wine glass against Tovi's. "I'd much prefer that. For now, I want to enjoy this lovely bottle of wine with my friend whom I've truly missed."

"I missed you, too, Evelyn."

The two friends smiled at each other, and as Tovi had promised, they didn't discuss Evelyn's returned flame again or what she planned to do now that it was back. They laughed and reminisced about old times. Tovi complained about her awful brother, and Evelyn mentioned her time with the McCarthy family.

A sense of good flushed through Evelyn. Talking with someone she trusted in a place she called her own, not looking over her shoulder and not worried about what came next, present in the moment only—she marveled at the simplicity of it all, enjoyed the experience for what it was.

Later, she'd figure out what to do.

Long after Tovi had left for the night, as Evelyn slept, howling screams blew through the town of Callum, like an omen on the salty wind.

Chapter Nineteen

Kade

As rain drizzled steadily the next morning, Kade helped Miss Patricia with bread loaves. They folded dough as the Runaway Radish's guests trickled downstairs for breakfast. A gust from outside swept through the inn, and Commissioner Doyle strode straight through the Runaway Radish's open door, his eyes downcast and gait determined. Bad news came with the spilling rain, like Callum knew something wicked had happened and wept. The news he shared rocked Kade, and he wasted no time seeking out Evelyn.

Readied in his traveling leathers, but with flour still fresh on his fingers, rain dripping down his cloak, and his inner wolf wary from the cold, he knocked twice on Evelyn's door. She swung it open after a beat, the hearth glowing behind her.

Her silvery eyes grew wide with shock. "Cyrus, what—"

He stepped past her and into the apartment, not thinking twice about it. "There's been another murder."

Evelyn shut the door behind her, muffling the sound of Callum's rain. Kade's werewolf hearing caught her heart beating wildly in her chest.

"Who was it?" she asked, crossing her arms.

The studio was quaint, a small kitchenette to the left, a single bed with ruffled sheets, and a kitchen table with four mismatched chairs. The exposed brick and the crackling fire gave it a cozy ambiance. The scents of coffee and breakfast lingered in the air.

"Fiona Kerry. A merchant's daughter two towns over. Her mother found her at Lake Glenn, an hour's ride from here." He looked out the north window into the adjacent alleyway below, overrun with rainwater.

Another young woman. Another murder. Another death. His gut twisted.

"Goddess," Evelyn breathed, and if it weren't for his wolf hearing, he would've missed it.

Kade pinched the bridge of his nose. Everything they'd learned from the castle ruins seemed futile now. It wasn't a single murder; it was *two*.

Evelyn paced behind him, the floorboards creaking under her weight. "How was she killed?"

"I'm not sure. Charles said they moved the body before he got there."

"They moved evidence. Fucking flames."

"I know," he said, still facing the window. "We should head to the Kerry estate to see the body."

"We'll have to be sure she won't turn," Evelyn said. "And find signs if it's more than one vampyr or not."

"I had the same thought."

Kade turned as Evelyn gulped down her coffee. Then his wolf howled. His blood ran hot. His breathing became shallow, and he sucked in a painful breath as his lips parted. He'd desired women before. In a crowded tavern where heated gazes met, wanting one thing and one thing only. During celebrations after much dancing around a bonfire, when sweat and anticipation led to tangled limbs and release.

But nothing, no one, had ever elicited this primal, all-consuming, maddening *want*.

"You're not wearing any pants," he finally said.

Black wool socks reached Evelyn's knees while an oversized tunic barely met her upper thighs, exposing her strong, slender legs. The sight of her like *that* awakened wicked thoughts. What would it be like to run his hands down her soft skin and hike a single leg around his waist?

Moons.

"Yes, and if I recall, you're the one who waltzed into my apartment," Evelyn said.

Kade threw out his hands. "It's half past nine. I didn't expect . . ." He took in her ruffled sheets, the fresh coffee in the air. "Wait, were you still in bed?"

"Not all of us are morning people, Huntsman." Evelyn's eyes narrowed.

He relished learning something new about her, but it only made matters worse. Her black hair had been pulled to the side and tied into an intricate braid, loose strands framing her face and tousled from sleep.

Unfamiliar feelings overcame him. Evelyn conjured something wild and ravenous inside him, something he feared and craved all at once. It unnerved him how out of control he became, how under-prepared he felt around her. It distracted him from what he was here for, what he'd come to do.

"This matter is urgent," he said, harsher than he'd intended. He peeled his attention away from her legs and met the gray depths of Evelyn's stare.

Which was a mistake.

Evelyn wore her aloof mask, but her eyes held a heat all their own, one she was failing to hide. *Moons,* she was attracted to him, too. The apartment buzzed with heat—not from the fireplace. Kade prayed to his god for restraint.

Thankfully, Evelyn broke the silence. "I apologize that the sight of my bare legs bothers you, Huntsman."

"Your lack of clothing does not bother me," he said far too quickly, and he kicked himself for how flustered he came across. What bothered him were these desires she awakened, ones that distracted him from the task at hand.

As Evelyn took a few steps to place her coffee mug on the kitchen counter, her thighs flexed, and Kade couldn't shake the thought of caressing that strong muscle.

Fiona Kerry.

There was nothing like the name of a murder victim to dampen the mood.

Kade scratched his beard. "I—"

"*Meow.*"

Kade jerked back, his wolf growling. His wolf hated cats, and this one was monstrous and sitting right at his feet. Yellow eyes stared up at him expectantly, tail whooshing behind like a pendulum ticking to his doom.

The feline creature seemed to feed off his discomfort, powering up a purr and sauntering between his legs as he backed farther to the window. Cold glass pressed into his shoulder but didn't cool his body. His inner wolf growled and snapped its teeth, ready to shift and fight the cat off.

"Saige, are you going to do something?" he said, realizing she had no idea the danger her pet was in.

Evelyn snickered, holding back a laugh. Kade sent her a glare, and she instantly recovered by biting her lip. "Cyrus, meet Maxie."

Kade looked at Evelyn expectantly, waiting for her to intervene, but Evelyn rolled her eyes. "Goddess, you act as if she's worse than the demons we faced yesterday," she said. "I'll let you two get acquainted while I change into something more suitable for our journey to the Kerry's estate."

She grabbed a few items from her bedroom area and fled to the bathroom, leaving Kade alone with Maxie. *Moons*, to think he'd almost met this creature in entirely different circumstances. He pinched the bridge of his nose, trying with all his might to remain calm.

He was interrupted as two plush paws pushed into his leg. Maxie stared up at him, her large eyes melting something within his chest. She meowed, the tone of it urgent. Kade's wolf even backed down, and Kade chanced picking her up. Her soft fur tickled under his beard, and her purring vibrated through his hands. Unsure what to do exactly, he held her at arm's length, nervous of her claws and anticipating a hiss.

Maxie curled her torso. He brought her into his chest, and she curled up even more, like a babe would while being held. Her purrs vibrated, and those yellow eyes locked with his, as if to say, *I know who you are*.

He scratched between her ears, the tufts of darker orange stark against his tanned skin, and tickled her white belly. In all his years, he'd never expected to hold a *cat*. Maxie's eyes fell to slits as she enjoyed his petting, and Kade's wolf sensed magic at play. What had Evelyn's sister called Maxie? Kade struggled to recall.

"*Oh*," Evelyn said as she emerged from the bathroom. She gaped. Her blush-pink lips formed an "O" under silver eyes wide as saucers. Her gaze darted between him and Maxie.

She'd changed into wool trousers tucked into boots and a maroon turtleneck that drew out the blue undertones in her gray eyes.

She cleared her throat. "I see you've made quick friends." She cast her gaze to the ground as she grabbed her cloak. Suddenly, the morning person he'd just met was in a rush.

Something bothered her.

"She's a sweet pet, isn't she?" Kade asked, trying to make conversation.

Evelyn scoffed. "Maxie's not a pet. She's a familiar."

Ah. That was the term Blair had used.

He placed Maxie down on the bed, and she curled into a ball on the sheets, assuming her new position. "Tell me more about what that means."

"Well," Evelyn said thoughtfully, "one's magic is connected to one's *familiar*. Like calls to like. A witch and their familiar speak to one another."

He joined her at the door. "Do all witches have them?"

"No. Witches keep pets, but familiars are rare. They find you—that's the difference. I was walking home with my sister—" Evelyn stopped, catching herself.

They stared at each other, the slip sitting in the air between them.

Kade opened the door, motioning her to join him outside. "Go on."

"Maxie scurried out from a bush about five years ago. Ran over my shoes. Scratched my feet. Followed me the whole way home. My magic recognized her the moment she appeared."

"Sounds like fate," he whispered.

"Indeed."

The rain had shifted to a slow drizzle. Kade pulled up his hood as Evelyn did, and they braced themselves together. Below the steps, Bleu waited. When they reached him, Kade helped Evelyn into the saddle, a question burning inside.

"Upstairs, you seemed surprised when I held her," he said. "Why?"

Evelyn stayed silent, hesitating. Then she sighed. "Maxie doesn't like others. She despises my friend Tovi, tolerates my family, and ignores strangers entirely. No one has ever held her like that but me."

Shock rippled through him. He swung onto the saddle to hide his reaction. Did Maxie's ease with him mean anything, or was it a coincidence?

"I'll chalk it up to my incredible charm," he said, not believing a word of it.

Evelyn snorted, and Kade pulled on the reins, urging Bleu to begin their journey to the Kerry estate.

The closer they came to their destination, the worse it rained. Dark, dreary clouds draped over Callum. Fog ghosted between hills, and gusts of mist pelted them.

By the time they'd made it to the Kerry estate, Kade swore the rain had drenched his bones. Evelyn's cloak repelled the rain, and he guessed it to be enchanted. Yet her face was wet, her lips rosy from the cold, and the loose strands of her black hair were matted to her forehead and hood. She appeared fierce, determined, and he ignored the swell in his chest.

She still trembled as she dismounted Bleu, taking Kade's hand and swinging her legs to the ground. When Bleu sidestepped, upsetting Evelyn's precarious balance, she squeezed Kade's hand harder and leaned into him for support. Kade sent her an encouraging smile as she avoided looking at the ground.

"Worse than the demons we faced yesterday?" he joked.

She scoffed. "Absolutely."

Once she was off Bleu, they gazed at the Kerrys' estate, so different from the McCarthys'. Unlike the white-washed cottage with the thatched roof, the Kerrys' home was a two-story, red-brick manor.

It reminded Kade of the wealthier homes he'd seen in Nūa that belonged to the affluent covens. A brick wall matching the manor stood at waist height. At each end, a cypress grew, their crooked branches bending around the estate as if shielding it from the outside.

The front door swung open with such force, it sounded like a thunderclap. A middle-aged man emerged and stormed toward them. Silver stubble lined his jaw, and his eyes were bloodshot. Kade assumed he was Fiona's father.

"Commissioner Doyle said you'd be here an hour ago," he barked. "You're late."

Evelyn stood still, her fierceness and confidence fading. "We apologize for the delay. The weather—"

Fiona's father held up his hand, silencing her. Anger shot through Kade, but before he could interject, the other man pushed between them in a rush, bumping his shoulder into Evelyn. "Follow me."

Kade saw red. He took a step toward the man, ready to say something, when Evelyn grabbed his wrist.

"Don't," she said in a hushed tone.

Kade gritted his teeth. "He can't treat you that way. We're here to help."

"He's grieving, Cyrus. We all process it differently."

Kade paused, knowing her words were true. He'd witnessed grief with his only family and pack after his mother had died. His father had become lost. Eldrick had become rigid. Lorkan had turned inward. He'd dealt with it his own way, too, putting all his efforts into defeating the vampyr and fulfilling the prophecy.

Evelyn's gaze followed Fiona's father, a knowing look there—sympathy, even.

"You've seen this before," he said, his tone questioning.

Evelyn released his wrist and didn't spare him a backward glance as she continued after Fiona's father. "We're here to investigate the murder. Let's go."

Evelyn was right. They were here to solve these murders, and the stakes were now higher with a second killing. But he struggled to focus, wanting to know more about Evelyn. Kade followed, his boots slopping through mud.

Maybe it would be easier if he were honest with her.

I'm Kade Drengr. Come back with me.

The request would be as easy as gaining his footing on the slippery path—difficult and near impossible. The young woman walking ahead of him wasn't Evelyn, his betrothed, but Saige Ferriwether, full of secrets and walls he'd yet to shatter. Impatience gripped him. He shut his eyes and entered the red barn's stable room.

Fiona's body lay on an unhinged door supported by two whiskey barrels. Her wet, tangled hair spilled over the door, strewn with water weeds. Sand stuck to her blue-hued skin. Her lips appeared shriveled, her skin slightly bloated like she'd sat in water for too long.

"Her mother wants to clean her, so be quick about it." Fiona's father sauntered out of the barn without looking once at his daughter's dead body.

As Kade reached Evelyn, his wolf hearing caught the hammering in her chest. He followed her gaze. Fiona's damp dress clung to her body except for a few shredded strands blowing in the breeze, the fabric stained by black smudges and mud.

A hole gaped in her chest, an empty cavity where her heart should be.

"She . . ." Evelyn swallowed. "Her heart was ripped out. Goddess—"

She turned and retched into the pile of hay beside her.

Her hammering heart, the sweat dripping down her brow, her rapid breathing. Kade should've recognized her fear. He rushed to her side, crouching over her as she retched again.

She was frightened to the point of illness. *Moons*, why? Had she not seen death like this? Surely she had during her time on the Guard. Kade placed a hand on her back, an instinct to help her awakening inside him as strong as the desires he'd felt earlier. She relaxed at his touch, her heartbeat slowing.

"I'm sorry," she said, turning to face him. Crimson colored her cheeks.

"Don't be." Kade pulled up his cloak, tearing at the edges.

"What are you doing?" she said.

Kade yanked and tore a decent piece off. "Here. I don't have anything else, I'm afraid."

Her brows furrowed, and her breath slowing. She took the scrap of fabric and wiped her face.

"Thank you," she said.

He helped her rise. "The sight of death can be jarring."

Evelyn stilled, stayed silent, and searched his face.

Moons, had he been wrong? "I'm so—"

"My parents. They were the ones killed by vampyrs. I was there when it happened, and . . . this reminded me of their deaths."

Kade went cold, realization dawning on him like a splash of ice water. *Of course.* He'd known yesterday Evelyn had been referring to her parents, but he'd forgotten she'd been there when they had died. She'd been riding out to meet his pack to discuss the terms of their wedding.

Guilt tore at Kade. He couldn't offer her the true depth of his condolences. He couldn't tell her that he'd wanted to be at their funeral, that he'd ridden to Sorin despite the Elders' orders but had hesitated. He couldn't admit that, to this day, he still regretted stopping outside the Wall and not finding her.

Evelyn moved toward Fiona as Kade struggled to respond to her omission. He let the silence hang over them and assessed Fiona further. Her lifeless eyes looked up as if she stared at and welcomed her fate. Her skin was ashen, opaque, and blue.

"She's been entirely drained like the last victim," he said.

Evelyn nodded. "And look where the bite mark is." She pulled back the dead woman's dress, revealing a bite mark under her left breast.

"Another intimate bite," Kade said.

"Do you think there's more than one killer?"

"Possible, but . . . there are too many similarities between McKenna and Fiona. Both are young women, both drained, both with intimate bites."

"And both are missing body parts."

One without eyes and another without a heart.

"Cyrus, this doesn't make any sense. Clearly these young women have been killed by a vampyr." She gestured toward the blue-hued skin and the bite mark. "Why take McKenna's eyes? At first I thought it was a vendetta or maybe a precaution so she didn't turn, regardless of how vile it was. Now, I'm not so sure. With Fiona's heart missing . . ." Evelyn shook her head like she couldn't believe it. "Vampyrs don't kill like this, Cyrus. Something isn't adding up."

Kade sighed, battling the growing desire to tell her he knew about her parents because he knew who she was. He could apologize. They could solve the murder faster, more easily. He wouldn't have to hold back, and neither would she. But he still didn't know *why* she'd left. If it was because of their union, the marriage, he risked her running away again. He needed to continue gaining her trust, and if he couldn't tell her the full truth, he could at least share a part of himself, show her he understood.

"I'm sorry," Kade said. "About your parents."

Evelyn pursed her lips into a sad smile. "It's difficult sometimes. The sight of Fiona"—she shook her head—"brought me back to that moment."

"My mother was visiting Sorin in the north on business and was killed by vampyrs." He returned his gaze to Fiona. He had to bend the truth so Evelyn didn't suspect anything. "I can't say with time it gets better, but it does get easier."

"How long ago?"

"I was fifteen, so a decade."

"Is that why you're a huntsman?"

Kade calculated his wording. "There are a lot of reasons I do what I do, and my mother's death is certainly one of them."

Evelyn assessed him, silvery gaze drinking him in. Kade waited for more questions. Discussing his mother's death was a risk, but it was something he could never lie about. Thanks be to the stars above, Evelyn said nothing more.

They left the barn, passing by the manor again. Bleu neighed in greeting, but a flicker of light caught Kade's attention.

Black candles, ones that hadn't been there when they'd arrived, lined all the windowsills. A mourning tradition for witches. The flame atop the black wax symbolized the sun above darkness, leading the passing soul to the afterlife.

"Are the Kerrys witches?" he asked, realizing his mistake too late.

Evelyn lifted a brow. "You've seen this before?"

Moons. "Yes. I've seen a witch's burial before, but there were hundreds of candles then." It wasn't a lie, but he hoped she wouldn't press him.

The air around Evelyn tremored, the beads of rain slowing. Seconds passed, and then it all stopped, the air snapping to normal again.

"My magic doesn't sense any other witches inside the manor. I don't feel magic nearby, and definitely not when we were around Fiona's body," Evelyn said.

"Then why the candles?"

"Maybe the Kerrys have a witch heritage. Callum used to have more witches than it does now." Evelyn clamped her mouth shut, as if stopping herself from continuing.

What would it be like to break her walls? What would it be like if she didn't hold back?

"I don't suppose we can ask Fiona's parents," Evelyn said.

"No. I don't think we can. We should consider going to the lake where they found Fiona's body, though."

Evelyn nodded. "I agree, but we should look into McKenna's journal first. I can't help but think it's interesting her journal was written in Olde Script and the Kerrys are practicing a witch tradition."

Kade agreed, and they headed back to Callum, his questions as tiresome as the rain.

Chapter Twenty

Evelyn

After seeing Fiona Kerry's body, they headed straight to Evelyn's apartment. At present, Cyrus showered in her bathroom, the sound of the running faucet making it quite difficult not to imagine him unclothed under the scalding water. What did his torso look like beneath his tunic . . . ? Heat spread through Evelyn's belly and across her cheeks. She became hotter than the fireplace, her toes curling in a pair of fuzzy socks.

Evelyn poured herself a glass of honeysuckle wine, her first gulp audible throughout the apartment. The alcohol did nothing to drive away her thoughts. It only made her belly warm like Cyrus's stares did.

Fucking flames.

Distracting herself further, she prepared some cheese, crackers, fruit, and bread for a humble dinner after their long travels in the rain. Aster was to join them shortly, and she hoped to pull herself together before then.

Evelyn bit her lip, staring into the hearth of dancing flame.

The truth was that Evelyn wasn't *just* physically attracted to Cyrus. In this partnership, they felt like equals. He respected her assessment of the murders, accepted her ideas. Neither of them led the other. They were a team. As Daughter of the Goddess, she'd experienced respect for her title from plenty of people, but they expected so much from her at the same time.

Cyrus didn't.

She'd not only heard his sincerity when they discussed her parents but *felt* it. Back home, some had told her they were sorry for her loss. No one understood it. Cyrus did.

Except she was telling him things he didn't need to know, and Evelyn hated how natural it felt to be honest with him. The words flowed from her, previous hope of working with him as partners be damned. After all, the beast of a man was taking a shower in her apartment for Goddess's sake. It'd taken one comment about missing running water, and Evelyn had offered.

Why?

Maxie bumped into Evelyn's ankle, and she gave her familiar a loving scratch behind the ear. After a few more bumps, Evelyn sighed and squatted down to dig into Maxie's cheeks the way she loved. Her familiar shut her eyes, and Evelyn recognized that look.

Trust.

Goddess, she was beginning to trust Cyrus. It was dangerous and illuminating, and Evelyn wanted to run from it and into it. It made no sense, her ease opening up to him, why she revealed what she did, and her treacherous traitor of a familiar was open to trusting him, too.

The faucet turned off, the sound replaced by the unrelenting patter of rain outside. Maxie abandoned Evelyn and ran to the bathroom door, awaiting Cyrus. Her familiar had never been so keen with anyone else before, not even her sister Blair or Tovi, whom she'd been around the most.

Worry grew in the pit of Evelyn's stomach. She and Maxie were bound, based on the connection to her magic, and she wondered if her growing feelings for Cyrus had anything to do with Maxie's behavior. What if Maxie's affection meant something? What if this attraction to Cyrus was more than she thought?

But Evelyn couldn't afford more. Not when she needed to solve these murders and leave. Entertaining a relationship with Cyrus felt like dragging him into a mess he didn't deserve. For one, if witches and werewolves from Sorin ever caught up to her, what sort of future could she promise? And if they did explore a future together, wouldn't she put him at risk? Sure, her flame was back, but if she lost it again and the vampyrs discovered she no longer had the Goddess-given gift they feared, she put those in her homeland at risk for war, and in turn, Cyrus.

Evelyn's heart ached, but leaving was best. Staying on the move. New place to new place. Yet leaving was getting harder and harder. Callum would be the most difficult since leaving her sisters. The kind people. The quaint town. The magical countryside. She couldn't throw in feelings and the memory of an amber-eyed stare. Her bruised heart couldn't handle it.

Cyrus emerged from the bathroom, steam following him into the main room. He tugged his tunic down, and Evelyn caught sight of the deep line of muscle leading into his trousers—

"I haven't had a shower in some time," he said. "I may pay you coin to use it from here on out."

Evelyn popped a grape and slab of cheese into her mouth, making it impossible to comment. Thankfully a knock at the door also helped her evade the conversation.

Aster entered from the rain before Evelyn made it to the door, a stack of books in one hand and a growler of wine with a parchment bag in the other.

"Damn dandelions, Saige. I love the rain, but some days it doesn't seem to stop." The stack of books with spines of greens, oranges, and browns obscured her face.

Cyrus took two steps to join them and grabbed the books before they toppled to the wooden floor. Aster pushed back her hood, her red curls springing free. Her eyes grew wide at the sight of Cyrus. A shriek of excitement erupted from her, and she launched at him. Unprepared, he rocked with surprise and staggered, the books crashing to the floor regardless of his efforts. Aster held on, giving him a welcoming hug. He sent Evelyn a look, but she laughed with a snort, enjoying his discomfort.

His eyes narrowed as if to say, *Help me.*

"Cyrus," Evelyn said, "meet Aster, Callum's finest book and plant expert, shop owner, landlord, and friend."

Aster released Cyrus, blushing a fierce crimson as she continued to stare with her large russet eyes.

"It's nice to meet you, Aster," Cyrus said, straightening his tunic and bending over to pick up the books.

Aster giggled. "Oh, Saige, you mentioned him being beastly, but you failed to mention how dreamy he was."

Evelyn froze as Cyrus caught her gaze. He brushed past her as he set the books on the kitchen table.

"You find me beastly, Princess?" he said with a smirk. Those eyes of his held a level of suggestion Evelyn couldn't handle.

"The description was not used as a compliment, Huntsman," she said.

Goddess, Cyrus's smile only grew.

Evelyn turned her attention to Aster, ready to change the subject. "What else did you bring?"

"Father's honeysuckle wine, five-year vintage." Aster held up the growler covered in dust.

Evelyn gasped with excitement, taking it off her hands. "He's a saint."

"And my mother's apple crisp cookies."

"Also a saint," Cyrus said, grabbing the bag of cookies and helping himself.

Hours later, they were gathered at Evelyn's makeshift kitchen table with open books scattered between them along with piles of scribbled notes. The fire danced rays of orange and red onto their goblets of wine. Maxie had curled herself in the middle of it all, sound asleep amidst their research.

Cyrus pored over a book about vampyr lore, the spine frayed from cracks threatening to split at any moment, while Aster deciphered McKenna's journal, jumping between one book to the next. Evelyn read through a large volume of *Callum and the History of Beasts*. She landed on a page depicting the rat-like demon she and Cyrus had defeated days ago, apparently called a confach. It had terrorized the ruins for three centuries.

Interesting.

The book itself held eight centuries' worth of history. Nothing depicted anything remotely close to the vampyr. It was not a creature of this land, as Evelyn had predicted. She searched for the possibility another creature could be at play, but nothing killed like the vampyr either or aligned with the state in which the victims were left.

One particular passage drew her interest regarding a young witch who'd transformed herself with dark magic and earned the name "banshee." Her coven had bound her magic, an extinct and outlawed practice amongst witches in the new age. A witch cut off from her magic often led to death, which sadly befall the "banshee". The people of Torren claimed the wind still carried her dying cries, but the story felt like a fable to warn children from staying out at night. It held no actual answers regarding the murders.

Evelyn sighed, looking over the list she'd made of the victims' situations. Both young women had been drained of blood and possessed blue-hued skin, and they'd both been bitten in intimate areas. Both had body parts missing, though which parts differed. Eyes and a heart.

In the margins, Evelyn had noted the small details related to witches, black candles at the Kerrys' home and McKenna's journal written in Olde Script. Evelyn struggled to find a connection.

"Anything with the journal?" she asked Aster.

"Well, it appears McKenna's notes are about magic. Research, really. Not necessarily how to use it, but about it. The history of it. The energies. Spells versus enchantments." Aster flipped to another page. "She never mentions *who* told her these things, though."

Cyrus ran a hand through his beard. "Let's forget who was teaching her for the moment. Why would *she* want to learn it if she's human? I thought magic was part of a witch, not learned."

Evelyn nodded. "You're right. It can't be learned per se, but perhaps McKenna *did* have magic."

"But you said the McCarthys weren't witches?" Cyrus said.

"They aren't," Aster said. "Though there's a chance their ancestors were. During the great burnings, many families stopped using their magic to protect themselves from persecution. Not using magic starves it, and it's possible over generations the McCarthys diluted their magic enough that it left their bloodline. Perhaps McKenna was one of the first to have it again. Rare, but not impossible."

"I agree." Evelyn nodded. "That is a possibility, but McKenna and her family would've noticed she had magic around age five. Doesn't it seem odd they never sought guidance from the covens close by? Why wait until she's twenty?"

Aster shrugged. "That reason alone is why I don't believe McKenna had magic. When magic resurfaces in families, it's celebrated, not feared." She gestured toward the book. "I think this is mere interest, not necessarily teachings or personal use."

Another dead end. They all sighed.

"Any mention of the vampyr?" Evelyn asked.

Aster shook her head. "No, but"—she turned the journal so they could all see it—"this word here means 'white.' She writes it often, followed by another word I can't translate."

"Does that mean anything to either of you?" Cyrus asked. He had learned Aster was a witch earlier in the evening.

"Not me, no," Evelyn said.

"Unfortunately, not to me either." Aster turned to Cyrus. "Anything in the lore of vampyr?"

Cyrus ran his hand through his hair and let out an exasperated sigh. "Sadly, no, nothing that I don't know already. I'm still wondering how it would've made it across the Sapphire Sea, considering sunlight and the need to feed. Thus far, we've only come across evidence of one vampyr. It would've taken a whole crew to get here."

"There's no way they would've gotten through Morrow's Harbor," Evelyn said.

Aster and Cyrus gave her questioning looks. She felt the need to elaborate, but doing so might reveal her ties to the efforts against the vampyr back home. Fine. They both knew she was a witch, and her knowledge of vampyr already gave away she was most likely from Sorin. The push and pull of keeping others at a distance and letting them close warred within her. It was becoming exhausting holding it all back, and the trust she had built with Cyrus and Aster so far made it difficult, too.

Evelyn's identity as a witch was out. The intricacies of the prophecy were deep-rooted in the witch culture back in Sorin, and Evelyn hoped it would take considerable time or luck before either of them drew conclusions that she was Daughter of the Goddess.

That'll be you one day, Evelyn. Protecting our people, defeating the darkness.

Evelyn's mother's words resurfaced from all those years ago. As she sat in her dimly lit studio with books all around her, a sense of purpose overcame her, despite being an ocean away from her coven. These murders were a part of the efforts against the vampyr, too, and though she didn't imagine this had been what her mother envisioned, it felt close enough, and revealing what she knew only helped.

"Morrow's Harbor is situated in northeast Sorin at the cusp of Drystan," Evelyn said. "It's heavily guarded by werewolves and witches alike. Though it's the nearest passage from the Void to the Sapphire Sea, there's no way a ship of vampyrs could make it through without raising an alarm and being taken down."

Cyrus considered. "I suppose that's a fair point. I'm sure news of such an attempt would've reached these shores by now if they'd succeeded. Anything on the beasts of Callum, Saige?"

Evelyn sipped her honeysuckle wine. "Well, I did learn we slayed the infamous confach, but other than that, no. There's one mention of an abhartach, a demon that drinks blood, but it doesn't turn their victims blue."

"True," Aster said, "and the abhartachhas been buried under a slab of enchanted rock for centuries. The chances someone released it would be slim."

Evelyn sighed. "What about where Fiona's body was found? Any significance regarding Lake Glenn? Castle Connacht had demons."

Aster mused. "Lake Glenn is a gorgeous sight, but folks have gone missing there for centuries. They say something lies in the deep, but no one's lived to say what, exactly."

Cyrus crossed his arms. "My guess is a kelpie. Water, dragged to the deep, never seen again. That demon fits."

"Right." Evelyn sighed. "But it doesn't fit Fiona's death or the rest of the murders."

Nothing in Aster's texts pointed to another creature, but the missing body parts didn't fit with a vampyr, either. *Something* wasn't right.

The fire crackled. Maxie's ears twitched, and she rose, stretching out all her legs and flailing her paws open. Evelyn expected her to come greet her as she always did after a nap, but her familiar, the cheeky cat, weaved her way over to Cyrus.

Aster pouted. "She wasn't that friendly with me."

Maxie rubbed her forehead against Cyrus's beard. He still appeared rather uncomfortable around Maxie, but he relented and picked her up. Maxie's eyes closed to half slits in contentment, and Evelyn melted from the tender sight.

Considering Maxie's behavior, Evelyn's feelings must've been brewing deeper than she'd realized. Whatever these feelings were, she couldn't act on them. She was Daughter of the Goddess, technically betrothed to another, and she was still on the run from her duty and title, the most important factor of them all. Two young women had just died at the hands of a vampyr. She needed to regain her focus.

She looked over her notes, tallying all the books she'd read through. One book she'd yet to open, green and weathered, sat under the title *Witches and Fae*. Pages of various lengths and shades stuck out, and the spine's leather cracked from repetitive opening.

Evelyn wedged it free and recognized Aster's last name, Arklow, etched in gold on the front.

"Is this your grimoire?" Evelyn asked.

Aster nodded, a steaming mug of tea in hand. "Started that beauty when I was four summers old."

It'd been some time since she'd come close to a grimoire, let alone held one. Her own sat in her old apartment in Nūa, most likely collecting a layer of dust. Her father and mother had created the book themselves, sewing the pages into the spine, enchanting the cover to recognize her, engraving the leather front with her name. *Just* her name. Evelyn Carson. No third-born. No protector. No Daughter of the Goddess. It'd been her gift at her sixth birthday, and Evelyn's childlike glee remained, overshadowing her nostalgia.

She ran her hands over Aster's emerald-green cover, made of a thick bark instead of leather. The buzzing magic felt different than her own, lively instead of hot.

Fitting.

"Do you mind?" she asked Aster.

Her new friend shook her head. "Not at all."

Evelyn flipped to the first page, settling on the first words of every grimoire.

"What does that say?" Cyrus peered at the first page, too.

"Well, that's easy," Evelyn said. "*Our eyes to the Sun, and hearts full of fire, minds open, and hands for good.*"

The words sent a chill down Evelyn's spine, familiar and old, stirring the magic in her blood. The words of her people. Old and New World.

Cyrus raised a brow, scratching behind Maxie's ears. "I thought you didn't know Olde Script."

Evelyn laughed. "This is different. Every witch knows this."

"It's the witches' creed," Aster said.

Ancient and old, the witches' creed was told like a nursery rhyme to children until it became a mantra each and every witch followed into adulthood.

Cyrus repeated it back. "Our eyes to the Sun, and hearts full of fire, minds open, and hands for good."

An inkling sparked in the back of Evelyn's mind.

"Say it again," she said, locking eyes with Cyrus.

He gave her a questioning look, but obliged, restating the creed.

She rose out of her chair in a rush, bringing the grimoire with her. Evelyn read the words over and over, hands shaking as she held it.

"What is it?" Aster asked.

Evelyn read the creed again, the creed she'd known her whole life, as if reading it would snap the pieces together in her mind. A creeping feeling crawled across her skin as the wood in the fire popped and sparks burst from the hearth. Evelyn's inkling grew, the clues clicking into place, one by one.

"Fucking flames."

"Saige, what is it?" Cyrus said, raw concern in his voice.

Evelyn said the creed again, looking at them both.

Aster laughed nervously. "Yes, we've all said it a few times now. You'll have to be more specific."

Evelyn struggled to explain. "The creed . . . the body parts . . . they . . . *align*."

Both Cyrus and Aster stilled, eyes growing wide, expressions suggesting she was maybe a little crazy.

Or right.

"Think about it." Evelyn placed the open grimoire back on the table and grabbed her notes. "McKenna's eyes were missing. *'Our eyes to the Sun.'* And then Fiona's heart was gone. *'And hearts full of fire.'* The missing body parts are in the witches' creed."

Aster and Cyrus remained silent, soaking in her words or unsure what to say, Evelyn couldn't guess. Nerves ate away at her. Was she wrong? Way off base? Did she sound crazy?

Yet, why did her gut twist with certainty? Like the flake of soot floating and landing on Evelyn's shoulder, it sat, melted deep, and eased into her.

Evelyn nibbled her bottom lip. "It's just a connection, and I'm not sure what it means, if anything at all."

Cyrus shook his head. "No, I think you're on to something." He rose and placed Maxie down. She scurried off under Evelyn's bed, out of sight. He took her notes and read over them, his brows pinched together. "Do you think the fact that there's some relation to witches is a coincidence?"

"No," Aster said. "If Saige is right, both of these murders are far more complex than any of us originally thought. The relation to witches means something, but I can't begin to guess what."

If Saige is right...

Aster's words resounded like an alarm bell in Evelyn's head. If she was right, there'd be more murders. She'd already felt fear from her twisted discovery, but now she felt sick, her stomach tumbling.

"There are two more body parts in the creed," she whispered. "Minds and hands."

Cyrus stared at her, his eyes growing wide. He began to pace, running his hands through his hair.

Aster gasped. "Damned dandelions, there could be two more murders."

"Not if we find the vampyr first," Evelyn said.

Cyrus stopped, staring into the fire. His eyes reflected the flames. He put his hands on his hips and faced Evelyn. Consideration flashed across his face, as if he struggled to say whatever he wanted to next.

"Saige," he finally said. "What if . . . what if this is bigger than us?"

"He's right. This isn't any regular murder case anymore," Aster said.

Evelyn wavered. They were right. This *wasn't* just any murder case, but she supposed it never had been. She'd known from the start the odd nature of it. None of the clues aligned with a regular vampyr attack. The intimate bites, the missing body parts, the rumors of a lover.

None of it made sense.

The sight of Fiona today reminded her of her parents' death. She understood loss, the weight of it. She *had* to protect those in Callum, regardless how complicated this case was.

"If there's a possibility of two more murders," she said, "the most important thing is to make sure we find the vampyr and put an end to all of this."

Cyrus shut his eyes, his shoulders dropped, and his jaw ticked. The fire crackled, the rain fell. "What of the other covens in Callum? Would they have any additional texts that could shed light?"

Aster shrugged, red curls bouncing. "It's worth asking. I can reach out to my coven if you'd like."

Evelyn turned to stone. If other covens learned a dark-haired witch was in Callum and made the connection . . . She'd been so wrapped up in solving the murders, she'd forgotten her secrets, what was at stake if others learned of her lost flame or that she was in Callum. Those in Sorin believed she'd married Kade and fought at the Void. They had no idea she'd run. Neither did the vampyr. More importantly, no one knew she'd lost her flame, the reason she'd left in the first place.

Evelyn's protective instinct warred within her—Callum or home?

She hated these decisions, but the threat at home was *war*, an entire army of vampyrs against witches and werewolves. So far, all signs in Callum pointed to a single vampyr. She could fight one vampyr without the help of the witches. She had to. Because asking for the witches' help would reveal her loss of power, would start a war. Evelyn shivered with nerves, an icy sensation prickling her skin. She had to choose, and *fucking flames,* she was going to be sick.

Cyrus smoothed his beard. "I think that's a good idea. We can come with you, too, if it helps."

Paralyzed, Evelyn blurted out, "*No*. No other covens. No other witches."

Cyrus's eyes widened. "I think we should try to and gain any insight we can."

Evelyn threw her hands into the air and gestured to her littered kitchen table. "We've already spent our evening reading texts, yet we haven't even investigated where Fiona's body was found. We should start there next."

Aster's russet eyes darted between Evelyn and the huntsman.

"Saige," Cyrus said, his amber eyes searching her face. The look made her uncomfortable, like he could read all her motives to sway the investigation as if they'd been tattooed on her skin. "We should consider—"

"I did not take on this job to consider. I took it on to solve these murders."

Cyrus scoffed. "Right. It's just a job for you. How could I forget?"

He strode from the fireplace and grabbed his cloak, reaching for the door.

"Cyrus—"

He paused, giving her the space to argue, but Evelyn didn't. She couldn't without revealing too much, without letting him in more than she already had. Evelyn had stayed in Callum to solve these murders, but she'd started to forget she was leaving after. She had a homeland to protect, too. Her partnership with Cyrus, their growing attraction for one another, the promise of something, had distracted her. Perhaps putting distance between them was best, despite the sadness souring her stomach.

She seized the opportunity by giving him nothing.

Cyrus shook his head, a flash of disappointment marring his features. "Fine. We'll do it your way, Princess." But this time when he used her nickname, his tone was biting and not playful. "I'll tell Commissioner Doyle what we discovered tonight while you visit the lake. We try to stay one step ahead of the vampyr from here on out."

Chapter Twenty-One

Kade

During the night, a storm had blown in from the west, making itself a lingering guest over Callum for the day and well into the evening. Between the chill and downpour, all the town had come for a bowl of Miss Patricia's warming stew and to hear a traveling band perform. They graced the Runaway Radish's stage, playing sad songs of the sea.

Kade used a rag to dry glasses at the bar. Barmaids bustled and passed out pints and plates of food as Miss Patricia busied herself in the kitchen, her hum matching the tune of the band's song. A draft from outside whirled its way in, the drizzle of rain trickling through the treble of the violin, and the wind howling alongside the accordion.

Evelyn, her cheeks rosy from the cold, entered with another young woman with damp hair as white as snow. The wooden door swung closed with a snap, and his betrothed's eyes met his across the room.

The crowd fell away. The music drowned out. And Kade's heart rose in his throat.

They hadn't seen each other or talked to the other since he'd stormed out of her apartment.

His betrothed's silver eyes only met his for the briefest of moments before flashing over the rest of the inn. Kade wasn't ready to face her after their disagreement the night before. Evelyn's shoulders drooped after her assessment of the tables and chairs, and she swallowed, seeming to mirror his sentiment.

But fate had different plans.

Not a single seat lay vacant except for the remaining bar seats. Whomever she'd arrived with must've not known about their quarrel or cared because she cut straight through the crowd to the seats as if she owned the place. A beauty in her own right, the woman drew appraising looks from some of the town's men as did Evelyn. Kade's grip on the glass he dried tightened, but Evelyn took no notice of the men sending glances her way, only biting her lip as she approached him.

"Hey," she said, saddling up onto the barstool.

The young woman sat next to Evelyn, swinging onto the barstool with grace and ease. Her brows scrunched over light green eyes that jumped between her and Kade. "You two know each other?"

Kade could've sworn Evelyn grimaced as she tucked a strand of hair behind her ear. "This is Cyrus. We're working on the murder case together."

Relief, Kade hated to admit, washed through him. After last night he wasn't sure where they stood. He'd told her to investigate Lake Glenn without him. *Moons*, she'd admitted they worked together, but it didn't lighten his frustration. With the missing body parts and the possible connection to the witches' creed, Evelyn, as Daughter of the Goddess, had to understand the gravity of the situation. Last night, she'd worn her mask. Kade couldn't gauge how she felt about the possible connection, only that she wanted to solve the murders.

Kade had left in a rush after those words, unsure if he'd let his frustration out and say something foolish or compromising. She'd started to drop her walls. Had revealed she was a witch. Had been vulnerable around him.

Then last night, it was as if she had built all these walls back up between them, and he could do nothing to stop it and still had no clue how to talk to her without demanding answers. Was she not unsettled that the witches' creed may be at play?

"You're *working* on the murders with someone?" The snowy haired woman's tone was high-pitched. Accusatory. And playful.

Evelyn fidgeted in her seat. Sighing, she said, "Yes, I . . . maybe I forgot to mention that."

"Right, *forgot*." The young woman's gaze met Kade's. "Because he's clearly *so* forgettable."

"Tovi," Evelyn warned.

Ah, so this was the friend Evelyn had mentioned knowing her identity as a witch. Kade observed her. Far as he could tell, she was human. His wolf didn't sense any magic or anything else, for that matter. Yet, why did Tovi know Evelyn was a witch? How had she gained Evelyn's trust to learn that secret?

"Forgive me for being curious." Tovi shrugged, a glint lighting her eyes. "You've never worked with anyone before, even on the Gua—*ow*!"

Evelyn kicked her friend so hard the slender woman swayed as her chair rocked. Evelyn widened her eyes and jutted her chin out as Tovi steadied herself.

Kade looked between the young women. Moons. They *knew* each other. Sure, Evelyn and Aster were friends, but these two shared a bond. A deep and long one.

He'd experienced sharing silent looks like that with his brother, Eldrick. Mischievous ones across the table during family dinners as pups listening to grown-up talk. Sly ones as they'd flirted and mingled with pack females during celebrations. The stoic kind, like the last one Eldrick had given him as Kade had ridden off to find Evelyn. He'd not needed words to say he didn't agree with Kade's choice.

He and Eldrick knew each other like no one else did. Like Tovi had attempted with Evelyn moments ago, Kade had tried to get under his brother's thick exterior and rile him up for the fun of it. And though Eldrick was his older brother, they were also best friends.

Like Evelyn and Tovi.

A bond like that took years to build with memories, occasions, and experiences.

Tovi had almost said Guard, Kade was certain of it, which meant Tovi was someone from Evelyn's past, and she had to at least know *something* of why Evelyn had left. Stars above, did she also know *which* witch she was?

"Are ya going to stand there all night?" Miss Patricia called from around the corner. "Serve the pretty lasses a drink! Saige, dear, extra turnips in your stew?"

"Please," Evelyn said with a laugh.

"And extra bread for me!" Tovi called as Miss Patricia disappeared back into the kitchen.

Kade grabbed a glass and poured Evelyn honeysuckle wine. The white liquid glinted the slightest green, and he slid it over to her without a word.

Bracing his hands on the bar, he looked to Tovi next. "What can I get you?"

The corner of Tovi's mouth quirked up as she stared between the glass of wine and Evelyn. She assessed Kade with those jade eyes, ones seemingly far older than her age.

"Your darkest red, please."

Kade pushed off the bar, heading to the end of the shelves. He took his time as he listened in on the hushed conversation behind him, hoping to learn something of value.

"*What?*" Evelyn hissed.

"Oh, don't you dare. I know exactly why you *forgot* to tell me about him," Tovi said.

Kade tapped into his werewolf hearing. Their voices barely made it over the traveling band's song, which had built into a jig.

"Stop. You're making nothing into something." A plea plagued Evelyn's tone. So did worry. Kade desperately wanted to understand. Did *he* worry her? Was it something else? Was it whatever was building between them?

Someone in the crowd cheered and another whistled as the band's jig built in tempo. Kade pretended to rummage through wine bottles while he concentrated on Tovi's next words, almost lost to the beat of the goatskin drums. As he rose, bottle in hand, he caught the tail end of her speech.

"Nothing into something? I guess pouring your favorite drink unpromoted and eye fucking you across the inn is totally nothing."

Kade almost dropped the wine bottle and knocked a line of glasses over, but luckily another "*Ow!*" muffled his fumble.

Moons, did he really stare at Evelyn that way? He couldn't help himself. Temptation seeped into his muscles, and he turned to face them. But Evelyn and Tovi's eye contact was inseverable, and they took no notice as he listened and watched this time.

Evelyn's cheeks shined ruby in the inn's firelight, and her grip on her glass turned her knuckles white. "You know it must be nothing."

Tovi's shoulders slackened, and she leaned closer into Evelyn, eyes sympathetic with a small smile. "Bloody hell, Eve—you actually . . ." Tovi shook her head. "You're right. I teased too far, and I'm sorry."

Evelyn gave her friend a weak smile in return, and their conversation was over. Done and gone before Kade learned much of anything, except that Evelyn had a reason for pushing Kade away, because whatever it was between them, it had to be "nothing." Her walls were purposeful, and from the looks of their forlorn expressions, Evelyn was struggling and Tovi hated it for her.

Kade sauntered back over to them, sliding Tovi's glass to her. He wished to meet Evelyn's gaze, wished to see in those incredible silvery gray eyes an answer as to why, but she focused on the band, lost to the music and sipping her wine.

Why run? Why keep secrets? Why push him away?

Stars above, Kade cared for her feelings, these whys she harbored so close, but it also only made him more frustrated. Remembering his mother's sacrifice, he couldn't forget duty no matter how hard he tried. Sympathy and frustration warred within him. He wanted to work with her on these murders, regain the progress he'd made with her, but he also wanted to declare his title and remind Evelyn of hers.

These murders in Callum only demonstrated their need to return home, fulfill the prophecy, and fight the darkness.

Together.

And yet, his betrothed likely had no intention of returning home.

If only he could say the right words, promise the right things—

The door of the Runaway Radish burst open, the storm's wind barreling into the inn and blowing the crowd's hair, cloaks, and belongings about. Lightning flashed outside, illuminating a frantic townsman, beard and hair matted with rain.

"The vampyr! It's here! In the streets of Callum!"

The hackles of Kade's werewolf rose. It took all his strength, all his training, to not jump over the bar and shift. Not only did Evelyn sit before him, but the rest of Callum had not yet seen his form. From the frightful screams and shouts of terror, they'd witnessed enough beasts for the time being.

Evelyn rose from her barstool without a backward glance toward him. *Stars above*, was she going without him? Of course, she was completely capable, and she might not want him beside her after their disagreement the night before. But he had no intention of letting her face the vampyr alone.

Kade grabbed his sword, tucked under the bar and never too far from reach, and jumped over the bar, all while resisting shifting into his werewolf form. It was so different, so maddening being unable to shift so easily like he did back home. His werewolf form was like armor, and it itched under his skin to be worn and used.

He breathed deeply and battled for composure as he moved through the frightened crowd with purpose. The townsfolk of Callum gave him a wide berth, allowing him to reach Evelyn at the door with Tovi in tow.

"Where?" he asked, voice booming over the crowd.

Evelyn spun toward him, that stoic indifference setting her jaw and pursing her lips, but she said nothing. They both knew they didn't have time.

"Pennington Avenue, near the print shop—"

"Riven!"

Tovi pushed them and ran out of the Runaway Radish and straight into the storm. Evelyn followed her, shouting her name over the thunder. Kade didn't think. He moved. An instinct, deeper than his protector duty, drove him forward.

"Saige!" he called. Wind pushed back his hair and rain pelted his face.

In the lamplight streets, he made out Evelyn's cloak tangling in the wind behind her. Tovi ran. *Fast.* Her snowy white hair beaming under the lamplights.

"Riven!" she called again, fear raw and raspy in her cry.

"Tovi, wait!" Evelyn pulled her shrunken staff out of her bun. Obsidian hair cascaded down her back as she extended her staff to its full size.

Two blocks from the Runaway Radish, Kade caught up to Evelyn and then to Tovi.

"It is too dangerous to run around the streets with a vampyr loose!" Kade said.

But Tovi either didn't hear or didn't care. It was as if she'd fallen into another world. Frantic, breathless, she ran relentlessly through the rain, wind, and storm. And Kade and Evelyn followed.

One by one they halted and skidded at the corner of an intersection, the brick street blending into cobblestones. Thunder boomed over the town. The Sapphire Sea, angry and wild, howled like a beast, and citrus wafted with the salt of the wind.

Vampyr.

Kade hadn't detected it once while in Callum, one of the reasons he'd wondered if the killer was actually a vampyr. But the sharp scent meant only one thing.

Enemy.

It was the scent of death laid in the villages of Sorin's plains and Vadon's mountains. The stench at the edge of the Void. Kade never failed to detect it. Even in his nightmares, the scent remained, coloring the moment of his mother's death and the attacks on his people. His werewolf itched and fought to be released. To defend. His hackles rose even further.

Stars above. He gripped his sword as the scene down the street became clearer.

"Riven!" Tovi's scream rang out with a clash of thunder.

A man with the same white hair as Tovi's turned his attention away from the raging beast gripping his chest. It unleashed a screech, regaining the man's attention. Eyes wide and frantic, the man held the bloodthirsty vampyr at arm's length.

"Tovi, stand back!" Evelyn yelled.

This time, Evelyn's commanding tone gained Tovi's attention, bringing her to a skidding halt. Evelyn slammed her staff into the cobblestone, a ricochet of magic blasting from the dragon bone. The force knocked the vampyr and the other man apart. Tovi rushed to the man, helping him to his feet. Her brother? The close likeness suggested so.

The vampyr rose, its movements jerky and stiff, too fast and too strong for its own good. Was it a scáth? It turned. Black hair and black eyes in pools of red, rimmed with black spidery veins. It wore tattered velvet pants and a tunic flapped in the wind, exposing sickly pale skin underneath. Its horrific stare fell onto Evelyn.

Kade buzzed with anticipation, raising his sword. The vampyr remained focused on Evelyn. Madness, hunger, and darkness swam in its stare. It held out its arms, flaring its clawed hands. The dark magic stained fingertip to elbow, as if it had dipped its arm into black ink. It bared its razor teeth, two fangs bulging over its bottom lip.

It let out an ear-piercing shriek, dwarfing the sounds of the storm. As it charged, Evelyn thrust out her staff, magic blasting across the street and knocking the vampyr down. It rolled, twitched, and staggered to its feet. It hissed like a wild animal, head turning and tilting to assess Tovi, who held Riven to her. Both appeared stricken, anguish furrowing their brows as the vampyr advanced toward them.

Kade approached from behind and swung his blade, the metal slicing up the vampyr's back. It screeched again, the sound deafening against the brick buildings. It whirled and wobbled, its speed volatile and jerky. Swinging its arms, the vampyr attacked.

Evelyn appeared to Kade's right. The two fought back. Kade swung his blade, and Evelyn used her staff. The vampyr's talons were strong like metal, catching Kade's swings hit by hit until it caught the sword in one go, tearing it from Kade's grip.

The blade clattered to the cobblestones, skidding out of reach. Kade wavered. Three steps and a dash away, but that left Evelyn alone with the vampyr. But if he slayed the vampyr, he'd follow his duty and in doing so, protect Evelyn. If he killed it, the murders would end, and he'd come clean to Evelyn. He'd be able to return home. With her. Fulfill their duties.

Kade lunged for his sword, turning his back to Evelyn and the monster for only a moment.

Long enough, though. Evelyn cried out, the sound ripping the air. Kade turned fast, but he was too late. The vampyr had slashed at Evelyn's shoulder, slicing through her tunic. Blood dripped off its talons.

"No!" Riven yelled, pushing out of his sister's grip.

"Riven! Wait!" Tovi cried.

He collided with Evelyn, pushing her out of the vampyr's path. The blood-hungry creature screeched, advancing toward Riven, who held Evelyn behind him. Something primal, something furious bristled under Kade's skin. He'd turned away and now another man guarded Evelyn, *his* betrothed.

Riven faced off against the vampyr. Kade readied his blade, calming his frantic heart. Rain poured around them. A crack of thunder sounded, and everyone went still. Lightning illuminated the street, and the vampyr jumped stories high to grip the shingles of an overhanging roof, escaping out of sight.

Part of Kade ached to run after the vampyr, yet his body took over, his primal instinct to protect, and he sprinted to Evelyn's side instead. Blood stained the frayed edges of shredded fabric, and he itched to touch the gashes in Evelyn's skin and care for them.

"Saige, are you all right?" he bit out.

She nodded. "I'm fine. It's already healing."

In the darkness, Kade watched as the blood slowed. Vampyr claws didn't possess venom or poison like their fangs. A witch could survive both injuries if treated quickly enough. A bite was trickier, but Evelyn healed quickly thanks to the flame in her blood, a gift from the Sun Goddess. Relief washed through him, as cold and jarring as the rain showering his face. He'd chosen his sword over standing at her side. Kade bristled. Thank the moon, she'd be all right in a matter of hours.

He met her stare, steely and tired, but magnificent still. Rain ran down the bridge of her nose and clung to her lashes like diamonds. Kade swallowed, fighting the urge to brush her wet, tangled hair behind her ear and away from her beautiful, sweet face. Instead, he helped her stand, his hands searing from holding hers as they rose.

"Perks of being a witch?" he said, somehow mustering the energy to make light of the situation.

Evelyn bit her lip. "Something like that."

Kade stilled, breaking his hold on her hands and averting his eyes. Her evasion of the truth snapped him back to reality. It was slight, but enough to build Kade's steely exterior again.

Evelyn Carson kept avoiding the truth, and Kade didn't want her to. He didn't want her to want nothing with him, and he didn't want her to push him away. Yet, he was unfair, and he knew it. He was Cyrus and she was Saige. How could he expect her to be honest about who she was when he was disguised as a huntsman?

Remember your duty.

His mother's last words echoed in his reeling mind. Kade traveled here to bring Evelyn home, and these murders and their attraction for one another was getting in the way of his purpose. Yet Kade couldn't shake the nagging question of why she had left. From her interaction with Tovi, Evelyn seemed sad. Her secrets hurt. A part of him wanted to understand, but another part simmered with frustration.

The rain slowed while Tovi and Riven approached them.

"I don't think I believed it until tonight. There is a vampyr in Callum." Riven clutched Tovi's hand on his arm, and the siblings shared a concerned look.

Kade turned to Evelyn. The wound on his betrothed's arm was another reminder of not only the threat they faced in Callum, but in their homeland. Without knowing why she'd left, Kade didn't want to lose the progress he'd made with Evelyn by revealing who he was, but he refused to lose sight of his purpose. Bit by bit, muscle by muscle, Kade straightened back into it.

Solve these murders, demonstrate they worked well as a team, convince Evelyn to fulfill their duty, and return to Sorin, their homeland.

"We should head to Lake Glenn tomorrow, see what clues we can find," he said.

Something flashed in her eyes. Relief? Unease? He couldn't tell.

"All right," she said.

"Tovi and I can walk you home," Riven said, taking a step toward Evelyn.

Kade angled himself in front of her, his body moving on its own accord again. "No need. I'll join her." He looked between Tovi and Riven. "You should both rest after the attack."

Tovi looped her arm around her brother's. "Cyrus is right. Let's get in from the rain."

Riven's jade eyes, similar to his sister's but with an edge to them that Kade sensed was predatory, lingered on him before the man followed his sister to the print shop.

Through the empty streets of Callum, Kade walked alongside Evelyn. The two of them said nothing to the other, but plenty of noise traveled between them. The lazy drizzle, the singing sea wind, and the unsaid secrets of who and what they were.

Chapter Twenty-Two

Kade

The next day, Kade's wolf became more and more restless the closer he and Evelyn got to Lake Glenn.

Thanks to the stars above, the rain had at least stopped, but a wintry chill brewed in Callum's air, crisp and cutting. A body of water sat nestled between two ancient mountains weathered down to hills. Feathery gray clouds floated over the peaks and onto the mirror-like surface, hovering just shy of the water.

Something within these lands was too beautiful. It unnerved Kade, the ancient darkness that once thrived here vibrating in the air like a façade, waiting to entrap its prey. He missed the Vadon Mountains. The proud trees, the songbirds, his ability to roam freely as a werewolf and not having to wake before anyone else in the town to shift and run.

As a werewolf should.

Evelyn walked ahead with her staff, her long hair tied together in a braid over her shoulder. Both of them had said little to each other. They'd dismounted Bleu half a mile back, inspecting the path leading to the lake closer up. Bleu grew agitated the closer they came to the water's edge, ears flicked back as if he too sensed the *other*.

Kade was disgruntled. While getting ready that morning, he come across the letter he never sent to Eldrick. He debated if now was the time to spend the silvers and send it. Of course, it needed updating. There was indeed a vampyr in Callum—he'd seen it, *fought* it. Not to mention the possible connection to the witches' creed. With that in mind, too, Kade recalled Evelyn's muince, taunting him with its pearly pendant and the truth. Like the letter, it felt like the right time to present it to Evelyn.

Telling her was the right thing to do. What he *needed* to do.

There's something I need to tell you. I'm no huntsman, but Kade Drengr.

Kade devised a speech in his mind and ran over the words. Emphasizing she could trust him, she did not need to fear him, that they had to warn everyone back home. Kade stood a breath away from spilling his secrets when his boots scuffed over the shore, knocking pebbles out of the way. The courage to come clean vanished, the task at hand taking precedence.

Slide marks cut through the sandy underlay of the lakeshore. Kade bent down, running his hand over mounds of rocks—it was as if boots and hands had made indents.

"Saige," he said.

She joined him, looking over his shoulder. "Signs of a struggle?"

"Yes, and possibly where the vampyr might have killed her."

But there were no droplets of blood, no iron scent in the air. The rain or lake might've washed away that evidence, but even so, Fiona had been drained. There wouldn't have been much blood left behind, same as at Castle Connacht.

With Evelyn so close, Kade couldn't use his wolf's magic to detect what had happened. *Moons*, tapping into his werewolf powers would be such an asset. He ran his hand through his hair, frustration giving him a headache.

"Cyrus, look." Evelyn pointed east, her brows furrowed and concern flashing across her face.

White-stone cliffs lined the right side of the lake's hill. A cloak billowed on a jagged rock in the faint breeze, red, bright and vibrant compared to the setting.

"I'll ride Bleu up to the peak and check it out," he said. "You stay here and look for anything else."

Evelyn observed him, frowning slightly. "Good plan."

Kade mounted Bleu. He didn't like leaving Evelyn behind in such a place, but he also needed to put space between them so he didn't say something rash. Despite warring reasons, he wasn't ready to tell her the truth yet.

Bleu galloped up the sodden path that shot straight up to the cliffs. The air grew thicker, the low drifting clouds kissing Kade's tunic and leathers with moisture. The path disappeared behind the bend of an overlook, obscuring the cloak.

Kade paused, the view stealing his breath. The lake appeared as still as glass, the reflection of the clouds as perfect as if it were a mirror.

Flapping fabric snapped in the wind. Kade dismounted Bleu and descended a hidden path tucked between rocks and sprouts of buttercups. The cloak came into view again, twirling its red fabric in the air as if to say, *you found me*.

The path dropped to an overhanging rock with an inlet underneath, and the moment Kade's boots landed, his wolf sensed the iron stench of blood. Smears of handprints and footprints of dried crimson stained the sand.

His wolf detected the blood belonged to a woman, and the other scent laced in the air was of death and a cloying sweetness.

Like licorice. Not the scent of a vampyr.

Kade closed his eyes, took a mighty breath, and channeled his magic. His wolf leaped with elation and sprang with eagerness at being used. He knelt down and planted his hand in the sand, connecting his magic to the scene. It awakened at the touch of the blood, the darkness intertwined with death, and after a beat, Kade's magic clicked into place. His surroundings blurred with colors as time lapsed.

Impossible to tell the genders or who was who. Two images appeared and sharpened, one smaller than the other. The smaller one shimmered red, and it billowed like the cloak snagged off the cliff. The other image slinked through the scene, black as night.

The two images pushed and shoved, fighting one another. Spurts of black fell from the red figure like flint falling from fire. The images faced off with one another until the red figure fell to the ground.

Pain, fear, and hunger lashed at Kade's magic, deeply woven into the memory. He held on to his magic, digging his fingers deeper into the sand. The images wavered with the wind, returning as the red figure fell backward off the cliff, and then the image snapped from existence.

Kade gasped back into reality. Sweat prickled at his temples, his heart thudding in his chest. The wind continued to blow his hair back as he studied the spot where he assumed Fiona had jumped. He peered over the edge. The drop was steep but manageable. No rocks broke the surface of the lake below. Perhaps Fiona had tried to swim to shore, only to find the vampyr waiting there to intercept her?

Kade surveyed the scene again. Her relationship with the vampyr had been much different than that of McKenna's. No lover. No picnic. Had she been lured here? If so, why?

Above Kade, Bleu let out a stream of neighs, stomping his feet on the cliff's edge. Kade left the inlet, finding Bleu trotting back and forth, nodding his head up and down.

"Whoa, there," Kade said, trying to grab hold of the reins.

Bleu relented, knocking Kade's shoulder back with his muzzle and forcing Kade to face the lake once more.

At the shoreline, Evelyn trudged shin deep into the water, yelling at—

Kade's heart plummeted in his chest. He sucked in a breath, willing his legs to move.

The water. The death.

The darkness.

I left her. I left her. Kade mounted his horse and sprinted down the path to Evelyn.

Who was yelling at a horse—or very likely *not* a horse—that looked exactly like Bleu.

Chapter Twenty-Three

Evelyn

While Evelyn searched the lake's shore, she caught a glimpse of her own face in the still water. Pale as the moon with hair as dark as night. Her gray eyes, tired and weary, looked fathomless reflected in the lake. Something felt off. Her magic sensed darkness. Fog dissipated as wind rolled down the hills—yet the lake was still. *Too* still. No birds chirped, no fish nibbled at the surface. Only the pebbles crunched under Evelyn's boots as she looked for clues.

Alone, she tried to dismiss thoughts about Cyrus and the wedge between them.

We'll do it your way, Princess.

She'd pushed him away, shut him out, and gave him no explanation as to why, and it seemed her efforts had worked. It had to be done, but then why did she care so much about what he thought? And why did it matter? Even though Evelyn hadn't decided yet if she'd return home, she'd leave Callum to go somewhere.

Alone.

Evelyn could no longer deny or tamp down the feelings forming for the huntsman. She liked him. Her disappointment this morning had been evident enough. Cyrus had not greeted her with his smile, and his eyes had not been bright. He'd been civil enough, but they'd said less than five words to one another on the three-mile trek to Lake Glenn.

She shook her head and stilled her thoughts as she looked for more clues. Evelyn extended her magic out and sensed death. One thing was for certain, Fiona had died here.

Was it her cloak off in the distance? Evelyn searched for the path Cyrus and Bleu had climbed but couldn't find them through the tall green weeds swaying in the wind.

A neigh from behind Evelyn jolted her around.

Bleu, Cyrus's gray steed, stood in the lake, pawing at the water. He neighed and thrashed, splashing cold water onto Evelyn.

"Bleu!" she called out. "You stubborn horse. Get out of the water!"

Where had Cyrus gone? She hated to think of the demons that Aster had mentioned slumbering in the lake. Her magic bristled with awareness. Evelyn gripped her staff, bracing for an attack. No doubt, Bleu wasn't helping. His hooves continued to stomp in the lake, trotting from side to side, surely calling forth whatever demons hid under the surface.

"Fucking flames, I hate horses," Evelyn said through gritted teeth.

She stepped into the water, cursing the beast and the cold and darkness. She reached to grab his reins, but he danced out of reach.

"Bleu!"

Evelyn's magic swelled in her chest. Darkness approached, brushing up against her light. Bleu halted, huffing hot breath onto her face. Rotten fish and salt churned Evelyn's stomach. She blinked through the horrid smell and found Bleu's milky white eyes staring back at her.

Evelyn stopped—

"*Saige!*"

Evelyn turned toward the frantic, urgent cry. Cyrus raced for the shore atop Bleu, his tanned face pale and flushed with exertion, his eyes wide and crazed. His knuckles shone white as he pulled on the reins, frantic in his effort to urge Bleu forward.

Wait, *Bleu*—

A hot, rancid puff of air hit her in the back. Evelyn gripped her staff with both hands, casting out a force field as she whirled back to the other Bleu.

A pristine, gray horse no longer stood in the water. Milky white eyes stared from the skull of a horse. Molars and razor teeth overlapped outside its jaw. Flesh and muscle hung from the black bones of a kelpie.

A dangerous trickster of a demon.

It neighed, a sound laced with a deafening screech that rippled across the lake.

Goddess, Evelyn was out of practice to be so easily fooled by a kelpie's oldest trick, transforming into an animal its victim knew. Evelyn conjured her flame, annoyed with herself that she'd missed the signs. Her magic had been warning her, and she hadn't listened.

She tapped into her frustration and lit her staff aflame. The kelpie cried again, charging at her. Before Evelyn could cast fire, Cyrus knocked the kelpie off course with Bleu. He unsheathed his sword, the iron crying out against its scabbard.

More screeches tremored through the lake, the fog thickening as the darkness surrounded the demon. Cyrus dismounted Bleu in one effortless move. From a sturdy stance, he raised his sword high. Strength vibrated off him like magic.

The kelpie charged Cyrus, but Evelyn cast a ball of fire to counter the attack. Flame met its shoulder, sizzling over rotting flesh. The kelpie rose on its hind legs and let out a cry that ricocheted off the lake and echoed from the mountains.

Unfamiliar confidence soared through Evelyn. She sent another barreling ball of fire at the kelpie. It made contact, but the enraged demon refocused on Evelyn. Cyrus swiped his sword at its hind legs, which buckled as it screeched in pain.

The water approached in aggressive waves, like an unseen beast beneath the surface unleashing its wrath. It knocked Cyrus back and dragged him under the lake's surface. Evelyn screamed, her magic bursting from her fingertips as Cyrus's hair peeked out of the water.

She pushed farther into the lake, sending a wave of flame toward the kelpie as she reached Cyrus. She gripped his shirt and yanked him up, pushing away the dark magic festering in the depths. Cyrus gasped. His eyes searched for her, wild and wide. They locked gazes, distracting her.

The kelpie clamped its teeth into her shoulder. It pulled her from Cyrus, and she lost her grip on her staff as pain shot down her arm. Cold, relentless currents washed over her. Her magic screamed.

Cyrus stood and slashed the kelpie through the throat. The demon crumpled into water, morphing into the lake. The darkness dove with it.

Evelyn scrambled toward the shore with Cyrus, but the magic in the water rooted her in place like quicksand as it swirled and tightened. Fear and pain battled in Evelyn. She tried to conjure her flame but couldn't.

Her fingers were stiff. Her bones turned cold. Her entire body was soaked.

The ancient dark magic, oily and slick against hers, embedded itself into her skin. It seized hold of her ankles and pulled her under.

Heaving, she pushed forward and screamed, "Cyrus!"

The lake yanked her back, the jagged stones scraping against her palms. Her next cry for help came out gargled, water rushing into her lungs. She couldn't see, couldn't breath—

Evelyn gasped as she was pulled to the surface. Cyrus held both her hands, holding her firm against the pulling current. His golden eyes glowed with resolve. *I got you*, they seemed to say. The water climbed higher up her legs, constricting.

Evelyn grimaced. Pain overtook her.

But a new, stickier essence weaved its way into the dark magic around them.

Death.

Chapter Twenty-Four

Evelyn

Cyrus kept a firm grip on Evelyn's hands, pulling her toward the shore. Bleu held on to Cyrus by the cuff of his trousers, starting a tug-of-war between them and the lake.

"You have to use your magic!" he said.

Evelyn shook her head. Words turned to ash on her tongue, and she said nothing. She couldn't tell him. She couldn't admit she was a damn fool for not noticing the signs of the kelpie. She couldn't admit she'd lost her flame or that she couldn't reach it now. Yet again, doubt consumed her, overriding her senses. Her mind flashed to the day on the riverbend, the vampyrs killing her parents. Her vision funneled into the small tight space her tutor locked her in as a child. Her failure. Her torment. She wasn't capable of winning this fight without her flame, but the huntsman didn't need to suffer.

"Cyrus," she said. Her voice broke as his eyes roamed over her face. "You have to let me go."

"No!" He roared it across the lake, tightening his grip on her hands and pulling her farther up shore.

"You must."

Her innate magic warred within her. Tears streamed down her face, the pain of the lake on her ankles, pulling her back.

Fear flashed across Cyrus's face. He pulled her so close, their foreheads touched. For a moment, the world stilled. It was just the two of them, holding on to each other.

"I've seen your power and strength," he whispered. "You're magnificent and you must believe."

Evelyn's breath shuddered. Such familiar words sank deep into her bones and reached for her heart. Words her father had used moments before he died, and a mantra her one kind tutor had used. Words often overshadowed by the terrors of her past.

An ancient chant, chilly like the air and haunting like the eerie land, sounded around them. She cringed in pain as the lake continued to pull, but she wouldn't let it take her.

Not today.

Evelyn channeled deep, reaching far within herself. Cyrus's words helped her reach that magnificent part. Her flame. A kernel of it flickered in greeting, awaiting Evelyn's grasp.

"You need to let me go," Evelyn said. "Grab your sword."

Cyrus pulled her closer, and Bleu took a mighty step up shore. "You must think I'm mad if—"

"Cyrus," she said. She darted her eyes toward his sword to the left of him. The silver blade glinted in the lapping water, the handle begging to be held. He would have to let go of Evelyn to grab it.

Evelyn's being beamed with something new. No fear. No doubt. Nothing but resilience.

"Trust me," she said.

Conflict warred in his eyes as he looked between his sword and Evelyn. Seconds ticked by.

"*Do it*," she said.

Chapter Twenty-Five

Kade

Kade released Evelyn and scrambled for his sword. Heat, light, and power unleashed in his peripheral vision. He took hold of his sword and turned back to Evelyn, her entire being engulfed in flame.

Flame danced at her fingertips. It whooshed her hair wildly. Red flame, blue eyes, black hair, the contrast both drastic and beautiful. Flame cascaded from her limbs and chest, hovering over the water and burning away the darkness, driving it from the shoreline. Bleu neighed furiously, as if cheering her on.

The kelpie manifested with the water again, rising into a giant humanoid figure. Its arms dragged across the surface, its faceless head tilting back and wailing. The very earth shook with the dark, ancient magic.

Water and fire intertwined. The kelpie hunched over, sinking into the lake as Evelyn's flame pushed it deeper and deeper. In one last effort, the kelpie reached out its watery hand. Kade took a single step aside Evelyn, swiped down and then back up. The kelpie's limb burst into water droplets, the dark magic dissipating into the wind like black smoke. The land quaked and shuddered as the kelpie fell under the lake's surface for the final time, bubbles bursting and hissing with steam.

Evelyn brought back her magic, the chanting in the air dying down as she did so. Flame dove into her chest, and Kade overflowed with admiration. It overshadowed his questions, his demands, his frustration with her secrets. He wanted to reach out to her. Touch her to make sure she was okay.

Moons, he wanted to . . .

Dark clouds rolled over the hills. Thunder announced rain.

Evelyn grabbed his hand and led him from the lake. "We must go. The darkness isn't done yet."

They retreated. Eeriness still lingered. Rain spilled. The sky stormed. Cyrus, Evelyn, and Bleu rushed from Lake Glenn, unsure if they heard the symphony of drums beginning or the thunderclaps of the storm above.

Chapter Twenty-Six

Evelyn

Thump. Thump. Thump.

All around Evelyn, there was beating.

The rain. The ancient drums. Thunder. Her heartbeat. Cyrus's boots on the path. Bleu's hooves.

Night had fallen as the storm raged. Behind her on the wooded path, Cyrus and Bleu's darkened silhouette followed behind. Lightning above the tree line cast flashes of pale light, illuminating his determined expression and Bleu's drenched coat.

They hadn't spoken since they'd fled Lake Glenn, two miles ago. The rain pelted the path, and the thunder rattled her ribcage. Her shoulder ached, and her arm was stiff. Her boots slipped through mud, and her balance wavered. She yelped as strong hands caught her waist and held her upright, but a glance over her shoulder revealed Cyrus behind her.

"We won't make it to Callum safely in the storm," he said, glancing at her wound.

Evelyn's stubbornness flared. She'd sunk an ancient kelpie. She could make it back to Callum, but sleep beckoned, her eyelids heavy. Evelyn had exhausted her magic, drained her energy.

"You're right," she relented.

Farther down the path, the trees thickened, but so did the rocky terrain. Cyrus grabbed Evelyn's hand, threading his fingers through hers and leading them off the path. Lightning flashed, revealing an inlet of rock, water trilling over the side but big enough to give them relief from the storm until it passed.

Thank the Goddess, Cyrus had seen it in the night. She released Cyrus's hand as he tied Bleu to the closest tree. Evelyn shuddered, unable to look at the gray steed without thinking of the kelpie. Its relentless bite was fresh on her shoulder, surfacing the memory of its teeth digging into her flesh.

But the warm rush of her returned flame was just as fresh. Evelyn teetered between relief and worry. Yes, it had come back. Again. It had also gone out, buried so deep within her that she'd been unable to reach it and use it. What good was her power if she didn't have the ability to tap it?

She wandered off to explore the small cave and found it empty, aside from the moss expanding over the walls, a plush shade of bright green that wouldn't look out of place in Aster's shop.

Evelyn unfastened her cloak and draped it over a large rock. She gathered a few lonesome logs and piled them nearby. Thrumming her fingers in the air and flicking her wrist, she felt excitement pulse through her as flame danced from finger to finger on her command. It was back. A part of her again.

She conjured enough energy to light a fire, the flames snaking down to the logs she'd stacked at the center of the cave. The walls glowed orange and green, flickering with her shadow.

A larger one entered the space. Cyrus. She took in his amber eyes, wet hair, taut jaw. He, too, removed his cloak to lay it out to dry. The top of his head almost reached the ceiling of the cave, and as he stood near the fire, Evelyn swore the cave shrank in size.

It was too small for two. Too small for both of them. *Fucking flames*, he was so close.

"Are you all right?" Cyrus asked, looking her over for what felt like the hundredth time since they'd left Lake Glenn.

Evelyn couldn't meet his gaze, unable to face whatever else lay beneath his stare. She memorized the dance of the flame, gripping her bruised shoulder from the kelpie's bite. She was grateful for her witch healing, running her hands over the puncture wounds that had closed over.

Flashes of their escape danced with the flames. Yanking Cyrus from the water. Their eye contact. Their wet shirts sticking together.

Evelyn shut her eyes, wishing the cave was bigger.

"Let me take a look," he said, stepping closer and taking hold of her shoulder all too quickly.

Evelyn gasped. Cyrus paused, apologized, and loosened his grip. He believed it to be pain, but Evelyn felt the electricity of his touch, flaring into something she'd never experienced before.

Cyrus ran his thumb under the sleeve of her blouse, eliciting a heat in Evelyn's belly. Her heart hammered as their eyes met in the dim light, the rain pattering outside the cave. Cyrus searched her face, the fire casting shades of gold and honey through his eyes. A question lay in them, asking if he should continue, waiting for her to say yes.

Evelyn stayed silent, tried to master her breathing, and nodded. With one gentle tug, Cyrus pulled the sleeve down past her shoulder, exposing the purplish-black bruise arranged in a half-circle. His nostrils flared, his jawline ticked. His usual kind and thoughtful expression shuddered into beastly brooding.

"Can you move your shoulder?" he asked, voice thick and low.

Evelyn nodded, shrugging and rolling her shoulder back despite the slight pain throbbing down her arm. "Nothing's broken."

Cyrus sighed, his expression relaxing. He ran his thumb over the biggest bruise, gentle and soothing, and lifted Evelyn's sleeve back over the wound.

The fire crackled, and Cyrus's gaze locked with Evelyn's, and they grew closer, like forces pulling each other inch by inch, a thread growing shorter and shorter.

Tugging.

Her heart thudded, her magic swelled. Eager and anticipatory. His breath tickled her nose, water droplets falling from his hair. A single bead landed and traveled down Evelyn's nose, leaving a cold path in its wake. Cyrus followed its movement until it dropped to her lips.

His eyes flared, and Evelyn knew in that moment, with his hand on her shoulder, the rain pattering outside, and the blazing sliver of space between them, that she wanted Cyrus to kiss her.

It was inappropriate. They worked together. Wrong and selfish. She'd leave after they solved the murders. And even more foolish and misplaced. She was betrothed to Kade Drengr, Son of the God. But Evelyn wanted it, nonetheless. Her heart thudded with need. She leaned closer, her magic egging her on.

Cyrus still held his breath. His brows furrowed in . . . Had Evelyn read the moment wrong? She swallowed, readying herself to pull back when, in an instant, Cyrus's lips crashed into hers with no warning. No way to prepare herself for the intensity, the smoldering contact, how quickly his kiss would consume her.

Or how unraveled and blissful she was as they came together.

Someone moaned. Maybe Evelyn. One of them growled. Definitely Cyrus. They kissed, their lips molding with excitement and anticipation and newness. Evelyn's stomach grew warm like a pit of fire fueled by the tension, the walls crumbling between them.

Cyrus's hand left her shoulder and moved to the nape of her neck. His strong fingers tilted her head, providing a deeper, more demanding angle as his other hand cupped her cheek. Evelyn grasped his shirt, craving his nearness, his skin on her skin, his lips against hers, the tease of his tongue as it explored her mouth.

She might combust with her flame. Her magic was joyous, full of hunger and desire, a sensation she'd never felt before.

She'd kissed, but not like this.

Their lips slowed, tenderly and begrudgingly. They broke away as if they'd both remembered they needed to breathe to survive, both of them gasping and shaking. Cyrus leaned his forehead on Evelyn's, dazed.

A beat passed. Rain spilled buckets. The fire crackled and danced behind them.

"I've wanted"—Cyrus paused, composing himself—"to do that for a while now."

"Since when?" Evelyn whispered, her cheeks hot and lips sensually bruised.

"Since you walked into the commissioner's office."

Evelyn took a step back, eyes wide with raised brows. "You're lying."

"I'm not," Cyrus whispered, kissing the edges of her lips and down her neck.

Breathless and elated, Evelyn fell into him. Their kiss and his words filled her with glee. She laughed. Goddess, it'd been so long since she'd truly laughed.

Eyes wide with surprise, Cyrus took every inch of her in, and Evelyn did the same to him. In the gilded light, the gold in his hair and beard glowed. The shadows flashed over a pinkish scar running through his beard, reaching to his cheek. Another scar cut through his right brow, over his eye. Cyrus had the face of a warrior, and Evelyn's insides melted. Curious, she reached up her hand and trailed a finger down the right scar.

"How'd you get this?"

Cyrus's mouth twitched to a half-smile. "An ialtóg."

Evelyn scrunched her nose. "Those are ghastly."

Ialtógs were bat-like demons, but ten times the size of a true bat. Fast, big, able to fly, and they were always hungry. For anything that moved.

Cyrus raised a brow. "You've encountered one?"

"Unfortunately, yes." Evelyn withdrew her hand from his scar, but Cyrus grabbed it and ran his finger over her knuckles.

"I'll tell you my story if you tell me yours," he said.

"About the ialtóg?"

Cyrus nodded, a playful smirk tugging at the corners of his lips. "But only if you go first."

She sighed. Seeing as the rain still continued with no signs of letting up soon, they had time to kill. She sauntered over to the fire, crossing her legs and soaking in the heat as it dried her clothes.

Cyrus joined her, resting his forearms on his bent knees as he waited.

Evelyn supposed she'd stumbled into this one particular story of her past. Maybe she *wanted* to tell him after such a magical kiss. Regardless, she could keep the details to a minimum so she didn't give too much away.

"I was . . . um, working when I heard the shouts of a man riding on a horse, frantic, an ialtóg chasing him. He was a farmer, and as you might already know, ialtógs have a large appetite for cattle. Anyway, it was chasing this farmer, who carried his injured father. The demon was triple the size of the horse."

"And what did you do?" Cyrus asked.

The two of them sat so close, shoulder to shoulder, as she told her story. Evelyn caught Cyrus's stare shimmering like golden jewels before the flame as he listened to her every word.

"I grabbed a rope and a lantern and ran out to meet it. After soaking the rope in the lantern's oil, I tossed it like a lasso at the ialtóg's feet. Took me three attempts to get hold of it. Now, I'm not strong enough to pull down a demon from the sky, but"—Evelyn flared her fingers on fire for a moment—"I set the oiled rope on fire and took the ialtóg down."

Cyrus whistled. "And the farmer and his father?"

"Alive and well." She waved her hand in the air dismissively, ready to move on before Cyrus asked any additional questions. Like where she worked or what town she was from. "It's your turn, Huntsman."

He shrugged. "A bit anticlimactic compared to yours."

"You still have to tell it."

He chuckled. "Well, I stumbled into the wrong cave at the wrong time. Came across a mated pair with their babes." He grimaced. "I ran, of course, but one managed to nick me before I reached the cave's edge." Cyrus pointed to his scar. "Anticlimactic, like I said."

Thoughtful, Evelyn tilted her head. "Was this before or after you became a huntsman?"

Cyrus paused for a breath, his shoulders going taut as if he rarely talked about this part of his past. "Before."

"Why did you become a huntsman?" The question left Evelyn before she could think more about it. She had no right to ask him, especially since she gave him so little.

Cyrus's gaze had become lost in the flames, a considerable furrow to his brow setting his jaw tight. "At the time, it seemed the best way to get what I wanted."

Evelyn fiddled with her hands, wishing she didn't care. She blamed that kiss, the growing bold, wrong feelings for this huntsman beside her.

Her next question was a whisper. "What did you want?"

He turned to her and reached for a flyaway strand of damp hair, tucking it behind her ear. "Can't say I remember, Princess."

Cyrus pulled her in close, and Evelyn rested her head on his shoulder, listening to the rain, the fire, and her happy, thumping heart.

Chapter Twenty-Seven

Kade

The next day, Kade washed and polished pint glasses behind the bar of the Runaway Radish. A howl hovered over the town, and Kade's werewolf hearing questioned if it was the wind getting trapped over the hills or the screams of a wretched creature. Yet, a newness sat in the air between him and Evelyn, overshadowing the ominous cries. His chest swelled with excitement while he wrestled with what he'd done.

At the end of the bar, Miss Patricia folded and formed bread dough, a first batch of loaves already baking in the oven and giving the inn a lovely, warm aroma. Only a few patrons sat at the long tables, the daytime slower than the evening hours.

"If you smile one more time, the shine might crack the glasses!" Miss Patricia called.

Kade laughed, appreciating the older woman's teasing. He had been smiling, thinking of Evelyn, remembering the kiss. *Stars above*, that kiss.

He shook his head, still at war with himself about what to do next.

You're lying, Evelyn had said.

Her words had meant something else entirely, and they'd rocked through Kade far more than he let on. He *was* lying. About who he was. Why he was here. What he wanted.

Moons, what did he want?

He didn't want to fracture what was building between them. He didn't want to let his guilt win.

He remembered her laugh. So happy. So relaxed.

Do that again, he wanted to say.

But couldn't, because she was Saige Ferriwether in that moment, he was Cyrus Skender, and no matter the force of their first kiss, Kade could not shake that he was Kade Drengr, lying to Evelyn Carson.

Miss Patricia took a break from her bread loaves. "May I ask if your mood is about a certain lovely lass?"

"What gave me away?"

"Aye, you're the talk of the town, smitten with the mysterious beauty."

Moons, was he that obvious?

Kade wasn't surprised. He was practically bursting with feelings for Evelyn, except she didn't know he knew she was Evelyn. His head pounded with a migraine. He placed a pint glass down and ran his hand through his hair.

"Now don't look so worried, lad," Miss Patricia said.

Kade scoffed, wishing it was only worry he felt.

"From what I hear, she's just as smitten," Miss Patricia went on.

Kade's insides twisted, more guilt eating away at him. Evelyn was smitten with a man who was lying to her. He *should* tell her. It was the right thing to do. If his mother was here, she'd suggest reconsidering what he wanted versus what was right. He wanted whatever between them to continue, but the right thing was honesty first. The nature of that kiss, the way she'd kissed him back, gripped his shirt, made it seem like she was as hungry for him as he was for her. The kiss wouldn't be the end of it.

Kade had to be honest.

He'd come to Callum to find Evelyn and convince her to leave with him. He'd never expected the murders, the vampyr. And now there were feelings and their kiss.

Miss Patricia placed her flour-coated hands on her hips. "Come on now, what's the matter? You're smiling one minute and solemn the next."

"How do I know what I tell you won't become the talk of the town?" he said with a brow raised.

Miss Patricia raised her hands in surrender. "Aye, I'll say nothin', keep it between us."

Kade sighed and decided to trust her. "I'm not sure how honest I can be with her about . . . who I really am."

Miss Patricia's brows furrowed in thought. Realization softened her features, and she nodded slowly. "I see." She sighed. "Well, my Da' always told me that bad news never gets better with age."

"I suppose that's true."

Miss Patricia wrung her hands together. "I dunno what you're keepin' from her, and I don't need to know. But what I do know: Saige was going to run and leave town I reckon she has been doin' that for some time now. And I know these murders started and she stayed to solve 'em, but I think something else, or *someone,* has also kept her here, too."

Kade blinked, digesting Miss Patricia's words. Evelyn had been less on edge lately. She'd opened up to him, revealed she was a witch. She seemed settled in her apartment. Becoming a part of Callum. It wasn't exactly what he wanted, but maybe he had influenced her decision to stay a while.

Before he could comment, the Runaway Radish's door burst open. Commissioner Doyle rushed in with two other men. They lingered by the door while Commissioner Doyle approached the bar alone.

"What ya barging in for?" Miss Patricia asked.

"Apologies, Patricia, here to see the huntsman. Cyrus, I'm sorry to bother, but I was hoping you could help me out with something that's not related to the vampyr business."

Kade's shoulders relaxed. He'd assumed the forlorn faces of the men by the door meant another murder.

"What's the matter?" he asked.

"There's been a kidnapping."

"A kidnapping?" Miss Patricia gasped.

Cyrus rounded the bar. "Who?"

Commissioner Doyle sighed. "A young woman named Tessa. She went to pick apples for this weekend's festival down by the Gray Wood. She didn't come back before supper." The commissioner nodded at the others, and they approached the bar. "This is Tessa's father, John Byrne, and her husband, Aaron Collins."

"Why do you think it's a kidnapping?" Kade asked.

Tessa's father cleared his throat. "Our farm sits near the Gray Wood, an ancient forest that's home to the Far Darrig."

Kade shook his head. "Far Darrig?"

"Aye, a tribe of faeries," Miss Patricia said.

"I thought the faeries were gone, abandoned these lands," Kade said.

Miss Patricia laughed, bitter and low. "The faeries never left. We don't see 'em like we used to."

Aaron nodded. "'Tis true, and we found this on our doorstep this morning."

He handed over a folded piece of parchment. Kade opened it, and as he read over the words, every inch of him that had relaxed earlier went taut, his protective instinct readying for action. He read over the words again to be sure, his knuckles going white as he held the note tighter. He shook his head. The commissioner was wrong. This kidnapping might be related to the murders, and Evelyn needed to see this, too.

Kade nodded. "Let me grab my things and find Saige. She'll want to help. Where is your farm?"

"Dinberry," Tessa's father said.

"I'll meet you there."

Kade rushed up to his room and grabbed his leathers, threw on his cloak, and gathered his sword. He paused at the small writing desk, looking over the spare parchment and unused quills. Still folded was the letter he'd planned to send Eldrick days ago as well as Evelyn's necklace from Blair.

His protector instinct screamed to write to Eldrick, his eldest brother. To tell him he found Evelyn, explain about the murders and ask his brother to send help. With the contents of the letter in mind, alerting the witches and the wolves was the right thing to do, the rational thing to do, but why did the idea make him sick?

He trailed his finger over the letter and necklace, while his other hand gripped the hilt of his sword with purpose. Perhaps *now* was the right time to give it to her. Kade's heart sank like stone in his belly. He didn't want to hurt Evelyn, couldn't lie to her any more than he already had and betray her trust. Damn that kiss. He shut his eyes, flexed his fists, and shook his head.

No, he'd tell her. *Soon*. He'd come clean and tell her after they killed the vampyr.

Until then, he would continue building their relationship, showing her they could be partners against the darkness.

Chapter Twenty-Eight

Evelyn

"To the Byrne family," Evelyn said, repeating the letter aloud again. "'At sundown, we take her head. Sincerely, the Far Darrig.'"

Cold, unrelenting horror coursed through Evelyn's blood, freezing her insides with icy anxiety. Cyrus had found her shopping in the market with Tovi, and when he'd recounted Tessa's kidnapping, they hadn't wasted any time in heading to Dinberry.

The sun shone high and bright, a much-needed reprieve from the last few rainy, dreary days. The roads snaking through the hills buzzed with activity and twice as many merchants and farmers as usual, everyone traveling south to Callum for the Autumn Festival. Evelyn had almost fallen into that contagious excitement earlier with her friend, had been fooled to believe they had a moment of reprieve from these murders.

Her head.

Evelyn shut her eyes in disbelief. "I hadn't wanted to be right, but fucking flames, Cyrus. The witches' creed, the body parts. Tessa's kidnapping could connect her to the murders. Head is the third body part in the witches' creed."

"I know," he said beside her.

They hurried up a thinner offshoot of a path and away from the main road. The stone shingles of a cottage came into view beyond the mound of a hill.

Evelyn paused, reading the signature at the bottom of the letter. "Assuming the vampyr didn't write this letter, why are the Far Darrig involved?"

Cyrus appeared as confused as she, brows furrowed, lips thinned. "Alliances? With the body parts, maybe these murders are more complex and the vampyr needed help. The signs have also pointed to a mature vampyr since the beginning, and we know they are more coherent than a scáth. It's not impossible for them to form an alliance."

Evelyn digested his idea. "Help with what, though? Why choose the Far Darrig, a *faerie* tribe? Why Tessa specifically?"

Cyrus ran his hand over his beard. "Maybe because they've had a feud with the Byrnes for so long, it was easy to convince them, and Tessa was accessible. There are also theories suggesting faerie magic created the vampyrs."

Evelyn blinked and glanced at Cyrus. He looked out across the land, seemingly lost in his thoughts. No one truly knew how vampyrs came about, but theories had been tossed around by scholars for centuries. The one constant in those theories: witches' bones.

What they'd been used for or how they'd been used had always been a mystery. Evelyn's head pulsed with a headache as she thought about the many mysteries before her. The murders. The origin of vampyrs. Now a kidnapping. She had a gut feeling she was missing how they were all connected.

Atop the hill, the Byrne farm came into full view. A white, squat cottage sat on the left, along with a large barn to the right. Cows grazed in a buttercup-dotted pasture, unbothered by the three men arguing outside the cottage. A woman beside them cried as she held on to a young girl, her eyes wide with fear. Evelyn recognized the Byrne family as the farmers who dropped milk off at the Runaway Radish, along with their son-in-law, Aaron Collins.

Poor Commissioner Doyle looked weary, his face flashing with relief as he noticed Evelyn and Cyrus. He rushed over to them.

"Thank the hills you're here. The Byrnes are a hot-headed bunch. Be ready."

The raised voices grated against Evelyn's headache. They didn't have time for arguing. Not with Tessa's kidnapping and the Far Darrig wanting her head. They already could have succeeded in aiding the vampyr's mysterious endeavor.

"I say we march into that forest and get Tessa ourselves!" yelled the youngest man, with a mop of red curls, pitchfork in hand.

"The Far Darrig and the Byrnes have a treaty!" John replied. "We all know that."

"Which they broke!" Aaron retorted.

Evelyn held up her hand, shaking her head. "What treaty?"

The family stopped, eyeing her and Cyrus.

John sighed. "My great-great-granddad forged it with their clan leader after the Battle at Byrne Farm. Every year we pay a tithe, a winter's supply of goods for no violence on our farm. We may have lost the forest, but for four generations, we've had no quarrel."

"Mischievous tricksters, but never violence," the woman Evelyn assumed to be Tessa's mother added. "Knocking over cows in the night. Switching sugar with salt in the cupboards."

"Aye, but they've stolen a few geese," Tessa's brother muttered.

"This is no goose. They have Tessa!" Aaron said. Unlike his in-laws, his hair was dark brown instead of red. He wore a gold band on the fourth finger of his left hand. "We have to do something. Bargain with something. Perhaps the entire farm? We can't enter the Gray Wood, but we have to get Tessa back."

Cyrus stepped forward. "This Gray Wood, what is it?"

"A forest," John said, "and the Far Darrig live in it and control it. Humans don't ever go in and those that do never come out."

"Is that where they took Tessa?" Evelyn asked, worry heavy like a brick in her belly.

Mrs. Byrne nodded, looking down at the younger girl clutching her waist. "We believe so. Jenny found her barrel of apples outside it."

The youngest, whom Evelyn assumed to be Tessa's brother, shook his head. "There shouldn't be a discussion. We march in and get Tessa back."

"Aaron is right. We should offer a trade, not march in and start more violence," John said.

The argument continued, Tessa's husband and her brother shouting at each other. Her father interjected, shaking his finger. Jenny watched, silent as a mouse while Mrs. Byrne attempted to calm them down.

Evelyn placed her hands on her hips and sighed while Cyrus pinched the bridge of his nose. They were going in absolute circles. If they didn't act soon, Tessa would no longer be the target of a kidnapping, but another name added to their list of murder victims. Evelyn's flame raged inside her, building and building until her fingers twitched and skin grew hot.

"We don't have time for this!" she shouted.

Her words cut through their raised voices, and everyone fell silent.

"We need to save Tessa before it's too late." She waved the letter in her hand. "Before nightfall, too, so we don't have to fight both the Far Darrig and the vampyr."

"Wait," Commissioner Doyle said. "You think her kidnapping is related to the vampyr?"

"What do you mean?" Aaron asked. "Tessa isn't like McKenna or Fiona. She's a married—"

"No one is insinuating anything about Tessa," Cyrus said, his tone direct and silencing. "We have a connection regarding the murders, and since the Far Darrig want her head, we have reason to believe they're working with or for the vampyr."

"Fine, let's say you're right. What do you plan to do?" Aaron nodded to Cyrus. "Do you think you're the first man to enter the Gray Wood with a sword? And you're just a young woman, one I hear used to be a mere barmaid."

Aaron's tired, angry gaze fell on Evelyn, but she didn't cower. She saw Aaron's doubt, and suddenly Evelyn was angry for ever directing such venom at herself. Her patience wore thin. She needed to protect Tessa if she was still alive and being a protector suddenly rose above everything else.

"I happen to be a witch," Evelyn said, setting her shoulders back.

The Byrne family stared, and Commissioner Doyle's mouth fell open.

Beside her, Cyrus straightened. He gave her a look that seemed to say, *Are you sure about this?*

No, in fact, she wasn't, but she was beginning to believe that maybe her doubt did her no favors. Doubting herself, doubting her sisters, doubting her flame. She needed to set those all aside at the moment.

If word got out that a witch with flame resided in Callum, so be it. If her sisters showed up, so be it. Even if Kade Drengr showed up on these shores, so be it. As long as she protected Tessa, this town, these people, nothing else mattered.

"It's all right, Cyrus," she finally said. She turned back to Aaron. "I'm a witch, and I have far more of a chance in that forest than any of you with rusty pitchforks."

Aaron's nostrils flared. "You think some spell or magic will protect you in the Gray Wood? Witches have tried and failed."

Evelyn's breath hitched, but not from Aaron's snide dismissal. A single word he'd used pushed the air from her lungs. *Spell.* Clarity snapped into place, all of it clicking piece by piece. She grabbed Cyrus's forearm for balance, unable to withstand the realization.

"It's for a spell," she whispered, but her words sounded like war drums.

Cyrus's eyes darted over her face, grabbing her shoulder to keep her steady. "What do you mean?"

Evelyn backed away, starting to pace in front of him, a sickening feeling setting into the pit of her stomach. "We may not know how the vampyrs were created, but every story included witches'—"

"Bones," Cyrus finished for her.

"Exactly," Evelyn said. "A witch's bones were involved, used somehow like items are used in a spell. We've been wondering why. *Why* the body parts? What if the body parts are for a spell, too?"

"A spell requires magic, and vampyrs don't have magic," Cyrus said with a frustrated shake of his head.

"But faeries do," Evelyn whispered.

Cyrus stilled, searching her face. His mouth opened and closed, and finally he cursed.

Faeries possessed a special, ancient power, wild and untamed. It wasn't magic gifted from the Sun Goddess or Moon God. It wasn't dark magic, but it wasn't good either. As Mrs. Byrne had said, it held trickery and mischief.

"If it is a spell, what is it for?" Cyrus asked.

Evelyn shook her head. "I don't know, but whatever it is, we can't let it happen. We have to save Tessa."

Cyrus nodded.

Evelyn gripped on to her role as protector. Her flame came to the forefront, her resolve hardening to a solid purpose. Save Tessa before sundown. Protect everyone in Callum.

And stop whatever plan for a spell the vampyr had.

Chapter Twenty-Nine

Kade

THERE'S SOMETHING I NEED to tell you. I'm no huntsman. I'm Kade Drengr.

Kade devised a speech in his mind, ran over the words as they traveled through the farmlands to the Gray Wood. The speech would emphasize the fact that Evelyn could trust him, she did not need to fear him, and that they had to call for aid.

With the threat of a looming spell at play, the time had come to tell the witches and werewolves of the west. Evelyn's own confession back at the Byrne farm had given him hope that he could come clean, too.

Bleu galloped over the waves of grass, and Kade counted to ten, readying to tell her. Then Evelyn turned. She sat ahead of him, relaxed into his chest, and tucked between his thighs as they traveled. Her gray eyes snared him. Trust shone in them, bright and dazzling, and *moons*, he couldn't fracture that trust.

"If you think for one moment I'm not going into that forest with you, Huntsman," she said with a shake of her head, "you're mad."

Kade couldn't help but smile because he *had* thought of that. Not because he thought she couldn't take care of herself or help, but because if he went in alone, he could possibly shift into his werewolf. Considering they were up against an entire tribe of faeries, his werewolf would come in handy.

Yet, he knew Evelyn would argue, and he hadn't wanted to lie and say he doubted her, which presented the perfect time to reveal who he was.

Please don't be angry, but I'm a werewolf.

She wouldn't run. She wanted to save Tessa. They needed her flame and his wolf in this fight—*stars above,* he knew it. If there was any time she might appreciate who he was, it would be now.

"Fine," Kade finally said, "I won't ask you to stay behind, but I will point out that you are a young woman like the other victims."

"Your point?" Evelyn asked, her tone flat and unamused. The wind wisped her hair in the wind, but she faced forward, leaving her expression a mystery.

"We have no idea why they're choosing these women. What's to say they won't take you instead of Tessa?"

Evelyn shivered, and she reached for her neck. She shook her head. "I knew when I took this job, there would be risks."

Kade sighed. He couldn't argue with that. Any fight against the vampyr held risks, and this was no different.

Bleu slowed without instruction, pausing on a hill overlooking a tangle of gray trees that stretched for miles.

Kade and Evelyn dismounted. Evelyn unfastened her cloak, as did Kade, and they readied themselves for the trek into the wood. Bleu eyed them with narrowed eyes—*you're both fools,* they seemed to say—and started grazing the pasture.

Kade would be wasting his energy if he continued to convince Evelyn to stay behind. She wanted to fight, to save Tessa, and he couldn't fault her. If they'd been back home at the Void, he'd never ask the Daughter of the Goddess to sit out a fight. This was no different. Instead, he gazed at her with admiration as she folded up her tunic's sleeves.

The leather bracelet she wore dangled from her wrist, a single stone at the clasp. He smelled the wolfsbane intercepting his wolf's senses, the herbs masking her magic.

"Why did you tell them you were a witch?"

Wind whirled over the hills, and Evelyn gazed at the horizon before she answered. The light of the sun hit her gray eyes, and they appeared like liquid silver.

"I've been hiding for some time now, burying away parts of me. And that part of me is desperate to solve these murders as if it were my responsibility . . . my duty, even. When Aaron Collins thought to doubt me . . ." She shook her head, holding back something.

Evelyn crossed her arms, met his stare and her gaze as strong as steel. "I have to do what I can to stop this vampyr, to protect those in Callum, but how can I if I keep parts of myself buried?"

She started down the hill, the light of the sun seeming to follow her as she shined bright and warm and proud.

Responsibility. Duty. Conviction.

Evelyn was so different from what he'd thought she would be like. The spoiled brat he'd imagined who'd run from her duty because she had no respect for it didn't stand before him. He heard her words, felt her conviction behind them.

I've been hiding for some time now, burying away parts of me.

He still wanted answers. Why would someone with such courage, such resolve as he'd seen, leave her people? Why would she abandon her duty?

Except a young woman's life loomed in the balance in the Gray Wood below. They didn't have the time, and Kade had already decided he would not reveal who he was. The longer he waited, the harder it was to be truthful.

He swore, though, that he'd shift during this fight if it ensured Evelyn's safety.

Chapter Thirty

Evelyn

Evelyn had never seen trees like the Gray Wood. Squat and twisted, the ash-colored branches extended no more than seven feet, creating a low canopy. Coniferous leaves sprouted at the top of the trees, leaving the trunks pale like crooked bones. In some sections, bark peeled to reveal a foxy-colored flesh underneath. At the center, like the Byrne family had promised, the trees formed into an opening path leading into the forest.

Yet, despite the Byrnes's description, Evelyn's magic did not sense darkness from the wood. In fact, compared to Castle Connacht and Lake Glenn, the Gray Wood was alive, buzzing with energy, but not full of dark magic. Evelyn's magic detected pain instead, as if something harmed it from within.

Cyrus joined her, his head almost brushing the trees' canopy. He crossed his arms and gritted his teeth, eyeing the Gray Wood with annoyance. "Why do I have a terrible feeling about this?"

"Probably because you're a beast of a man," Evelyn said.

Cyrus smirked. "I do love your compliments, Princess."

"Actually, come to think of it, it might be best if you sit this one out." Evelyn bit her lip, fighting a smile.

"Not happening." Cyrus stepped around her, peering down with a scowl.

"What? Don't like being left out?" She raised a brow, crossing her arms.

”Sa—”

Evelyn grabbed his tunic, pulled him close, and planted the briefest of kisses on his lips. Her assault happened so quickly, done and over with before Cyrus had the time to react. She left him standing there with his arms braced out, utterly stunned into silence.

“Let’s go, Huntsman.”

His eyes had softened, more honey than gold, yet he’d not relaxed. He followed, ducking under the branches with disdain. He appeared to be a giant compared to the Gray Wood, and Evelyn had to remind herself why they were here in the first place in order not to laugh.

“Has it ever occurred to you that we enter these places without so much as a plan?” Cyrus asked.

Evelyn stopped on the path, turning to face him with wide eyes. “I thought saving Tessa was our plan.”

Cyrus pinched the bridge of his nose and sighed. “Lead the way, Princess.”

As they continued their walk into the forest, Evelyn wondered why the Byrne family or anyone in Callum believed the Gray Wood to be dark. Her magic danced about, curious of the other magic around them. No darkness. Just life, old and restful with a hint of pain, like an aged bruise.

The branches of the trees warped farther down the deeper they went, causing both Evelyn and Cyrus to duck and bend. The roots and branches twisted and turned together into a tunnel, so thickly woven that the sunlight couldn’t breach the canopy and no dirt brushed beneath their boots.

Evelyn’s legs burned from crouching, her magic skirting out to sense any danger present in the forest, though there appeared to be none. She twisted her fingers and wrist, conjuring a small orb of flame that floated and lit the way.

She turned to Cyrus and found him scowling and brooding behind her. His head tilted and his eyes went wide. He grabbed the back of her tunic to stop her.

“Listen.”

Evelyn concentrated, her orb of fire stopping and hovering over them as a sound like the distant rumbling of thunder pounded toward them through the forest. Not thunder. Drums—a persistent, percussive rhythm. Up ahead, the end of the path glowed with wavering light like the glow and sway of fire. The low beat of the drums matched the flickering of the shadows.

It reminded Evelyn of the dark eerie drums that beat at Lake Glenn, surrounded by the dark magic of the kelpie.

Evelyn leaned in close, making sure her words were hushed and only for Cyrus. Except it left them a breath apart, her head so near his chest that she could smell a forest after rain—his scent. More than the drums, it made her heart beat faster, her palms sweater, her fingers itch to caress his face, his neck . . . everywhere. The drums beat louder. Goddess. She couldn't be feeling this way right now. She shook the bone-deep, body-altering attraction away and cleared her throat. "What if it's the Far Darrig?"

If they continued to head down the path, they risked exposing themselves to an entire tribe of faeries.

Cyrus seemed to have the same idea. He looked around the tunnel of trees, his eyes landing to the left of them. "Don't suppose we could try and go around."

The branches parted in a slight gap, large enough for Evelyn to fit through but not large enough to check what lay on the other side first. As for Cyrus making it through, they'd have an issue. Evelyn laid her hand on the branches, finding the foxy-colored bark and ash shavings to be soft and plush. Her magic met the other, and it tingled in greeting.

"I'll go through first, making sure it's clear, and try to open more of a gap for you," she said in a whisper. Without the sunlight above, they had no idea how much daylight remained, how much time they had left before potentially facing off with a vampyr.

Cyrus grabbed Evelyn's wrist, her breath catching and her magic humming at his touch.

"That's too risky," he said.

"Walking straight into whatever is down there is more of a risk."

Cyrus didn't let go of her wrist, his hold firm but gentle. Apprehension swam in his stare. Evelyn pulled her hand from his grasp, took hold of his hand, and gave it a squeeze.

"I know sometimes I doubt myself but . . . I trained all my life to protect," she said. "This is what I know, what I do. Trust me."

Now wasn't the time to tell him everything, and she didn't have the courage to even if they did, but maybe if he learned this small part of her, she could reassure him.

"Saige . . ." He opened and closed his mouth. Evelyn waited. Crickets and drums built in tempo together in the background. "I have never felt this way about anyone, let alone imagined ever feeling this way about someone," Cyrus said, tucking a stray strand of hair behind her ear and cupping her cheek. "I *believe in you*, Saige, and it frightens me."

Evelyn's heart dipped and swayed, while her physical body stayed rooted in the tunneled darkness of the Gray Wood.

"So it is not doubt you see and hear, but fear," Cyrus said.

Truth and sincerity rang in his tone.

She had no idea what to say, what to do, so she tilted up and kissed him again. It was slow at first, and then the same hunger from their first kiss awakened, burning like fire in her belly. Cyrus filled her with elation, his kiss igniting something fierce within her.

Evelyn pulled away, reminding herself why they were here. She stepped through the small gap. Cyrus's words gave her hope, and she appreciated his confession, but her own thoughts sent cold guilt through her. His view of her was skewed. He did not truly know her.

A part of her relished that he didn't see her as Daughter of the Goddess, that he'd established a perspective without her title, her fate, marring his opinion of her. Another part of her worried about how he'd react when she finally told him who she was. How would things change between them? Evelyn recentered on the task at hand, storing the elements of her complicated relationship for later.

Her orb of fire followed her through the gap, illuminating the crooked white trees scattered about. Soft moss and blackened dirt covered the forest floor. Slivers of sunlight peeked through, these trees taller and the canopy less tight. Relief coursed through Evelyn. They still had time.

Evelyn faced Cyrus again, taking in his golden features—tanned skin, golden brown hair, amber eyes. In the light of her floating fire orb, he appeared ethereal and bright. His jaw ticked and his eyes blazed, as if at any moment he planned to barge through the branches.

"There's nothing here," she said. "Relax."

Cyrus didn't falter, unconvinced. He tracked Evelyn's movements as she placed a hand on each side of the tunnel gap. She reminded herself that her flame, a warm fiery magic, was still energy. She channeled that simple essence, connecting it with the energy of the forest.

It answered, linking with her magic. She sensed that pain again as if the forest wanted her to, and Evelyn brushed a gentle caress of her magic, giving some to the Gray Wood in an exchange for the request to grow.

The branches answered, the trees creaking and cracking as they widened.

Chapter Thirty-One

Kade

STARS ABOVE, *RELAX*?

Nothing in Kade's entire being could relax.

His heart raced with each passing second he was separated from Evelyn. His werewolf pushed against his skin, demanding to be released, needing to be by her side again. Protecting. Guiding. Near her. He pushed through the moment the trees widened enough and released a silent sigh of relief.

Evelyn's magic buzzed through the air, and even though her bracelet blocked most of her witch, his wolf was on high alert, reaching out to be sure she was close.

Maybe it was the unease that made his hackles rise. Maybe it was the low-hanging, thick canopy crowding in on him. It was like being trapped in a box. Unleashing his werewolf form wouldn't do him any favors in a place like this. It left him unable to protect Evelyn, and that didn't sit right.

He rose to his full height but kept his attention alert and his stance ready for battle, assessing the area around them like a beast in the night.

"Let's keep moving," Kade said.

Evelyn didn't object as he took the lead this time and she followed, silent and stealthy. Kade hoped it was because she didn't doubt his trust, his belief in her.

He'd meant what he'd said. What she could become, what they could be together, what she meant to him. Believing in the possibilities scared the shit out of him.

Because he still didn't know why she left, and he wasn't convinced he could tell her who he really was. He had his duty to think of: bringing her home.

Ahead, the woods stopped to reveal a drop-off, and the light and smell of burning wood assaulted Kade's senses. They reached the edge. Anxiety pinched through his skin, his wolf almost vibrating to join them.

Evelyn came around, her eyes growing wide. He covered her mouth with his hand, stifling her audible gasp. Kade pulled her into his chest, Evelyn's heartbeat ricocheting through his ribcage as they assessed the situation below.

A young woman with the red hair of a Byrne knelt before a block of stone, blindfolded and hands bound behind her. Tessa. She shook, her shoulders shivering, her head twisting frantically. Kade's werewolf sight noticed the rusty stains left on the chopping block and growled.

Faeries didn't live in Sorin. They were the ancients of Torren that Kade had only read about in books, but he'd never seen a depiction of the Far Darrig before. They were short, appearing to reach the height of a human's knee. Large eyes, rosy cheeks, hair the color of snow. Each of them wore rags for clothes and matching red caps.

They gathered around the platform where Tessa knelt. Four surrounded her, one holding an ax three times its height. At the farthest end, a single Far Darrig stood alone. He wore a long, gaudy cape threaded with gold and a red cap larger than the others'.

Kade focused on holding Evelyn, the rise and fall of her chest against his forearm calming his werewolf, which was ready to fight the darkness.

"We need to do something," Evelyn said, pushing against his hold.

"Wait," he said. "We need to think about this."

"We do not have time!"

Moons, save him, Evelyn's will to protect others challenged his own when he wanted to protect her more. It was maddening.

He took a deep breath. "We are clearly outnumbered."

Evelyn gestured to his build. "You are literally the size of ten of them!"

Kade threw up his hands. "That has nothing to do with it. If we're overrun, not only will we die, so will Tessa."

Evelyn gritted her teeth, her nostrils flared, and her left brow furrowed more than the other like it always did when she became frustrated. Kade was frustrated, too. He wanted to fight the Far Darrig, but they needed to be smart.

"Whatever we do next," he said, "it has to ensure we save Tessa."

Evelyn looked down at the gathering, her gaze following the smoke of the bonfires billowing upward through holes created in the forest canopy.

An idea dawned on Kade. A sense of excitement zapped through him as the plan formed step by step. Hope filled him. It reminded Kade of his time back home, working with his team. He supposed working with Evelyn wasn't much different. He was fighting darkness with someone he trusted, someone he—

"Can you manipulate another flame, one that is not yours?" he asked.

Apprehension shifted through Evelyn's steely gray eyes. "Yes, if I am close enough. Why?"

Kade nodded. "I have an idea."

Chapter Thirty-Two

Evelyn

Nerves rattled Evelyn's ribcage. The intricacies of Cyrus's plans went against everything she believed in about fighting darkness, and it terrified Evelyn to her core. But he believed in her. Tessa needed her. And she wouldn't dare admit her doubts out loud.

Luckily, the music and cheering of the Far Darrig tribe drowned out the sounds she and Cyrus made descending from higher ground. Past the drop-off and over the edge, the Gray Wood sloped down a dramatic hill.

Mounds of moss, tree stumps, and protruding roots made their climb down easier. From one perch to the other, skirting between trees to hide from sight, they made it ten feet from the edge of the oblivious crowd.

Evelyn swore the Gray Wood's magic urged them on, rooting for them in the fight. One second, they'd deliberate their next move and then a stump or root would appear. Then a larger tree shuddered and curved to hide both Cyrus and Evelyn from the crowd of Far Darrig.

A large horn blew long and deep. Cyrus stood behind Evelyn, his chest up against her back as they listened, holding their breaths. The cheering died, the music stopped, and the crowd quieted.

"My good tribe," the caped Far Darrig said, its voice shrill and raspy. A shiver traveled down Evelyn's spine. Razor-sharp teeth gleamed from its wide smile. "Our time has come. For too long we've been underestimated. But now"—he gestured to Tessa—"a new time has come, a new age. With this sacrifice and gift, we will gain a powerful ally."

Evelyn and Cyrus made eye contact, seeming to agree the Far Darrig referred to the vampyr.

Fucking flames, why? Why did the vampyr need allies? Why did it need Tessa's head or any of the other body parts?

The questions gave Evelyn a headache, as did the Far Darrig's terrible voice. Cyrus tapped her shoulder. Four bonfires sat at each corner of the gathering, and he pointed to the farthest left.

Evelyn nodded. They slunk from their hiding place. Her magic wanted to unleash itself, to use a spell to mask them, but in order for Cyrus's plan to work, Evelyn needed to reserve her energy. Controlling fire she had not conjured could be a tricky thing. She'd done it before, during the times she'd tried to get her flame back, but the energy was not her own and often difficult to grasp.

Far Darrig stood and sat upon stools of seeping and steaming mushrooms. The mushroom caps shined the same red as the wool caps they all wore. The stench of rotten eggs assaulted Evelyn's senses, her magic detecting dark magic in proximity. No moss or trees grew near here, and Evelyn guessed the mushrooms were not native to the Gray Wood.

A crack and hiss sounded. Behind her, Cyrus muttered a curse.

Evelyn stopped and whirled. Cyrus had frozen, eyes wide, muscles tense and ready to strike. He'd stepped on a lone mushroom, and a foul green gunk oozed out of the destroyed fungus and steamed across his boot. Other mushrooms around them began to burst, popping and oozing. The stench of rotten eggs now overtook the smoke from the bonfires.

The sound and stench gained the attention of the Far Darrig. The leader's speech faded, and all eyes fell on them.

Silence ticked like the drums of doom.

The tribe erupted into high-pitched cries and commotion. Cyrus unsheathed his sword and knocked down the first wave of faeries with an unrelenting swing of his blade.

"Go! Get Tessa!" Cyrus cried. His blade and onslaught only riled the crowd more, drawing their attention to him and not her. Evelyn undid her bone staff from her low bun, extended it with her magic and used it to knock back any Far Darrig who ran in her way, using strength instead of magic.

Reserve energy. Get to Tessa.

Cyrus's battle cries and slicing blade resounded behind her as she reached the first bonfire. She sensed the warmth and heat radiating off it. Holding her hand to her side and flexing her fingers, she tried to connect with the energy. It fleeted and flared, difficult to grab hold of. Sweat trickled down her temple, her heart racing in her chest.

It was not her own flame, but it was not unfamiliar.

She could do this.

A surge of flame burst from the bonfire, twisting and turning like a living entity. Evelyn's magic grasped hold of the fiery energy, wielding it like her own. She cast the surge of flame toward the other bonfire, creating a line of flame between the two.

Some Far Darrig perished. Others ran from the wall of fire she created. She ran toward the center, and before they ran back into the Gray Wood and she lost grip on the bonfire's flame, she flicked her wrist from the far-right bonfire to the left one, another wall of fire rising between the two.

Above, the forest's canopy opened to allow more smoke to escape. The Far Darrig leader screamed, his twisted wooden crown falling lopsidedly.

Evelyn collapsed, exhaustion weighing her down.

You're nothing without your flame.

In her moment of weakness, the same resounding doubt ricocheted in her mind. But she didn't need her flame to do this. Not yet, at least. She needed to keep going, to fight. Looking up, she caught sight of Tessa kicking a Far Darrig trying to get hold of her.

Evelyn could not fail Tessa. Flashes of her parents' last moments helped her stand. She would not let darkness take someone else.

Rushing toward Tessa, Evelyn used her staff to beat down the Far Darrig. The blindfolded young woman struggled with her bonds. Evelyn grabbed her shoulder, but the woman screeched in fear.

"Tessa! It's all right," Evelyn said, ripping down the blindfold. "I'm here to help."

The young woman's eyes glistened with relief and tears. Evelyn sent a spark of flame around the rope on Tessa's wrists, snapping it loose.

"Take my hand!" Evelyn said.

Just as Tessa did so, something hit the back of Evelyn's knees. She fell, bringing Tessa down with her. The leader of the Far Darrig screeched, wild and feral, its needle-like nails scratching Evelyn's skin as he crawled up her body.

Wrinkled skin and black, pupil-less eyes met hers as tiny hands gripped her throat. Evelyn struggled to pry the Far Darrig off. For Cyrus's plan to work, she couldn't conjure her flame, and it went against her instinct, everything she believed to be true.

That she was nothing without it.

But the plan worked only if more Far Darrig focused on Cyrus—the one with the sword cutting them down. If she brought her flame forth at her fingertips, Cyrus wouldn't be the main distraction as she put their trap in place. She also needed to keep her energy, reserve her power for the last part of the plan.

The razor nails of the faerie cut at Evelyn's neck. Her vision went in and out, the sky above blurring and focusing. She fought and pushed the Far Darrig but failed, her staff out of reach. Fear chilled her blood. Her magic urged to be released. Images of her parents' death flashed through her mind. The comments of her cruel tutor rang in her ears.

Along with the last words of her late father.

Believe, Evelyn.

Evelyn didn't need her flame to win this fight. She could do it herself, not depend on it. She *had to*. Belief coursed through her, something new, a magic she'd never felt before.

She reached out farther, her fingers landing on her staff. She grabbed the familiar weathered bone and hit the leader of the Far Darrig, bludgeoning the faerie until its grip loosened.

Regaining her breath, she gripped its wrinkled neck, tossing it off her. The Far Darrig rolled, its red cap and wooden crown falling off. It screeched and bared its teeth. Evelyn stood, using the blunt end of her staff to hit the leader of the Far Darrig into the raging bonfire.

The Far Darrig tribe screamed at the loss of their leader. Tessa fought three, kicking them down and tossing them away. Evelyn rushed to her aid, knocking the few faeries back with her staff.

"Thank you," Tessa breathed, taking Evelyn's hand.

Evelyn nodded. "Stay close."

Behind them, Cyrus swung his blade, slaying and pushing the Far Darrig onto the platform. Evelyn set her sights on connecting the far-left bonfire to the next, but her boot crushed something.

The Far Darrig leader's crown.

Darkness screamed against Evelyn's magic. Picking up the crown, she sensed the wretchedness within it. The Gray Wood around them writhed in pain. The trees and crown were one and the same, ash-colored branches braided and looped together, patches of foxy underbark visible. Whatever darkness was weaved into this crown, it controlled the forest.

Evelyn had no time to wonder any further; she looped the crown through her arm to examine it later. She focused on the bonfire. Exhaustion gripped her like a storm, blood trickled from her wounds, and bruises pulsed around her neck.

Determination thrummed like magic in her blood, drowning out everything else. Evelyn lifted her hand, twisting her fingers to regain control over the flame of the third bonfire.

Like called to like. Her flame, the one tethered to her soul, was a part of her. Not separate. Not independent. Evelyn grasped what she knew, strong enough to manipulate it without using her power.

"Damn dandelions," Tessa breathed next to her.

The third bonfire burst upward, and Evelyn swayed the snaked flame to the next. A third wall of fire whooshed as they connected.

Far Darrig screeched behind them. The ones fighting Cyrus turned and rushed atop the platform toward Evelyn and Tessa.

As Evelyn and Cyrus had wanted.

Taking Tessa's hand, Evelyn rounded back, leading the horrid, tiny faeries around the platform until she reached the one side open and without fire.

Cyrus nodded, a glint of something in his eyes she could not decipher.

"Push them back!" he cried.

Together, the three of them fought and pushed the Far Darrig onto the platform. Evelyn used her staff, thrusting and hitting Far Darrig. Tessa held her own, kicking their attackers one after the other. Some of the tribe members threw poisonous mushrooms, but Cyrus charged, the sight of his blood-soaked blade sending horror through the faeries as they retreated.

Above, the Gray Wood shuddered. Roots slithered, trunks trembled, and branches swayed. The darkness in the crown, still looped through Evelyn's arm, cried out. She eyed the mysterious, enchanted object. Again, her magic slithered with caution, sensing it was a wretched and wrong thing.

Evelyn took hold of it and the Gray Wood sent out a desperate plea, its magic reaching out to her like a hand reaching for help. Most of the tribe had been pushed onto the platform, the plan almost complete.

It was time Evelyn ended this.

She'd needed her energy to complete the walls, and she needed the Far Darrig to fight Cyrus and not her, all so she could trap them, herd them like cattle into the walls of fire. She threw out her arms, reaching out to the two bonfires, the last ones standing unconnected. She shut her eyes, gritted her teeth. She didn't need her own flame.

Strong enough without it, she felt belief and will flourishing through her.

This time, the bonfires answered her pull like old friends answering a call to arms. They listened, bent to her will as if she'd made them her own, rallied them to her own magic and being.

With her last bit of energy, Evelyn pulled as if she held chains, yanking the powers from either side. The last wall of fire formed, dancing oranges, yellows, and reds flaring upward. Tangled, hot, and hungry, the flames trapped the faeries.

The Far Darrig cried out. Pain. Fear. Despair. Evelyn possessed not an ounce of mercy. They'd tried to kill her. Hurt Cyrus. Behead an innocent young woman. *No.* Whatever this was, whatever dark magic was at play, it was Evelyn's fight, her duty to protect those in Callum against it.

Evelyn tossed the crown into the fire, flames turning black and green, spitting and hissing until wisps of red and orange took over, engulfing the branches and destroying the dark magic.

The Gray Wood trembled again, and the canopy opened to the light of dusk.

Chapter Thirty-Three

Kade

The Far Darrig tribe's cries of agony and anger rang out like a warped chorus of victory.

Evelyn's gaze snagged Kade's. Sweat trickled down her brow and soaked her blouse, clinging to her heaving chest. Kade breathed deep, his attraction and respect for her growing, his stomach fluttering.

Stars above, Evelyn was willing to take risks to protect and save others.

The forest tremored, and an ancient magic, one that reminded Kade of the Vadon Mountains back home, awakened beneath their feet. Ash branches braved the walls of fire, grabbing and tossing the Far Darrig into the flames. Roots broke through the platform, dragging the faeries underground or constricting them with brutal strength.

Whatever power the crown had possessed, it had controlled the Gray Wood, and not only had Evelyn trapped the Far Darrig and saved Tessa, but she'd also set the forest free by destroying the darkness.

The Gray Wood fought back.

"Saige!" he cried, joining her side.

Tessa stood close behind, cuts bleeding through her dress but otherwise unharmed.

They had no time to discuss or celebrate. The cries of the Far Darrig rang out over the roaring fire. Trapped inside the Gray Wood, they came to a brutal end. Portions of the Gray Wood canopy snapped and fell.

Kade grabbed Evelyn's hand, and she grabbed Tessa's. Together, the three of them ran through the Gray Wood, following the sides of the tunnel for guidance. It widened, the roots receded, and the canopy opened. Dusk broke over the hills beyond, illuminating the exit in a peachy pink.

As they emerged, the sunlight shimmered over the Byrne farmland like a beacon of hope. Breathless, covered in ash, they all fell onto the plush green grass.

Kade held Evelyn's hand, blinking away the stinging in his eyes, never daring to let go. By the way she squeezed his fingers, she didn't seem keen to let go any time soon either. They locked eyes.

Kade sucked in a breath. *This*. Their hands joined. Working together. Was this even about duty anymore? Or was this about what he wanted? At first, he had thought them the same. Find Evelyn. Convince her they could work together. Bring her home. Except he had proven they worked well together, and he hadn't admitted the truth. He still wanted to fulfill his duty with her now more than ever, but the idea felt far away, distant. Different. *Not them*. Realization quickened his heart, had him squeezing Evelyn's hand tighter.

Behind them, the Gray Wood groaned and crashed.

Evelyn whirled to the trees, her mouth agape. A final touch, like *thank you*, tickled around them. It caressed Kade, and must've touched Evelyn too, because her eyes shut in contentment, a small smile stretching her rosy lips.

Stars above, he wanted to kiss her. To tell her how proud he was of her. And that he needed to—

"If the Gods aren't already talking about the two of you, they damn well are now," Tessa said, staring at them both with eyes wide and a brow raised. Her red hair was wild in the wind.

Wild and free.

Evelyn snatched her hand from Kade's, angling her body away as she reached out to help Tessa stand. His betrothed's heart hammered in her chest, as fast as a doe fleeing a wolf.

Horses galloped over the hills. The Byrne family rushed to Tessa. She broke from Evelyn and embraced Aaron, fierce and desperate, tears of happiness streaming down both their faces.

One by one they hugged Evelyn, shook Kade's hand, praised them and gave their thanks. Commissioner Doyle applauded their bravery, but all the while, Kade couldn't stop staring at Evelyn, conflicted now more than ever on what to do.

Tessa's words hadn't been far off the truth. The God and Goddess had spoken of him and Evelyn for some time now. But they weren't Evelyn Carson and Kade Drengr. Evelyn wasn't falling for him—not really. She was falling for Cyrus Skender, a huntsman. How would she react if she learned who he really was? She *had* run from her duty in Sorin, and yet he still didn't know why. What if she'd run from him, run from Kade, her betrothed?

He feared that was why. He feared how she'd react to the truth. He feared *losing* her. And Kade's fear paralyzed him.

Chapter Thirty-Four

Evelyn

Evelyn and Kade found lodging at an inn in Dinberry to rest for the night before heading back to Callum.

In a steaming tub, Evelyn scrubbed from her aching feet to her stiff thighs, over her rounded shoulders and down her sore biceps. Her sponge snagged on her wrist, and a snap echoed in the tub. Evelyn's magic fluttered around her, her enchanted bracelet floating near her breast in the sudsy water. For a breath, Evelyn stared at the severed leather until her heartbeat thudded rapidly like drums in her ears. She dropped the sponge and grabbed the bracelet, inspecting the frayed edge.

Scorched black, it must've caught fire and loosened without her knowing it in the Gray Wood. Bare, open, unhidden. *Fucking flames.* Evelyn hadn't been without it in over two years. A witch or werewolf could sense her now, her magic detectable.

Why did she feel light without it instead of skin-prickling anxiety? She hadn't moved from the tub, hadn't checked the lock on her door. She slumped back into the tub, stretching out her body in the warm water, stretching out the sense of being free and unafraid.

Hours later, clean, full, and with her wrist now bare for the time being, Evelyn fought sleep, restless and riled.

She and Kade had *saved* Tessa, successfully staying one step ahead of the vampyr's plan, whatever that was. Yet, Evelyn felt their victory was overshadowed by the ever-wavering doom of who she was.

Perhaps she did not need the bracelet now, did not need to hide and run. She'd defeated the Far Darrig without her flame, after all, with nothing but her own wits, courage, and magic. If she could do that, perhaps she would not fail to protect her people if she returned to them.

Ever since she'd been a little girl, she'd been defined by her Goddess-given gift. That was why she was "Daughter of the Goddess." With her birth order as a protector and with her flame, she'd defeat the darkness.

Alongside Kade Drengr.

A pang twisted in Evelyn's gut. A certain huntsman's amber eyes made her forget her betrothed, title, and even the prophecy. Cyrus had not left her side until they parted to sleep at the inn in Dinberry but had said little. So much had transpired between them. Evelyn ran her hand down her face, thinking of their moment in the tunnels of the Gray Wood, warmth spreading to her belly at Cyrus's admission of feelings.

She worried Cyrus would ask more questions or make conclusions on his own and learn who she actually was. What would he do? What would he think? Evelyn closed her eyes, frustrated. She wanted to tell him, to trust him enough to reveal her secrets, but her all-familiar doubt withered those desires. What if he judged her for failing her parents? For running from her people? Could she stomach dragging him into her mess?

There was also the fact she was betrothed to another. She'd never met Kade Drengr, but she still felt guilty betraying their betrothal. Yes, she'd had relationships during her time at university, *been* with men before, but nothing emotionally serious, knowing she was to marry another and bind her soul. For the last two years, she'd believed she'd never marry Kade. Yet now that she'd regained her flame, she could. But could she while her heart yearned for another?

The fireplace to the left crackled, the inn silent in the late hours. Eventually, Evelyn's reeling thoughts succumbed to sleep, her tired and healing body's need for rest winning out.

It did not last long.

Images of her parents' deaths, their lifeless bodies on the other side of the riverbank. Evelyn's flame buried within her. She tried to run to them but found herself in a dark room, locked inside. She begged to be let out. Banged on all the walls. Her hands were small, too small to be her own; they were the hands of a child. *Her* hands as a child. Nightmares and memories blended together. A certain rake-thin tutor appeared, standing over her.

"You are nothing without your flame, Evelyn Carson!"

She sprang awake, sweat sticking the bedsheets to her bare legs. She clutched her hand to her chest, a phantom pain pulsing through the bones of her fingers. The fireplace had gone out, smoke wisping from the ash. Evelyn took a deep breath, her throat raw from the screams of her night terrors.

A single beat passed, and the door to her room crashed to the floor. Cyrus stood on the other side, panting and searching her room with crazed eyes. He'd knocked her door straight off its hinges, bursting the dead bolt through the door frame.

"I heard you scream," he said as if in explanation.

Evelyn only stared, her heart thudding in her chest. How was she supposed to process this? He'd broken the door down to *get to her*. She rose from bed, eyeing Cyrus and the destroyed door.

"I . . . it was just a nightmare," she breathed.

Cyrus nodded, evident relief flashing over his features. "A nightmare."

No one in the Dinberry inn stirred, the hour so late that others must've been dead asleep, as the two of them continued to stare at the other. Evelyn couldn't bear what this all meant, couldn't shake the depths of his stare. The intensity left her feeling as if he saw every inch of her. The heat made her insides smolder, her only desire for Cyrus to touch her, to run his hands down her sides.

Only his touch would give her relief. From her fears, from this growing tension between them. If she gave in, she'd shatter and be free of this growing desire for him.

Stupid, irrational thoughts.

Evelyn shook her head, gripping the sheets of her bedding so tightly her knuckles went white. She stood, reaching for a shawl and searching for her boots.

"What are you doing?" Cyrus asked as he stepped into her room.

"I need a walk," she said.

"A walk?"

"To see the moon," Evelyn said, pulling on her boots. She imagined she looked ridiculous, boots with no pants, her sleeping tunic, a shawl for a cloak.

Cyrus took a step back, staring at her with wide eyes as if she were mad. "The moon?"

Evelyn barely caught his question as she laced her boots. "Yes, the moon." She tightened the final knot and stood. "The sight of it calms me."

"The sight of the moon calms you," Cyrus repeated, his eyes glowing in her dim room.

Evelyn nodded. "Would you care to join me?"

Cyrus swallowed. "Saige, it is frigid out, but there happens to be a view of the moon outside my room." He stared down at her door, the wood chippings scattered about. "I hope you don't find me too forward, but I don't believe you'll be sleeping here for the rest of the night."

Evelyn teetered. He'd invited her to his room. Goddess, she couldn't breathe, couldn't think. It was *just* to see the moon, she told herself. And to sleep. Maybe.

"I suppose that might be a better option," she whispered.

He nodded and led the way to his room at the end of the hall. Outside an open balcony, the moon sat in a starless sky, opal and bright. Evelyn's hammering heart slowed, her magic calming.

Her Goddess may be the sun, but the moon tempered her soul from time to time, like an element of peace tied to her very essence.

"You weren't lying," she whispered.

The view of it in Cyrus's room reminded her of her apartment in Sorin. She'd gazed at the moon then, too, when she needed time to think, to feel calm. Cyrus had also been right about the cold. The temperature had dropped, a threatening winter chill in the air, but to the right, a lively fire kept the small room toasty. A chair sat at the cusp of the room and open balcony, his bed untouched.

"You're up late." Evelyn turned away from the moon.

Cyrus still stood by the door, staring at her. The fire reflected in his eyes, gold against orange. He wore a pained expression as he gazed at her, then turned away.

"I couldn't sleep." His voice came out gruff, and Evelyn's toes curled on instinct.

He grabbed a bottle of whiskey and held it up to her. "Would you like a drink?"

Evelyn nodded, noticing the glass by his chair. Cyrus poured her one, handing it to her.

"It's not honeysuckle wine, but it should help with the nerves after your nightmare," he said.

"Thank you." The liquid reflected the orange hues of the fire and the pearly glint of the moon behind her.

Cyrus brought over another chair, setting it beside his. They sat, the tension between them as evident as the battling warmth of the fire inside and the cold outside.

"We did well today," Evelyn said, twirling the whiskey, amber and warm, like the eyes she felt staring at her.

"*You* did well," he said.

"It was your plan." Evelyn met his gaze.

"A plan you executed flawlessly."

Evelyn raised a brow and took her first sip of whiskey. It burned as it ran down her throat, a soothing warmth, like a fiery caramel. No, it was no honeysuckle wine, but she found she enjoyed it as much.

"Like I said, *we*. Your plan, my skills," she said. "You know, I think we make quite a team."

The words tumbled out of her, like a small part begged to admit it.

Cyrus gave a short laugh. "That we do."

She faced him, obsidian hair catching in the evening breeze and twirling around her face. "What's funny?"

"You wanted nothing to do with me in the beginning, didn't even want to work together." Cyrus sipped his whiskey, staring up at the moon.

Evelyn laughed. "And here we are."

"Here we are." Evelyn swore she heard a bit of sadness in his tone. He sighed. "I suppose you won't tell me what your nightmare was about."

There seemed no reason to withhold the information. "The night my parents died."

Cyrus looked away from the moon and searched her face. "I see. Do you get them often?"

Evelyn sipped her whiskey and shook her head. "No, only when I'm desperately tired."

He nodded, twirling his own glass.

They sat in silence for a little while, the moon above them, the fire crackling beside them, their whiskeys dwindling.

"What are you thinking?" Evelyn asked.

"About you," Cyrus said. "And all your secrets." He downed the rest of his whiskey.

"I'm sorry," she whispered.

Cyrus turned to her. "For what?"

She didn't meet his gaze. "For my secrets, for holding back."

Cyrus sighed, sitting up and leaning his forearms on his knees. "It doesn't bother me like it used to."

"Why not?"

Cyrus shrugged. "I suppose we all have secrets. What and when and how you tell me pieces of yourself is up to you." He rose. "More whiskey?"

Evelyn took the last swig of her drink. "Please."

Cyrus filled up their glasses, silence stretching between the two of them. Maybe it was the whiskey, maybe it was the mood, and maybe it was Cyrus, but Evelyn wanted to unleash her secrets. Even her magic danced at the thought, to be seen, to be heard.

Cyrus returned, handing her more whiskey.

As he sat back down, she started. "I think I've been keeping secrets—who I am, what I am—for so long that I forget what it's like to even talk about them."

She'd been Saige Ferriwether in Callum, but each place she'd had a different name. With each place, each name, she moved farther and farther away from the truth.

She wrestled with her doubt. What if his opinion of her changed? Yet, today's victory gave her a spark of bravery, and she continued.

"I can't tell you everything," she said, taking a large gulp of whiskey. It warmed her knees, bloomed in her chest. "Partially because I don't know where to start, partially to protect you, but mostly because I'm not fully ready."

"Saige—"

"I left my coven," she said. "I left my life behind two years ago."

Cyrus went still, as if he wasn't even breathing. He waited, silent, as if any movement or question might shatter the moment.

Evelyn shook her head. "Actually, 'leaving' puts it lightly. I ran away."

No judgment flickered in Cyrus's eyes, just interest. A smile played on his lips. "Let me guess. From a marriage? A man you had no interest in marrying?"

A snort left her as Evelyn shook her head, staring deep into the depths of her whiskey.

She'd always been willing to marry Kade Drengr, to unify their souls and fulfill the prophecy, until she'd lost her flame.

"I believe he's a good man." She took a swig of the whiskey, the truth burning. "But I'm certain I wasn't, well, what he needed. Let's put it that way."

"You're wrong." Cyrus rose in a rush, anger shaking his shoulders. "*Need* you? Any man would've been lucky to have you at his side."

Evelyn sank deeper into her seat, a blush scorching her cheeks. Cyrus's words settled over her, only increasing the heat of his intense stare. Goddess save her, she was a wretched person for appreciating his words. They were talking of her betrothal, a man she'd been promised to marry but left behind.

Desperate to move on, she shrugged. "It doesn't matter anymore. I'm fairly certain he wants nothing to do with me now and has most likely moved on."

The usually calm, collected huntsman appeared frazzled, unnerved. He ran his hand through his hair, then braced his hands on his hips. Cyrus's chest heaved as he calmed.

Maybe admitting she'd been betrothed had been a bad idea. Evelyn swallowed. "Cyrus—"

"If it wasn't him, then why did you leave? What did you run away from?"

What a question. Evelyn wavered, torn between telling Cyrus everything and stopping there. Yet, doubt trickled in. If he learned who she was, what she'd done, how she'd failed . . . She didn't want to risk losing whatever this was between them.

"An idea of me that does not exist."

Which was true. She didn't have her flame fully back. It came and went. Without the Goddess-given gift, she doubted her ability to fulfill the prophecy.

She faced the moon, admiring its white smooth surface, the silvery hue around its circumference. She felt light, relieved she'd told him something.

Cyrus sat back in his chair and considered her words, sipping his whiskey. He leaned over on the arm of his chair, reaching out to tuck a stray strand of hair behind her ear.

"I think if your coven could've seen you today, they'd be proud, no matter what they expected of you, whatever they wanted you to be." There was nothing but honesty in his tone.

Evelyn shut her eyes, appreciating his words. She had saved Tessa. She'd even released the Gray Wood from dark magic. They sat back in their chairs, enjoying the light of the moon, soaking in the warmth of the fire.

Soon, their whiskeys were empty, and Cyrus stood and cleared his throat.

"I stand by what I said earlier. Sleeping here might be best without a door in your room. I'll take the floor, and you can have the bed."

Evelyn rose in a rush. "Cyrus, that isn't necessary."

He shook his head, reaching for the small blanket at the end of the bed and the extra pillow. "I don't mind—"

"Cyrus."

"Saige, I will not put you in a position that may be uncomfortable or—"

"*Cyrus,*" Evelyn said, grabbing his hand, making him look at her. "I trust you."

Chapter Thirty-Five

Kade

Under the moon and stars, Kade had sipped the burning whiskey to bury his torment. To tell Evelyn. To not tell Evelyn. To have her. To lose her. Then pain had shot through his chest, so violently, so suddenly, it rocked him back like he'd been stabbed by a phantom dagger.

Evelyn.

The moon and stars had seemed to whisper her name.

Evelyn. Evelyn. Evelyn.

She was in danger. He'd felt it. Felt her. Felt her pain. And she needed him.

Kade had moved without thought, like he did so often when it came to her. Get to her. Protect her. They'd been the only thoughts consuming his mind as he'd abandoned his chair, run to her room, and barreled through the locked door, crashing it to the ground.

Mate. Mate. Mate.

Unlike other werewolves, Kade had never dreamed of having a mate. Since he was promised to a witch, it wasn't possible. Witches and werewolves couldn't be mates. Even with the prophecy, his union with Evelyn would be a forced bond by magic and rituals. Their destinies were intertwined by duty, not by souls and hearts.

Or so Kade had thought.

The moment he'd gazed into Evelyn's eyes as she stood there in a sleeping tunic, the silvery gray of her stare ensnared him with the soul-binding truth. The absolute, unwavering knowing of who and what Evelyn was.

His mate.

Now, he stood before her, harboring that truth, his gaze not daring to flicker to her bare wrist. Because Evelyn had taken off her enchanted bracelet, and with her magic unhidden, his wolf had finally met it, recognized it, cherished it.

And Evelyn's words rocked through Kade.

I trust you.

Her gray eyes searched his face, her cheeks flushed from the whiskey. He tuned into her heartbeat, her level breathing. *Moons*, she meant it. Kade could throw up from the guilt twisting his gut. She should not trust him. He was a liar, a fool, *manipulative*. He'd had ample opportunity to tell her who he was during their discussion as she'd told him secret after secret.

Stars above, the moon calmed her. He should've told her right then and there. *You're my mate.* She'd left because of her coven's idea of her, of what she needed to be. He should've told her he related, that he shared the pressures of being prophesied. He should've told her she was incredibly, most certainly, and devastatingly wrong. Her betrothed *needed* her, and she was his mate.

But all he said was, "All right."

He dropped the pillow and blanket back onto the bed.

"All right," Evelyn whispered.

She readied for bed, unlacing her boots. Kade shut the balcony door, put away the chairs, and fed the fire so it lasted through the night. He, too, readied for bed, removing his tunic but keeping on his britches. He found Evelyn already tucked under the bedsheets, her obsidian hair spilling over her pillow. Her shawl was slung over the chair to the left, her sleeping tunic still on.

He joined her under the sheets, and Kade had made the decision the moment she'd declared they'd sleep in the same bed. That was all they'd do. Nothing more. He kissed her forehead, putting his arm around her waist, pulling her back to his chest, and tucking her into him. Holding her close, keeping her safe.

Her body melted into his, and Kade tamed his wild wolf.

"Goodnight, Saige," he said.

"Goodnight, Cyrus." Evelyn's heartbeat slowed.

With the fire crackling in the night, the scent of cedar and vanilla surrounding him, and the moon shining outside, Kade drifted off to sleep.

When Kade woke, he felt the most rested he'd been in ages. He found his hand splayed over Evelyn's belly, her tunic's fabric a barrier between their skins, rising and falling as she breathed in her sleep. She slept on her back, one arm above her head. She appeared content, less like a witch troubled by her secrets.

Outside the glass balcony doors, the sun had replaced the moon. A few clouds drifted through the sky, birds singing to signal morning. The fire lingered, a few sparks still alive. Evelyn stirred, turning to face him. Her eyes opened, her sleepy, silvery gaze meeting his.

Kade stopped breathing. His heart lurched from the sight.

He wanted to marry her.

Not because she was Daughter of the Goddess or to fulfill their duty, but because he wanted to wake up to her every morning. He wanted this privilege, this simple, fantastical part to be in his everyday life.

Evelyn said nothing, tracing her fingers over his jaw through his beard. Her hand fell to his shoulder, trailing down the muscles of his arm. Her touch awakened his wolf, elicited desire in his blood.

Their eyes met, and Evelyn kissed him, that primal, magical hunger overtaking both of them. Kade pushed himself over her, and Evelyn ran her hands through his hair, pulling him closer. He traced his fingers down the side of her thigh as their lips molded together. Her skin was as soft as he'd imagined, the muscle as strong. Feeling her magic, his wolf entangled with her flame, putting him in thrall to want and need.

Kade's hand found the back of her knee. He hiked Evelyn's leg up and over his waist, like he'd dreamed of doing many times, and pressed himself to her core. Evelyn's eyes grew wide at the feel of his length, of the promise of what he planned to one day give her.

She whimpered and writhed underneath him, her lips swollen, hair a mess, eyes glazed with lust. Kade smelled need between her legs. He bent to continue their kiss, but Evelyn had different plans.

Stronger than he thought, his mate pushed him onto his back and straddled him with those maddening legs of hers. *Moons*, he felt the wetness of her core through the fabric of his britches. Her hair spilled over her shoulders; her nipples poked against her oversized tunic. The sight of her on top of him was almost his undoing.

Then Evelyn reached to pull her tunic off. Slowly. Lifting it, first to her hip bones, then inching it over the skin of her belly, then revealing the bottom crescents of her breasts.

Kade snapped back to reality.

He couldn't do this. If she undressed, *stars above* save him. The first time he lay with her, it would be as Kade Drengr, not Cyrus. Out of respect for both of them. He gripped Evelyn's forearms, halting her progress.

"Saige, wait!"

Her brows pinched in confusion, her cheeks flushed with embarrassment.

"What will you do after this?" he asked in a rush.

"I don't understand," Evelyn said, her words breathless and wary.

Kade pulled down her tunic and lowered his hold to her thighs, brushing her skin gently with his thumbs. "When we solve the murders, after we kill the vampyr, what will you do? Where will you go?"

He rose up, bringing his chest to Evelyn's, and wrapped his arms around her as he waited for her answer. Their hearts hammered against one another's.

She looked down, toying with a loose thread in her tunic. She shook her head. "I don't know."

Disappointment overcame Kade. Why had he hoped? There was still something she kept from him, secrets he wasn't privy to. And maybe he didn't deserve them because of his own secrets.

"But . . ." Evelyn paused, taking a deep, mighty breath, and meeting his eyes.

That foolish hope rushed through Kade again. He tightened his hold, encouraging her to keep going, wishing and waiting.

"Whatever I do, wherever I go, I want you to be a part of it," Evelyn whispered.

Kade's heart soared in his chest. His wolf howled. He took hold of her face in both his hands and kissed her, fierce and fast. "Saige, there's something—"

"Housekeeping!" someone said, banging on the door. "One of you better have an explanation for that broken door down the hall! We expect full payment to fix it!"

Evelyn laughed into her hands, and Kade's courage evaporated. She swung off him, taking his chin in her hand and giving him one more delicious, auspicious kiss.

"Let's get going, Huntsman," she said.

She gathered her boots and her shawl. Kade watched her and his chance of coming clean to her falling through his fingers, like trying to grasp the wind.

Chapter Thirty-Six

Evelyn

In the time they'd gone, Callum had transformed. An apricot-colored banner read "Autumn Festival" above the entrance of the town, and towers of gourds leaned on either side. Carved pumpkins sat on bales of hay. Wreaths of dried leaves hung from the doors, garlands of apples cascaded from balconies, and vendors, booths, and games packed the streets, filling the day with cheer and celebration.

Eventually, the townsfolk recognized Evelyn and Cyrus and stared as they passed, Bleu clopping alongside them.

Evelyn sighed. "I assume word is out."

The whisperings of the townsfolk reminded her too much of those back in Sorin, everyone seeing her as Daughter of the Goddess, judging her abilities, pointing out what she lacked. Callum knew her as Saige Ferriwether, the mysterious outsider, but now they knew her as a witch with flame, and she worried how long it would be before they drew their own conclusions as to who she was.

Cyrus threaded his fingers through hers, too quick for anyone to notice, but his discreet touch gave her comfort. "I hope you find it in you to forgive Commissioner Doyle. I imagine keeping the defeat of an entire faerie tribe in the Gray Wood a secret is near impossible."

Evelyn didn't blame Commissioner Doyle. She'd told Cyrus she wanted him to be a part of whatever she did next, and she wanted to control the news as it trickled back home to Sorin. She feared how word would travel across the sea to the Carson coven, the Drengr pack. Anxiety tickled through her, hiking her fear so it threatened to unravel her.

"Hey," Cyrus said, slowing Bleu as they reached the Runaway Radish. He turned to face her, using Bleu as a wall to shield their conversation. "Why do you look so worried?"

Evelyn shook her head.

"Don't tell me it's complicated," he said in a playful tone.

Evelyn bit her lip and then laughed. She supposed *everything* was complicated at this point. Her secrets, her relationship with Cyrus, the murder investigation. Yes, they'd saved a young woman's life. Yes, she'd been honest with him. And yes, they were very much, undeniably, falling for one another.

She eyed his jaw line, appreciated his broad shoulders. She remembered the feel of his taut chest underneath her fingers, that unimaginable promise he'd teased against her core. She felt hot thinking about their morning, and it was *not* due to the heat of her magic flaring inside with hunger.

Evelyn wanted him.

A gleeful screech gained their attention as a small but mighty force barreled into Evelyn. Aster wrapped her arms around her, holding her in the tightest of hugs.

"Oh! I've missed you!" she said.

Evelyn laughed, hugging her friend back. "I've missed you, too."

Aster's chin reached Evelyn's breastbone, and she rested it there as she looked up. "I hear you're a hero, and I better get the first account of what happened right from the source!"

Evelyn grimaced at the word hero, hating it. She'd hated it back in Sorin, too, and in Callum the word still filled her with dread and heaviness. She didn't deserve the word.

She pulled her friend's arms free. "I will, if you promise to never call me a hero again."

"But—"

"I brought something for you," Evelyn said. She rummaged in Bleu's side saddle, handing Aster the ruined crown of the Gray Wood—Tessa had given it to her as a reminder of what she'd done. It had not burnt entirely to ash but had hardened to black stone under her flame's heat, never to hold dark magic again.

Aster took it, her small hands trembling as realization dawned on her. "Damn dandelions, do you know what this is?"

Evelyn shrugged. "Not exactly, but it was dark and wrong, and I think the Gray Wood is free now."

"Thanks to you," Cyrus said, his brows raised, expectant, as if annoyed she'd left that part out.

"Wait," Aster said, eyes going wide. "You did this?" She raised the blackened crown, devoid of any power. "But this is the Dark Crown of the Gray Wood. It would take considerable power to destroy it. You'd have to . . ."

Aster paused, taking a step back as if seeing Evelyn for the first time. She was speechless, her eyes growing wide and then flicking to Cyrus and growing wider. Evelyn guessed her friend had figured out who she was, but thank the Goddess she was too speechless to say anything out loud.

Beside her, Cyrus stiffened, his hold on Bleu's reins tight. Had he recognized Aster's reaction as realization? Evelyn worried it wouldn't be long before he drew conclusions himself, but perhaps she wouldn't say anything until he brought it up.

If he brought it up.

"Can I keep this?" Aster asked, running her fingers over the calcified branches.

Evelyn nodded. "Of course. Kept it for you."

Aster smiled. "Thanks. My parents are in town for the festival. They won't believe it!" She eyed both Evelyn and Cyrus. "Damn dandelions, you're both attending the festival, right?"

"What does it celebrate?" Cyrus asked, more relaxed now and undoing Bleu's saddle.

Aster beamed. "The new harvest, the fall crop, the end of storm season! We enjoy the autumn splendors and kick off the harbor opening back up."

Dread doused Evelyn like a bucket of cold water. The end of storm season only reminded her that with ships and trade, news would spread to the shores of Sorin. It was inevitable.

"When does the storm season officially end?" Evelyn asked, her throat dry, her hands cold.

"One week!" Aster said. "It's great to see the docks full again, the market booming. Helps my shop, too."

When we solve the murders, after we kill the vampyr, what will you do? Where will you go?

Cyrus's question from that morning resounded in her mind. If she went back home, she could come clean to her sisters, admit the truth. She'd left because she'd lost her flame, but now it was back. How would they take it? Would they be angry? Disappointed?

What of her betrothed?

Evelyn looked to Cyrus, who was discussing with Aster the booth her parents had down the street.

She'd meant what she said that morning. Whatever she did next, she wanted him to be a part of it, and *felt* the need for him to be. Her growing feelings for Cyrus and her magic's draw to him filled her with equal parts fear and excitement. She knew the possibility of what this could be, but feared he'd reject her the moment he learned everything.

Cyrus's kind eyes met hers. *Fucking flames*, why had the Goddess done this to her?

"It sounds as though this is an event we cannot miss," he said.

"Miss the Autumn Festival?" Aster said, laying a hand over her heart. "I absolutely forbid it. You must attend!"

Evelyn laughed, despite her never-ending thoughts, the still-hovering doubt, and the ache in her stomach from worry. Aster's perspective on life had a way of overshadowing things, her light far too bright for any shade of darkness.

"What do you say, Princess?" Cyrus asked. "Will you accompany me to the festival?"

His polite tone, hopeful eyes. How could she say no?

"Huntsman, if I didn't know any better, I'd say you were asking me on a date," she said, unable to not smile.

Aster threw her hands in the air. "Well, of course he is! He's absolutely smitten with you."

Evelyn's mouth dropped open. "Aster!"

"What? The entire town knows it! He can't even take his eyes off you for a moment."

Mortified, Evelyn was close to dragging Aster from the scene, but Cyrus laughed, a pure and genuine sound spilling from him. "Aster is undoubtedly right in her assessment. Therefore, I will be devastated if you turn me down."

Aster gripped Evelyn's arm. "Did you hear? Devastated, Saige. Put the poor man out of his misery and say yes."

Evelyn smiled, warmth spreading in her belly.

"Yes," she said. "All right! I'll go!"

Cyrus's smile grew, and Aster clapped with glee.

Evelyn knew she had things to figure out. What about the prophecy? What about going home? Her duty and homeland nagged at her and yet . . . the thought of an evening with Cyrus filled her with so much hope, so much eagerness she refused to let her worries overshadow it all. She sighed them away. She'd figure out what to do next. How to tell Cyrus everything.

Later.

First, she'd give herself the evening, the festival, and time spent with the handsome huntsman she was falling for.

CHAPTER THIRTY-SEVEN

KADE

EVELYN HAD LEFT TO shower and dress for the festival and promised to meet Kade within the hour at the Runaway Radish. He led Bleu to the town's stables but sensed someone following close behind.

He turned, finding Aster, her narrowed eyes and pinched brow catching him off guard.

"Aster—"

"You have to tell her," she demanded. Her head of ringlet curls barely reached his waist, short yet so fierce.

Kade stilled, searching her face. She couldn't know. "What are you talking about?"

Aster crowded his space, taking step after step, peering up at him with rage in her russet-brown eyes.

"I know who you are, Kade Drengr."

Cold fear ran through him, his heart racing in his chest. "You're—"

"Wrong? Mistaken? I've known you were a werewolf since the first night I met you. Necklaces like the one you're wearing don't work around us witches tied to the earth."

"And you said nothing until now?"

"It wasn't my business. But now it is." She shoved the crown in front of him. "Only a witch destined to defeat the darkness would have the ability to save the Gray Wood. I've known Saige was a witch with a secret, and today I learned she is Daughter of the Goddess."

Kade shook his head, dread creeping over his shoulder. "What does that have to do with me?"

"Why else would a werewolf be in Callum?"

Bleu neighed as if agreeing with her, and Kade pinched the bridge of his nose and struggled to find the words. He'd fought at the Void. Battled vampyrs. Slew demons. Yet, Aster's opinion and demeanor frightened him. She clearly cared for Evelyn, but so did he.

"You think I haven't tried or wanted to?" he hissed, but luckily, they were in the stables with only the horses to hear them, and he could speak openly.

She pointed at him, and he took a step back. "If you truly wanted her to know, you would've done it by now!"

Kade shook his head, releasing Bleu's reins. The horse seemed happy to walk off and munch on the available hay in the corner.

"It is not that simple," he said to Aster.

Aster shook her head. "Of course it is—"

"What do you think she'll do once she learns who I am? Run like she has been for the last two years."

"You're right," Aster said. "She is falling for you, *Kade Drengr*. And running is exactly what she'll do if you don't come clean before it's too late. This time, she may run, and you'll never see her again."

Kade balked, the thought sending cold chills through him. He feared losing Evelyn more than anything else. He didn't think of the prophecy. Of her agreeing to go back with him. He thought only that he wanted to be with her, for her to stay with him.

"I don't know how," he breathed, running his hands through his hair.

Aster's russet eyes softened. "You really do care for her."

"Yes," he whispered. He shook his head. "I didn't know this would happen. I thought . . . *Moons*, I don't know what I thought. That I would find her and convince her to come back. I didn't know I'd fall—"

Kade stopped himself, but Aster's small smile and wide eyes showed she knew what he'd been about to say. She took his hand, giving it a gentle squeeze.

"I will not tell her, but I can't lie to her forever," she said. "You must tell her soon."

Aster left him alone in the stables. He heard the truth in her words and didn't fear she'd reveal his secrets.

Instead, he feared he'd lose Evelyn, no matter what he decided.

Chapter Thirty-Eight

Evelyn

A few hours later, Evelyn and Cyrus had consumed a helping of all the food and drink the Autumn Festival had to offer.

Cups of warm apple cider. Danishes filled with pumpkin cream. Fried potato slices sprayed with vinegar. She'd even dragged Cyrus to the docks to visit her favorite fish stand. He'd assumed they'd split one, and Evelyn laughed and ordered two. Afterward, Cyrus admitted he wouldn't have shared a single bite of his, which earned him a shove into some hay bales from Evelyn.

They'd laughed until tears sprang into their eyes. They bobbed for apples and shot arrows at scarecrows, which Cyrus happened to be wickedly good at. They even visited Aster's parents' booth, appreciating the samples of honeysuckle and mulled wine.

For a few hours, Evelyn forgot about the murders. All of Callum seemed to as well. She thought not once about her failures and her doubts, or of being Daughter of the Goddess.

She enjoyed her time with Cyrus, and that was all.

Full of joy and food, Evelyn rested her cheek on Cyrus's chest as they slow-danced in the Runaway Radish. Miss Patricia had moved all the chairs and tables, leaving the inn grand and open. A larger band than usual played a slow, steady song.

A magic fiercer than any witch's had taken over the atmosphere. Evelyn didn't want to admit that infamous, otherworldly feeling pounding in her chest, settling in her gut, and tingling her toes.

She glanced up at Cyrus. His eyes, bright like honey tonight, twinkled with happiness. Their hearts beat in tandem. Evelyn's magic soared, ready to burst.

In that moment, with their hearts in sync, swaying together to the violins of Callum, the weight of what this was dropped on Evelyn like a gentle rain.

Fated.

The thought of it was not her own, but a whisper, like the flicker of flame in the night. Her heart skipped, shock and delight coursing through her. Her magic spoke, telling her what she'd already suspected.

Fated.

"Are you all right?" Cyrus asked. They slowed. With his brows slightly furrowed, he searched her face, but nothing dulled the light still in them.

Evelyn was far from all right. Doubt riddled her. Cyrus was *human*. Why would she be prophesied to Kade, who could never be her fated as a werewolf, when her soul belonged to the kind huntsman before her?

If he learned the truth, would Cyrus understand? Or would he turn the other way?

No.

Evelyn couldn't doubt this. Wouldn't. Not him, not something as precious and rare, magical, as this.

Fated.

"Saige?" he said.

Goddess. She'd been staring, saying nothing. So she kissed him. Slowly. He didn't falter, meeting her lips, pulling her closer. They kissed in the Runaway Radish, sweet and lazy. Just like their day, their dancing.

They pulled apart, and Evelyn swore she was more drunk from Cyrus's kiss than elderflower wine. "Cyrus, I need to—"

"Huntsman!" Miss Patricia called from the bar. "I'm gonna need your assistance!"

The poor woman had a line out the door. Jolly festival-goers trickled in from outside, overtaking her inn. Evelyn had been so consumed by her emotions, she hadn't realized the late hour and the change in the festival.

Cyrus sighed and looked down at her. He tucked a stray strand of her stubborn hair behind her ear. "You were going to say something."

Evelyn shook her head. "It can wait. Go help Miss Patricia and earn your keep, Huntsman."

He smiled. *Goddess*, it was beautiful. "Stay," he murmured, kissing her cheek, down her jawline and neck. The hairs of his soft beard grazed her skin, raising goosebumps and sending shivers through her. "And I'll walk you home."

A promise hung in his husky voice and heated gaze. Evelyn's throat went dry. She wanted to agree, wanted to tell him on the walk home, wanted him to understand—

"*Saige*!"

Aster appeared, pushing through the patrons. She carried a basket of apples, her cheeks matching the red of the fruit, a leaf garland hanging around her neck. She eyed Evelyn and Cyrus, her lips pressed into a thin line.

"Saige, this is the part of the festival when things get a little rowdy," she said in a whisper. "I'm headed home and wondered if you'd walk with me."

"Go," Cyrus said, nodding to the exit.

Evelyn's heart soared, her feet planted in place. Her next words came out in a rush. "Will you come to my place for dinner tomorrow night?"

Cyrus blinked, swallowed, and searched her face. Evelyn almost took it back, ready to tell him to forget it when he said, "Yes."

Dancers began to bump into them as the band started a faster jig. Miss Patricia called Cyrus's name from the bar.

"Six o'clock?" she asked.

"Six," he said, planting one final, parting kiss on her lips before heading to the bar.

Aster pulled Evelyn through the crowd, and they held hands the whole way home. Evelyn twirled and gushed, and Aster laughed.

"He's my fated, Aster," she said to her new friend. "Goddess, I can't believe it. Cyrus Skender, a huntsman and human, is my fated."

The Autumn Festival continued on for the night. The joy, the warmth of it, stayed thick in the air, lulling Evelyn to sleep, readying herself for the evening to come when she'd tell Cyrus everything.

Chapter Thirty-Nine

Evelyn

Nerves as flighty as the butterflies in Aster's shop swirled in Evelyn's stomach.

She ran her hands through her hair a dozen times. Straightened the forks at the dinner table at least twenty times. Tasted the meal cooking away more than she wanted to admit.

With Cyrus as her fated, her union with Kade Drengr could never happen. She'd consider going back home and helping him defeat the darkness, but she wouldn't bind her soul to him.

Not when it sang for another.

First, Evelyn had a plan. More of a speech, really, ready for Cyrus. She'd tell him over dinner, over the food, after their first glass of wine. Goddess knew she needed the wine. Then, if the conversation went well, they'd figure out what to do next together.

She spun her freshly made bracelet around her wrist. She'd debated keeping herself unhidden, but with Cyrus being her fated, she wanted to control what would happen next and had made another, woven with the same herbs. Whispers of a witch with flame would soon reach the shores of Sorin, but at least by then she'd have somewhat of a plan.

A knock sounded at the door. Evelyn froze, her pent-up anxiety rooting her in place. Could she do this? Would he understand? Would he even want her after he learned the truth?

Evelyn took a deep breath, tucked her hair behind her ear, checked the table, reined in her magic, and took a step toward the door.

Cyrus stood in the evening drizzle, eyes as bright as the lanterns down the street, and not for a single second more did Evelyn doubt her decision.

"Huntsman," she said.

"Princess," he said.

She opened the door wide, and he entered her apartment. He held a bouquet of flowers, marigolds, and tuberoses. Red and orange contrasted with the trumpet-shaped white petals, and something itched at the back of Evelyn's mind, but her nerves didn't let her think much more on it.

"They're beautiful," she breathed. He handed them over along with a bottle of wine, sea-green glass covered in time and dust.

"What's this?" she asked, brushing away crusted dirt to read the label. She gasped as the date on the bottle became clear. "This is as old as I am!"

Cyrus laughed, but Evelyn noticed how he swallowed. His shoulders were taut, hands flexing.

"Miss Patricia gave it to me from her cellars. Told us to have a good time."

"Tell her I said thank you," Evelyn said, moving to the kitchen.

With her magic, his presence, the closed door, and the crackling fire, the apartment became hot and full of static. She fought the urge to tell him now, to unleash her secrets, to say it already. She needed to wait for the right moment.

I believe you're my fated.

"Are you hungry?" she said, conversation an attempt to distract herself.

She turned to Cyrus, who was looking even more rigid than before.

"I'm sorry?" He laughed and rubbed the nape of his neck. "I think . . . I think I'm a little nervous."

Goddess, him, too. For what?

Evelyn would tell him she was nervous as well if it wasn't so obvious already. Yet, to him, tonight should just be dinner, right? Had someone told him? Maybe hinted at it? Had Aster given him a heads up? No, her friend wouldn't do that. Maybe someone else in the town had, or maybe he'd figured it out himself, and he was here to end it. Perhaps he'd finally figured out who she really was and had come to confront her about it.

Evelyn's heart dropped, her doubts surfacing. She called forth her magic, using it to ease her nerves. It gave her comfort, dancing at Cyrus's proximity, reassuring her this was real.

"Here." Evelyn rummaged in one of her cabinets, finding an empty milk jug. "You can use it for the flowers." She stood on her tiptoes, planting a soft kiss on his cheek. "And thank you."

Cyrus's entire being softened, lightened, at her kiss, tension in his big, broad, muscular body seeming to ease.

The fire's flame dwindled, indicating the spell Evelyn had cast for a timer had finished. Diner was ready.

"I made shepherd's pie tonight," Evelyn said as Cyrus put the flowers in water. She worked on opening the wine.

"Sounds delicious."

The flowers appeared beside Evelyn. Cyrus lined his chest against her back, running his hands down her arms. Even through her thick, wool sweater, her skin burned from his touch. He leaned down, running his nose up the side of her neck, brushing a tease of a kiss halfway up, scorching her skin with his lips. He inhaled, really inhaled, and Evelyn couldn't help but giggle.

"Are you smelling me, Huntsman?" she asked.

Cyrus laughed, a deep rumble that vibrated through her ribcage. "And what if I was?"

Evelyn couldn't think straight, not with him so close, leaving kisses on her neck, her core heating.

"You smell like cedar, warm and exotic," he whispered. His voice shook. "There's an underlying sweetness." He wrapped his arms fully around Evelyn, planting a kiss on her temple. "Like vanilla."

"Is that what you imagine?" Evelyn asked.

Cyrus stiffened behind her, then turned her around. A smolder shone in his eyes, like browned sugar and butter. He stared, and she stared back. Not in a stand-off, but taking the other in. Tonight felt big. For both of them. Cyrus side-stepped, reading over the cookbook. He clasped her hand, soothing the back of it.

"Thank you for cooking," he said. "And to your earlier question, I am hungry."

"Then let's eat," Evelyn whispered, stepping out of Cyrus's orbit to breathe.

He brought the wine as Evelyn summoned the skillet with her magic. It lowered to the table, set with makeshift plates, silverware, and cups, all Evelyn had in her humble apartment. The pie smelled rich and beefy, steam rising off the golden potato crust.

Evelyn spooned them each a portion, lamb, peas, onions, and carrots swimming in red wine gravy on Cyrus's plate.

"Saige, this looks amazing," he said.

Evelyn smiled, her heart hammering. She couldn't muster words. Her pie tasted bland, and her nerves festered, tingling her fingers, and making her skin flush.

She had to get on with it. She *had to.*

"There's something I need to tell—"

"I need to be honest with you," Cyrus said at the same time.

Silence crashed down on them as their gazes locked.

Suddenly, the static in the room wasn't just nerves. It was something else entirely. The beat of the unknown. Whatever lay between them dangled in the air, hanging over their heads. The seconds ticked by as the fire crackled behind them, each waiting for the other to go first.

Evelyn set her fork and knife down, the metal on the wooden table booming in the silent apartment. She tried to smile, but Cyrus wouldn't look her in the eye. Her empty glass called to her, and she managed to say, "Wine?"

Relief flashed over Cyrus's face. "That's a fine idea."

They both scrambled, reaching for the bottle at the same time. Their hands collided, innocently, awkwardly. Cyrus's fingers brushed over Evelyn's wrist, barely a touch, barely anything at all, and yet—

Cyrus exploded.

He grunted—no, *growled*—as he erupted out of his seat. His chair fell back, clattering to the floor. As he clutched his wrist to his chest, smoke drifted up and through his clenched fingers. The unmistakable smell of his *burning* flesh had Evelyn's stomach roiling.

She glanced at her wrist, at the leather-cord bracelet sizzling from Cyrus's skin.

Then her mind reeled.

Her bracelet had wolfsbane, the only element there capable of harming another.

"You're a werewolf," Evelyn whispered, the words bitter and laden on her tongue.

"Evelyn, I can explain," Cyrus said.

Time stopped. Silence rang. Wretched, dreadful cold drenched her like an ice bucket being dumped over the fire in her veins.

Her name. He'd said her name.

"What . . ." Evelyn couldn't speak. "How do you . . . ?"

Cyrus blinked. Then his eyes went wide as if he realized his mistake, as if he'd been close to slipping up before, revealing whatever he'd been hiding, revealing that he knew who Evelyn was.

He had to be from the Drengr pack sent by her coven. *Goddess*, did her coven know she was here? Did her betrothed know?

The floodgates of worry, doubt, and questions opened in her mind. For so long, she'd evaded everyone. Months. Years. She'd run with her secrets, and the threat of them coming to light was too great. Fear ran through Evelyn's blood, icy hot. She rose from her seat and used her magic to flip the table over and put space between her and whoever this werewolf was.

Their dinner, plates, and glasses crashed and shattered. In the corner of the apartment, the fire roared to maximum capacity, surging with the flame in Evelyn's veins.

"Who are you? How do you know who I am?" she demanded. She didn't recognize her own voice, icy and soulless.

"Please," he said, taking a step closer to the table.

Evelyn ignited her fingertips with flame, ready to attack, ready to defend if she needed. Maxie meowed underneath the bed, hunkered down, and watched them both with wide yellow eyes. Evelyn frowned at her familiar. Who was this werewolf who had pretended to be a huntsman and entered their lives?

"*Who are you*?" she said again.

Cyrus sighed and swallowed, looking her dead in the eye. "Kade Drengr, third-born son and Son of the God."

Chapter Forty

Evelyn

The world tilted. Evelyn's magic, just as stunned as she was, retreated inward. The fireplace both whooshed out, and a new cold settled in her apartment.

Evelyn rocked back a step, her mouth going dry. "You're lying."

The words came out like a wish. Please. She wanted it to not be true.

Cyrus shook his head, pain and anguish in his eyes. "I'm not, I swear it."

Goddess, she heard the truth in his voice. Her betrothed stood in front of her.

I suppose we all have secrets.

Everything she'd built with the huntsman, Cyrus Skender, crumbled. Dread descended on Evelyn. All this time, it had been Kade. His questions about her secrets. Fishing for the reason she'd left her coven. Evelyn felt violated, manipulated. Why hadn't he told her? Their first kiss, their dance at the festival, the words of encouragement he'd given her. Evelyn felt sick. He'd always known—pretending to care, pretending she meant something to him. She'd been ready to believe him. To tell Cyrus everything. She wanted to scream, to cry, to unleash her flame.

"I can't sense your wolf. Why?" she whispered.

He hesitated, then reached to the collar of his tunic and pulled out a leather-braided cord, a knot tied at the center. Round and intricate. Evelyn had seen that type before. It buzzed, powerful. Not even her own magic would've detected it, not without seeing it first. She tunneled her magic toward it, investigating.

Evelyn gasped.

Her sister Blair's magic laced the necklace. Her very own bloodline. Evelyn took a defensive step back, reaching out to the wards of the apartment. Nothing. Yet, a cold realization crept over her, her heart racing in her chest. What if her sisters knew where she was? What if the Elders and Alphas did, too? According to Tovi, she was supposedly at the Void *with* Kade. Was that no longer the ruse? *Fucking flames*, had the vampyrs learned of her absence?

Evelyn stepped over the overturned table and rushed to Kade. "Who knows I'm here?" Her voice came out hoarse as she shouted, desperate for answers. "Did you tell anyone?"

Kade shook his head as his eyebrows drew together. "What?"

"Did you tell anyone I left? That I'm in Callum?" she shouted.

"It is only me." Kade raised his hands, concern flashing across his face. "No one knows I'm here."

Only me.

"Evelyn, can we just talk?" Kade whispered.

"Talk?" Evelyn scoffed, clutching her chest as if her heart might beat out of it. "Talk about how you've been lying about who you are?"

"You've been lying all this time, too, *Saige*," Kade said, using her fake name like a jab.

Evelyn balked. "That is different!" she hissed. "I was planning to tell you, to tell Cyrus. It's why I invited you over to dinner. To come clean, to be honest, and what a fool I would've been, as you already know exactly who I am," she said, her voice breaking.

Evelyn stared down at the dinner she'd made, the warm scent of meat pungent and overly rich. The spilled wine soaked into the floorboards. She'd been so nervous, so frantic. All for nothing.

Kade took a step toward her, proud and sure. He tilted his head, a gleam in his stare that put Evelyn on guard.

"You had me over for dinner just to be honest about your true name?" He raised a brow, surveying her, his implication as clear as Callum's sky after three days of spilling rain.

He knew.

Evelyn's heart dropped even further than it already had.

You're nothing.

Evelyn grimaced, the words reminding her that it didn't matter that he recognized they were—what did werewolves call it? Mates? Evelyn didn't have the energy to care. It was in his eyes; he knew what he was to her. She shut out the memory of his arms around her moments ago. His lips. His touch. Her heart felt torn and bruised as the worst truth of all settled over her. She could never have this, never have him.

Her fated.

Because he was Kade Drengr, the Son of the God, tied to the prophecy she could not fulfill without her flame. If they chose each other, they'd travel home. The Elders and Alphas would expect them to defeat the darkness, but how long would it take before others learned of her lost flame? Before the vampyrs learned of it? Evelyn, for the sake of her heart, would put the entire continent at risk. As a protector, Evelyn couldn't entertain the possibility of war, even if it meant not being with Kade.

He took one step and then another until he reached her, nose to nose. The flecks of gold in his eyes tugged at her aching heart. What she'd give to reach out, to rub the anguish from his tight brows, thread her fingers through his beard, and soothe his ticking jaw.

Evelyn kept her hands by her sides, nails digging into her palms.

"I'm sorry," Kade said, reaching out to run his thumb over her cheek. He caught a tear Evelyn hadn't even known she'd shed. She closed her eyes, shuddering at his touch. He cupped her cheek, making her look at him. "I should've told you, and I'm sorry."

His apologies made Evelyn weak, made her second guess. Evelyn shook her head, fighting the pull to lean into him, to forgive him, to be honest.

"You don't understand." Evelyn managed a small whisper.

Kade shook his head. "Perhaps. But I do understand there is something between us. My plan tonight was to come clean as well. To tell you who I am. The truth. And that I want to be with you—"

"We can't be together."

Kade stilled. "What?"

Evelyn swallowed, crossing her arms. "You have to understand—there are reasons I left."

"Ah, yes . . . why did you? Because I still haven't figured that out. From what I've seen, it's not because you don't care or aren't a protector."

Evelyn's heart skipped a beat. She blinked back tears. "Kade . . ."

His brows furrowed and his voice came out small and weak, unlike she'd ever heard it before. "Did you leave because of me?"

"No." Evelyn shook her head wildly. "No, I would've married you, had every intention of doing so."

"Then come back with me, Evelyn. Please." Kade stepped toward her and reached for her.

Evelyn retreated, backing away from his outstretched hands. "You don't understand. I lost my flame!"

Her admission came out in a blurt, shame showering over her as her most coveted secret came to light.

Kade's eyes widened. "No . . ." His brows scrunched together. "I've seen your flame. It's magnificent—"

"It left me, Kade." Tears made Evelyn's voice break. "The day my parents died, it went out and I couldn't reach it and . . . they died. I hadn't wielded it in two years until the day at Castle Connacht only weeks ago."

Kade's sun-kissed skin had gone pale. "But it's back."

"No." Evelyn paced, arms locked around her middle as the truths spilled from her. "It left me again at Lake Glenn. I barely got it back in time. Even now . . . I can't feel it, Kade. It's not a part of me like it used to be. Like the prophecy says."

"That's not possible."

Evelyn scoffed and stopped dead in her tracks. "What's not possible is my place in the prophecy. I can't fulfill it without my flame. You and I both know that."

Kade opened and closed his mouth. "We will figure it out. We can fix it."

Evelyn blinked away the tears stinging her eyes. He didn't say it outright, but she heard him loud and clear. Fix *her*. Fix her brokenness. Fix her lost flame, the power that differentiated her in the prophecy. She'd never told anyone for this very reason—seeing Kade's judgment, his doubt, was worse than what she'd ever imagined...

"You don't think I've tried?" Evelyn jabbed her finger into her chest. "For two years I've traveled to every temple, every library, everywhere, to figure out how to get it back. I don't possess this Goddess-given gift foretold in the prophecy. I am not . . . I am not what Sorin needs. I can't defeat the darkness."

In two long strides, Kade was in front of her. He cupped her face in his hands, making her look at him. Evelyn held back tears, looking upon the man—no, the *werewolf*. The one she'd kissed in the rain. Drank whiskey with under the moon. Fought against demons with in a ruined castle.

Kade leaned his forehead against hers. "We won't tell anyone. No one else has to know. Only you and me. Just us."

The word *us* sent goosebumps up Evelyn's arm, grasped at her magic, sounded like the chorus of peace and truth and joy all in one.

But as Kade's suggestion sank in, Evelyn's heart dropped. *No one else has to know.* He wanted to keep her lost flame a secret, and yes, Evelyn hadn't told anyone, harboring it alone. Except going back home, pretending she was worthy of the prophecy, was different. *Wrong.* Shame wrapped around her bruised heart like a wretched thorny vine. Lying to the people of Sorin would only mean that there was something wrong with her, that Kade saw something wrong with her. Her lost flame would become a dirty little secret they kept to themselves, all while still putting their homeland at risk.

She pulled away from his embrace. "There can't ever be an 'us.' What do you think will happen if vampyrs discover my flame leaves me?" Evelyn didn't wait for Kade to answer. "After all this time, why did you even come after me?"

Kade threw out his hands. "I left to find you, to convince you to come back home. I just . . . I wanted to show you we could work together, that we could fulfill the prophecy and fulfill our duties."

Convince. Duties. Prophecy. Evelyn's stomach churned with bile.

"Do you not hear yourself, Kade? You came to look for me because of the prophecy. I can't help you, not when my flame leaves me."

Kade ran his hands through his hair. "And what is your plan, exactly? To keep running from your duty like you did two years ago?"

Evelyn sucked in a breath. Kade's words were like a dagger stabbing between her ribs. She had run. He spoke the truth, but his tone—harsh and disapproving—demonstrated he didn't understand. Deep down, she was a protector, and she'd protect Kade and those she loved, even if it broke her heart to do so. She'd rather have scars on her heart than the threat of war.

She marched over to the door, easing it open and allowing the drizzle of rain to enter the tense apartment. "If that is what you think, then there's nothing more for us to say. Please leave."

Kade swallowed. "Evelyn . . ."

She opened the door wider. "Kade, please."

His boots beat against the wooden floorboards of her apartment, Evelyn's heart hammering in unison with them. Kade paused at the door, and Evelyn soaked in his stare. The kindness, the light. A mirrored pain.

And then he left.

The instant the door clicked shut, Evelyn's magic retreated so deeply inward, she collapsed to the wood floor. Pain throbbed in her chest. It was her heart, her soul breaking in two.

A sound, one fueled by physical and emotional pain, came out of Evelyn. A miserable, devastated cry. Her soul gaped open, empty, and vacant. Hot, wet tears streamed down her face. She sat against the door, the weight of loneliness and what she'd lost too heavy to bear.

Chapter Forty-One

Kade

Kade left in a rush, his wolf fighting against him as he sprinted down the stairs from Evelyn's apartment. She'd wanted him to leave, and Kade couldn't face the hurt in Evelyn's silvery eyes. The hurt he had caused.

Stars above, he wished he could take it all back. He wished he'd told her in the commissioner's office all those weeks ago. He hated that this was how she'd learned who he truly was.

His wolf whined, unsure why his mate had pushed him away, crying at the memory of her in pain. What if she ran? What if he never saw her again? Kade debated. He could go back. Talk it out. Apologize. But a glaring truth hit him in the gut. Evelyn had lost her flame.

All of his life, he'd trained as Son of the God. He'd been taught that his union with the Daughter of the Goddess would defeat the darkness. With the power of the Sun, Evelyn's flame, and the power of the Moon, his wolf, they'd become a team and fulfill the prophecy. Why did twenty-five years of belief suddenly feel wrong?

Pain shot through Kade with every step he took from Evelyn's apartment. His chest hurt. His eyes stung. His soul twisted. It had been a decade since pain of this nature had assaulted him, and like last time, his wolf took over. His bones creaked and muscles stretched, shredding his clothes as he shifted. He fully turned on the outskirts of town, sprinting off into the surrounding hills.

Thankfully, his beast did not turn back to its mate. He ran, wolf and man, around the village farms, through the old faerie ruins, to the edge of the sea cliffs. Hours passed, and Kade struggled to shift back. He grew anxious, flighty, but it was no use.

His pain drove him to the state of his beast, his wolf adamant on staying.

Like when his mother had died.

Yet, this pain felt more raw, more fearful. When his mother had died, it had been laced with grief. She was gone. The pain he carried now was heartache. Evelyn was out there, in her apartment, possibly readying to *leave*. The thoughts of what would come next were limitless. There was no end.

Kade stayed as a werewolf for three days. He patrolled the outskirts of Callum. The days crisp, nights chilly. The moon waned above, mocking him and his mistakes. The sun shined bright but offered no comfort or warmth.

At least, praise the moon, only one rain shower drenched his fur coat, his paws sticking with mud. He ate a few rabbits to keep his energy sustained. The village never left his sights, and he found the perfect vantage point to keep tabs on Evelyn's apartment. It felt wrong keeping an eye on her, monitoring for movement, but he never spotted her. Aster came and went from her shop. Kade grew restless. What if Evelyn had used her magic to cloak her departure? What if she was halfway to her next destination already?

Wretched screams on the wind tore him from sleep on the second night, but nothing moved about on the hills or in the streets of the town. It was Kade, the foggy night, and his thoughts.

The next morning, Maxie left the apartment from the bay window. The sight filled Kade with hope. Evelyn would never have left her familiar.

She'd stayed.

Kade's renewed hope, little as it was, allowed him to reconnect with his wolf, tapping into the need to shift back to his human form. He fully shifted in the alley behind the Runaway Radish, hidden behind stacks of barrels. Sweet whiskey and malty mead seeped into the air. He stood, stark as a newborn babe. He hadn't shifted in enchanted clothes, shredding his previous attire in his haste to leave Evelyn's apartment.

"Aye, lad." Miss Patricia stood at the back door, arms crossed, her expression sorrowful. "I have a pair of clothes for you on the step. I'll see you inside."

Thank the *stars above* only his head reached above the barrels, the rest of him out of sight. She went inside the inn, keeping the door open. A pair of his trousers and a tunic sat folded on the step like she'd promised. Checking the alleyway and street, Kade dashed to his clothes, changing quickly before anyone saw him. His dirt-covered feet slapped against the stone ground as he entered the Runaway Radish, the tavern empty aside from one guest eating lunch by the fire.

Miss Patricia stood in the kitchen, ladling a bowl of steaming soup. "Now sit."

Chapter Forty-Two

Evelyn

For three days, Evelyn stayed hidden in her apartment, riddled with emotion. Yet again, her flame had died, unreachable in the depths of her soul. She tried reaching for it, grasping it or stretching it like a tired muscle, but it never reached back out. Its absence only solidified her decision to reject Cyrus—no, *Kade*—no matter how violently her stomach twisted into knots.

On the first day, she'd gathered her things to leave. Packed her satchel, laced her best boots, even fastened her cloak to travel. She stood at her door, Maxie at her side, but couldn't.

And what is your plan, exactly? To keep running from your duty like you did two years ago?

Kade's hurtful words replayed in her mind, rooting her feet to the floorboards of her apartment. Yet, he was right. It *had* been her plan. But when she shut her eyes and remembered Kade's judgment, she couldn't do it. Leaving felt wrong, horrible. With a vampyr on the loose, Callum still needed her. The murders were a mystery she could not abandon. Not with the witches' creed involved, not with other lives at stake.

So she unpacked and cleaned, scrubbed and tidied her apartment instead, doing anything and everything to not think of Cyrus. Every time she did, she reminded herself he was actually Kade, then her thoughts would spiral out of control until she found something else to clean. The cycle never ended. Her immaculate apartment could not cure her heartache. Abandoning her duty, lying to her sisters, running from her coven . . . Evelyn had believed those had been the hardest things she'd ever done, but pushing Kade away, denying herself her fated, was the hardest.

In the days of being alone, Maxie side-eyeing her on occasion and choosing to sleep on the windowsill instead at the foot of her bed like she always did, a nagging part of Evelyn wondered if any of it had been real with Kade. Their shared moments. His kindness. Their kisses. Had it all been an act to convince her to come home? An unwavering part of her didn't doubt them. No. What was between them was real. He was her fated and she . . . Thinking about how real it had been, the promise of what could've been, only hurt worse.

When Evelyn finally found a few hours of sleep, she tossed and turned as screams on the wind jostled her awake. She blamed her turbulent thoughts for her weariness, but as sleep overtook her again, something bellowed in the hills, finding her deep in her dreams.

A knock sounded on the morning of the third day. Evelyn envisioned Kade outside her door, flanked by his pack and her coven. Her thoughts ran wild, anxiety rooting her in place. How could she face him so soon? What would she say to her sisters?

"Evelyn, it's me, Aster," her friend's sweet voice said. "We haven't seen you in three days. Is everything all right?"

We?

"It's Tovi, too, Evelyn," her best friend said. "Let us in."

Irrational thoughts still spiraled in Evelyn's mind. What if it was a trap? What if her sisters stood out there, pretending to be Aster and Tovi? No. She was being ridiculous and paranoid. There was no way they'd make it here during storm season. Evelyn moved to the door and eased it open. To her relief, she found both her friends on her doorstop, alone.

"Oh dear," Aster said, worry scrunching her brows.

"You look worse than I thought," Tovi muttered.

Evelyn glared.

Aster held up a large brown paper bag, breaking the tension. "We went by Finn's fish stand. Turns out their special was seafood chowder."

Food didn't interest Evelyn, but Aster's lively energy did. She opened the door wider, still prepared for Kade to jump out at any moment, but her betrothed, Son of the God, was nowhere to be seen. Why was she disappointed?

Evelyn's sour, desperate mood had soaked into every inch of the apartment. No fire glowed at the hearth and the sun, obscured by a thick layer of slate-colored clouds, cast a low light through the window. But Aster brightened the space and Tovi's smile washed away the creeping discomfort of being alone with her doubts for three days straight.

"What happened?" Tovi whispered.

Evelyn leaned against the kitchen counter, watching as Aster unboxed and laid out a Finn's fish stand feast. Without her realizing, tears had begun to stream down her face. Her words spilled from her as she explained what happened between her and Kade. She held nothing back—no detail, no emotion, no secret.

Tovi gathered her in her arms, holding her tight. "My word, Evelyn."

Aster's lips thinned, her eyes downcast. A blush bloomed on her cheeks, and her friend shoved a few fries into her mouth.

"Fucking flames, you knew," Evelyn whispered.

"Damn dandelions, Saige, I mean *Evelyn*," Aster said. "Please don't be too mad at me. I only learned who he was days ago, and he promised he'd tell you himself. I knew he was a werewolf the moment I met him. But I didn't know he was your werewolf—"

Evelyn peeled herself from Tovi's arms. "Aster—"

"I guess I shouldn't say that, should I? It's . . . I knew you were a witch but didn't realize you were Daughter of the Goddess until you set the Gray Wood free and—"

"Aster," Evelyn said. "I'm not mad."

Relief flashed over Aster's features. "You're not? Wait, why? How?"

Evelyn snorted. "For one, you're an impossible person to be mad at, but I've been lying and keeping secrets for so long. I'd be a bit of a hypocrite if I was mad at you for doing the same."

"So, you're not mad at Kade, then?" Tovi asked.

Evelyn shook her head. "I didn't say that."

Aster shook her head, curls bouncing. "No, you said—"

"You're an impossible person to be mad at, which makes it easier. He, on the other hand . . ." Evelyn gazed out her window, wondering where he'd gone.

"You care for him," Aster said.

"That's precisely the problem." Evelyn hugged her arms around her waist. "I can't care for him."

"But you said he's your fated," Tovi reminded Evelyn. "You *know* that's a huge deal. Prophecy aside, witches and werewolves can't be fated. Or mates. But you are? Somehow?"

Evelyn's soul twisted. "That doesn't matter." It felt wrong to say he wasn't her fated. She knew it like she knew breathing.

Aster rounded the counter. "How can you say that? Fateds are rare. Precious. It's a calling for your soul, self, and magic."

"I'm well aware," Evelyn said, her tone biting. She sighed, seeing hurt flash across Aster's russet eyes. "My flame is gone, Aster. It leaves me from time to time." She shook her head, feeling so tired of all of this.

Tovi took a tentative step toward her. "And you think he won't care for you because of that?"

"What? No. If vampyrs learn that I'm not what the prophecy entailed, there would be war. I put Kade at risk, too. How could I possibly be any sort of partner to him when I have no control over my magic, like some witchling still in training?"

"Your magic isn't the problem."

Evelyn and Tovi turned to face Aster. She'd crossed her arms over her magenta turtleneck, eyes narrowed into angry slits.

"What's that supposed to mean?" Evelyn asked.

Aster shook her head. "You have no faith, no belief. Did you forget that you're the one who destroyed the Crown of the Gray Wood? Evelyn, that crown was created with the darkest of magic. No witchling in training could defeat it."

"That . . ." Evelyn shook her head. "That's different."

Aster appeared ready to pounce, and Evelyn took a step back. "How? Last time I checked, your flame didn't decide to solve the murders. It didn't figure out the connection to the witches' creed. Damn dandelions, I even heard you barely used your magic at all to save Tessa from the Far Darrig. The problem is that you think you're nothing without your magic, but in fact your magic would be nothing without you."

Evelyn balked. Aster's words tried to sink in, but all her life, she'd been told she was nothing without her flame.

"Aster . . . has anyone ever told you that you're frightening when mad?" Tovi asked, jade eyes wide.

Evelyn held her palms up. "Aster—"

A bang on the door interrupted them.

"Miss Ferriwether, it's Commissioner Doyle."

They all shared a concerned look. His arrival usually meant bad news. Evelyn answered the door, and Commissioner Doyle entered with a sad expression. Evelyn noticed the dark circles under his eyes. He didn't appear to be getting much sleep. Worry wafted off him in waves.

"Don't tell us there's been another murder," Aster whispered.

"Aye, I'm sad to tell you there is," Commissioner Doyle said.

He explained about Sheila O'Brien. She'd gone for a ride on her family's horse, something she liked to do in the evening light over the hills of Callum. After she didn't come home, her family and friends found her body still atop her horse's back, sitting upright, hands on the reins, but without her head.

"She wasn't drained of blood," Commissioner Doyle said. "No blue skin or bite marks either, but the missing head fits."

Aster slumped into a chair at Evelyn's kitchen table, while Evelyn leaned against her counter, arms crossed. Tovi joined her, planting a hand on her shoulder.

Another murder, another young woman, and another missing body part.

Minds open.

Evelyn had been so consumed with learning Cyrus's true identity as Kade, she'd almost forgotten the murders. Frustration gripped her. She'd saved Tessa, but another young woman had taken her place. The killer she fought against was relentless. Whatever their plan was, Evelyn needed to figure it out soon, before a fourth and final murder happened.

"Where were her body and horse found?" Evelyn asked.

"Just over the hills of Callum, near the cliffs," Commissioner Doyle said.

They talked further of clues and findings until there was nothing else to discuss and the commissioner left. In a matter of minutes, Evelyn made her mind up. She put out a bowl of milk for Maxie, then grabbed her traveling cloak and boots.

"What are you doing?" Aster asked.

"Going to investigate where they found Sheila's body," she said.

"Wait, don't you think you should tell Kade about this first?" Tovi asked.

"No," Evelyn said, final and flat.

Aster rushed from her chair, following Evelyn as she gathered her clothes. "Evelyn, hold on, wait a second."

"I agree with Aster, let's let our emotions settle," Tovi said.

Evelyn whirled. "The vampyr or killer isn't waiting. They have a plan, which they seem fairly intent on following through with."

Goddess, Sheila's death felt like another failure. If she hadn't been so caught up in her feelings with a huntsman, who wasn't even a huntsman, she could've put a stop to this.

"Evelyn," Tovi said, biting her lip. "I think you need to consider telling Kade. He will want to help."

"I have no idea if he is still in Callum. There's no time," she said, knowing her words were bullshit.

She didn't want to face him. She wanted to solve this murder on her own, fix her shortcomings, prove her worth.

"Well, he's definitely still in Callum," Aster said, teetering foot to foot.

Evelyn pretended not to care, pulling on her boots and lacing them up. She made for the door, but Tovi stood in front of it, arms crossed.

"Don't be stubborn, Evelyn," she said. "I know you don't want to see him, but you can't go out there alone."

Evelyn seethed, gritting her teeth. She hated to admit it, but Tovi was right. They'd faced the rats at Castle Connacht, a kelpie at Lake Glenn, and the Far Darrig in the Gray Wood. Who knew what she might face at the cliffs. She may not have her flame, but she did have sense.

Evelyn sighed. If she went out there alone, it would be foolish. She'd put herself and perhaps others in danger, and Evelyn's protective instinct, her years of training, warred against the idea. She didn't fear facing the threats alone, even without her flame. What she feared was facing Kade and his judgment.

Yet did it really matter what he thought? Fated aside, Evelyn *was* a protector and she'd signed up to solve these murders. She'd even agreed to the job when she hadn't had her flame. She didn't fear the mission—she worried about facing the truth with him. But she couldn't let that get in the way of finding the vampyr, not when more young women were being killed. When it came to the prophecy or her duty, she didn't know what to do. Not about Kade. Not about her future. Not about her next destination—whether to keep running or return home.

As she shut her eyes and fisted her hands so tightly she felt her nails digging into her palms, Evelyn grasped the one thing she did know.

She protected others.

She would solve these murders, find the vampyr.

Even if she had to face Kade and manage her broken heart.

"Fine," she finally said. "Do you know where I can find him?"

Chapter Forty-Three

Kade

Kade sat, eating his soup as Miss Patricia scowled at him. She reminded him of his mother when she was cross and disappointed. Unlike those times, Kade was too tired to argue. He only thought of Evelyn, wondering what she'd do, wondering what *he* should do.

"How long have you known?" Kade asked.

"Saw you shift a few weeks ago in the early hours of the morning," Miss Patricia said, cutting a barmbrack loaf.

"But you never said anything," he whispered.

"Aye, not my business, so not much to say."

Miss Patricia put the soup in front of him and a plate of bread. He didn't feel like eating. His stomach twisted with guilt, frustration, and sadness. Not even Miss Patricia's cooking could conjure an appetite.

"But tell me," Miss Patricia said. "What's your real name?"

"Kade Drengr."

"Where ya from, Kade?"

"The Vadon Mountains, in Sorin."

Miss Patricia nodded, her flyaway curls shaking. "And why'd you come to Callum?"

Kade mused. "To find . . . to find Evelyn, my betrothed, and convince her to return with me. I think I should mention that you know Evelyn as Miss Saige Ferriwether."

A sad smile spread on Miss Patricia's rosy face. "Now, that wasn't so hard, was it?"

Kade blinked, eyeing the older woman. In minutes, she'd had him admitting who he was, and he hadn't realized it.

He crossed his arms, sending her a glare. "It's not that simple."

The older woman chuckled. "Oh, things are always simple until we make them complicated."

Kade ran a hand through his hair, leaning over the table and staring endlessly into the bowl of steaming soup. He blamed the murders. The never-ending clues. Evelyn for leaving her duty in the first place. The damn prophecy. But in the end, he had lied. He supposed *he'd* made this situation complicated by not telling Evelyn.

"Is that why you're still in Callum?" Miss Patricia asked.

"What do you mean?"

"Are you still in Callum to convince Evelyn to leave with you?"

Kade's heart skipped a beat, and he paused. That was what he'd told Evelyn, wasn't it? He'd spoken of duty, fumbling over his words, saying the things he *thought* he should say. The wrong things.

Had he stayed for duty? At first, yes, he'd stayed to solve the murders and kill the vampyr. Yet, along the way, he'd lost track of that mission. He'd still wanted to kill the vampyr, but he'd wanted to learn why Evelyn had left, then he'd wanted to build their relationship, and—

"I'm in Callum for Evelyn. Not because she's my betrothed, not to bring her home." Kade still wanted those things, just in a different way. "But because I care for her."

And that mattered more to Kade than his duty. *Evelyn* mattered more than his duty. He'd been so caught off guard by Evelyn's admission, he hadn't said the right things.

Miss Patricia sighed, pushing the bowl of soup and bread closer to him. "I think that's what you need to tell her."

"I don't know how. How do I know she wants to talk, to even see me?" Kade shook his head, Evelyn's tearful gray eyes flashing in his memory. He'd cared so much about his purpose, was so worried about losing the ability to fulfil the prophecy when he learned about her lost flame. He'd panicked. But Miss Patricia was right. He hadn't stayed for his duty or the prophecy. He'd stayed for Evelyn, and not for her magic, but her beautiful bravery. *Stars above*, what had he done?

Miss Patricia sighed. "Well, look at it this way—you won't make the same mistake twice. Saying nothing about that got you nowhere."

Kade considered Miss Patricia's words. It'd been three days since Evelyn learned the truth, and maybe it was time he tried again to tell her what he felt, that she was his mate, and that he was sorry. She might leave. He feared that more than anything. But in the end, he'd rather be rejected than let her go without trying.

"You're right," he said, standing.

"Oh, I know it," Miss Patricia said. "But I suggest you take a good long shower before seeing her. You smell like dog."

"Wolf," Kade corrected.

Miss Patricia rolled her eyes, then shivered as a wind from outside wrapped around them and the inn's door hit home in the frame with an unexpected bang. Commissioner Doyle approached, bringing the cold in with him, and he drummed his fingers down the bar as he walked.

"Good day to ya, Charles," Miss Patricia said.

"Thank ya, Nance," he said, spotting Kade at the end of the bar.

"Surprised to see you here after the latest news," he said, eyes grim.

Kade's instinct clicked into place. "What news?"

Commissioner Doyle shook his head. "The third murder."

"Another one?" Miss Patricia said.

"Aye, Sheila O'Brien. Found atop her horse without her head," Commissioner Doyle said. "A sight I won't soon forget. I thought Miss Ferriwether would've told ya by now, Cyrus."

Kade snapped to attention, standing from his chair. "Wait, Evelyn knows?"

"Evelyn?" Commissioner Doyle asked.

"Charles, there's a fair bit ya don't know about those two," Miss Patricia said.

He looked between Miss Patricia and Kade. "You're not a huntsman, are you?"

Kade shook his head.

The commissioner assessed his bare feet and dirty exterior. "I don't suppose I have you to blame for the giant wolf sightings from the last few days?"

Kade winced, scratching the back of his neck. "Apologies."

Commissioner Doyle took a large swig of mead and cursed. "I think I'll retire this year, Nance. Gettin' too old for these surprises. Don't catch 'em like I used to."

Miss Patricia patted the commissioner's arm. "You have a job here if you ever need it."

They stared at each other, and Kade saw affection between the two. He sighed, staring into his soup. Had he and Evelyn been that obvious? Had everyone else noticed what had been brewing between them?

The patter of rain broke the peace of the inn, the main door easing open and slamming shut. A familiar scent, one warm, sweet, and woody, caught Kade's attention. He glanced back as Aster and Tovi entered. Behind them, a cloaked figure waited in the rain. Kade didn't have to see their face. His wolf, his entire being, recognized her.

Evelyn.

He rose from his seat. Had she come to see him? Was she ready to talk? Relief and hope showered over him like the drizzling rain outside.

Aster and Tovi approached the bar. Tovi's lips were in a thin line while Aster's steps were hesitant. The two glanced back to the closed door where Evelyn stood, unseen and in the rain.

"Is she—"

"If you're about to ask if she's all right, you're being daft," Tovi whispered.

Kade flinched. The bite in Tovi's words froze his burst of relief and hope.

"She is here to see you, though," Aster said with a small smile. "To investigate where they found Sheila."

Kade nodded, his sights set on the door and his mate beyond it. His soul fought for his legs to move forward, but his heart thumped rapidly in his chest, the quickness pinning him in place.

Tovi laid a hand on his arm and swallowed. "Evelyn . . . She's not ready to talk, and I'm not getting in the middle of whatever it is you both need to figure out, but remember, Kade, she's a protector. That's all she's ever wanted. Perhaps if you don't push her, she'll tell you more herself."

She released her hold on his arm, and Kade used Evelyn's best friend's words to fuel his resolve and head toward the door.

Outside, Evelyn stood under the scant overhang of the Runaway Radish's doorframe. Rain droplets clung to her black hair, reflecting like beads of ink. Her hands were tightly clasped in front of her, knuckles white. When she finally looked up at him, his heart squeezed from the sadness threaded in her silvery-blue gaze.

"Did Commissioner Doyle tell you about Sheila?" she asked.

"He did."

Evelyn nodded. The silence stretched before them. The things left unsaid. The way they parted. The secrets they still held. It grated against Kade's skin, scratched against his heart. He wanted to shatter the silence. He wanted to admit everything.

"Evelyn—"

"We need to investigate where they found Sheila's body. The killer, vampyr or not, only needs one more body part for the spell. We need to stop them before they kill again."

We.

Kade tried to not read too much into Evelyn's words, but his hope flared back to life. She was determined to solve the murder and find the killer. With him. She planned to stay, and she wouldn't cut him out of the investigation.

Again, Kade struggled to silence the words of his heart. He wanted to come clean, to apologize, to make amends. Yet, he hesitated. Evelyn stood before him, ready to investigate the murder site. Was she telling him something he shouldn't dismiss?

Don't push her.

Tovi's words from earlier rang in the back of Kade's mind. No. He'd say nothing about them. He'd follow her lead, help with the murder investigation, and hold on to the hope that he hadn't messed up so greatly, they couldn't work this out.

Kade nodded. "Let's head to the cliffs."

Evelyn shut her eyes and exhaled. When she met his stare again, determination gleamed. "There's something else."

Dread dropped in Kade's gut, but he didn't let it show as he said, "Go on."

"If we're to work together on this, head to the cliffs, and face the possibility of a vampyr, you have the right to know my flame is gone. I've tried to reach it, tried to get back, but I . . . can't." Evelyn exhaled a shaking breath.

Kade relaxed, his heart soaring in his chest. Like Tovi advised, he wouldn't push Evelyn, but he wanted—no, *needed*—her to know, she was more than her flame.

"All right."

Evelyn stood there, still as stone. After a few moments, her eyes widened, and her brows drew together. "Wait, that's it? All right?"

Kade shrugged. "Has it not occurred to you that I haven't used my wolf once during these last few weeks?"

"That's—"

"Different?" Kade shook his head. "We're more than our duty, Evelyn. More than our powers and magic. Like I haven't needed my wolf the last few weeks, you don't need your flame to be my partner solving these murders."

Evelyn's silvery eyes searched his face. She opened and closed her mouth, and by the increase in her left brow's furrow, the wheels were turning in that magnificent mind of hers.

Kade knew a few words wouldn't do, and like Tovi had said, Evelyn wasn't ready to talk, and he had no intention of pushing her. Instead, he could show her.

"We should head to the cliffs soon, so we'll get there before sundown."

Evelyn nodded, and with that, they set off to their next investigation site.

Chapter Forty-Four

Evelyn

THE MIST TURNED INTO an insufferable drizzle, escaping past Evelyn's hood and frizzing her hair. Her cloak became sodden with rain. Soon, the moisture bled into her trousers and blouse. Sticky and frigid, Evelyn's hands grew stiff, and her cheeks burned. Kade hadn't bothered with his hood, his hair and beard shining with droplets, wet clothes sticking to his broad frame, and Evelyn kept catching herself staring. Somehow he'd become more rugged, more werewolf, and she couldn't look away.

You don't need your flame to be my partner solving these murders.

She blinked away his earlier comment, not daring to hope what more he meant. Yes, they were solving the murders together, but what else had he implied? The prophecy, their duty, returning home. Did he still think that possible without her flame? Doubt swam around like a frenzy of parasitic worms deep in her belly, her years of training at war with the idea.

Ahead, the path narrowed and snaked north. A wall of fog hovered over the grass until the grass disappeared, giving way to a sheer cliff and the never-ending ocean of fog that rolled beyond it. Unseen, waves crashed against rock and gulls squawked.

Nothing appeared until the dirt path became littered with rocks and pebbles, and the salt of the sea hung heavier in the air. The fog parted over the remnants of a cottage, its roof caved in, the stone walls overtaken by ivy. Trees and underbrush grew from within it, as if the cottage had exploded with vegetation.

Kade dropped to his haunches, laying a hand on the ground and threading his other through the grass.

"What are you doing?"

Kade glanced up at her and smirked. "Tracking magic."

She studied him as he closed his eyes. His forehead smoothed out as he inhaled, and his shoulders relaxed. The wind whipped by, ominous and wild. Evelyn's chest ached as Kade used his werewolf abilities. Something about it, something about him, made her so curious. What else did she not know about him? What else could she learn?

Kade's eyes flashed open, and his jaw ticked. "Sheila was here." He stood to his full height. "There's also . . ." His nostrils flared as he sniffed the air.

Evelyn let out a giggle, then clamped a hand over her mouth.

He narrowed his eyes, but mirth lay in his stare. "What?"

"I'm sorry." She shook her head. "I just . . . you're sniffing the air."

"I am a werewolf. We have heightened senses."

"Trust me." Evelyn held up her hands. "I haven't forgotten. What are you sensing?"

Kade's eyes flashed with something she couldn't read, and then he said, "Licorice. I also smelled it at Lake Glenn."

"Licorice? Like the candy?"

Kade nodded. "I think it belongs to someone."

"Is that what vampyrs smell like to you?" Evelyn approached closer to the cottage.

"No, vampyrs smell sharp, almost like a lemon."

More curiosity, more interest, sparked in Evelyn, but she dismissed it. "I'm going to check the other side."

She didn't wait for Kade's response, circling the perimeter of the cottage. She found no signs pointing to Sheila's murder. No blood. No signs of a fight. On the other side, the fog thickened, becoming as dark as smoke, the wisps and tendrils moving like a crowd of ghosts.

Evelyn sent out her magic. An oozy energy, like tar, slid against her. She'd never felt anything like it before and her instinct told her something was off. Her heart hammered away like it would after having a nightmare.

She assessed the cottage further as she neared the other side. Had this been another meeting place between a victim and the vampyr? Between the caved-in roof and overgrown vegetation, Evelyn doubted it, but she also questioned if a vampyr had killed Sheila. Commissioner Doyle said her body was missing a head, but she hadn't been blue or held a bite mark.

Evelyn wondered if Kade, with his werewolf senses and tracking magic, had discovered anything new, but when she rounded the corner, he was gone.

"Kade?"

As Evelyn searched for him in the thickening fog, the air dropped a rapid ten degrees. A gust of briny wind ripped Evelyn's hood back. It howled, sending shivers up her spine. Sensing the change in atmosphere, she readied her magic.

A raspy, throaty laugh echoed behind her. "Oh, hello, Evelyn Carson. I've waited so long to meet you."

Chapter Forty-Five

Evelyn

Evelyn whirled. Her cloak billowed, and fog moved in its wake, unveiling a woman with eerie features standing in the thicket of trees growing from the doorway.

Only her face was visible between two vine-like branches. The woman twitched and tilted her head, blinking in a slow, animalistic way. Evelyn dared to think she'd once been beautiful, but her white, gaunt skin appeared sickly. Inky black hair, long and tangled, shined with grease. Beady red eyes, as if the woman rarely saw the light of day, assessed Evelyn with a predatorial interest.

Was she another faerie working with the vampyr? More importantly, where in the *fucking flames* was Kade?

"Daughter of the Goddess at last," the woman said. Her voice echoed across the cliffs, as if she shouted from elsewhere.

Evelyn took a cautious step back and reached for her bone staff pinned through her bun—

The woman tsked. "I can hear your heart, you frightened witch. I can also taste your magic, sweet and hot," she said. "But you need not be frightened. I don't wish to hurt you."

Evelyn found no comfort in the haunting woman's words, and Kade's sudden disappearance unnerved her. Was he all right? She stepped back again, hoping to find the narrow path, but her back hit a solid wall. She swiveled around, the fog dense and dark. She tried to step out of the perimeter of the cottage but again hit a wall. *Goddess*, had the fog been enchanted? Who had done it?

Evelyn took a deep breath, stifling her fear. She was alone and trapped, but she couldn't allow whomever she faced to sense her doubt. She set her shoulders back and asked, "Who are you?"

The woman's head twitched again, her lips spreading into a frightening smile. Pointed teeth, thin as needles, gleamed. "I'm the White Lady."

Evelyn remembered McKenna's journal, along with Aster's translation. *This word here means "white." She writes it often, followed by another word I can't translate.* The missing word was "lady."

"You knew McKenna," Evelyn said. "You taught her magic."

The White Lady sneered. "Oh, McKenna McCarthy, what a troublesome young girl, but with such gorgeous eyes."

Her smile sickened Evelyn. How had this woman managed to teach McKenna magic? Had she been the one to kill her? Signs had pointed to a vampyr as the killer, but there had always been a different edge of darkness surrounding the murders, one Evelyn and Kade had yet to figure out. The witches' creed and missing body parts had stumped them because it wasn't usual vampyr behavior. What if—

Evelyn assessed the cottage, searching the details more closely. She'd been so busy looking for clues regarding Sheila's murder, she'd missed the signs. The markings above the door were scorched words of the witches' creed, and the plants growing around the front weren't just any weeds, but nettles.

"You're a witch," Evelyn said.

The cottage walls shook, rustling the trees inside. The White Lady hissed, baring her needle-like teeth, her eyes blazing with anger.

"You claim to not know my story, Daughter of the Goddess." The White Lady's voice boomed.

Evelyn shook her head and took a brave step forward, tired of the woman's antics.

"I'm not here for your story. I'm here to learn more about the deaths of McKenna, Fiona, and Sheila."

A sound, much like a wheeze and laugh, shrieked from the woman. "Are you saying you actually care about what happened to them? You're a liar. Like all witches. From what I hear, you're a spoiled and selfish runaway witch who abandoned her people. I know what you are, Evelyn Carson."

The White Lady's words stung, no matter how much Evelyn tried to ignore the insane woman's taunts. It was an echo of the beliefs she harbored about herself, rooted deep within her bruised heart.

The cottage shuddered again like something large pushed to be unleashed. The stillness of the cliffs resonated in the thickness of the fog as if the world had transformed to a darker, more sinister dimension far from the cheer and charm of Callum.

Beady red eyes raked over her. "You fail and hurt the ones around you, don't you?"

Evelyn said nothing, a retort laden on her tongue, but images of her parents' mutilated bodies haunted her. Kade's judgement when he'd learned she'd lost her flame yanked at her heart. The hope radiating from her sisters before she ran away sank her stomach. All the deaths of the young women in Callum made her feel worthless.

You're nothing without your flame.

Evelyn was empty, unable to meet anyone's expectations. She couldn't be the daughter her parents believed her to be. She'd never be the partner Kade needed. Or the Daughter of the Goddess her sisters hoped for.

The White Lady's smile only widened at Evelyn's internal turmoil. "After all these years, witches haven't changed, have they? I wanted to save our people, set us free, and defeat the humans long ago, but my people, *your* people, condemned me. Tried to destroy me."

Which meant The White Lady was a witch. Evelyn thought of McKenna's journal, the woman's sickly appearance, and the wrongness in the air. Witches would only condemn another witch if—

Why hadn't Evelyn thought of it before? The missing body parts. The possibility of a spell. Vampyrs didn't have magic, and they'd assumed one had banded together with the faeries to make use of it. She'd never considered those who *did* have magic.

"You found dark magic," Evelyn whispered.

The woman tsked. "You catch on quick, Daughter of the Goddess. But yes, my coven called it dark magic, too. You know what I call it? *Freedom*. I could've defeated the humans, even the vampyrs, if my coven hadn't banished me."

"You're lying."

The White Lady blinked, slow and unnatural, her head tilting to assess Evelyn. "Why would I lie?" She spoke with deadly calm.

Evelyn channeled her magic just to the surface, and it hovered at the ready. Even if her flame did not arise, she at least needed her innate magic. "You want me to doubt my people."

"But you already doubt your people, or you would've told them your secret. You ran from a prophecy that declared you their savior against the so-called 'darkness.' I think you doubt quite well enough without me needing to spew lies. What I want is to enlighten you. *Show* you the possibilities, and that your doubt in your people is not misplaced."

Evelyn gritted her teeth, trying to shake off the constant reminders of her failures. She had stayed in Callum to solve these murders, to fight against the darkness again. The White Lady only meant to rile her, but Evelyn had so many questions. How did the White Lady know so much about her? Was she also working with the vampyr? Unless all this time she and Kade had been completely and utterly wrong, and there wasn't even a vampyr involved.

But what about the scáth they fought outside the printshop?

The dark witch wavered in the cottage. "I can see you have questions. Come with me, Daughter of the Goddess. You and I aren't much different, you know? Revered by our people. Misunderstood. Powerful. Destined for greatness. I can show you my ways and show you how magnificent you can be."

Disgust rolled through Evelyn. "You're mad if you think I'll come with you. You've been killing the young women, haven't you? You're a monster." Evelyn bit out the last comment.

The White Lady's grin widened, and her red eyes raged with delight. "Willing or not, delivering you to the darkness will be my biggest accomplishment."

The scream the White Lady unleashed reminded Evelyn of the low howl she'd heard on the wind all these weeks. The night before they found Fiona's body. In the market the day Tessa had been kidnapped. Last night as she lay in bed, hollow and lost, mere hours before she'd learn of Sheila's headless body.

The ballad of death in the air.

The trees shook more while the walls of the cottage cracked. The White Lady's face twitched, shimmering out of focus like a fading mirage. Branches snapped, the main doorway crumbled, and the cliffs quaked.

A *demon* emerged from the cottage. Evelyn had never seen the likes of it before, so she couldn't name it. Six bone-white legs pounded into the grass as it approached. They protruded from an abdomen with wiry fur and bent at a harsh angle like the legs of a sea creature.

The demon advanced, still wearing the face of The White Lady, greasy hair draping down an elongated neck. Her face flickered again, revealing a snake-like face with even sharper needle-like teeth.

Evelyn gasped, side-stepping as the demon approached. The force of its six legs shook the ground, and Evelyn fell back. She panted and pushed away on her forearms as the demon slashed a pincher-claw at her. Evelyn rolled, the pincher indenting the ground where she'd been, grass and mud spraying in the air.

"Do you think I'd face you in the flesh?" the shimmering image of the White Lady's face screamed.

Evelyn had no time to think of what the dark witch meant. She could do that later, once she survived. She rolled again and again, the demon's attacks missing her by a hair. Her heart pounded, fear flooding through her veins. She stood and pivoted to avoid the demon's advances. She grabbed hold of her bone staff just in time to enchant it to its full length, using it to block an attack.

The demon's screech chorused with the White Lady's laugh. Evelyn slammed her bone staff down, ricocheting the power of her innate magic across the cliffs. The demon stumbled back, legs digging into the grassy ground. It regained its footing and charged. Evelyn wasn't ready for its speed, retreating at the last moment. A pincher grabbed her staff and thrust it away.

Fucking flames.

Evelyn would have to do without. She assessed the cottage, looking for anything she could use. She stumbled over stones surrounded by dead buttercups. Hurt the demon and then run. Not her proudest plan, but it would keep her alive.

Evelyn dug her nails into the dirt, releasing the rock.

Evelyn threw the rock, hitting her target spot on. The rock grazed against its eye, and the demon's head and the White Lady's face pulled apart, screeching.

Evelyn's assault had only angered the demon. It charged, legs pounding into the dirt. It swiped, hitting Evelyn right into the gut and throwing her into the air. She landed with a thud, head spinning and bones aching.

Flashes of her parents fighting the vampyrs years ago blurred her vision. Kade's hurt expression as he left the apartment punched her in the gut. The names of the murdered young women echoed in her mind.

How would she prove herself if she couldn't fight? How could she make it right with Kade if she didn't figure out her flame? How would she defend Callum?

Turmoil, fear, and a shred of hope pushed Evelyn to roll once, twice, a third time as the demon beat and thrashed at the ground. She rolled out of the bludgeoning pincher, but on the fourth roll, the demon anticipated her move.

The razor-sharp blow came crashing down right above where she landed on her back. She wasn't fast enough to move out of the way and braced her arm over her face. Razors on the claw tore her skin. Evelyn cried out, clutching her arm. Pain blinded her, and Evelyn's muscles shook with defeat.

The White Lady laughed. "Pathetic—"

A roar, deep and demanding, thundered through the hills. Even the fog seemed to recede over the cliffs. Evelyn's heart thudded in her chest. She'd never heard that roar, but her soul knew, recognized the beast.

The White Lady sneered as the fog trembled and gave way, a large mass charging toward them and breaking through whatever dark enchanted wall had trapped Evelyn.

She had no time to think of the incredible strength it took to break down such a spell, because the most beautiful creature Evelyn had ever seen leaped through the air and landed, putting himself between her and the demon. The face of a wolf turned and gazed at Evelyn with unmistakable amber eyes, spreading hope through her.

Kade.

Wonder and awe gripped Evelyn as she took in the hybrid version of the man she knew and his werewolf magic. The beast she'd always sensed, the energy she'd always known, crouched before her. His large stature was bulked by fur and more muscle. He possessed the head and legs of a wolf, even a tail, and his golden-tanned skin was now fur the color of his sun-kissed hair, shimmering gold-brown head to paws.

He rose from his haunches, and Goddess, he'd grown an extra foot with elongated hind legs. Arms hung at his sides as the abdominals of his torso shook with tension. Those strong, callused hands that had held her face and brushed away tears were now clawed and deadly.

Kade turned his attention to the demon and bared his ferocious canines as he growled. His tufted ears flicked back. The mane of fur on his neck and back thinned down his chest and shoulders and billowed in the wind. Wicked and dangerously fast, he lunged at the demon in a blink.

The last flicker of the White Lady's face, wide-eyed and fearful, vanished. Left was the screeching demon, its head a cross between a snake and an insect.

Kade grabbed one of the pincher-claws and yanked it clean off. The cry of pain cut through Evelyn's ears, and no doubt all of Callum heard the cry despite the distance.

Evelyn's energy started to drain. Feeling feverish, she clutched her arm and saw black poison spreading through her veins. She pushed upward, reaching the walls of the cottage and keeping her sights on Kade.

Strength, the power of the Moon, and magic emitted from him. Her soul soared at his proximity, her essence tethered to his.

The demon used its one pincher against Kade, but he didn't back down. He avoided it, dodging and rounding the other side, swiping with his claws. The demon used its long neck to swipe Kade off his hind legs. His werewolf form flew through the air, breaking the fog to reveal the edge of the cliffs yards away.

Evelyn lurched forward, calling out his name. Beads of sweat trickled down her temples, and her heart sank like a stone in her belly. Her pain didn't matter. All she could think was that Kade needed her, and she had to do something. *Fucking flames*, Evelyn was Daughter of the Goddess, a witch gifted with flame. She *could* do something.

Kade rolled and stopped, hunching on all fours as he recovered. He snarled, baring his teeth ashe stared down the demon charging at him.

Determination filled her, and Evelyn's magic awakened, her flame dancing at her fingertips. Despite her energy draining, her eyesight closing in around her, and the coldness in her toes, Evelyn brought forth her flame. She channeled every last bit of it, every essence of power in the tendrils of fire that coursed through her veins. All she could think about was that she needed to save Kade.

A sphere of flame formed in her hand, round and spinning. She channeled hope, belief, and something she felt deep in her soul into the sphere. Aster had been right. Her magic was nothing without her. Nothing without her thoughts, feelings, and soul.

Evelyn slunk up against the cottage, gaining balance and stability as she geared up to attack.

She unleashed her flame. It soared and barreled into the demon's neck, exploding on contact. Debris and embers blinded its eyes.

Kade didn't hesitate, launching at the demon and biting its neck. His claws dug in too, dragging the demon to the ground. Its six legs scampered and twitched, and it screeched to no avail. Kade's grip didn't falter. With one final bite and tug, he tore the neck clean in half. The demon's head tipped and fell, rolling across the ground as its body slackened with a deafening thud.

Relief flooded through Evelyn. Kade was okay. The demon was dead.

Why did she feel so cold?

Black poison spread farther up her arm, the cut from the demon's claw oozing black gunk. *Fucking flames.* Evelyn wanted to sleep, wanted to sigh and rest knowing Kade had come. He was here. Safe. He was safe.

"Evelyn!"

She blinked, mustering the energy to open her eyes, and found Kade rushing toward her. He'd shifted to his human form. Goddess, he ran stark naked, his bare tanned skin, muscles, everything visible—

She averted her gaze to meet his. Relief went through her again. That color, the kindness in them. Yet, she saw pain swimming there too. The same pain from three nights ago.

You're a spoiled and selfish runaway witch who abandoned her people.

The White Lady's words brought her back to the darkness.

You're nothing without your flame.

Her tutor's voice joined the chorus of doubt.

That'll be you one day.

Her mother's false hope brought Evelyn farther into the darkness. It beckoned her like a heavy blanket, tucking her in for a rest.

You fail and hurt the ones around you, don't you?

Fucking flames, she needed to sleep, needed to fall away from the resounding doubt ricocheting in her mind.

"*Evelyn!*"

The cry was distant, but it reached deep within her. It tugged on her soul, her magic, begging for her to open her eyes. She tried, but she craved silence, a place where no doubt could reach.

She submitted to an oblivion of darkness.

Chapter Forty-Six

Kade

Kade had not doubted it, but now there was no question. Evelyn *was* his mate. Witnessing her against the demon, watching as it attacked her, hurt her, turned him feral.

Protect her. Save her. Defend her.

As he delivered the final blow to the demon, Kade and his wolf relished saving their mate. Yet, his victory had been rocked by an all-consuming fear when he laid eyes on Evelyn. The light in her gray-blue eyes, the silver he cherished, dimmed.

She was dying.

He ran. Faster than he ever had before. Black poison crawled like vines up her slender arm. Kade's heart hammered in his chest. Fear strangled his heart, tore at his soul.

Reaching her side, he pulled her into his arms. *Moons*, she'd grown so cold, like ice to the touch.

"Princess, stay with me."

Her eyes wouldn't focus on him.

"Hey, love. Come on, love. No. *Evelyn*." Her eyes fluttered completely shut. Her body went slack. Kade heard her heart skip. Felt it within him. Skip, skip, skip.

"No, no, no."

Kade channeled his strength, tried to channel it into their mating bond. A flutter of her magic met his, familiar and welcoming. Her heart thumped once. Twice. Her chest swelled with breath and the slow rhythm of her heartbeat resumed. Kade almost sobbed with relief.

He shifted, bringing Evelyn into his furred arms and clawed hands, the black poison spreading to her neck, spilling like ink from her obsidian hair.

He ran with her to Callum and prayed to the Moon and Sun, pleading with them to pull Evelyn from the darkness.

Chapter Forty-Seven

Evelyn

Sleep weighed Evelyn down, threatening to pull her back under. She fought it, regaining her senses. A fire crackled nearby. Pattering rain sounded against a window like a lullaby. A layer of blankets warmed her muscles. A familiar weight sat atop her feet. Rose and ivy filled her senses. Evelyn's head pounded, her mouth dry. Lying there, succumbing to sleep, seemed to be the wise choice. Her body begged for it.

Then she stiffened, images of the White Lady coming forth and reminding her of what had happened.

Her eyes flashed open, and Evelyn found herself in her apartment, a quilt brought up to her chest, Maxie curled at the foot of the bed. She tried to sit up, but a gentle hand held her shoulder.

"Whoa, there," someone said.

Evelyn blinked, her vision blurring until she made out the sharp jawline shaded with scruff she loved.

Kade.

"Take it easy. You've been out for three days," he said.

Evelyn gaped. "Three days?" Her words rasped out of her.

Kade nodded, releasing her shoulder. He leaned over her bedside table and poured a glass of water, handing it to her. Evelyn's hands shook as she held the cup. She was embarrassingly weak, but driven by a maddening thirst, she drank. Water trailed down her throat, settling into her stomach.

"The demon was called a *scairp*," Kade said. "According to Aster. And one of the deadliest demons to roam our world. Your heart almost stopped beating from the poison. You almost died, Evelyn." His last words were a mere whisper, as if it hurt him to say them.

They assessed one another. Evelyn couldn't find words, worried she would say the wrong thing. Kade appeared hesitant and tense, his jaw tight.

"Do you want me to leave?" Kade asked, eyes downcast.

Evelyn realized with a sinking feeling in her gut that Kade was gauging how she'd react to him being here, in her apartment. If she asked him to leave, he would. She knew it. Yet, that was the last thing she wanted.

"No." It was all Evelyn could muster, her breaths shallow as she waited for his response.

Kade relaxed, leaning back in his chair. Worry and exhaustion still weighed on his shoulders. He ran a hand through his hair. They sat in silence. There was a comfort in the air, a settling sense of having him close to her.

Evelyn turned away from him, staring into the flames of the fire. It danced and twisted, beautiful tendrils of red and orange. She remembered the sphere she'd conjured against the demon. The wretched things the White Lady had said. Kade's speed and strength as a werewolf.

They had so much to talk about. The development in the murders. A new foe at play. None of those things seemed to matter, though. Even a week ago, Evelyn would've used those as an excuse, ignoring whatever this was between them. She didn't want to now. Kade deserved to know the truth. All of it, even if he made the decision that they couldn't be together for the sake of their homeland. She took a long breath, deciding to get it over with.

"I'm sorry," Evelyn said in a rush, setting the cup of water back on the bedside.

Kade's head snapped up. "For what?"

"For making you leave that night," she said.

Kade winced, and he shook his head. "Evelyn, I lied to you and said hurtful things. You had every right to be angry with me—"

"I lied too, Kade. After all, I was the one who left in the first place."

His gaze roamed over her. Evelyn expected to see anger or resentment, but all she witnessed was that deep-rooted kindness mixed with longing.

Evelyn sighed, her breath shuddering as she held back tears. "The day my parents died, I was riding out to meet your father and brother."

"I remember," Kade said.

"Well, I was a bucket of nerves and feeling like a prize peacock. Anyway, there I was, annoyed to even be there, frantic to meet my betrothed's family, and worried about what they'd tell you, not knowing it would be my last moments with my parents."

Maxie prowled up the bed, plopping into Evelyn's lap. Her familiar felt her pain and began to purr. The feline hum calmed Evelyn, and she stroked Maxie down her back, finding enough resolve to continue.

"Then the vampyrs attacked. It all happened so quickly. The sun set, and they came out of nowhere. We never expected them, but we fought. Hard. But then one threatened to tear my mother's throat . . ." Evelyn sucked in a breath. She'd felt so helpless watching the life drain from her mother's eyes, the vacant hole burrowing into her chest. "I lost my flame."

Kade's eyes widened, but it was the only reaction Evelyn witnessed. He said nothing, gave away nothing of what he was thinking.

"My power just left me. I couldn't grasp it, couldn't wield it. It didn't matter how much I'd trained as Daughter of the Goddess. It did not matter that my own mother needed me. My father realized, saw me struggling. Despite the pain of watching and *feeling* his fated's death, he saved me by casting me across the river. Then he was killed, too."

Tears streamed down Evelyn's face. Maxie nuzzled her cheek into Evelyn's chest, and she pulled her familiar closer, thankful for the contact.

"I need you to know, I tried to get it back. Day after day, night after night. Months went by, and I told no one. Not even my sisters. Then Mirella announced our wedding date, and I knew I couldn't marry you. I wasn't the Daughter of the Goddess. How could I be? Not without my flame." Evelyn released Maxie to stare at her hands, recalling all the times she'd tried to make her flame come forth. "I'd only be false hope, a liability, and if news ever reached the vampyr that my flame had left me, I feared war would break out."

Kade leaned forward and braced his forearms on his knees. "You left to protect everyone."

"I know it sounds cowardly—selfish, even. But I didn't know what else to do," Evelyn said, looking at Kade. He appeared astounded. "Why aren't you angry?"

Kade scoffed, leaning back in his chair, as if overcome with exhaustion. "Oh, I *was* angry. When I first heard you went missing, I'd been worried. Then when we all realized you'd run, all I could feel was anger. You'd left your duty, and I couldn't fathom it."

Evelyn flinched.

"I carried that anger for two years. Felt it even on the shores of Callum. And then I met you in the commissioner's office, appearing lost, sad, but determined. I saw the light in your eyes, your need to protect the people of Callum from the vampyr. I recognized your bluff of taking on the job for money immediately. You cared. You wanted to protect people."

"That's all I ever wanted," Evelyn whispered.

"I know," Kade said, crossing his arms. "Why didn't you come to me? Or tell me the truth?"

"Tell the most admired general, Son of the God, that his betrothed failed and was inadequate for the job?"

"You think I have not failed? That I have not made mistakes?"

Evelyn scoffed. "I read about you in the papers. The valiant, courageous Kade Drengr making mistakes?" She shook her head. "I couldn't imagine it."

Kade sat forward. "You know how my mother died?"

Evelyn paused, studying him. "Yes, at the Battle of Morrow."

Kade nodded. "Well, I was fourteen at the time, a little reckless and dimwitted. My brother Eldrick and I were five years apart and spent most of our time together."

Evelyn fidgeted, sitting farther upright and concentrating on Kade's next words.

"We had the bright idea to skip our training lessons one day. We left the Vadon Mountains, trailing my mother's unit all the way to Morrow. We thought ourselves clever werewolves, not once getting caught until we came upon the fortress. My mother was angry, disappointed in our recklessness. Traveling alone? Leaving the Vadon Mountains? I was Son of the God and needed to learn my duty, take it more seriously. But I was young and let some things go in one ear and out the other. We stayed for two days and then left the fortress with a small unit."

Kade paused. Outside, the rain no longer drizzled; it poured in sheets against the window. The lively fire continued to crackle. Evelyn didn't dare to say anything, unsure where Kade's story was heading.

"Vampyrs attacked less than an hour after we left. We witnessed the horde of them breach the fortress wall. Eldrick and I sprinted back, ready to defend and help our mother. As I jumped the wall, I found twenty vampyrs circling her. We locked eyes. I knew before she even shook her head. She wanted me to stop, to not engage. Her last words as the vampyrs swarmed her were, 'Remember your duty.'"

Evelyn wanted to reach out to him, to take his hand or place a comforting touch on his arm. Maxie had a similar idea, moving from Evelyn's lap and jumping to Kade's. His pained expression relaxed. He held Maxie close, and she purred, golden eyes staring up at him as if to say, *Go on, now.*

He did. "As it turns out, the horde of vampyrs had trailed me and my brother for miles. We'd led them to Morrow. If it weren't for me, my mother would still be alive."

"Vampyrs killed your mother," Evelyn said.

"As they did your parents, but the choices I made led to my mother's death. I failed her in being foolish. I do not judge you, Evelyn. I do not think less of you.

Your flame may have left you, but that moment does not define you. Your flame doesn't define you."

Evelyn squirmed and twiddled her fingers. Familiar, treacherous words resounded in her mind. They fought against his kind words, making it hard to believe him. "My tutors always told me that without my flame, I was nothing against the vampyr."

"I don't know who your tutors were, Evelyn, but they can rot," he said. Maxie leaped back onto her bed, assuming her favorite position at the foot. Kade leaned forward, grasping Evelyn's left hand. "I can't take back the things I said. I was wrong. Please know, I'm sorry." The look he gave Evelyn stole her breath, and she had to look away, had to focus on something else.

She wasn't ready to talk about Kade being her fated. The magnitude of it sat in the air, unhinged and frightening. Admitting to him why she had left and hearing his acceptance and apology was enough.

"You need more rest," Kade said, tucking a stray hair behind her ear.

Evelyn wanted to argue, but sleep weighed on her. "We need to discuss the White Lady and the latest murder."

"We will," Kade said. He stood, gathering his cloak.

"Where are you going?" Evelyn asked, sitting up straighter, worry lacing her words.

"Not far," he said. "You gave more than me a scare, Evelyn. The people of Callum were beside themselves when I ran into town with you in my arms."

Evelyn relaxed, raising a brow. "Are you sure that had nothing to do with you as a werewolf?"

Kade laughed. "No, their concern for you outmatched their shock. I need to let Miss Patricia know you're awake or she'll wring my neck. At least that's what she promised. Aster and Tovi also deserve to know you're awake."

Evelyn went to stand, but Kade stopped her.

"Remember needing rest? Did I mention you almost died?"

"I can go with you," she muttered. "I want to see them."

Kade sighed. "If I promise to bring them back with me, will you sleep?"

Evelyn eyed him. Then a yawn escaped, her body betraying her. "Fine."

Kade stood, looked at her, sighed, and then nodded. He turned in a rush and disappointment flushed through Evelyn.

"Kade," she called as he made it to the door.

He whirled. "Yes?"

"Thank you."

Kade smiled, and Evelyn's chest swelled. Her heart soared and her stomach dipped. He said no more as he left, and Evelyn hunkered into the bedsheets, finding her body had indeed betrayed her, and she floated back into sleep.

Chapter Forty-Eight

Kade

Kade took a deep breath, inhaling the scent of electricity and the promise of a storm in the air. Behind him, Aster bounced in her rain boots as she clutched the feast Miss Patricia had sent them with. She gave him a wide, toothy smile. Tovi, on the other hand, stood regal and proud like she always did.

As he eased open Evelyn's apartment door, he expected to find her in bed, maybe sleeping, and he cursed the moment he spotted her on shaky legs. She hung on to the edge of her kitchen table, wearing only the long white tunic Aster had dressed her in when she'd helped him heal her. Evelyn's hair fell over her shoulder, untamed and long.

She shot him a scathing look. "Don't."

He fought a smile and said nothing, but Aster pushed him out of the way.

"Damn dandelions, Evelyn!" she said, dropping the bagged food on the table. "Are you mad?"

"No, just stubborn," Evelyn said.

Aster's frustrated expression fell, and her eyes grew wide. She launched into a hug, squeezing Evelyn tight along with Tovi. Kade had to intervene in order to stop them from toppling to the ground.

"She almost *died*," he said.

Frustration laced his tone. Was he the only one who remembered three days ago? His wolf howled at the reminder, the air whooshing from his lungs. If his wolf had any say, he'd lock everyone out and oversee Evelyn's healing himself.

"So you keep saying," Evelyn said with a raised brow as he helped her into a seat.

Dark circles rimmed her eyes, but not as dark as the ones from that morning. The natural rosy hue on her cheeks had returned. Kade felt relief, thankful that rest had been good for her.

Evelyn studied him, her brows furrowing.

Kade swallowed, walking away as Aster and Tovi checked on Evelyn. He busied himself with the food. Barmbrack loaves, meaty stew, roast potatoes, and cinnamon scones. Miss Patricia had outdone herself.

"Thank you for the salve, Aster," Evelyn said, and Kade stilled.

"Oh, that wasn't me," Aster said. "That was Kade."

He turned, finding Evelyn wide-eyed and staring at him. She'd been referring to the green gunk on her arm, and Aster had been right. He'd done that, but he hadn't been ready for this conversation yet.

"You did this?" she whispered. "But . . ." She stared down at her arm and shook her head. "This is a witch's salve. I've watched my sister use it. How did you know?"

Aster stood between them, her russet eyes going back and forth. She coughed, taking a step back from Evelyn. "We came by to make sure you were all right, but Kade gave us strict instructions that you needed rest, and we weren't to stay long."

Kade gaped. "I said—"

"I also have to go close up the shop for the evening." Aster gave Kade an expectant look only he could see.

"Plus," Tovi added, "Aster and I are grabbing a drink at the Runaway Radish. We certainly need one after the last few days." She raised her brow and crossed her arms. "We'll come after the storm passes through and check in again."

"All right," Evelyn said. "Thank you both for . . . making me see reason."

Aster kept her petite hand on Evelyn's shoulder. "Of course."

Tovi gave Evelyn's hand a tender squeeze, the best friends' eyes locking in a silent conversation only the two of them understood. Evelyn's friends left, and the pattering of rain grew louder as the door opened for a moment, and then silence stretched between Kade and Evelyn.

Evelyn's silver gaze, one that had almost gone out a few days ago, roamed over his face. Her expression begged for answers, but Kade needed a moment to figure out how to tell her so much.

"Are you hungry? Miss Patricia sent us enough to feed an army," he said with a slight smile.

"If I eat, will you tell me where you learned how to make the salve?" Evelyn asked.

Kade sighed, running his hand through his hair. "Your entire healing regime cannot be based on bargains, Evelyn."

"I'm fine, Kade."

He almost argued, a retort ready, but his name on her lips stopped him in his tracks. He prepared Evelyn some stew, a few slices of barmbrack, and a single scone with butter. He sat next to her, plated his own dinner. It wasn't lost on him that a week ago, they'd sat in similar places, before their world had unraveled. He'd been about to spill his secrets, and now he readied himself once more to admit something, make himself vulnerable.

"A witch taught me," Kade said.

Evelyn stilled. "A witch?"

"After my mother died, each of my brothers and my father mourned differently. My mother and father were mates."

Evelyn's eyes flashed.

But Kade continued. "We all assumed my father would die, as most do after losing their mate. Instead, his health declined, but he didn't succumb like other werewolves. Eldrick, my older brother, leaned into becoming the next Alpha and became consumed with it. My middle brother, who is a latent wolf, receded into himself, never leaving his books and potions."

Kade paused, remembering Lorkan and those dark times. Rain continued outside, the sound a calming current urging him on.

"Guilt gripped me with an iron hand, and I turned to my duty. Training to fight the vampyr, but I also knew I'd one day marry you, binding my soul with another." Kade set down his spoon, leaning back in his chair. "Werewolves take marriage seriously. I witnessed it with my parents, and yes, they were mates, so fate played a part, but they were partners. And I decided, if we were to defeat the vampyrs, our powers alone would not be enough. We would need to be a team, partners against the darkness.

"Except I knew nothing about witches and, of course, the Elders forbid us to meet each other, something I hated and respected. All the while, I kept thinking, if I could learn what it meant to be a witch or something about the magic of being a third-born, I could gain your trust. I traveled deep into the Vadon Mountains and found Carena, the first Daughter of the Goddess."

Evelyn shook her head. "That's not possible. Carena died. My tutors told me she hadn't survived after her bond with Finton was severed."

"They weren't mates," Kade said. He wanted to add, *not like us*, but refrained. "It's true Finton died in a battle against the vampyr, but Carena lived for decades without him. Scáths eventually raided her village, and she died protecting her pack."

Evelyn leaned back into her chair, picking at her scone. "So she stayed with his pack? She didn't return to her coven?"

Kade sighed. "I gathered she preferred a quieter life. Carena and Finton had not been mates, but they had grown to love one another. She missed him every day, and I think a part of her didn't want to leave a land that reminded her of him."

"And the werewolves, Finton's pack, never told anyone she'd lived?" Evelyn asked.

"No," Kade said, shaking his head. "I think they respected her enough to let her live the rest of her life in peace."

Evelyn sat up, swirling her spoon in her stew. "She taught you remedies like this?" She nodded at her arm.

Kade nodded. "I hoped that maybe, when we did meet, I'd know something about you to help understand you. Even if it was one thing. And I never expected anything from you. Carena told me she and Finton had become friends, and that over time friendship grew into love, and I hoped we'd at least find the same. But I'd settle for partners with the same goal, to defeat the vampyr, if that's what it came to."

Evelyn didn't say anything, her brows furrowed. Kade listened to the hammering of her heart and feared he'd said something wrong. She suddenly stood, staggering a few steps as she did so.

"Evelyn—"

She moved before he could catch her, taking a few steps closer to the fire and bracing her hand on the mantle.

"Is that what you still want?" she whispered. "To be partners?"

Kade stood, joining her by the fire in two long strides. He cupped Evelyn's cheek, making her look at him.

Words didn't seem right for the moment.

The fire in the small apartment crackled beside them. The spilling rain surrounded them in a small sea town far from their homeland. The pounding of their hearts beat like thunder. Between them was the electric charge of what they were to one another, what they'd been through, and who they wanted to be.

So Kade kissed her.

His passion overrode reason, and he kissed her fiercely, like he hungered for her. Evelyn met his kiss, one hand grasping his tunic and pulling him to her, and the other hand threaded through the waves at the nape of his neck.

Kade gave her his answer with lips molding over hers, cupping her cheek as he kissed her. His hand found her waist, pulling close, and teasing his fingers on the start of her backside. As he parted her lips and explored deeper, drawing out gasps from his beautiful brave mate, Kade told her yes.

Yes, yes, and yes.

He wanted them to be partners, but also so much more. He'd never wanted anything more. It outmatched his duty, his hope to defeat the vampyr. Kade wanted Evelyn by his side. He wanted her in every way he could have her, and the new hope he harbored was that she would want him the same.

And by the way she continued to tug him closer, kissing him with her own sweet fierceness, Kade knew she wanted him, too.

He pulled away, resting his forehead on hers. "Do not doubt that I want you. *Need you*, Evelyn."

She shuddered at his words. "I don't know how to not doubt myself, not yet anyway, but I trust you."

Kade kissed her forehead. Her cheek. Her other cheek. And then her lips.

"I know I said I came to convince you to come back with me and fulfill our duty, but my focus shifted. I wanted to get to know *you*. I wanted to understand you. Not because of your title or that you were my betrothed, but because of you."

Evelyn melted into his arms, resting her head on his chest. A long sigh escaped her, and Kade held her tight.

Chapter Forty-Nine

Evelyn

The next morning, Evelyn awoke earlier than Kade. Sound asleep, her werewolf lay on his side, one hand splayed across her belly. Serene and calm, his features were at ease, and he breathed deeply and steadily. The fire lit the dim room, casting glints of gold through Kade's tousled bed hair. Evelyn's roaming fingers likely had something to do with his disheveled look, too.

Which had been the only exploring she'd done last night after Kade had enforced an obscenely early bedtime, because she needed "rest" and she'd "almost died," which he'd reminded her at least a dozen times. She was surprised he wasn't the firstborn with his overbearing and keenly attentive healer-like qualities.

Except Kade had destroyed Evelyn with his lips, and she knew what he wanted.

Her. Them. *Us.*

She should never have doubted him. His feelings for her were true, and she needed to trust that no matter how her heart raced with doubt every time she thought of it.

Rain still poured outside, the lingering aftermath of a sea storm. Evelyn could barely make out Callum through the steady stream of rain and the gliding droplets down her windows. Between the winds and the downpour, no one would be out in town. They certainly weren't going anywhere either.

She stretched out her arm, stiff as a board but no longer throbbing. She glided her hands over the salve Kade had given her, noting how dry and cracked it had become. Mirella would tell her it was safe to wash off, so Evelyn eased Kade's hand off her side and slid from the bed. In her place, Maxie walked up to the bed and nuzzled herself into Kade's chest.

Evelyn almost laughed, amazed she'd missed the signs. No wonder Maxie had grown attached to Kade. Her *familiar* had sensed Kade was her fated.

Well, fated mate.

Evelyn bit her lip, nervous they had yet to talk about that or about going home. She'd hoped Kade would've brought it up. He'd mentioned his parents being mates, even how Carena and Finton hadn't been.

She tiptoed to her dresser and grabbed a fresh oversized tunic and knee-high socks. Mindful of her sleeping fated, Evelyn continued to tiptoe to the bathroom. A hot, steaming shower would do her thoughts some good.

The scalding water soothed her creaking muscles. Rest and sleep had helped her body heal, but the better Evelyn felt, the more restless her energy became. She needed to do something.

Like find the White Lady.

She scrubbed and washed her body, taking care to ease the salve off her forearm. A fleshy pink scar ran up the side, slight but nonetheless a reminder of what had happened. Considering she'd almost died from a demon's venom, Evelyn would take the scar.

She inhaled the herby steam from her soap, letting the shower cascade down her body and trickle through her hair.

Fated mates, the White Lady, deadly demons.

Evelyn sighed, turning off the shower. Who exactly was the White Lady? Was she behind the murders or working with a vampyr? If so, why? With the storm, Evelyn and Kade would be going nowhere, which meant she'd have to face another conversation entirely. She'd told Kade the truth about her parents' death, and it hadn't deterred him. How was the gravity of this any different?

Drying herself and readying her hair, Evelyn realized more decisions lay on the horizon. Despite wanting one another, despite being fated mates, they were still Daughter of the Goddess and Son of the God. They had a duty to uphold back home with her coven and his pack.

Goddess, Evelyn didn't want to face her sisters. Or the Elders. Or run into a particular tutor. Worse, she couldn't fathom facing Kade's pack, his brothers, after she'd run away.

No.

Going home, facing what she had done, and navigating her flame—it would be challenging, scary at times, and it would take courage, but for Kade, she would.

Refreshed, clean, and comfy, Evelyn exited the bathroom to find her bed made, Maxie curled in the middle of it, and Kade making coffee in the kitchenette. She tripped on the floorboards when he turned, the bastard not bothering to wear a shirt. The sight of male muscle zapped any remaining sleepiness from her. There was nothing like a bare-chested beast of a man to wake a woman up.

"Good morning," he said, planting a kiss on her lips as she reached him.

Evelyn smiled, unable to hold it back. "Good morning and thank you. You're a saint." She took the mug of steaming coffee he handed her. For a brief moment, Evelyn wished *this* was their normal. Waking up on a rainy morning, sipping coffee together.

No murders. No prophecies. No duty.

"You're overthinking," Kade said over the rim of his coffee mug. He leaned against the counter, taking her in.

Evelyn sighed. "How do you know?"

He scoffed. "First, your heart races a little when you do. And"—he ran his fingers over Evelyn's brow—"you become quite serious. What are you thinking?"

Evelyn took the first sip of her coffee. "The other unions, the previous Son of the God and Daughter of the Goddess, they weren't . . ."

"Like us?" Kade finished. "No, they weren't."

Evelyn shut her eyes and swallowed. She stood before Kade, summoning that courage.

"Fated," she whispered, opening her eyes to catch the flash of gold in his as she said the word.

"Fated?" Kade asked, taking a step closer to her and running his thumb across her bottom lip.

She shuddered from his touch. "Last night, you said mates for werewolves. For witches, we call it fated," she said.

Evelyn didn't meet his eyes, setting her coffee mug down and taking in his build. His jawline. That chest. Those arms. His Adam's apple bobbed as he swallowed under her perusal. The leather-corded necklace caught her eye and an idea struck.

"Take this off," she said, slightly pulling it with two fingers away from his neck.

Kade's breathing hitched, and after a beat, he did as she'd asked. Moments ticked by as he reached behind, unclasped the back, and pulled it from his neck.

The moment it landed on the counter behind him, Evelyn staggered back, his magic, his wolf, barreling into her. The onslaught of Kade stole her breath and made her knees weak. Evelyn felt every bit of Kade. He hummed with an energy of his own and her magic brightened, like his magic made hers more alive. All the senses she possessed were taken over by *him*.

Her skin heated, and she swore she smelled the forest after the rain, and she saw a deeper, crisper version of him.

Kade straightened. "Evelyn, are you all right?"

Evelyn nodded, smiling, almost laughing at the feeling of him, of their magic intertwining.

Evelyn looked down at her own bracelet, using her opposite hand to singe it into oblivion with her flame. The ashes had yet to reach the ground before a deep growl erupted from Kade, and before it had finished vibrating around them, he'd pushed her against the wall in the kitchenette.

Breathless, he gazed down at her, shaking. "I'm sorry. Your magic . . . my wolf . . ."

Evelyn nodded. "I know."

She kissed him, curling her hand around his neck and pulling him closer. Pure ecstasy overwhelmed them.

Kade pushed her arms above her head, grasping her wrists and placed them against the wall. Evelyn whimpered at the exposure, the sensual power and control of it. The taste of him, drove her magic mad, swirling around him, reaching for his wolf like it was a lifeline. Against her own lips, she felt his smirk, but he didn't stop molding his lips to hers, exploring her mouth with his tongue, stroking it against her own.

Evelyn bucked her hips into his groin, and a deep gravelly growl of approval and distress vibrated through her. He finally backed away, still leaving her arms locked above her. Kade blinked and released her arms, his eyes roaming over her face.

"I didn't mean to lose control," he said, easing away from her but still keeping her in his orbit.

"Stop talking," Evelyn said, pulling him back to her.

They kissed, a fiercer version than the night before. A hunger, one manifesting deep in Evelyn's core and unlike one she'd ever had before, consumed her.

Kade's hands trailed down her bare thighs, pushing up the fabric of her tunic. Evelyn hissed, the touch of his fingers driving her mad.

He stilled. Entirely. "Do you want me to stop?"

His eyes were dead set, and Evelyn knew at that moment, no matter what she wanted or what she said, he'd always respect her, her decisions, her wants. He'd stop it all if she asked.

"Don't you dare," she said.

"Thank the Moon," he breathed, his lips crashing back to hers.

She'd never wanted anything like this before. The hunger. The desire. The maddening need of wanting him closer, to feel his skin burn against hers. Fire flared in Evelyn's veins, a heat she knew all too well, but with Kade's magic connecting to hers, it was like a burning inferno. Never-ending.

His wolf and her flame called to the other.

She bit and tugged at his bottom lip. He pushed farther into her core with a growl and *that sound.* Deep and beastly. Why had she not said anything sooner? Fucking flames, why had it taken her so fucking long?

He broke their kiss, Evelyn far too breathless to object. He trailed his tongue from her jawline down her throat. Goddess, the things she imagined him doing with that exquisite tongue.

Kade continued to pull up her tunic until her legs were completely exposed. Her skin tingled, alive and sensitive enough that the fabric brushed over her flesh like electricity.

Pulling away, Kade studied her face. Male intent glinted in his stare. Evelyn sucked in a breath as he slowly lowered to his knees, never breaking eye contact.

"Moons . . ." he whispered. "You want me."

"You sound so confident."

"I can smell you."

"*Oh.*"

Kade laughed, his warm breath tickling the inside of her thighs. "I plan to taste you, Evelyn. Every inch." He looked up at her with heat. His voice, gravelly and full of longing, had her core pooling with need.

He pushed her tunic up farther, and she relieved him of the task by gathering its fabric and fisting it to her chest, her breast peeking out, nipple hard with arousal. Kade laid a kiss on one thigh, and a single kiss turned Evelyn molten. She feared she couldn't handle much else.

His teeth grazed her undergarments, and he rumbled with another growl, dominating and hungry.

"Black lace, Evelyn?" he breathed. "You will be the death of me."

Evelyn released a small laugh, and then gasped as he looped his thumbs under her underwear, his touch hovering over her shivering skin. Goddess, she wanted his hands on her hips for eternity. Kade pulled them down slowly, a dangerous taunt, piercing her with his heated gaze. She stepped out of them, one leg at a time, certain she shook.

He discarded them to the side and returned his attention to her sex. Again, he painted her thighs with kisses, reaching higher and higher. The higher he went, the more his kisses turned to nips. Gentle and painful, the sensations made Evelyn warm, buzzing for more.

Kade gripped the back of her knee and swung her leg over his shoulders, opening her legs and allowing him better access to her core. His first lick through her folds was slow and methodical, like he intended to take his time as he tasted every inch of her.

She gasped and leaned her head back against the wall. He did it again, and Evelyn writhed, but Kade gripped her hips to keep her steady. He licked and relished it until he found that spot, her knot of nerves, bundled and swollen. Ready. He kissed, sucked, and twirled his tongue in a rhythm of glorious torture.

Panting, whimpering, Evelyn held her tunic for dear life with one hand and threaded her fingers through his hair with the other. Her desperate hold only encouraged him, unleashing a frenzy of sucking on that single spot.

Flushed and hot, Evelyn felt something building, wave after wave of sensual tension, and then Kade slipped a finger into her wet core. The combination of his tongue on her clit and his finger inside was too much. She screamed. In pleasure. In anguish. In the promise of release.

His twirling tongue gathered rhythm, the waves building higher and quicker. Adding a second finger, he pumped slowly. Then sped up. His tongue and fingers in tandem and cadence together, a final wall of tension built and crashed. Crumbled. Bursting with sensation and light, Evelyn unraveled in a never-ending ride of bliss.

Kade removed his fingers slowly, looking up at Evelyn with wicked male satisfaction. He gave one last kiss to her clit, swollen and spent, peeled her leg from his shoulder gently, and then stood, kissing up her neck as she came down from the climax with ragged breaths. Evelyn released her bunched-up tunic, her knees weak and senses off-kilter.

Suddenly, Evelyn was airborne as Kade lifted her, wrapping her legs around his waist. He planted her on the counter, still smiling a devilish grin.

"Feeling all right, Princess?"

She kissed him once, smoothing back the hair she'd grabbed and displaced earlier, tucking the waves behind his ears. "More than all right."

Warmth blossomed on her cheeks, but Kade's touch, pushing her own hair behind her ears, made her feel a way she'd never felt before. Warm. Seen. Adored.

"Tell me more about what you said earlier," Kade said. "What do witches call their mates?"

"Fated," Evelyn said. "Not only does one's soul connect to the other, but so does their magic. They collide on every level."

"It's similar for werewolves. It's our wolves connecting, sensing each other on a deeper level. Evelyn, I feel your magic like it's my own. Sense every fiber of your being."

Despite the dim lighting in Evelyn's apartment, his eyes glowed.

"I . . ." Taking a calculated and brave breath, Evelyn said, "I felt you long before you took your necklace off, Kade. I've sensed you. Not like I do now, but all this time, a part of me always knew who you were to me."

Kade leaned his forehead against hers, and Evelyn's heartbeat slowed to normal. "I don't regret how we fell for each other, Ev. I wouldn't change a damn thing."

Ev.

No one in Evelyn's life had ever called her that. Ever. But on his lips, with his voice, with that tone . . . Goddess, she wanted to hear it at every hour of every day.

"Say it again."

"I wouldn't change a damn thing."

"That is lovely, but I meant the name."

Kade smiled that dashing, wide, knee-wobbling smile. "Ev." He kissed her collarbone. "Ev." He pressed one, two, three kisses up her neck and whispered into her ear, "Ev."

She wrapped her arms around his neck, tangled her fingers in his hair.

Content but unable to shake the gravity of it all, Evelyn said, "This will change things."

"What do you mean?"

"Everything. The prophecy, our union. If you and I are, well, I guess, fated mates, it means something."

It had to. The other union before them had not been connected this way. Their connection had been based on the magic of their marriage ritual, not fate. It meant something and had to relate to the prophecy. It also meant they must return home. Face Evelyn's coven, her sisters, and meet Kade's pack. Not to mention figure out her flame. Except there were the murders in Callum. The mystery of the White Lady and possible vampyr—

Kade gripped her chin, stilling her running thoughts. "I don't want to talk about the prophecy or our union—"

"Kade."

"I don't," he said. "What I want to talk about is how my beautiful, brave *fated mate* admitted what we are."

"But what about—"

"And I want to enjoy this morning. Slowly. With some coffee. I'll even make us pancakes. Please."

Evelyn slumped her shoulders. It seemed Kade, too, wanted to relish the moment. She couldn't deny him, because her soul soared at the thought of letting things settle, basking in this newfound connection to one another.

"Fine, but I'll hold you to those pancakes."

"It'll be my pleasure," Kade said. "As you know, I am a fan of sweet things on my tongue." He winked, and Evelyn didn't miss his double meaning.

Chapter Fifty

Evelyn

Evelyn, as promised, had given them the morning.

While Kade cooked pancakes topped with sugar and lemon juice, his family's favorite way, she told him about her parents being fated as well as her eldest sister Mirella. She sipped her coffee while he talked of his own parents being mates, along with his good friends Bétar and Yennifer. They shared stories of what it meant, how it was celebrated, how it was cherished.

Over pancakes and crispy bacon, they talked of their homelands, the things they missed about Sorin. Kade told her about his pack and his team, the Gray Fenris. She'd read about them in the papers, but hearing who they were in his eyes was different. He smiled wide when he said their names and predicted she and Yennifer would make quick friends.

Evelyn told him of her coven and sisters. How Mirella was stern but kind, and Blair was the smartest and most fashionable witch she'd ever met. Evelyn promised to take him to her favorite bakery in Nūa one day, and Kade promised the beauty of the snow during winter solstice in the Vadon Mountains and knew the perfect place to see it.

They somehow ended up in front of the fire atop a pile of pillows and blankets, talking until their throats were hoarse. Evelyn drifted into a nap, and when she awoke, the shower was on and Kade was nowhere in sight.

Water and steam escaped from the bathroom door, and Evelyn considered joining him. The prospect sent a nervous thrill through her, but a hunger, one fueled by sexual need, built within her.

Evelyn couldn't shake the image of him naked in there, the hot water cascading down his taut muscles. Similar thoughts had invaded her mind weeks ago, but now, they'd been intimate.

Evelyn stood, warmth spreading through her body as she wavered foot to foot, contemplating her next move. Kade had obliterated her senses, and she wanted to do the same to him.

She craved it.

Mustering courage, Evelyn stripped her clothes off as she made her way to the bathroom, leaving a trail through the apartment as she undressed. She eased open the door and entered the bathroom naked, the steam clinging to her aroused skin. No word from Kade, no indication he heard her approach.

She pulled back the curtain, meeting his bare backside as Kade scrubbed his face under the shower. He stilled and turned. His amber eyes flashed, his nostrils flaring.

"Evelyn, what are you doing?"

She pulled the curtain back more, revealing her nude body. Her nipples hardened in anticipation, her sex already growing warm. She stepped into the shower, Kade watching her every move. She hoped he saw the intent in her eyes. Goddess, he'd smelled her earlier, so there was no doubt he knew.

Kade turned, his tanned skin covered in droplets of water that gave it a sheen. He'd pushed his wet hair back, and his beard glistened. Water traveled down his toned stomach to his deliciously wet and hard length. She sucked in a breath at the sight of what she'd come in here for. His length bobbed against his thigh, long and erect.

Clearly, he did smell her arousal and knew her intent.

They stepped closer to each other, and Evelyn didn't allow Kade to say another word. She pulled him into a kiss, grabbing his hip and crushing their bodies together. He palmed her bare ass, sinking his fingers into her cheeks. The pain went straight to her core, and she kissed him with fervor. Tasting him, twirling her tongue with his, moaning into his mouth.

Her heart pounded as she reached for his length, stroking it once and tightening her grip around the tip slightly.

Kade groaned, pulling away from their kiss.

Breathless, he said, "I didn't exactly imagine the first time we lay together to be in the shower."

Evelyn bit her lip and shook her head. "That's not why I'm here."

Lying with Kade sounded amazing; her toes curled from the thought of it, but she craved something else entirely tonight. That next step would have to be discussed as it would bind them for life, completing their fated mate bond. Evelyn wanted that. One day. But they needn't rush it. There were plenty of other ways to have fun.

She knelt, and Kade's eyes widened and darkened, conflict brewing in them.

"Evelyn, you don't—"

"I want you in my mouth, Kade," she said, looking up at him. "I want to taste you."

Kade shut his eyes and dipped his head back. "Stars above, save me."

Taking that as permission, Evelyn set her focus on his daunting length. She ran her hand up it again, stroking it. It grew longer and harder, until she feared it might unleash under her touch. Looking up at Kade, Evelyn licked from the base to the tip, watching him shudder and his brows furrow as she did so.

She'd done this before, pleasured a man with her mouth, but never once had she so badly wanted to do it to please the other. She wanted to relish Kade, enjoy him, and pleasure him as he did to her that morning.

Evelyn used one hand to hold it as she licked the tip, getting it wet and ready. When she finally took him into her mouth, Kade growled, and Evelyn took more of him, his pleasure driving her forward. She tasted him, felt him. Putting her hands on his hips and holding on, she bobbed on his length.

Kade released a string of curses, saying her name like a prayer.

Using her tongue, tightening her hold, and humming low, Evelyn worked Kade's length. As he grew tighter, his breath quickening, she used one hand to stroke his base and increased her pace as she sucked his tip.

"Evelyn."

She felt the tremor, the tautness in time. Evelyn popped his length from her mouth. Kade slumped, one hand bracing the shower wall as he released onto her breasts.

Evelyn stood, washing remnants of him from her chest, and sent him a sly smirk.

Kade took hold of her neck, kissing her with a new roughness Evelyn enjoyed so much she almost came undone. He lifted her, wrapping her legs around him.

"You have no idea what you just started," he said, turning off the shower and carrying her to her bed.

Evelyn squealed, anticipation hot and heavy around her, more than certain she'd enjoy whatever plans Kade had in store for her.

Chapter Fifty-One

Evelyn

The next morning, Evelyn felt spent. Kade had somehow managed to unravel her senses and send her over the edge four times. She'd pleasured him as well, but it seemed he'd never allow her to outmatch his fingers and tongue. A few times, Evelyn had been tempted to straddle him and take him, craving him inside her, but Evelyn still didn't want to rush it, and Kade didn't seem inclined to do so either.

The storm had passed in the night and the screaming wind with it, and Evelyn was recovered from the demon attack. With the sun out, birds singing, and the streets filling with townsfolk again, she and Kade decided it was time to refocus on the murders.

Down the steps from her apartment, Kade parted from Evelyn with a kiss, heading in the direction of the Runaway Radish. He'd promised to return after collecting more of his things. In the meantime, Evelyn planned to find Aster and do more research. With one body part left from the witches' creed, time wasn't on their side.

Callum had only begun to stir. Shopkeepers turned their signs to "open," children sprinted off to school, and merchants dragged their carts to the harbor market. Wind carried the scent of winter and the sea. It funneled into the street, twirling Evelyn's dark, silky hair.

The Pages and Leaves' open sign was already flipped, and Evelyn found the front door unlocked. It was a few hours earlier than usual for Aster to have opened up, and the shop bells chimed into a deafening silence.

Evelyn froze. Her magic sensed something off. *Wrong*. Aster's magic—

Evelyn sucked in a breath. Death and decay had overtaken the shop. Flowers had wilted, green had gone gray, an ashen color drowning the shop in the presence of darkness. Not a single petaled butterfly flapped its wings. Evelyn tried to step over their lifeless bodies scattered on the ground as she moved farther into the shop.

Then she stopped, searing dread coursing through her like a bolt of lightning. *She knew*. Her heart ached, her chest tightened.

Aster.

"Aster!" Evelyn called out, but she already *felt* her friend's lack of magic, her missing light, and knew deep down her friend would not answer.

Her magic sensed only death.

"*Aster!*"

Evelyn ran to the back of the shop. Skidding and halting at the sight of the body—

A wretched scream rang deep from Evelyn's belly, powered by the pain of her soul and magic. She collapsed and shook, crawling to Aster's dead and lifeless form. Evelyn brought her poor, petite frame into her arms, wetness soaking into her trousers, slicking her hands, soaking her hair. Aster's red curls. The horrible angle of her neck. Red blood on her lips. There was so much blood.

Red. Red. Red.

On the ground. On her body. On her arms.

She tried to unsee it, tried to make it not real and—

Evelyn's heart fractured, and her magic flared alive with another cry of anguish. Aster's hands. Her small freckled fingers. The hands she potted plants with, grew life with, cast magic with, laughed into.

Gone.

Evelyn screamed again, the sound so inhuman she wasn't sure it belonged to her. Between the ringing in her ears and the pain coursing through her, her magic threw out a wall of flame, shielding her from the outside world. Her sweet and innocent friend was dead. She kept muttering to herself that it wasn't true, wishing she'd wake up from this nightmare.

Someone called her name behind the barricade of her magic, yelled out for her over the ringing of heartache.

She'd been upstairs with Kade in their cocoon of exploration and bliss, and her friend was dead. She'd set aside her duty for a moment—

"Evelyn," the voice said. Evelyn slumped at the familiar tenderness, noted the sheer worry in Kade's tone as he reached her. Her barrier of flame dropped, and he rushed toward her.

When his sights fell on Aster, he sank to the floor.

"She's dead," Evelyn said. "She's . . ."

Evelyn sobbed, and Kade pulled her into his chest, Aster's body draped over her lap. So small, so fragile, so lifeless.

"Evelyn," Kade whispered, pulling her in close. His magic nudged hers, his wolf nuzzling against her flame.

"She's gone," Evelyn rasped, barely a whisper. She was so, so empty. As vacant as Aster's shop without her friend's bright light. She'd failed her friend like she'd failed her parents. A gaping hole opened in her chest, a hollow ache.

"Breathe, love," Kade said. "Breathe."

"She's dead," Evelyn said again, her throat raw from her screams and sobbing.

All those young women. All the body parts. Evelyn had never once thought the vampyr would take someone she knew, someone she *loved*. First her parents and now Aster. What good was she if she couldn't even protect the ones she loved?

Maybe it was hours or maybe it was mere minutes—Kade rocked and held her. Evelyn couldn't take her eyes off Aster's still, cold body. Her russet eyes shone with no eagerness, none of that light Evelyn had grown so accustomed to. All gone.

Aster's skin was not a shade of blue. Not a vampyr bite in sight. Blood soaked her, a deadly slash lining her neck.

"I didn't protect her. I couldn't save her."

Evelyn breathed the words over and over, eclipsing herself into a darkness of her own making.

Chapter Fifty-Two

Evelyn

They laid Aster to rest two days later.

It didn't rain, but the sun never broke through the thick blanket of slate clouds casting Callum in a solemn and still gray. Every window in the town had been lined with black candles, honoring Aster's heritage. More than two hundred people marched in her procession. At the front, Kade led in his werewolf form on all fours, as it was customary for his people to shift in mourning. His werewolf form had received glances, but the people of Callum had put Aster's passing above all else. Behind him, Evelyn rode atop Bleu. Tovi walked beside her, head bowed, eyes red and wet. Her friend had been silent and sad the whole walk.

Everyone traveled three miles over the hills to reach the forest where the Arkwood coven laid their dead, and instead of black, everyone wore green.

For Aster and her bright, beautiful magic that grew life.

They burned her over a pyre, as witches' tradition demanded, releasing her soul into the afterlife. Evelyn had used her flame at the request of Aster's parents, placing a hand on a single branch and allowing the fire to overtake the bed of wood. It burned for hours, the flame twisting and swallowing the pyre until it reached Aster's clothed body.

Even as the red and orange blazed, the entire pyre engulfed, it did not feel real. Evelyn stood like a shell, hollow and empty. Her feet had weighed heavy as lead during the procession, and her hand had shaken as she'd conjured her flame to burn her friend's body. When she'd stepped back, Tovi had grabbed her hand and held firm. She'd turned and met her friend's jade gaze, her eyes glistening with tears. A comfort, a hope, a gesture of strength she needed and was grateful for.

Hours later, Kade had not left her side, not even as the flames died. Smoke rose through the forest's canopy from the pile of blackened rubble. No one remained, not even Aster's coven or parents. They'd invited her back to their home for refreshments, to share stories of Aster, and to honor her memory. Tovi had left, giving her hand a squeeze and whispering something to Kade as she parted with them.

Evelyn could not leave. She *knew* deep in her bones that the White Lady had killed Aster, but responsibility still gripped her heart with an iron hand. If she had solved the murders already, had killed the vampyr, or had learned more about the White Lady, Aster might still be alive.

Yet again, Evelyn had failed someone she cared for, and the weight of it sickened her. The thought she could not shake was that this murder had been purposeful. Her friend's death had not been a coincidence. Aster had been killed for her hands, but also targeted. Whoever killed her did it to get at Evelyn.

They knew her history; it should scare her. Break her. Two years ago, Evelyn would have crumbled from Aster's death as she had with her parents'. Rage and determination filled her now. Her bruised heart had been wrapped with thorns of guilt. The world had lost a beam of light due to Aster's death. Evelyn could not bring that light back, but she could fight for it.

"For you, Aster, I swear it," Evelyn said to the wind.

The forest bristled. Birds sang from branches. The wind came to life. It felt like an answer. *"We hear you."*

Behind her, Kade moved off to the side, leaves and twigs cracking under the weight of his bulked werewolf form. Out of sight, bones snapped and cracked.

Skin rippled. Shifting sounded dreadful. According to Kade, it didn't hurt. It felt like an intense stretch as his magic did the work.

He joined Evelyn at her side, wearing an untied tunic and loose trousers. He took her hand, rubbing his thumb across her knuckles. Evelyn shut her eyes, fighting the tears. She'd already cried so much and had remained strong in front of Callum and the Arkwood coven.

"Evelyn, I know you want to stay in Callum," he said, taking a shuddering breath.

She snapped her eyes open, assessing Kade's tight jaw and the apprehension swimming in his eyes. Why did she feel a *"but"* would come next?

"But we should consider returning to Sorin, seeking your coven and my pack," Kade said.

Evelyn pulled her hand from Kade's, his words like ice water.

"No," Evelyn said. "I can't. Not yet. Not until I kill whoever is responsible for these murders. I must do this. For Aster. For McKenna, Fiona, and Sheila." She shook her head, her decision unyielding.

"I know you want vengeance for Aster. I want whoever did this to suffer, too."

"It is not vengeance, Kade, it is justice. The right thing to do. I will not abandon Callum like I did my people."

"Leaving to get reinforcements is not abandoning them, Evelyn." His tone was gentle.

"It feels like it, like I'm running because things have gotten worse," Evelyn whispered. She stepped closer to him, taking hold of his hand. "Kade, if we are right about a spell, they now have all four body parts from the witches' creed. We still have no idea what they intend to do—"

"Which is precisely why we need to go home. This is beyond just the two of us. This mysterious White Lady knows who you are. Evelyn, you cannot dismiss the severity of that fact. You are Daughter of the Goddess."

She did not need to be reminded.

"I will not abandon Callum!" Evelyn yelled.

Kade sighed, running his hands through his hair. He released Evelyn's hand, bracing his hands on his hips. "I know you feel like you failed Aster, but staying will not undo her death."

"No—I mean, yes, a part of me does feel like I failed her, but this feeling is different. I do not feel lost. I feel I need to do this."

"Evelyn—"

"Going back will not be as simple as you believe. I left. There will be consequences. You think the Elders will allow us to shift their priorities because of some murders in Torren? No. All they care about is the prophecy. We will be wed within hours of arriving in Sorin—"

"*Moons*, I don't give a fuck what the Elders want or what they think. Screw the prophecy. We will not marry until we're ready, until you're ready, *if* it is something you ever want, my duty be damned. All I want is us."

Us.

Evelyn shut her eyes, swallowing her tears. Kade meant every word he said. Her magic soared from his conviction, and his tone sent shivers down her spine. She didn't know how badly she had needed to know those things, be reassured of them, but it did not negate that they still had an unsolved murder and people to protect in Callum.

"Evelyn. I want us to be safe, to be together, and I know in my bones that these murders related to the witches' creed are far more than they appear." Kade searched her face, his own etched with worry.

Evelyn said nothing. She could not say the words he wanted to hear. At this moment, they did not agree.

After a few beats, Kade's eyes widened, as if he too realized she would not change her mind. He moved past her, walking away.

"Kade, wait," she said.

He stilled.

"I'm sorry," she whispered.

Kade did not turn back to face her. He continued walking, and in the thicket of trees, Evelyn watched his body shift into his werewolf form. Bleu sauntered over to her, nibbling at her hair. With one last glance at the pyre, Evelyn headed back to Callum.

She rode Bleu straight to Aster's shop, disappointed that she and Kade had gotten into an argument. She thought of her parents, how they'd get in disputes when she was a child. They'd been cross but never yelled or used words to hurt the other. In fact, oftentimes they'd spend some time apart before coming back together. At such a young age, Evelyn hadn't seen it for what it was, but now she understood.

Sometimes emotions needed time to settle.

Evelyn would give Kade space and hope the rift between them was not too vast.

She sighed, bracing herself in front of Aster's shop. Being surrounded by the people of Callum and seeing Aster's parents had made today so much harder. It didn't matter that Aster had been murdered by someone else—Evelyn would carry the weight of her death as if she were solely to blame.

But as she'd told Kade, her grief and failure did not hold her down. It gave her resolve, a deeper eagerness to solve these murders once and for all. She entered Aster's shop, the lock clicking undone in the presence of her magic. The shop still held no life, but Evelyn had worked hard to clean it up. Dead plants sat on the shelves, but no decay littered the ground and not a single stain of blood remained.

Evelyn recalled meeting Aster for the first time. She hadn't met a fellow witch in so long, her magic had hummed to life in greeting. Frightened, she'd cowered from her own kind, but Aster had been welcoming—despite the slight attempt at blackmail, which Evelyn would be forever grateful for.

Staying in Callum, renting Aster's spare studio apartment, and working with Kade had been the best decisions she'd ever made. She believed deeply that she'd been meant to make them as if all those years ago, maybe she had been supposed to leave in order to get to these moments. Fate had an interesting way of laying a path down.

She walked the perimeter of the shop, trailing her fingers over the pots Aster had painted, her delicate handwriting displaying the types of plants and prices, and the bookshelves threatening to lean and topple without magic to keep them up.

Even without Aster's magic, it still felt like *her*.

Evelyn sighed, her tears all spent. She sulked to Aster's workstation and poured herself a glass of honeysuckle wine. She sat, taking in the last projects. A pathos propagated to the left. A fiddle and fig sapling recently potted. A bushel of pinecones bagged for selling.

Evelyn buried her face in her hands, gritting through the heartache and anger. She'd never see her friend again, hear her bubbly laughter, or appreciate that wide smile. She hated the vampyr, hated the White Lady, and wished she knew which one had killed Aster.

To the right of the table, a stack of books and notebooks sat, notes scattered about. Evelyn caught the list she'd written weeks ago, listing the first two murders. Aster had added to it in her handwriting, the attempt on Tessa and death of Sheila. Evelyn wanted to vomit. How cruel was it that Aster had written this list, not knowing her name would be added to those who'd died?

Evelyn flipped through other notes, discovering that not only had Aster learned the unknown word in McKenna's journal had been "lady" as well, but she'd also dug up significant research on the mysterious woman. Evelyn scanned over the documents, completely immersed in Aster's findings. She read over her neat handwriting, flipping through the pages more than once to be sure.

Fucking flames.

She and Kade had been wrong all along.

Chapter Fifty-Three

Kade

Kade sat under a tree that grew upon a hill just above Callum. The town appeared empty and silent. After Aster's funeral, the townspeople had left the rest of the day to mourn. Silver lined the horizon where the sun dipped low, past the luminous clouds stretching for miles against a darkening sky. The earth seemed to mourn too with shadows and silence, recognizing the beacon of light it had lost.

Kade hurt from the loss of a friend, but he hurt most for Evelyn. The sight of her horror leaning over Aster's body would haunt him, and he hoped his mate would never feel such pain ever again. Yet, with the murders and their impending fight against the vampyr back in Sorin, Kade's hope felt futile.

Movement below on the path leading to his perch caught his attention. Evelyn's black hair blew in the breeze. She hugged her dark green sweater closer to her figure as she climbed to meet him. His chest swelled at the sight of her. No matter what she came to tell him, even if she hadn't changed her mind, he was glad she had sought him out.

"However did you find me?" he said.

She gave him a small smile and plopped next to him. With her near, Kade calmed, relaxing with a deep exhale.

"Miss Patricia," she said. "Though you're not exactly inconspicuous in your werewolf form. Half the town saw before you shifted. If ships were at sea, I bet they'd even spot you, too."

Kade bumped his shoulder against hers, appreciating her mood. She turned to him, gray eyes roaming over his face like she could read his soul. She ran her hand through his hair, brushing her fingers over his beard. She held his cheek as she made him look at her.

"Kade, I have to see this through."

"I know," he whispered. Of course he did. His brave mate. He should never have suggested she do otherwise.

She picked at the grass. "But after this is all over, I will return to Sorin with you. I swear it. I want there to be an 'us', too," she said.

Kade shut his eyes and pulled Evelyn into him. She sat between his legs, her back flush to his chest. Kade rested his chin on her shoulder, breathing in her warm and sweet scent.

"Whatever your coven, sisters, or my pack throw at us, we will get through it. Together. I will be by your side, Evelyn."

"I know. I wouldn't have survived the last two days without you."

"I am sorry. Aster was . . ."

"Special."

"Yes."

The two of them sat in silence. Being together, Kade realized, was enough. Always would be. He'd not known Aster like Evelyn had but had met a fair share of people in his time. Aster had been special, was special. Magic like hers was rare, and he'd not soon forget. All his life he'd trained to defeat the darkness and nothing of late had swayed that desire, only deepened it.

Night was on the prowl. Lights down in Callum twinkled like fallen stars coming to life. The deep blue of the sea diverged to black. Rumblings of thunder in the distance matched the intensity of the wind.

"As much as I'd like to sit here in your arms for all my days, there is something I came to tell you," Evelyn said, turning to face him.

"What is it?"

Evelyn pulled out a folded stack of paper from her pocket, handing it over to him. He opened the pages, scanning the notes as she explained.

"All along, we thought it was a vampyr, but after the cliffs, we started to question if it was the White Lady," she said. "Aster was one step ahead of us. She'd fully translated McKenna's journal. Apparently, the White Lady had once been a witch during the Great Burnings. She had wanted to use dark magic against the humans, but her coven refused. Eventually, worried about the power she'd succumbed to, they tried to bind her magic. The account of it gets murky, but there have always been whisperings that she'd never really died. Screams in the night, shrieks before people died like she'd manifested into a ghost. She earned the name banshee."

Kade followed Aster's notes, reading over the abilities of the White Lady.

"From what Aster hypothesized, it seems the White Lady could feed off darkness. Aster didn't note what the White Lady's intent was, but it makes more sense a witch using dark magic collected the body parts for a spell."

Kade shook his head. "True, but what about the blue-hued skin and the intimate bites?"

Evelyn nodded, riffling through the notes to show him a certain page. "A vampyr bite turns their victim blue as a result of the darkness in their venom. Though we don't know how vampyrs were created, Aster wondered if it was simply dark magic. Only the first two murders, McKenna and Fiona, had blue-hued skin with bitemarks.

"It could've been easy to manipulate how they appeared after their deaths—even the bite marks, if she'd wanted. Aster also believed the White Lady drained her victims of blood for sustenance, though she isn't a vampyr. We both saw her teeth. The bite marks could match."

The clues and findings fit, except for one. "But McKenna had a lover, a *male* lover."

Evelyn nodded, her brows furrowing. "I know, it was the only clue that didn't match Aster's theory. I went to Commissioner Doyle and, well, it turns out a sailor's body had been pulled from the bay the same week of McKenna's death. He hadn't been bitten, hadn't been drained of blood. They assumed he'd fallen into the water drunk. It happens often during storm season when sailors have little to do."

"You think he was McKenna's lover?"

Evelyn shrugged. "What if he was? A young man winds up dead the same week as McKenna—I'm not sure we can chalk it up to coincidence. What if the White Lady had been pretending it was vampyr attacks all along so witches in Callum didn't realize it was her? Think about it. Maybe the White Lady lured McKenna with the promise of magic. She learned McKenna went to Connacht Castle with her lover and killed them both when she had the chance."

Kade considered Fiona Kerry's murder. The images he'd seen hadn't been clear enough to decipher whether the killer was a vampyr or a human; he'd simply assumed. The dark and wrong energy from the figure could fit the dark magic of the White Lady as well as that of a vampyr. It also made sense that the creature born of this land would gain the backing of the other dark creatures. The kelpie from Lake Glenn, the demons at Castle Connacht, the Far Darrig in the Gray Wood.

"What about the scáth like vampyr that attacked Riven? Did it look like the White Lady?"

Evelyn shook her head. "No, I wondered about that, too, but that vampyr behaved oddly. It didn't go for any of us, for our blood. What if it was another ploy to make us believe a vampyr was behind the murders? A spell, an enchantment? Dark magic of sorts?"

"The missing body parts would eventually have led to someone believing it was for a spell," Kade agreed. "Then a witch."

"Exactly."

Kade sighed, digesting everything. After all this time, it was hard to adjust to the idea that the killer wasn't a vampyr. He supposed the White Lady had been clever, keeping witches off her trail and creating quite a frenzy amongst those in Callum, but he still felt like he'd missed the signs. The last two murders hadn't pointed to a vampyr, and all along the missing body parts hadn't aligned with a vampyr either. Frustration flushed through him. They'd been fooled. According to Aster's theory, there hadn't been a vampyr at all.

But there was something else, something more important.

"What about the White Lady knowing who you are?" he said. "I still find that unnerving." He rubbed his thumb across the back of her hand. He didn't like the White Lady knowing who Evelyn was. It didn't sit well with him and had been his driving reason to travel back to Sorin.

Evelyn bit her lip, looking down at the grass. "That is the part I'm afraid to tell you."

Kade waited, his stomach twisting into knots. The White Lady had almost killed Evelyn, and he feared that if they had to face her again, they couldn't win without help.

"Go on," he whispered.

"We all assumed the victims had one thing in common, being young women. Yet, Aster traced their bloodlines, their ancestors. It appears they all trace back to the original Carson coven, even Aster."

Kade's breath left him, and his heart stopped. "They . . . they all share your bloodline."

Evelyn fiddled with her fingers, appearing unnerved like he was. "Yes. All of them are distant relatives, barely even cousins, and only Aster was a witch."

"I'm suddenly realizing why you're telling me this last and after declaring you're seeing this through."

"I don't want to argue," Evelyn said with a shake of her head.

Kade sighed, gripping her hand tightly in his. "No, there's no sense in it. We have to see this through, even if there are a lot of unknowns."

Evelyn squeezed his hand back. "I know I am Daughter of the Goddess, and the Carson coven bloodline must mean something to her spell, but we don't have time to figure that out. If we defeat her, those unknowns won't matter."

"Let us hope so." Kade sighed. "If one were to craft a spell like this in nature, from the little I know of witchcraft, they'd need a powerful place to do it."

"Aster thought of that, too." Evelyn found the last page of notes. "It is an ancient faerie tomb built into the mound of a hill named Newgrange. At five thousand years old, it was the oldest faerie ruin in all of Torren. It sits north of Callum."

"Other than its age, what significance does it have?" Kade asked.

Evelyn pointed to a sketch Aster had drawn. "The entrance of the tomb allows the light of the sun to cast straight through the center, but only on one evening of the year, autumn equinox."

"Which is when?

"Tomorrow," Evelyn breathed. "That's if she has all the parts of the spell."

Kade muttered a curse. That gave them little time to prepare against the White Lady, if she planned to perform the spell then and there.

"With the age of the tomb and the power of the sun's light, the White Lady could conjure any spell she wished, even with the forces of dark magic," Evelyn said. "There is a chance she does not have all the parts of the spell, though. The body parts could be a portion or only a small part."

"True, but we cannot afford to assume that is the case. It is too much of a risk."

"I agree."

For a few moments, Kade sat in silence, night fully upon them. They had so much to plan, and so little time to do it, but he believed they could.

"Together," he said. "For Aster."

Evelyn gave him a curt nod. "For Aster."

Chapter Fifty-Four

Evelyn

Kade and Commissioner Doyle had spread the whisperings of a vigil to honor the women who had passed on. By midday, said whisperings were so wild, they'd threaded themselves into the wind. Those who lived in the villages outside of Callum, even those from towns miles over, had ventured to the harbor.

Yet, the whisperings were only whisperings, not plans to light candles and talk of the dead. They were a distraction, something to egg on the White Lady to follow through with the spell or whatever she had planned. Everyone had gathered together to wait out the fight, too.

Kade encouraged strength in numbers. He instructed everyone to stay indoors once the sun went down. Miss Patricia had cried as she watched them leave, holding her apron for dear life as Commissioner Doyle put an arm around her shoulder.

Many had offered to accompany them. McKenna's brother and father. Aster's parents. Tessa and Aaron along with her family. Even Mr. Kerry, Fiona's father, had shown up, hatchet in hand. Yet, Kade and Evelyn had refused. They appreciated the support, the sentiment, and witnessed Callum's honor in wanting to bring justice to those they'd lost, but they'd asked everyone to stay behind to protect one another. Evelyn and Kade needn't shed more blood and also needed their wits about them. They couldn't afford to protect anyone while they focused on killing the White Lady.

On foot, they ventured northeast toward Newgrange. Kade wore a sleeveless tunic and linen trousers and assured Evelyn they were enchanted to grow with him when he shifted into his werewolf form. Made from the silk of prairie worms, they appeared dainty but were utterly indestructible. He winked when he explained that fighting in the nude wasn't ideal.

Kade also wore his Drengr sword strapped to his back, the crest visible at the hilt. He'd had it stamped that morning after Evelyn had encouraged him to, adamant he go into this fight as Kade Drengr. He'd not argued, seemingly content to restore his sword to its original glory.

Evelyn wore leather trousers, tighter than she was used to and a leather corset strapped over a tunic, one easy to move in but enchanted to act as armor. She'd twisted her hair around her staff, keeping it smoothed away from her face. She felt secure, oddly armored as if she were again on the Guard back home. Kade took her hand, running his thumb over her fingers. They said nothing. Everything shone in their eyes. His gold, reminiscent of the sun setting, and Evelyn's silvery blue, like the rim of the moon still awaiting nightfall.

They'd devised their plan before they'd left Callum. Discussed every possible scenario. They'd studied the few layouts of Newgrange. They both knew what they needed to do.

As they continued over the hills and into the first few moments of the sun's descent, the mound became visible beyond a rolling hill patchy with rock and wilted buttercups. It appeared like a rising green sun in the distance, too perfect to be a hill and rimmed with a base of stone.

"Do you think it's powerful enough for a spell?" Kade asked.

Unlike Castle Connacht or Lake Glenn, no darkness lay in the wind or air here. The breeze over the land smelled of the winter prowling from farther north, but Evelyn's magic detected nothing else. Not even the spirits or souls buried within or whomever it honored. Compared to the Gray Wood, it didn't appear alive either.

It was simply a tomb, but its age and intactness were breathtaking—older than witches or werewolves. It was a wonder time had not left its mark.

Evelyn nodded in answer to Kade's question. "Its age alone could be enough. Dark magic is also different from regular magic. Wickedness and intent can feed it. Considering the White Lady's power, I'd say this spot would work well for her."

As they grew closer, they saw smoke against the evening sky rising from the center. Through the open entrance, a fire flickered.

"Someone's inside," Evelyn said as they crept down the hill.

Kade nodded. "I can hear them moving about. A woman's voice. Muttering. I've also detected a scent. Familiar, too."

"A scent?"

"Licorice."

For a moment, Evelyn tried to hear and sense what Kade had mentioned, forgetting his werewolf senses outmatched hers. Though he wasn't Cyrus the huntsman any longer, he was still the same man. Kind, thoughtful, loyal. She supposed he'd been Kade all along, and it had only been his werewolf that had been missing, something she was still learning more and more about.

Anticipation prickled Evelyn's fingers the closer they neared, the muttering becoming clearer to Evelyn. The shrill voice belonged to the White Lady, and so far, Aster seemed to be right.

They had no vegetation, no rock to hide their approach. Evelyn stretched out her magic to muffle their steps.

But Kade laid a hand on her arm and whispered, "Save your energy and magic for the fight. There's a chance she assumes we're already coming. The effort would be a waste."

His eyes roamed over her face, and Evelyn nodded in agreement. She turned away, but Kade held her firm. He said nothing of what was to come, what lay inside the tomb, or whatever they faced.

He kissed her.

With passion, eagerness, rightness, and adoration. Feverish and sweet, his lips moved with hers, in a defining tandem, a physical declaration that he was with her. Through it all.

They pulled apart, taking one last glance at each other, and then Evelyn continued to lead them on. At the cusp of the entrance, the White Lady's mutterings echoed. Chants of Olde Witch, of words Evelyn didn't recognize, anger and hatred laced within each one.

Evelyn faced Kade. His nostrils flared, his jaw ticked. She could tell—maybe it was even their bond—that he didn't want to leave her side, but they had a plan.

He nodded, and Evelyn faced forward.

She tiptoed down the corridor leading to the fire, sliding against the walls. Swirls and circles carved the stone, and Evelyn's fingers grazed the grooves as she continued inward. At the end of the path, she stopped.

At the tomb's center, a fire burned but no one stood manning it. Across the way, a single swirl had been carved into the stone. The rest of the walls were smooth, untouched. The falling sun's glow reached across the tomb's floor, casting a sliver of orange light onto the wall as well. A hair stood between the light and the carved swirl. Minutes before the tomb reached its full potential.

"Daughter of the Goddess," the White Lady's voice sounded through the tomb, except this time, the White Lady was here. Her voice was close, and it sent shivers over Evelyn's skin. Despite the grating evil in the White Lady's words, Evelyn stood tall, proud, believing in what she came here to do.

A flash of darkness fizzled in the space, and the White Lady appeared. This time, she possessed a body. Dressed in a long white cloth draped around her like a cloak, her bony frame jutted in places, her frail arms stretching outward as if welcoming Evelyn to the tomb.

That was when Evelyn noticed the vacant space behind the White Lady, stone pushed away to reveal a hole large enough for a body. There was nothing in the ancient tomb that she could sense—no magic, energy, or life. The White Lady had been surviving off it, lying dormant like a beast slumbering during winter. She'd been buying her time, waiting to awaken.

The White Lady snapped her fingers, and the flame in the center of the tomb flared to black fire. Gray and onyx danced.

"I sense that you're alone. Did the werewolf finally see you for who you are? A coward. A runaway," the White Lady said.

Evelyn stayed silent. She had no time for doubt. She had no time for the intrusive thoughts that would keep her from her task.

"It appears your friend's death did the trick. You and I aren't so different. Both seeking vengeance."

"Do not speak of her," Evelyn said. Calm. Collected. Determined.

"Aster Arkwood?" the White Lady sneered. "An earthly witch, the very kind who turned their back on their sisters as they were burned at the stake. You stooped low to be her friend."

Evelyn snapped her fingers, extinguishing the black fire between them with her power. She took a step farther into the tomb, meeting the White Lady's beady red eyes.

"She was full of love, light, and life," Evelyn said. "Things you know nothing of." She withdrew her staff from her hair. The dragon bone's power vibrated through her hands, and she lit it aflame, then slammed it to the stone ground.

The White Lady took a step back as the flames danced her way.

The light beamed across her gaunt cheekbones and sickly white skin. Sneering, the White Lady hissed and bared her razor teeth. She used her shawl to hide from the light, and even if the White Lady hadn't pretended to be a vampyr, Evelyn couldn't help but notice the similarities. She supposed dark magic affected everything in the same way.

The White Lady thrust her gnarled hand out over the tomb's stone floor. Evelyn sent her fire, hitting the wall of darkness the White Lady had manifested. Gold and black collided with one another.

"You're weak!" the White Lady yelled. "You failed your friend, and I took her hands! You are nothing but a façade of strength and power."

Evelyn shut out the memory of Aster's dead, mutilated body and held her ground, believing she could. Their powers collided, and the White Lady pushed her farther over the center of the stone.

Aster's words rallied Evelyn. *Your magic would be nothing without you.*

Evelyn felt those words and put all her hope and belief in them. Her friend may have been gone, but her memory would never fade. Evelyn would never forget what Aster had taught her, reminiscent of her father's last words.

Believe, Evelyn.

The White Lady curled her hand, jabbing her magic and breaking Evelyn's wall of flame. In that instant, the beam of sunlight, the perfect minute of the day, hit behind the White Lady and illuminated the carved swirl. It caught fire, molten rock searing red.

Throwing one hand in front and the other behind her, the White Lady cast her dark magic in both directions. The light spreading through the carving of the tomb turned black and the stone ground began to crack, the sound echoing through the entire tomb.

At the center, a fracture split through the rock. The ground shook again, and Evelyn used her staff for balance. Rubble and rock crumbled into the steaming liquid that bubbled from beneath the ground. Death, decay, and darkness seeped into the air. The spell. The potion. The White Lady had used not only the age and time of the tomb, she'd used its structure.

Evelyn stood her ground, not losing hold of her flame. She met her fear head on, manifesting it into power and feeding her conviction to fight for those women who'd lost their lives to the darkness. She gave no stock to doubt, only her belief.

In her plan, forged with Kade. In her power. In herself.

The White Lady slumped, spent from her magic. Her already pale and weathered skin appeared to age before Evelyn. Her bones peeked through, stretched tight over darkened eye sockets and a hollow nose. She retrieved a sack from her shawl, full and heavy.

Evelyn's heart sank, her magic sensing death.

The body parts.

Evelyn whipped her staff, sending her flame toward them, attempting to destroy those parts of the spell. Her ball of fire ricocheted off the sack and rounded back.

"No!" she shouted as the White Lady thrust the parts into the bubbling liquid. Black fire flared to life, the liquid morphing also to black. The sack sank, the liquid eating away at it.

The White Lady began to chant.

"With the gouged eyes, the ripped heart, the severed mind, and the lost hands, shield us, oh darkness! With the blood of the light, shield us, oh darkness! In this powerful hour, grant us cover, oh darkness!"

Movement caught Evelyn's eye, but she paid no mind to the figure stalking the perimeter of the tomb's cave in the shadows and in silence.

Evelyn approached the White Lady, whose eyes had rolled into the back of her head, and moved around the bubbling potion. Acid shot up in bouts from the center. Black fire flared around the White Lady. Black inky poison, like the one Evelyn had endured, inched its way like ivy up the White Lady's arms.

Evelyn prepared to deliver a blow with her staff, but the White Lady's eyes snapped back and met her gaze. She cast her magic, sending Evelyn flying across the tomb. Airborne. Until she hit the stone. Her bones hurt, her side throbbed, and her head rang.

The White Lady advanced.

"It is too bad I cannot kill you, Daughter of the Goddess," she said. "For we need you."

Evelyn stayed put, holding her stomach as if in anguish.

The White Lady cackled, mere skin and bone as she stared down at Evelyn. Her beady red eyes were now bloodshot, glistening orbs of full crimson.

Evelyn's own magic cringed in proximity to the darkness. At what cost had this dark witch done this? She'd lost herself. Destroyed herself. And for what? Why?

"Did you really think you could take me on?"

"Yes," Evelyn breathed. "We did."

The White Lady's eyes went wide.

But it was too late. A roar vibrated through the tomb. Kade in his werewolf form broke through the smoke and darkness, his jaw wide. He launched straight for the White Lady's shoulder, embedding his teeth into the nape of her neck. She screamed. Screeched. Bellowed in pain.

In a single move, Evelyn rose to her feet. Kade thrust the injured White Lady into the center, over the rocks overlooking the steaming liquid. Death and darkness came from beneath. The spell had started.

Evelyn felt her bond with Kade, the fated mates magic giving her strength—tethered, intertwined, unbreakable. She couldn't fathom the depths of their power when they finally bonded their souls in unity, knowing how strong the connection between them was now, how their magic danced effortlessly with one another.

Kade stood by her side, massive in his werewolf form. A warrior. A protector. His cross between man and wolf bulged with muscle and menace. The dark magic fled in fear from his unwavering strength. He growled when the White Lady moved, baring his sharp teeth, his eyes alight with lethal promise.

Her wide, red eyes looked up at him, mouth agape. "I didn't sense you! How are you in my tomb?"

Buried in the depths of his long mane, Kade lifted Blair's enchanted necklace. For this one fight, he'd put it back on to mask his wolf and presence. He tore it off, casting it into the flames. The last of his disguise burned away, as if the last of the lies between Evelyn and Kade were vanquished.

Evelyn cast her flame atop the liquid. Flame ate away at the darkness, spreading through the fractures and cracks of the floor.

"No!" the White Lady screeched, more animal than woman, scrambling toward her spell. Her shawl fell into the flaming liquid, catching fire. Screaming, she turned back to Evelyn.

And laughed.

"You still have no clue what is at play, Daughter of the Goddess and Son of the God!"

No, they didn't. But it didn't matter. The White Lady was wicked and wretched and lost to the darkness. Whatever she had planned would end, too, with her death.

"This is for Aster. For McKenna, Tessa, Fiona, and Sheila."

Evelyn flicked her wrist, feeding her flame to the end of the White Lady's shawl. Shock fell over the dark witch's features.

"Wait," she cried as the fire climbed up her body, eating at her darkness. "Stop! You don't understand! No!"

The White Lady rolled and writhed as Evelyn's flame consumed her.

Evelyn looked away, the sight jarring and sickening.

"Wait! My Dark Prince! Please!" she cried over the flames.

Before Evelyn could think more of the desperate ramblings, the tomb shook around them. Kade grabbed her hand, and she found the pads of his paws plush and soft.

They pushed toward the entrance, Evelyn's flame rising and falling over the darkness as they retreated from the tomb. Assured her magic would hold—the White Lady lay unmoving, one arm dangling in the potion—Evelyn continued on.

Down the hallway, the tomb shook again, knocking the two of them apart and into the stone walls. Kade hoisted Evelyn into his arms and ran.

They exited into the evening light, their eyes meeting for the first time. Hope and triumph soared in Evelyn's chest, but then the center mound concaved inward. Dust and debris blew past them. Kade knelt, held Evelyn close, and shielded her from the debris. She gripped his fur, holding on as the world seemed to quake all around them.

The grassy ground trembled, the tomb collapsing into a pile of rubble with a final boom. Kade still held Evelyn for a few breaths, the only sound against the quiet backdrop.

No screams from the White Lady. No hissing from the potion. Her flame had been snuffed out, and so had the ancient power of the tomb.

Nothing but the evening wind, awakening stars, the swaying grass, and their triumph.

"Fucking flames, we did it," Evelyn breathed.

We did.

Startled, Evelyn jumped and gripped the fur on his chest tighter. Kade's voice had sounded in her mind.

A snort came from his snout, and his muzzle tightened and exposed his canines into what Evelyn imagined as a smile. It was a terrifying and hilarious sight.

"Is this a werewolf thing?" she asked, heart still racing with adrenaline.

We call it mind-linking.

Whatever it was, Evelyn liked it almost as much as she enjoyed being in Kade's arms. His hold on her granted a comfort she'd not known she needed.

My brave mate, he said.

Goddess, when he looked at her with those eyes, even in his werewolf form, she believed those words. They were sweet, and she appreciated them. Didn't mind hearing them one bit. And what made it sweeter: Evelyn agreed.

Because Evelyn did believe. Instead of believing in her flame, she'd believed in herself. Her Goddess-given gift no longer controlled or defined her. *She* controlled her power, possessed its strength and potential all herself.

Protector. Defender. Daughter of the Goddess.

She was brave. And she'd defeated the White Lady.

Chapter Fifty-Five

Kade

Outside, the sun shone over Callum on the first wintry day. Frost embedded in corners of the windows, and the fire blazed with extra strength against the cold.

Tangled in their half-nakedness, Kade and Evelyn had explored every inch of each other the last two days as they came down from their victorious triumph. He trailed her spine with his fingers as she slept. She released a sigh at his touch, and Kade couldn't get enough of how responsive she was. Her sounds. Her cries.

The way she said his name before she fell off the edge of sexual bliss.

He also loved how she drove him mad with need. Her touches. Her kisses. *Stars above*, the way she worked him.

They'd yet to lie together and complete their fated mates bond. The way their eyes met during passion, the question brewing between them. Where Kade would be over her, so close to her entrance, or when Evelyn would straddle him, her wetness coating his length, and evidently ready for him.

Physically, they were both ready.

Yet, Kade wanted to know if she was with him. She'd promised, but he wanted to be sure. Storm season was over. Ships were coming and going from the harbor.

Before they shared that depth of intimacy, before they fully bonded with the flesh, Kade needed to hear Evelyn was with him. That they'd leave Callum and travel home to Sorin together.

They'd solved the murders. They'd defeated the White Lady.

He felt selfish. Horrid, even. Her feelings for him vibrated through their bond. He knew her intentions, knew her truth, and yet he feared his desire to fulfill their duty would drive her away.

You're staring again, Evelyn said through their mind-linking.

He smiled, impressed that his mate had mastered a werewolf ability so quickly. It had come in quite handy in the sheets when they were too breathy to manage words. As she turned, he stared at the ceiling instead of her nipples pressing against her tunic, ready for him. If he wasn't careful, he'd go against what he wanted.

"Kade," Evelyn said with concern in her tone. She reached over and drew her fingers through his beard. He turned to face her.

She lay on her stomach, leaning on her forearms. Her dark hair spilled over her shoulder. Sleepiness still rimmed her silvery gray eyes, but moons, they were ethereal, ensnaring Kade like the first day they'd met.

"Come home with me," he whispered. The words fell from his mouth in far more of a plea than he'd anticipated.

For a moment, Evelyn said nothing. Moved nothing. Her breath stopped. Her hesitation pushed Kade into a spiral of disappointment, until Evelyn rose, draping her leg over his hips and sitting atop him in a glorious straddle.

Ever so slightly, she rolled her hips over him, and stars above, he wanted to take her right then and there. His earlier goal to wait be damned.

"And why should I do that?" she whispered, cupping his cheek.

Though there was a little playfulness in her tone, Kade knew what she wanted to hear. Not because it was their duty. Not because she was Daughter of the Goddess. And not because they had vampyrs to defeat.

Because I love you.

Kade did not say the words or mind-link them. No. He stared at her, at her beauty, at her ability, at the sheer force of this woman and what she could do to him. And then she smiled. Wide and happy.

"Because I need you," he said, running his hands up her thighs. She shut her eyes at his touch. "Because I've never wanted anything more in life."

It was the truth. He wanted her more than defeating the vampyr. He wanted her more than fulfilling his duty.

"I know your sisters and coven—"

"No," Evelyn said with a shaky breath. "I may be afraid of what they'll say and think. Goddess knows I'm more petrified of what your pack will think of me, too. But"—she paused, staring so deeply into his eyes, she may as well have been talking to his soul—"I will not let that stop me from being by your side. It's what I want, too, Kade. *Us.* I promised after we found justice for Aster that I would come with you, so I am ready when you are."

Relief rushed through Kade, and he kissed her. Fervent and happy. She wanted to be with him, to go home and stay at his side. He broke their kiss and held Evelyn to him as he leaned over the side of the bed. She squealed as they moved as one, laughing into the nape of his neck.

"Kade, what in the world are you doing?"

He rummaged in his sack, feeling what he'd been looking for. He tipped them back upright, holding Evelyn to him with one hand and clutching a necklace with the other.

A white, pearly stone that shimmered with the colors of a rainbow hung in the center of the chain, the winter sun illuminating it like the moon.

"Blair told me to give this to you when you were ready," he said. "I figured now felt like a good time."

He'd been a different man when Blair had handed it to him. Duty above all else, frustrated beyond belief.

Now he knew that what he wanted mattered more, that his duty didn't define him.

Evelyn's eyes widened. She stared at the necklace, silent, and then laughed. She laughed so hard she cried, grabbing hold of the necklace and staring at it as if it might disappear.

"Ev, what is it?"

"Do you know what this is?"

"Your muince, yes," he said. "Blair gave it to me."

"Yes, you're right, Kade," she said. "But do you know what it can do?"

Evelyn laughed again, lacing the necklace around her neck. His silence was her answer.

"It tracks the whereabouts of whoever has it," she said.

Kade held Evelyn tighter, shaking his head. "Evelyn, I swear to you, I never knew."

She put a finger on his lips and planted a small kiss on his cheek. "I know, Kade, and knowing my sister, I am sure she left that detail out on purpose."

"You don't seem mad enough," Kade said, searching her face.

In fact, Evelyn appeared lighter. Relieved.

She held the pendant in her fingers. "You've been in Callum for months, which means Blair has probably known you found me. Storm season may have prevented my coven or your pack coming for us, but storm season ended over a week ago. If they aren't here or haven't sent word, I don't think they're coming at all."

"Which means?"

Evelyn sighed. "Blair probably didn't tell anyone she knew where you were. It also means Blair forgives me for leaving, and she respects my decision to return home when I am ready."

"And are you ready, Ev?" Kade asked, pulling her into him, resting his forehead on hers.

Before she said anything, an urgent knock sounded at the door. Evelyn shared a nervous glance with Kade, and he feared the worst, thanks to the last few weeks. Yet, they'd killed the White Lady. Another murder hadn't occurred. He hoped. Evelyn moved off him as another knock sounded on the door.

"Coming!" Kade said.

He threw on the closest trousers he could find, and Evelyn wrapped a wool blanket over her, staying in bed as he answered the door. A hooked-nose man stood there, waiting. Kade recognized him as the courier from weeks ago, a letter in hand.

"Kade Drengr, is it?" the man asked.

"It is, yes."

The man nodded, stretching out his hand. The navy wax seal caught Kade's attention. He'd recognize that crest anywhere.

"Miss Patricia said I'd find ya here. Have a good day." He sauntered down the steps.

Kade held the letter, the weight of it heavy, as if the words it held amounted to an omen.

He shut the door, unfolding the letter as he did so. Evelyn rose from the bed, joining him in the center of the apartment.

"Kade, what is it?" Evelyn said.

It was addressed to him, and he read over the words written in Eldrick's hand. Neat and tiny. He read the letter a second time. Only on the third time did it all make sense for Kade. The words began to blur, the news they reported tilting his world off-kilter.

"Kade?" Evelyn asked, taking a step forward.

"My father," Kade said, looking up at her and away from the words breaking his heart. "He's dead."

Evelyn sucked in a breath. "Oh, Kade . . ."

He pushed past her, leaving the letter in her hands. "Vampyrs. They attacked his convoy from a pack meeting." Kade recounted Eldrick's words, more to himself than her. Maybe if he heard them out loud, he'd believe them. *Stars above*, his father was dead.

For years, Kade had assumed his father would die from his broken heart. He never imagined the vampyr would take down his strong, wild father.

He began collecting his things, moving without thinking. "I have to go home. I've been gone for too long."

Evelyn said something, but a ringing began in his ears. He folded his cloak, retrieved his boots, ignored Maxie as she danced between his legs, meowing over and over.

Father is dead. As your new Alpha, I command you to come home. Our pack and all of Sorin need you.

Kade had been wrong. He'd deviated from his duty, had dismissed what needed to be done. And now his father was dead. Like when his mother had died, Kade had allowed what he wanted to get in the way. He was Son of the God, prophesied to defeat the vampyr, and it was time he began remembering that—

"I love you," Evelyn said.

The words didn't register as Kade continued to gather his things, throwing them into his worn-out pack. His father, dead. The leader of the Drengr pack. Eldrick would take over as Alpha, and Kade would need to be there, to help and support him. He'd also need his cloak and boots. Where had he put them last?

"Kade, I love you," Evelyn said. "And I'm coming with you."

He stopped. His heart quickened, and Evelyn's words touched his soul.

She loved him.

He turned, inch by inch, to face her, as if turning too quickly might fracture the moment or reveal it to be entirely an illusion.

Evelyn's silvery gray eyes glistened with tears, and she stared at him, waiting for a response. Those words . . . Kade felt them deep in his bones. They were true for him, and Evelyn meant them, too.

"I wish I'd told you sooner or at a different time entirely, but I need you to know the truth, Kade," Evelyn said. "I need you to know I'm with you through this."

Moons, he'd lost himself. He'd let his grief get the best of him. He'd lost who he wanted to be and what truly defined him. Love, loyalty, friendship, and hope. Not duty. Duty was not what drove him to pack his things and rush home. It was love for his father, loyalty to his pack. It wasn't duty commanding his soul as he stared at Evelyn. Moons, she was a beauty, and her love grounded him in the present.

His brave mate.

In two long strides, Kade grasped hold of her hands. "No, I needed you to say them. I needed to hear them. Stars above, Ev." He rested his forehead on hers.

"I'm so sorry, Kade," she said, squeezing his hands.

He shook his head, the threat of tears stinging his eyes. His father's health had been declining for years. He, his brothers, and pack knew the inevitable: his father would die from a severed mating bond. Never had he expected his father to *be* killed. Not like this. His grief snuck up on him, given the circumstances of how he lost his father.

"Oh, Kade," Evelyn said, cupping his cheek.

She pulled him down into a hug and held him.

"Losing a parent is not easy," she whispered. "But I swear it to you, Kade, you will get through this."

Kade found himself listening to Evelyn's heartbeat; it grounded him again. Her touch, her arms holding him close. Her cedar and vanilla scent.

He wasn't okay, but she made him feel safe.

He believed in her and in them. Whatever they faced, may it be Eldrick's transition as Alpha, her coven's scrutiny, the demands of the Elders and Alphas, or the threat of the vampyr, they'd face it together.

Chapter Fifty-Six

Evelyn

Evelyn and Kade had packed all their things, and with the funds between them, they'd purchased passage across the Sapphire Sea on a ship that left at sundown destined for Nūa. She had an hour before she joined Kade with Maxie at the docks. They'd already said their goodbyes to Miss Patricia and Commissioner Doyle, and they'd even written a letter to Aster's parents with the last month's rent for her Callum apartment.

Evelyn, though, had one more goodbye before she left, and she hurried her way through Callum to make it. She'd miss the cobblestones, the forever promise of rain in the air, and the sweet, warm smiles of its people. None of that mattered, though, not with Kade's father dead. Evelyn frowned and blinked away tears, sadness for her fated still fresh.

With the death of the Drengr Alpha, Evelyn also feared conflict with the vampyrs was only getting worse. Unease traveled up her spine but resolve tightened her muscles. It was good they would travel back to her homeland, but it would not be easy.

Evelyn had her flame. With or without, she would fight the vampyr alongside Kade, whom she loved.

Deeply.

His kisses. His amber eyes. The sadness he carried now because of his father's death. He needed her, Sorin needed her, and she was determined to let go of Callum, let go of her doubts, and push forward. For Kade. For her people. And most importantly, for herself. Doubt was darkness too, and she'd learned to defeat it. Whatever came next, she could face it.

The black painted brick building sat eerily between two townhomes, the print shop's name swinging on its rusty hinges. Evelyn knocked, hoping to make this quick. Saying goodbye to Tovi would be difficult. She hadn't seen her since Aster's funeral, and they hadn't had time to discuss everything that had happened. That Kade was her fated. That the White Lady had been the killer. With the rush of leaving to head back to their homeland, this goodbye wouldn't be enough with her best friend.

Twisting her pendant necklace in her fingers, Evelyn imagined seeing her sisters. Even knowing Blair had given her time, she was still a bundle of nerves. But Kade was worth it, and believing in herself made it easier.

Evelyn shut her eyes, rallying her breath.

The door swung open, but Riven answered it. Evelyn's shoulders slumped. She'd come to say goodbye to Tovi. She didn't have time for Riven.

He smirked. "Miss Carson."

He held the door open for her to come in, and Evelyn entered, heading to the parlor, and hoping to find Tovi. She found it empty, dark, and cold. The fire lay dormant. Black curtains covered the windows. Not a single sign Tovi was here. She *really* didn't have time for this. The boat left in an hour.

"To what do I owe the pleasure?" Riven asked, hands in his pockets as he slunk his way back to his desk. He wore an ensemble of silk pants and a matching vest with an open tunic, baring his pale chest. "Can I offer you a glass of wine, perhaps?"

Evelyn shook her head. "I came to say goodbye to Tovi. Do you know where I could find her? I'm leaving Callum today."

Riven looked up like a cat would when its prey moved. He stood, bracing himself over his desk. "Leaving?"

Evelyn's instinct flared. Riven's movements, his tone. Something was off about them. She took a hesitant step back, one tracked by Riven's jade eyes.

Something flashed from the left near the back stairs, barreling into Riven. Dark hair, talons, fidgety movements.

Vampyr.

Evelyn didn't have time to think more on it as Riven and the vampyr tussled. Tovi's brother had strength far more impressive than Evelyn realized. Why was the vampyr in the print shop? How had it gotten in here? And why was it attacking Riven again?

The vampyr threw Riven into his desk, and the wood splinted in the center on impact. Evelyn ignited her hands, flames flaring at her fingertips. She took a step closer, flicking her wrist and thrusting a shot of flame at the vampyr. It screeched, turning from Riven, setting its sights on her.

It widened its arms, a black inky substance traveling up its skin to its elbows. Evelyn breathed in her power, centered on her flame. She didn't hesitate.

Evelyn unleashed her magic.

She thrust both her hands out and sent her flame at the vampyr. Power, heat, and flame flooded out from her. It was her, and she was it. Flame overtook the demon, eating away the darkness. Red and orange consumed black shadowy mists. The vampyr writhed, crumbling into itself like a dry, folded leaf until it became a burnt, black corpse, tucked into a ball in the center of the print shop.

Breathless but smiling with relief, Evelyn sprinted to Riven to check on him.

He lay turned away, and she gripped his shoulders to pull him upright—

Evelyn scrambled back, her heart thudding in her chest as she gasped. Riven's eyes, spidery black veins rimming them, stared at her. His hands had transformed into inky black talons. His head tilted and he flashed an elongated fang.

Evelyn reignited her flame, a whoosh resounding at her sides as she stood. "You're . . . you're a vampyr."

Evelyn's head pounded with the hundreds of questions warring for attention in her confused brain. Had the vampyr bitten him weeks ago? Had he turned as a result with no one noticing?

Riven was a vampyr, though, and a threat. Evelyn held out her hand, flame dancing at her fingertips. "Don't come any closer."

She needed to get back to Kade or warn him that she needed him. Evelyn channeled their bond, reaching out in her mind.

Kade.

She sent out his name as a call. It bounced back as if hitting a wall. Frustrated, Evelyn tried again. Maybe she wasn't doing it right. She tried again, again, and again until a searing pain sliced through her head. Evelyn's knees buckled, and she cried out. *Fucking flames.* Why couldn't she get through to Kade?

"Your werewolf won't be able to sense you here, Daughter of the Goddess. One thing the White Lady was good for was wards and protection spells." He held out his hands and gestured around the room. Discreetly placed volcanic-rock wards sat on nearly every surface.

Evelyn stilled. She looked between the dead vampyr corpse still steaming from her flame and Riven. "How do you know the White Lady?"

Riven placed his hands in his pockets, calm and cool as she stood there with her flame ignited. "We had a working relationship. Business partners, you could call us."

"You were working with the White Lady?" Evelyn's flame flared as her anger grew. At herself. At the situation. "*You* killed the young women." Evelyn shook her head, disbelief rooting her in place. Everything had aligned with the White Lady killing those in Callum. She'd been conducting the dark magic and had all the body parts. They'd thought she'd created a decoy, but all along it had been Riven's servant.

A vampyr.

Anger seared through Evelyn. These past few days she'd thought they'd defeated their enemy. What involvement did Riven have and why?

Suddenly, a cold, unrelenting dread traveled up Evelyn's spine. *No. No. No.* She'd already lost Aster. She couldn't lose another friend. She couldn't fail someone else she loved.

"Where's Tovi?" she demanded.

Riven tilted his head back and laughed.

Evelyn took a step closer, flaring her hands even more. "Where is she?" She bit out the words. The temperature of the print shop rose with her flaring anger.

"Indisposed at the moment." His eyes tracked her slowly. "But don't worry. As my sister and princess of Drystan, I cannot kill her."

Evelyn's flame flickered, her heart tinging at Riven's words. What did he mean by princess of Drystan? Yes, they had a king, but not a princess. Unless . . . Evelyn shook her head, refusing to believe it. Tovi wasn't . . . *No.*

"You're lying," Evelyn said. "*Tell me where she is.*"

Riven stood, laughing. The spidery black veins retreated back into his skin, the color vanishing like disappearing ink. His talons retracted, leaving him with human-like hands.

Evelyn swallowed, blinking away what she'd witnessed. Riven appeared normal again, as if he'd never been a vampyr at all.

"Neat trick, isn't it? I'm sad to tell you that Tovi can do the same exact thing. She has been fooling you into friendship."

The White Lady's last words rang through Evelyn's mind: "*Wait! My Dark Prince! Please!*"

Evelyn couldn't breathe. Her ribs tightened. She held the hope that Riven was wrong. Tovi? Her best friend? A vampyr? No. She refused to accept the piercing pain that drove into her heart. "I don't believe you."

Riven shrugged. "Believe it or not, Tovi is a vampyr. One of the first, I might add."

Betrayal seared through Evelyn like a white-hot burn. Her flame mirrored her anger, threatening to engulf the entire room. She'd trusted Tovi like a sister, had been her friend for years. Tovi had known she'd lost her flame. Why hadn't the vampyr king attacked with that knowledge? Why had Tovi befriended her at all?

Fucking flames, how had Evelyn not realized? Her magic should've sensed the darkness. Even standing in the room with Riven, her magic detected a threat, but not the vampyr curse.

"Why don't you look like other vampyrs? How can you walk in the sunlight?" Evelyn demanded, stepping closer to Riven and raising her flame to her elbows.

Riven's jade eyes snagged on her flame, and he held his hands up in surrender. "I can see you have questions, Daughter of the Goddess."

"Answer. Them."

"Do you know what is in your blood, Miss Carson? Flame, yes, of course. An element that can kill a vampyr. But as vampyrs, we feed off blood, and your blood, my dear, gives us light. We discovered it after killing Carena, the first Daughter of the Goddess. With it in our system, we can walk in the sunlight and mask our true selves. Poetic, don't you think? The one destined to defeat us is also our savior?"

He began to pace as sweat trickled down Evelyn's neck. She felt Kade's absence, and Tovi's betrayal weighed on her as Riven spoke calmly.

"Yet, during our attempt at capturing you two years ago, we discovered your parents' blood did almost the same. The ability to walk in sunlight is within your bloodline. Thanks to some dark magic, we were able to preserve such blood."

Evelyn's flame fell back down to her wrists.

"Tovi drank my parents' blood?"

"No." Riven shook his head. "Tovi is a thorn in my side, and on the opposing side of the court back home. A fucking disgrace to the vampyr race," Riven said, picking lint off his shoulder. "After so many years against the witches and werewolves, I began to wonder what it would be like if all my people could walk in the sunlight."

Evelyn's mind reeled. Vampyrs walking in the sunlight. Because of her bloodline. It made sense. The body parts. Her ancestors. The spell. Whatever the—

"That's why you were working with the White Lady," Evelyn whispered. "She could create the spell."

Her gaze dropped to his ink-stained hands.

The black smudges hadn't been dirt on McKenna or Fiona. They'd been ink.

Riven was the missing piece to the mystery. The reason *why* she and Kade couldn't shake the feeling they'd missed something. Yes, they'd killed the White Lady, but they'd never learned what the body parts or what the spell had been for. Now, Evelyn knew, and dread filled her. They'd been right all along. This was bigger than they'd ever anticipated.

"But the White Lady is dead," Evelyn said. "I burned her a fortnight ago, but you knew that, didn't you."

She remembered the White Lady's shocked eyes as Evelyn's magic brought her down, as flame engulfed her and ate away her dark spirit. How did Riven intend to succeed without a dark witch by his side, without the body parts?

"Ah, yes. The White Lady," Riven said. "I guess I have you to thank. Her screams were quite a delight."

"You let her die," Evelyn said with a shake of her head.

"She took McKenna's eyes before I had the chance to turn her. Went against *my* orders. I swore we'd find enough descendants, but that witch had an agenda of her own, and hung McKenna's body as a message. She believed herself to be in charge."

"McKenna's lover was a sailor," Evelyn said with another shake of her head.

Riven said nothing, but his eyes flashed with a dangerous gleam.

Evelyn wavered between keenness and self-preservation. She wanted to know the truth, but she also wanted to get back to Kade. She thought of everything they'd learned. The clues. The unanswered questions.

"You promised McKenna forever, didn't you? *You* were the lover she had and met in the night."

"After the White Lady derailed my plans, I had to kill a sailor and cover my tracks. I only killed McKenna so I could turn her while the White Lady took care of the rest. She took such delight in killing, feeding her dark magic. Though I believe the White Lady's last choice in descendants did cost her life, and I warned her about using your friend, but she did not particularly like you."

Evelyn's hands burst with more flame. At the mention of Aster, her desire for justice rose again.

Riven's jade eyes—fucking flames, so much like Tovi's—tracked her hands. Not with fear, but with curiosity.

"But all that does not matter," Riven said with an edge. "I have all I need now."

"What about the Far Darrig, the kelpie . . ." Evelyn said.

A cool breeze wisped by Evelyn.

"Allies of the darkness," Riven whispered into her ear from behind. "You have no idea what has started since you left Sorin."

Evelyn's instinct almost made her jump, but she would not balk from fear or intimidation. She kicked the desk forward, toppling it and creating space for her to step forward and attack. She pivoted, shooting her flame upward.

Riven's movements were unlike the vampyrs Evelyn had fought. He was agile, not flighty and jerky. He fought like one would dance—fluidly. He moved enough for her flame to miss, his blond hair swaying, his eyes alight with mischief.

Then he attacked. She countered his blows, which were full of force and hard like stone. She cried out when he landed a blow to her gut, but sent a wave of flame that grazed his black vest. Riven writhed and discarded his vest before the flame reached too much of his skin. Welts formed on his chest, steam rising and a putrid scent filling the air.

Evelyn rushed toward the door, intending to run into the street and call for help. To warn Kade and all the rest who the vampyr was.

Yet, Riven beat her to it, a predatorial glare overtaking his previously playful demeanor. He'd not enjoyed her flame, then.

Good.

Evelyn mastered enough flame to rise past her elbows. The room was getting dangerously hot, her confidence searing the air. "I will burn you where you stand, vampyr."

"On the contrary, you will comply," Riven said as he stepped toward her.

Evelyn did not waver. She did not blink. Nor did she calm her flame.

"You are the last element in the spell. The blood of the Daughter of the Goddess is the final piece I need to allow my people to walk in the sunlight. *You*."

He lifted a vial from his pocket. Dark crimson in nature, the liquid inside shimmered gold as if glittering sun had been transmitted into the blood.

Evelyn took a mighty step forward, coming toe to toe with Riven. He stared down at her, jutting fangs inches from her neck. He was too fast in the too small of a room—she had to be smart, calculated before she made for her escape. But first, she had to destroy that vial.

"You will never use my blood for your people," she breathed.

Before he could retort, Evelyn bashed her forehead into his nose.

He stumbled, and Evelyn reached for the vial. Together they fell. Wrestled and rolled. Until Evelyn thrust the vial against the walls of the townhome. The glass shattered, the glittering blood inside evaporating into rays of light.

Hope and triumph flushed through Evelyn, her lungs swelling with relief.

In a blink, Evelyn gasped for air. A cold, bony hand gripped her throat. She blinked, her vision blurring as Riven came into view. She struggled for air, clawing at his hands.

"Did you really believe my plan hinged on a single vial?" Riven asked.

No, she wouldn't let him take her. *Never*. She was the Daughter of the Goddess and she believed. Evelyn took a mighty breath, grounding herself in that belief. It swelled within her, powering up her attack. Evelyn gripped Riven's hold with one hand while the other burst into a flame, ready to kill him, end him—

"Don't or Kade will die," Riven shouted.

Evelyn stopped, her heart lurching in her chest.

"If you kill me, my death will be the catalyst for more death and dismay in this town you so dearly love. The first casualty, your werewolf betrothed. His head will be at your feet by day's end if you do not put out your flame."

Evelyn's blood went cold. Her heart pounded in her chest. She'd believed she'd known fear, but this was all-consuming. Maddening. Her magic soared to protect Kade. She could think of nothing else but keeping him safe.

"You're bluffing," Evelyn muttered through Riven's hold on her neck.

Riven tilted his head, smirking. "What if I am? What if I am not? Is your love's life worth that risk?"

Evelyn cried with frustration. "If you touch him—"

"It'll not be me he needs to worry about. I have allies, Evelyn. You may have killed the Far Darrig and driven back the kelpie, even destroyed the infamous White Lady, but that only angered those who support me. If my ship with black sails does not leave the harbor within the hour flying a red banner blowing from the back, they've been instructed to destroy this town and everyone in it."

Evelyn gripped Riven's hand, kicking her feet. She put out her flame, sending him a glare of death, of promise. He lowered her to the ground, setting her down. She gasped for breath, massaging her neck.

The clock behind Riven's desk chimed the hour, the long clangs stretching in the silence between them as she made her decision. The sound mocked Evelyn and her lack of options. For all she knew, Riven was lying, bluffing his way into capturing her.

But she would not fail someone else she loved.

"Do you swear it?" Evelyn asked.

Riven clucked his tongue and shook his head. He reached for something on the bookshelf, leaving Evelyn alone in her defeat. He rejoined her with two black metal bracelets. Matte, they seemed to swallow the darkness all around them. Evelyn's magic scurried underneath her skin, sensing the wretchedness laced within them. Evelyn's heart sank, knowing what the bracelets were for.

"I will never swear to any witch, not even you, Daughter of the Goddess," he said. "Give me your hands."

Deep in her soul, Evelyn knew she could burn this entire building down. She could end Riven right here, right now. She didn't doubt her ability, her power, or desire to do so. Yet, it didn't matter. Risking Kade's life was out of the question. Even if no army of darkness surrounded Callum, she would never endanger Kade. She loved him. The thought of losing him almost buckled her knees. Her heart and soul twisted.

She couldn't in good conscience put the people of Callum at risk either. The sweet, kind people of this town did not stand a chance against whatever darkness sided with Riven.

She held out her hands, meeting Riven's victorious stare. She did not cry. She did not shy away from his touch as he snapped a bracelet on each of her wrists, trapping her magic. She felt it still but could not unleash it. Riven had bound her.

He gripped her arm, pulling her along with him. Out the back door, a carriage awaited. Evelyn didn't catch whoever steered it before Riven opened the door and thrust her inside. It was designed like a black metal box, similar to her bracelets, and tamped down her magic even more.

"Welcome to your new life, Daughter of the Goddess. You will give me your blood." He lowered himself to Evelyn's level. "And you will help finish the spell the White Lady began."

Evelyn wanted to rip his eyes out and spit in his face. She charged him, but Riven shut the carriage door before she could, and she slammed her fists into the metal, releasing her anger.

In an instant, they were moving. The wheels bumped over the cobblestones. She heard nothing, saw nothing from the outside world, her fate as desolate and bleak as the black metal box.

Evelyn did not cry. She did not weep. She didn't let an ounce of doubt trickle in or a fraction of fear. Even as the carriage halted and the ebb and flow of the ocean made her realize they'd driven straight onto Riven's ship. Even as time ticked and

Evelyn realized with a breaking heart that Kade would stand alone on the docks of Callum, waiting for her.

Yet, Kade was safe, and Evelyn did not doubt her decision or herself.

She was Evelyn Carson, Daughter of the Goddess, and Riven, prince of Drystan and vampyrs, had allowed his greatest enemy access to his lands and people.

From the inside out, she swore to burn them all.

ACKNOWLEDGEMENTS

First and foremost, I'd like to thank my kind and encouraging husband. Drew—you've been so incredible since the moment I told you I wanted to write this story in 2022. Not once have you doubted me or my ability to bring these characters to life. When the idea of indie-pub was a mere spark, you never once doubted that either. You've encouraged me to go for it and motivated me along the way. I appreciate you letting me vent about plot problems even though you had little to no idea of what I was talking about. I love how Kade and Evelyn have become household names thanks to you, and when times got challenging you asked, "What would Evelyn do?" I love you and thank you for setting the standards for book-*husbands*.

A huge thank you to my family. Dad—thank you for introducing me to the world of fantasy with Lord of the Rings marathons, listening to the same Harry Potter audiobook over and over on long drives, and being the one who planted the indie-pub idea and also telling me to go for it. Mom—thank you for always telling me to never stop writing. Ian—thanks for being the best fantasy-loving sibling a girl can ask for. One day, I promise I will play DND.

To all my friends—thank you, thank, thank you. There are too many of you to shout out by name but writing this book and getting it out into the world has shown me I have such an incredible group of friends supporting me. Writing has always been a part of me, but sadly the part I talked about the least or even admitted. The more I wrote and the farther I got along in this process, the more

I started discussing it with friends. I mean when you do something every day it tends to be what you talk about. . . Not a single friend batted an eye. All of you sent love, support, excitement, and warmth my way. To the friends who told me to bold, to the ones who came to my college poetry readings, to the ones you made *Of Faith & Flame* double-date night dinner talk.... It means so much to have you all in my corner, cheering me on—thank you.

Dear Neerali—I used to say I owed you dinner, but at this point, I owe you about ten. . . You've done so much to help get this story out in the world: FaceTime calls, rereading the same chapter five times until I got it right, dealing with my random plot ideas that didn't fix anything, and being Kade's biggest fan. You've been with this story since day one and thank you so much for being the best critique partner and fellow writer-friend an author can ask for.

My writing group, the Critique Chicks. You've all been with this story since the early plotting days, and it wouldn't be where it is today without all of your feedback, accountability, words of encouragement, and enthusiasm surrounding *Of Faith & Flame*. Birgit Schreiber, Rachel May, and Pandora Pierce—thank you for being a fantastic group.

To my beta readers: G.W. Prouse, Emily Michel, and Nanna. Thank you for all your kind words and genuine excitement after reading *Of Faith & Flame*. Your positive and constructive feedback was so valuable.

Ginger and June: thank you for being my first internet writer friends. We started meeting during the pandemic when I revisited writing after a four-year hiatus and talked about all things writing, books, and life. Our late-night conversations over Zoom were such a delight. Thank you both for letting me know it's okay to shelf a story that isn't working—if I hadn't, *Of Faith & Flame* would not be on shelves today.

I'd like to thank and shout out two writing communities. First, Writing with the Soul and WWTS Drafting Club. WWTS workshop was instrumental in connecting me to my inner storyteller and I'm forever grateful. The WWTS community is also so uplifting, and the Drafting Club has been the perfect place to surround myself with like-minded writers while I sprint and sprint some more. Second, Tenacious Writing. I'm so grateful to have stumbled upon this group on the gram—thank you so much for building an amazing space for creatives.

Lastly, Evelyn—ultimately, her story is about belief. It's about being bold and brave even when doubt trickles in. I didn't know how much I related to Evelyn until the very end of editing this story. Here story is my story, and I'm honored to have learned the same lesson she did while bringing this story to life.

About the Author

A lover of fantasy since childhood, C.C. discovered her passion for storytelling during high school. With a bachelor's in creative writing and psychology plus a master's in mental health counseling, she likes to blend romantic fantasy elements with an understanding of the human psyche. Beyond writing, she's obsessed with a good latte, and can often be found enjoying one with her husband as they set out on adventures of their own, traveling to various places fit for a fantasy-novel backdrop.

If you want to stay up to date on C.C.'s book news, updates, and bonus content, sign up for her newsletter at authorcctyler.com or follow her on Instagram.

instagram.com/authorcctyler

Made in the USA
Columbia, SC
26 September 2024

42462652R00226